RIO

KNIGHT EMPIRE
BOOK 3

LILY ZANTE

AUTHOR'S NOTE

RIO is the third book in the KNIGHT EMPIRE series, a steamy, contemporary romance saga based around a family of six brothers and their tyrannical father.

The series begins with the prequel, THE DARKEST KNIGHT. The first book is JETT, followed by DEX, and then RIO.

Each book can be read as a standalone, and is about one couple, but it is recommended to read these books in order for the best reading experience.

THE DARKEST KNIGHT

JETT

DEX

RIO

ZACH (pre-order, releasing in February 2026)

CHAPTER ONE

RAQUEL

CARACA. MY STOMACH FEELS ALL FLUTTERY.

I have a Knight in my hotel room. It feels so dangerously wrong on so many levels, and yet I'm the one who invited him in.

A Knight of all people.

He was kind enough to see me back safely, and that scorching hot chemistry between us is as strong as ever. That surprises me. Shocks me, that someone like me could ever feel anything for something like *him*.

I don't know why this man has such an effect on me, but he does, and I haven't stopped thinking about him since that night at the Manhattan bar when I was spying on Dex and Dani. Tonight, at their wedding reception, it was impossible to ignore how much in love they are, but it still strikes me as odd that everything has happened so fast.

The Dani I know wouldn't do this. She's not just a friend, she's like a sister to me, even though we were from such different worlds when we met. Against the odds, we became best friends at the private school I was lucky to attend. Our paths would never have crossed were it not for the government-funded scholarship I got to one of São Paulo's most elite schools. The type of school I never knew even existed. The type of school that had what I imagined only the grandest homes would have: marble staircases, tennis courts, swimming pools and perfectly landscaped grounds.

When I stepped into that school, I entered a world that was alien to me. A world I didn't belong in. In my early days, armed with nothing more than a sharp tongue and death stares, it made me more determined than ever to rise. To show these people that I was more than my tattered shoes and clothes. That's when I met Dani. She was nothing like the others, even though she looked perfectly at home here.

I taught her how to swear and she taught me how to control my anger and use it to fuel something I could control. I vowed then to be someone who could make things better.

We grew close and kept in touch through the years, and then we lived together in the U.S. while I was doing my Master of Laws degree at Georgetown. We've always known what was going on in each other's lives, but I never thought she'd keep something like this from me. Her marriage to one of the Knight billionaires. She kept Dexter a secret for so long, I wonder if she fell in love and lost her head.

Some women do.

But the way Dex kissed her this evening, in front of everyone, it was plain to see that they're in love. I'm so happy for her. I am. But I'll be watching Dexter. He's a Knight, so he doesn't get a free pass from me.

"Nice room, princesa."

"Why do you keep calling me that?" I ask, turning to the Knight in my room.

"Because you are."

I kick off my heels to find Rio stands, taking up the space like he owns it. Hands in his pockets. Calm. Relaxed. He laughs. His voice is too low, too smooth, too flirtatious. He's the kind of man who's hard to forget, and I know he's bad for me. I know he spells trouble, which is why I keep my distance. But now, he's only a few strides away, filling the room with his aura. His magnetism.

He's Dani's new brother-in-law. I mustn't forget that. I was tempted to kiss him in that Manhattan bar when I thought he was just another sharp-dressed, cocky businessman. Then I discovered who he was.

As a corporate environmental lawyer, I know all about the dirty tactics Knight Enterprises uses. I've seen too many cases where they've wreaked havoc across the globe.

The Knights mean trouble, and I've only let this man in to be polite. I'm going to send him back to the wedding reception soon. Dani might not realize I left the celebrations early, but I had to.

Work commitments, unfortunately.

The law firm where I work, Tovey & Roth, is one of the best firms in Miami. It was founded by two partners, but only my boss Pierce Tovey remains at the helm. William Roth retired years ago and faded quietly from the legal scene.

Pierce has been on my back all week. Pressure from the job, I can take. But a shiver of revulsion slithers through me every time I think of him. He's a corrupt, misogynistic blot on my day. The subtle innuendos he makes when others aren't around, the way he looks at me, how he brushes past me "accidentally" are all things that can't be used as evidence against him. He's careful, and knows exactly what he's doing, but he knows how to stay clean.

I love what I do. It's my passion. It's what fuels me. I'm a corporate environmental lawyer who occasionally takes on pro bono cases, though Pierce prefers I stick to billable hours that keep the firm's profits flowing.

Having Rio around is a little distraction. A little harmless fun. Nothing will happen, but I'm curious, and I have been, about him, for months. This one is rare, I feel it in my gut, but I've just got to find a way to stop thinking about him.

Though sometimes I can't help but wonder what he'd be like in bed. I don't usually think like that. But with him? I haven't been able to stop. He should've been easy to dislike. Easy to walk away from. I knew we'd meet at the wedding and I managed to keep away from him for most of the day, but then he found me in the gardens. And now he's here.

"What'll you have to drink?" I head toward the wet bar.

"You're offering me hospitality?"

"Just one drink. Knight, before I send you on your way. What will it be?"

"I'm not going to drink. I just wanted to make sure you got back to your hotel room safely."

He's chivalrous, if a little forward. I turn around to see if he's joking or being real and his eyes dip down to my bare feet. I'm suddenly feeling hot and bothered. I reach up and undo the big bow at the side of my high neck; not that it's going to help much. This dress which tapers in at the waist and fans out into a wide skirt, is elegant and perfect for a wedding, but now, with its full sleeves and that neck, it feels suffocating. The silky fabric clings to my skin, too hot and sticky, even though the air conditioning is on.

"You don't need to strip for me, princesa," he murmurs. The corners of his lips turn up into a lazy smile.

"In your dreams. I'd never strip for you."

"You have no idea of my dreams." His voice, thick and raspy, makes my brain fog over because his words sound like a confession. I'm suddenly too afraid to fire back. My mouth usually doesn't let me down. I can match wit and humor, easily. But tonight? I'm at a loss.

Despite my earlier resolve, I need a drink, so I reach for a small bottle of white wine, but then I remember I can't have it. I need a clear head, for work but also because I also can't let my guard down, not with this man in my room, looking like he wants to eat me.

How I want him to.

I shake my head, hating myself for feeling so hot, and tingly all over and grab a bottle of sparkling water instead. He hasn't even touched me yet, and already my breasts feel heavy. Heat begins to coil low in my belly.

Needing to show that I'm in control, even if I don't feel it, I turn around, place a hand on my hip and stare at him. He's made himself at home, dropping onto the edge of the armchair like he owns this room, but now his gaze trails over me slowly, and I fold my arms in disapproval. We stare at each other, tension crackling in the air. Suddenly everything feels too intense. The hot, sultry night fills with heated anticipation.

"I've changed my mind. I'll have uh …" He pauses. "I don't suppose they have much in there?"

"Stale peanuts or overpriced chocolate?" I ask him. Then, "There's no aged tequila."

That earns me a grin. "You remembered, princesa."

Me and my mouth. "Jack Daniel's?"

"That'll do."

I grab a mini bottle of the Jack Daniel's, walk over and hand it to him. The rough calluses of his fingertips scrape lightly across my skin. It's heat and fire. Electricity and shock. Just from one touch. A delicious shiver tingles along my spine. I assumed that as a pampered Knight, with his smooth suits and inherited money, his cocky self-assuredness and not a worry in the world, he'd have baby smooth skin. But now my imagination runs wild as I wonder what it might be like to have those big, rough hands all over me.

I immediately step away.

"You been thinking of me, huh?" He twists of the cap and downs half of it without blinking."

I don't bother replying, but move away, needing to keep some distance between us, even as my heart hammers in my chest and I try to phase out sinful thoughts running rampant in my head. My breasts feel heavy, and as I stare at Rio looking so comfortable, so casual, I wonder if he can tell I want him. He looks so at home with his legs wide apart, one hand resting lazily on the armrest, the other holding his Jack Daniel's.

"I see you've made yourself at home."

"You haven't kicked me out." His gaze slides over my body again. If looks could undress, I'd be naked now. I shift from one foot to the other, feeling the need to squeeze my thighs together, to relieve the buildup of pressure making my insides combust. "I think you like me being here but you're too stubborn to admit it."

The audacity of the man. "My mother raised me to have manners and I'm too polite to kick you out just yet."

He's nothing but a pompous, confident ass, sitting on my armchair, looking like he's never going to leave. I almost, *almost,* look him over again.

"You're not nervous are you, princesa?" He grins before taking another gulp.

I laugh. "I don't scare easily—"

"I didn't say you were scared. I asked if you were nervous."

"Same thing, Knight." I sip my water, the bubbles fizz as they go down my throat. He watches me so intensely, I feel goosebumps skittering across my skin.

"We're two adults in a hotel room, alone. Very innocent, princesa."

"I said no flirting."

He holds up a hand. "No flirting. Just sitting. Watching you pace around barefoot like some kind of goddess who hates me."

I snort. "Goddess?"

He nods. My eyes avoid his, but it's the heat I feel, from everything being so overpowering—his gaze, his presence, his cockiness.

"You hot?" he asks.

I stifle the sigh threatening to cut loose from my throat. This man can read me like a book, and this is something I'm not used to. This is why he intrigues me. Why he's constantly in my head. I feel sweaty all over, with a dampness under my arms, between my legs, down my back.

He sits forward. "You left your best friend's reception early. Why?"

I shrug. "Too many people. Too much noise. And I hate small talk."

"Hmm." He studies me, like he doesn't believe me. "That wasn't all of it."

Damn him. I have work to do. Pierce is going to call soon and demand an update. But Pierce and work are the last thing I want to think about right now. "Dani's happy. She has someone who sees her. Fights for her. It made me realize … how lucky she is."

He frowns, and I feel like I've said too much. "You could be lucky." He winks. "All you have to do is not push me away."

"I know what kind of man you are."

"You know what kind of man my father is. Please don't ever make the mistake of thinking that I'm another version of him. I'm not."

He stands up and places his now empty mini bottle of Jack

Daniel's on the table next to him. My heart thunders inside my chest, but I manage to hold my ground until he closes the distance between us.

"You think I'm dangerous, arrogant, and spoiled," he challenges, his husky voice reverberating through me.

"I don't *think* you're spoiled. I know it, Knight. You brothers with your billion-dollar trust funds."

"We're not trust fund brats, but you have been thinking about me." He reaches out and brushes a strand of hair behind my ear. Gone is the cocky grin, replaced by a more serious, intense look. He's looking at me like I'm the only woman in the world. Like we're already intimate and he knows everything about me. I look up into his eyes—so dark they look black, just like his hair, slicked back today. He looks sharp and dangerous, like he could sling me over his shoulder, and walk out of here, and no one would dare stop him. That charm of his sometimes borders on predatory, and my insides heat up in a way they shouldn't.

My eyes go to the soft dimple in his chin, and I'm tempted to touch it; to run my fingers over the dip. But I don't. I scarcely breathe. His tone is softer now, almost a whisper.

"You still let me into your hotel room, and I have a feeling you're not about to tell me to leave anytime soon."

My breath hitches, but I don't move away.

He's right.

"What are you doing?" I manage to say, feeling a trail of heat where he touches me.

His hand lingers around my jaw. "You can keep hating me tomorrow, but right now, tell me you don't want this."

I swallow, and my voice is barely a whisper. "I don't."

"What's changed, princesa?" He walks back a few steps like the shock of my words physically punched him. "When we first met in Manhattan, you were all smiles and flirtation."

"I didn't know who you were back then."

"But you shut me down fast enough."

I don't flinch. I don't smile either. "Because once I found out, everything changed." It's not that I hate the rich. I don't. There are many rich people who do good, but the Knights are not those people. I was raised by a single mother in a favela on the outskirts of São Paulo. I've seen poverty up close. I've experienced the struggle and the injustice.

"Because of my last name?"

"Because your last name destroys rainforests and bribes politicians," I snap. "Because Knight Enterprises is the kind of monster I've built my whole career fighting."

The words seem to land harder than I expect.

"Then tell me, what am I doing in your hotel room?"

I narrow my eyes. "I know how to keep my distance."

"By letting me in?"

"By being nice to you because you saw me back to my room safely."

"You think you're safe from my charm here?" he murmurs. "I think you still want me."

He's infuriating, and not wrong. But I'd rather die than admit that. I tilt my chin up in defiance. "You think very highly of yourself. All of you Knights do."

"I think very highly of what I see, and what I want." He does it again, his gaze taking its sweet time trailing over me, slow and deliberate, every cell in my body vibrates. Heat flares at the base of my belly. I want to lift my dress up and have him be on his knees, pleasuring me.

Damn this man.

Damn my thoughts.

I force a light laugh, but it's laced with challenge. "You're wasting your time here. I don't do men like you."

"*Do?* That's an interesting choice of word, princesa." His

eyes glisten with mischief. "What exactly do you mean by men like me?"

"The type of men who think the world revolves around their name, their money, and their ability to get whatever they want."

His smile is lazy, full of undisguised interest.

"What type of men do you *do*, then, Raquel?"

My name on his mouth sounds like temptation and sin. I love the way he says it. Slightly dirty, and in his voice thick, and raspy. Stupidly, I step forward and place a finger on his chest. "I do men who can keep up."

I start to walk away, but he grabs my wrist, gently, but firm.

"I can keep up, princesa. What are you offering?"

CHAPTER TWO

RIO

I TOLD MYSELF I WAS BEING POLITE WHEN I OFFERED TO WALK her up to her hotel room.

That I'm not hoping for anything. But the way Raquel's eyes cut to me over her shoulder—half dare, half danger—makes my restraint unravel one thread at a time.

I take off my jacket and toss it over the back of a chair. "It's too damn hot for all that formality."

I can tell she's getting hot in that dress. So hot, she had to untie that big fancy bow at the neck. I wonder if she's planning on getting changed into something more comfortable.

Now that I've downed a Jack Daniel's, I wouldn't mind downing a few more because of the way she's looking at me, dark eyes, full mouth, lips stained in a rich red satin lipstick. She makes it impossible for me to look away. Those big, dark Bambi eyes, framed by thick lashes, are hard to look away from. I can see myself falling, deep, deep, deeper into them. Losing my mind and my morals. Her loose hair tumbles over her silky dress in waves, and she's barefoot. Just seeing her painted toes, oddly intimate, ties me up in knots.

It's a teasing glimpse into the woman who seems to keep her walls up around everyone, especially me. Not only is she sensual and beautiful, not only do I find myself immensely attracted to her, but she's also a mystery. One I desperately want to unravel.

I want to kiss her, and taste her, and do so many things *to* her, *with* her. But she's fighting this attraction between us. We could be fucking like wild animals on that supersized bed of hers, but she can't get past that goddamn moral compass of hers. She hates me, and while I love the thrill and chase when it comes to a beautiful woman, I don't like wasting my time.

Clearly, she doesn't like me. My family. The Knight name. Who knows which of these it is? She's not seeing me as someone separate. She's not feeling what I'm feeling so there's no point sticking around any longer. "I should go."

"Let's play a game," she offers.

We both spoke at the same time, and now we're staring at each other. Did I hear correctly? She wants to play a *game?* I guess I shouldn't be surprised that she can't fight it, her attraction to me. She doesn't want me to leave. This woman wants to party. I knew it. I goddamn knew it.

I'm in.

"A game, huh?" I swipe a hand over my beard. "What are we talking here? Hangman, Scrabble?" I need to make sure we're on the same page.

"You play poker?"

Hot damn. Her question brings a smile to my lips. *Poker?* This is my kind of woman. I knew it from the moment she sidled up to me at the bar in Manhattan. "You offering money or something better?" Anticipation makes blood course through my veins and my pants suddenly feel tighter.

Her brow lifts, cool and lethal. "Clothes."

She says it like a challenge, as if she's daring me to break first. And damn me, I've never been more ready to lose.

"Clothes, princesa? You sure about that?" She's wild, and I'm a lucky, lucky, lucky guy.

"You scared, Knight?" Her eyes widen. Her mouth parts, just a little. Enough to have me thinking about the things I'd like to do with her.

Not scared, princesa. Just fucking excited.

I grin. "Never."

She smiles, wide and full. I couldn't drag my gaze away from her lips if I tried. I want those luscious red lips on mine. Wrapped around my cock, on my stomach, kissing me all over. It's incredible to think that we haven't even kissed.

Yet.

We've done nothing but dance and bicker around one another. The slow burn, slow-building tension is heating up, and it's slowly killing me. I'm usually more of an instant gratification kind of guy but this battle of wills between Raquel and I is more intoxicating and dangerous than any foreplay. It makes me wonder how explosive we'd be in bed.

Would we even survive it?

I hope I'll get a chance to find out.

"We need a pack of cards." This night has quickly turned from a near disappointing disaster to something filled with endless possibility.

"Luckily, I have one." Raquel walks over to the desk near the window.

"You always carry cards with you? You always play these games when you're traveling?" For a second it pinches, that I'm not the only recipient of such a night. Of such games. But I wave the thought away. We're about to have some fun. That's all this is. Nothing too deep. Nothing meaningful.

"What if I do?" she throws back.

I don't have an answer for that but I wonder if she's the type of woman who has an insatiable appetite.

"There was already a pack of cards in here. Feel better?" she snaps. "You think I carry these around all the time, playing games with strangers in my hotel room?"

I open my mouth and close it.

Because she's damn right. Now I feel like a prick for being so judgy.

"We get five cards each per round," I say, taking the cards out of the pack and shuffling.

"Okay." She eyes her desk, but it's cluttered. "Let's just play on the floor." She sits down, cross-legged.

I sit down, or try to, but it's not comfortable. Still, I'm not going to make excuses, not now that we're playing strip poker. "We get five cards each. No bluffing, no bets, just the highest hand wins. Standard rankings. Nothing fancy or convoluted. Just enough to get you in trouble." I flip the cards in my hands like this is my full-time job and I'm an expert.

She raises a perfectly shaped brow, then licks her lower lip, making my cock twitch in my pants. "Sounds good to me."

"Let's iron out the rules."

We eye one another like hungry predators. I wonder if she's imagining me down to my boxers, because I have a visual of what I'm expecting to see before this night is over. My hard-on is becoming painful unbearable and, when she's not looking, I need to adjust myself in my pants.

"Loser removes an item of clothing," I say, stating the obvious.

She looks at me carefully. "They can remove an item of clothing *or* answer a personal question."

"Or answer a personal question," I echo.

"Remind me again of the hierarchy, Knight?"

"Oh, princesa. I'd be happy to break it down for you." I gaze at her like I'm going to win. "Top of the food chain? Royal flush. Ace, King, Queen, Jack, 10—all one suit. Untouchable. Like me."

She scoffs, but her eyes glint with fire.

"Next? Straight flush — five in a row, same suit. Four of a kind? Four cards, same rank. No mercy."

"Go on."

"Full house? That's three of a kind, two of another."

Her fingers toy with the hem of her dress. "Okay, I get it. I've played this before, Knight. I'm no poker virgin."

"I don't take you for one, either."

"Want another drink?"

"I'll have another Jack Daniels."

She gets up and walks over to the wet bar again, and I watch her intently, admiring her as she stands with her back to me. I'm still incredulous that I'm here. Playing strip poker.

Wait till I tell Dex.

She hands me the drink. For herself, she has a small bottle of water.

"You're not drinking?"

"I have work to do."

"What? Work, *now?*"

"I have a caseload. My sleazy, nasty, boss has cracked his whip."

"Sleazy?"

She shrugs, sits back down on the floor again, takes a sip of water then puts the lid back on. There's more to this than she's letting on. Something I don't like the sound of.

"How old is he? Is he married?"

"Why so many questions?"

"Just answer them, princesa."

"He's not married, and as for the "sleazy." I can deal with

him." She picks at something on her dress. "I have work to do, Knight. So if you want to play, I suggest we get on with it."

"Okay."

"And once we've finished playing, you're leaving soon after I've gotten you down to your boxers."

I grin. "Who says you'll want me to leave once you see me in my boxers?"

"You're so sure of yourself."

"You know you want me. This is just a tactic for getting me down naked."

She chews her lower lip, then fans her face. I can see the color rising to her cheeks. She mumbles something about it being hot.

"You keep fanning yourself," I say. "How about you change into something a little lighter? I'm sure that satin must be hard for your skin to breathe through."

She flaps around with the high neck of her dress, as if trying to let in some air.

"You could get changed into your pyjamas or something more comfortable," I suggest.

"I'm fine, but I bet you a hundred dollars that by the end of this evening, you'll be in your boxers and I'll be fully clothed."

"You've played this before." I suddenly realize why she wants to play this. "Do you cheat?"

She gives me a wide smile. "I don't cheat. That's something you Knights are masters at."

"Five cards. No bluffing, no folding, no excuses." I ignore her comment and continue shuffling. She thinks the worst of me. Fine. That's her prerogative. Dani obviously would have told her how the old man tricked her father. It shouldn't be a surprise to me that Raquel thinks badly of us.

Still, I'm not my old man, and neither are my brothers. Not even Jett, Dex and Zach. Turns out, we're surprisingly better, despite having Paul Knight for a father, and given the trauma we've all suffered.

"Fine."

"I can't wait to start." I deal out the cards.

"We're not doing anything stupid," she says flatly.

"Define stupid."

Her eyes flash. "You. In my bed."

Now there's a visual. Did she have to go and put that in my head? "Then let's keep it safe."

She picks up her cards and fans her face with them. "You first, since you dealt."

I give a lazy grin. "Two pair."

She studies her hand, her expression unreadable. Then she lays down her cards. "Flush."

My smile dies in my throat. She beats me. She leans back, lifting her arms behind her head like a queen expecting tribute. "What are you going to do, Knight? Strip or answer a question?"

"I'm going to strip." I stand up, my hands reaching for the zipper of my pants. Her eyes turn dark. Her lips part. I know that look. I can sense her desire. It's so obvious that she wants me. I undo a cufflink.

"A cufflink?" she cries, her body sagging slightly. It's like she's releasing a breath she's been holding in. If I'm hard with anticipation, she's also feeling something too, but it's such a pity that she's in denial about it.

"Slow burn, baby. You love the tease."

She doesn't smile. She fights to keep on the mask. Trying to look calm, but I know she's not. We play again, and three rounds in, I've lost a sock and two cufflinks. She's lost her earrings.

We're toeing the line, and the air between us grows heavier by the second. Then I win the next hand, but barely—

a lousy two pair. But smile fades, and that tells me everything.

"Your move," I murmur. "Is that dress coming off, princesa?"

She leans back, arms crossed. "No."

"I get to ask you a question, then?"

"Maybe."

I can't help but notice the tight set of her jaw, the flicker of something defensive in her eyes. "Maybe?" She's not playing coy. She's hiding.

Then she bends down, reaches up her dress, and, *hot damn* if my cock isn't going to start leaking cum. She hold up her lacy black thong, and my breath stalls. My cock presses uncomfortably against my boxers and if this continues, I'm going to shoot my load right now.

Damn it if she doesn't go and dangle her panties from her fingers. My mouth waters at the slip of lace and satin in the stringy thong she's twirling around. A sharp grunt escapes my mouth before I can stop it. It's the kind of sound that betrays just how close I am to losing it. My brain hazes over, every thought vanishing before I can grasp it.

She throws her panties onto the bed, good job, too, because I'm so tempted to reach for them and sniff. And then another rock lands on me. Underneath that dress she's *naked* from her waist down.

"Cheat." My voice is hoarse.

"How?" She sits back down. Cross-legged.

Cross-legged.

But she makes sure her dress covers her legs, spilling onto the floor, so I can't get a peep. *She's cross-legged and bare.* I want to crawl along the floor, lift up her dress, and feast on her pussy. I'd bet a million dollars, she's dripping wet.

"How am I cheating?" Her voice is steady and calm, her

expression cool as ice. She looks like a movie star from the fifties in that elegant dress which covers everything. Clearly she doesn't want me asking questions, which means, we need to play a few more rounds, and fast.

"Because you can take your panties off, while keeping your dress on, and I can't do that."

She chortles. "You sound like a little sulky boy, Knight."

Sentences elude me right now, so I focus on the game. We each pick up our cards. She grins. I groan because I lose.

"What'll it be, Knight?"

I stand up and slowly undo the buttons of my shirt. She gives me one of those hungry stares I'm accustomed to. Encouraged, I slowly peel off my shirt, feeling thankful I have a body worthy of her to look at.

She licks her lips, as I sit down, then clears her throat and twiddles with the high neck. She must be roasting in that dress. A thin sheen of sweat lines her face. I know she's hot. I'm feeling hot myself.

We play another round. She sets the cards down, looking jubilant. "Straight flush." She looks at me, but her gaze soon drops to my chest.

"Oh, princesa." I set down my cards. I got super lucky. "Royal Flush." I lay down my cards, all diamonds, high hands, in order, and look up, feeling gleeful.

She looks uncomfortable. It occurs to me later that she's wearing a watch and a bracelet. She took off her earrings, and she could have taken her watch and bracelet off next, but she chose to take off her panties.

Now there's a tease if ever I met one.

We play a few more rounds, and she loses, again.

I want that dress off.

Unless she's going to fiddle around with her bra and take that off? That'll only get me more aroused. I lean forward—as much as my stiff-as-a-rod boner will allow me to. "Are you stripping for me now, princesa?"

She arches a brow, trying to stay cool, but her dewy face, and the tightness around her eyes, gives the game away. She sits upright, her spine stiffening, and I know she's trying to figure out how to dodge it.

She doesn't want to strip.

"How about a question then?" I ask.

She clenches her jaw. "Fine. One question. Make it count."

She's all hard edges, with steel walls around her. I sense she doesn't want me probing, but I so badly want to dig and unearth all her secrets. Even the painful ones, because I know this much. Despite her armor, despite that quick tongue and sharp mind, Raquel's hurting. She's hiding something.

"Why do you invite me in and then push me away, princesa?" She seems to have an internal battle whenever we're close together, and her actions confuse me, but I can't walk away because she's different. There's something about this woman that catches my curiosity more than it should.

"I can't make my mind up about you."

"You're trying very hard to resist me."

"Not resist. I'm struggling with my morals."

"Morals? Who needs morals?" I cry. "How about we abandon them for tonight?"

She laughs, shaking her head and staring at me in disbelief. "I figured you'd be the type of man to do that."

I sit up, gut hardening. "What type of man?"

"The type who screws around and leaves. Not that I'm looking for anything more than fun from someone like you."

"Someone like me?"

"A playboy. Someone who probably has a woman in every city. Someone who uses women for pleasure. Nothing wrong with that, either. Women use men for pleasure. I do, too, sometimes."

She's so wrong about that. I like to think of myself as a man of honor. "Then what do you hate about me, apart from my name?" We could both use one another for pleasure, but I have a feeling she's not the type of woman I'd screw once and discard.

"Who you are. I have no patience for entitlement."

"You think I'm entitled?"

"I've had to work twice as hard for half the respect, but for people like you it's guaranteed, just because of your wealth."

"Must you always hold that against me?"

I feel like she has a deep buried pain. I can see it, just like I could see it in Mama, in the early days, when the old man ripped all our lives apart.

She looks at me, eyes sharp. "Do you so badly want to get me in your bed, Knight? Is this the part where you try to get to know me, pretend to care, and listen, so that you can salve the hurt and—"

"No." I shake my head, slightly confused, trying to figure her out. She could so easily tell me to get lost, but she hasn't. "I would like to end up on that bed, with you," I say carefully, "but that's not my main driver for wanting to be here. I just want to know more about you."

She looks at me as if, after all this time, she still needs a reason to validate why she shouldn't let me in, but she can't find one.

"I want to know what makes you look at me like I'm a grenade lying at your feet." There. I said it.

She opens her mouth to protest, but I hold up my hand, halting her. "You hate the Knights. Allegedly you hate me because I'm a Knight, and yet not only have you allowed me to come into your hotel room, and offered me a drink, but we're playing strip poker, your idea, not mine. And now I'm shirtless, while you're panty-less." My cock, on cue, twitches again. "All that to say, if you didn't feel anything towards me, we wouldn't be here, like *this*." I wave my hand between us.

She swallows, her eyes narrowing. For a second I don't think she's going to answer.

"I despise myself for wanting you."

Not the words I was expecting. They hit hard, like a gut punch I didn't see coming, and which knocks the breath from my lungs. My quickfire quip would be to grin, and tell her that I knew she wanted me, but there's a solemnity in her eyes, something raw and unspeakably fragile. Something that makes me take notice, and want to peel back more layers, and get to know her better.

"Why?" I barely recognize my low whisper.

"I mistrust men like you, and families like the one you come from. I've grown up hearing the very worst about these people, and I know one thing: the rich cannot be trusted."

"If this is about the old man and AO Eletronica, we outplayed him and managed to get Dani's father's—"

"It's not just that. It's about the stories I heard, from my mom, growing up in a favela on the outskirts of São Paulo."

"You grew up in a favela?" I flinch because she's hit me with something that I can't reconcile with the image of the woman I see. I don't care where she grew up, but her words surprise me, because it's the last thing I expected her to say. It's the way she says it, as if it's a confession shrink wrapped in shame.

It kills me. She shouldn't feel ashamed. It's a shock, for sure, that this polished, glamorous, supremely smart and confident woman—grew up in a favela. My brain short circuits for a while but I'm filled with admiration and disbelief.

"You're shocked, and you're disgusted."

"No. Not disgusted. In shock, yes, because I would never know. I'd never have guessed."

"That I clawed myself out?"

"No, because you have balls, and confidence and grit. That's what attracts me to you, but you telling me about where you grew up, well, that's a big surprise, a shock, even, but in the best way, not in a way that makes me think less of you, Raquel. You have the wrong impression of me. Give me time to help you see me for who I really am." I'm scrambling to not piss her off because I can tell she's judging me, and watching how I react. I get up and sit back in the chair. "Tell me more," I say softly.

"What do you want to know?"

"Everything."

"I can't tell you—"

"Tell me what you can, please."

She sits down again, her expression softening, like she didn't expect this. She shrugs, and I sense that this doesn't come as easy as her verbal left hooks. Being vulnerable is hard for her, like it is for me.

"My mom was a teacher by day, and in the evenings she helped out a small volunteer clinic. It was just a tiny operation in our neighborhood and it offered free legal support to the underserved. It was run by a retired judge and a few former law students who wanted to help the people no one else would. As I grew older, I would sometimes go along with her."

"That's where you got your love of the law?"

She nods. "My mom taught me that knowledge is power, and that fighting injustice wasn't about shouting louder, it was about knowing the system better than the people who built it." She gives me a bitter smile.

"And you push me away because?" This is what matters in this moment.

"You're dangerous not just because of who you are, but because of how good you are at pretending to care."

I take umbrage at her accusation, but I don't want to get into an argument. She's feisty and hot headed, and while I'm not one to back down from a confrontation, this moment is fragile. "You think I'm like the other rich people you don't like?"

"I didn't grow up disliking them for no reason. I wasn't biased just because we were poor," she shoots back. "I'd hear my mom and the judge talking about cases they were involved with, and it told me the rich cannot be trusted."

"We're not all like that," I protest, wondering how I'll ever convince her to give me a chance. She's opinionated, and she's already labeled me. The old man's manipulation of Dani's father hasn't helped. If anything, I'm sure it's only confirmed her bias.

"I heard about toxic waste being dumped near a school once. Children got sick, but officials said it was a coincidence. The legal clinic tried to file environmental claims but the multination corporation got away with it. They always do. A young boy died later, because he was so sick." She looks away, as if the pain is still fresh and when her eyes meet mine again, there's fire behind those rich, dark irises. "I learned that corporate greed can kill, and no one will be held accountable unless someone fights tooth and nail."

"And you're that someone to hold people accountable." I look at her in admiration. This woman is a warrior. I knew it from the day I met her. I just didn't figure what type of warrior she was. "Your mom must be so proud of you." I beam at her, because in that moment, this stunning beauty with a razor-sharp mind and wit, and with a heart full of love and compassion, is exactly the type of woman I want. Fate led her to sit next to me at an upscale bar, and now with Dex and Dani, fate has linked us together forever.

"She is." There's a soft smile on her lips as she peers down at her feet. "I bought her a nice apartment in a middle-class neighborhood. It's near a library and a park. She misses the community of the favela, but she appreciates the quiet and the independence."

She took care of her mom, like I have with Mama.

"She's waiting for her grandkids now," she says, a faraway look in her eyes. "But that's not what she's getting any time soon."

I chuckle. "My mom says the same."

She looks at me. It's weird how we have some things eerily in common.

"I never knew my father," she confesses, and that bombshell hits hard. Another thing I wasn't expecting. My mouth opens and I start to wonder if this is also a part of her having her guard up. Her father's absence must have affected her. Maybe that's why she's wary of not just me, because I'm a Knight, but of all men. "I'm sorry."

"I'm not. I didn't know him, never met him. He left before I was born. My mom says he vanished as soon as she got pregnant. She's never badmouthed him. She's far too noble and classy for that." The defiance has gone, but her expression grows distant and somber, as if she's trying to distance herself emotionally from it all. Her voice turns softer, smaller, hurt leaching into it and softening the defiance, even as she tries to feign indifference.

My mind whirs with all these little jigsaw pieces, but instead of making a flat cardboard picture, I'm beginning to weave together a rich tapestry of Raquel's life from the snippets she's shared with me. It explains so much.

Yet again, we have something else in common. Daddy issues. She never knew her father, but I know the asshole that is mine. The asshole that turned up at our door one day, looking so different to how we'd usually see him. The asshole who had to tell us that he was a cheater, and a liar. The asshole who'd been keeping a dark and dirty secret.

"Was he rich?" I want to know.

She lets out a hard laugh. "No, he wasn't. That's not where my mistrust comes from. He was like us. He just didn't want to accept responsibility." Her eyes lock with mine. "I don't hate you because my father let me down." She pauses abruptly. "Did yours let you down?" Her tone changes, like she's remembered something. I'm sure she knows our family history. I'm sure Dani would have told her.

"He did, but I expect you already know that."

"I want to hear it from you."

"The old man let us all down. Not just my mom and brothers, but Dex's mom and his brothers."

She sits taller, leaning forward, looking eager.

"I grew up believing my father was a man of honor until we discovered the truth about him living a double life."

"It must have been devastating for you all." Her eyes soften, like she feels the hurt, too.

"It was. That betrayal wrecked my sense of trust, especially in the old man. After Aurora, his wife, Dex's mom, died by suicide, my mom fell apart. I think she felt partly to blame, but she had no idea that he was married. It was a shock to her."

Raquel shakes her head. "She wasn't to blame."

"Overnight he went from being this happy, smiling, wonderful man—"

"Paul Knight, *happy?*"

"Crazy, right? You can't imagine Paul Knight ever being happy, genuinely happy."

"Or laughing, or being wonderful."

"These aren't words I'd ever use now." I breathe in deeply, like I need the extra oxygen to survive the retelling of that terrible time in our lives. "He was no longer the Papa we were used to. I was ten years old, so I didn't understand why Mama banished us all upstairs, and he and Mama talked for hours. I didn't know then why Mama looked so sad, why her face was so blotchy, her eyes so red. She told me to keep Matteo and Enzo busy. She never shouted, neither did the old man, but that day, their voices were loud, and angry. I knew something was very wrong. He left, without so much as playing with us, without talking to us, without hugging us. He was a changed man that day."

She blows out a sigh. "Your poor mom."

"My mom is the center of my world. She's the reason I still believe in integrity, and loyalty. I saw her pain that day, saw the way her hands shook, how she tried not to cry in front of us. It etched something permanent in me, and from that day forward, I made a silent vow that no one would ever hurt her again."

Raquel slumps back. I think I might have heard a "Wow," from her. Or maybe that was wishful thinking.

"My mom is too good for the world she got thrown into. Later, she told me, not the others, because they were so young, that we wouldn't be seeing Papa much anymore."

"Rio." Raquel looks like she wants to come over and give me a hug, but we're not those people yet. We don't have that easy going familiarity around one another. "I'm so sorry."

"It's not anything you have to be sorry about."

"Did your mom tell you about Jett and the others?"

"Not directly, but I found out by listening to her talking to her friends on the phone, and when they came to the house. Mama thought we were sleeping, but I was wide awake, and sitting on the stairs and listening. That's when I discovered that Papa had another family. A wife, and three young sons in the US. He and Mama were never together after that. He moved us to the US after that, and put us up in a house in Manhattan. It was tough for her to leave her friends and family in Italy, the only country she'd ever lived in. He must have threatened her, or made her an offer she couldn't refuse. She stayed with us until we were able to stand on our two feet, then she returned to Italy and lives in Soave now. We visit her as often as we can."

"How did they meet?"

"She was a shop assistant, working in a haute couture boutique. He was shopping for clothes. He wined and dined her, charmed her, but didn't tell her he was married or that he had children. He cheated on them both. Dex and I are only a year apart in age. He was having babies with both women."

"Ugh." Raquel looks horrified.

I nod.

The old man is the scum of the earth.

A most despicable man.

And, unfortunately my father.

"I'm not a playboy. I don't have a woman in every city. I don't screw women for pleasure. I like giving them pleasure, and receiving it from them. I guard my heart with steel walls, and I don't trust easily. I keep my emotions under lock and key, even when it costs me the very thing I want."

"What's that?"

"Real connection."

She stares at me, wide-eyed, like she can't believe I've just said all that. Hell, I can't believe it either. I don't have out pieces of myself. I don't let women peek behind the armor, yet here I am, laying down my cards for her, and I don't know if it's because I want her to understand me, or because some part of me wants her to break through those walls.

Her face hardens as our eyes hold. "I don't want you to feel sorry for me, or underestimate me, Knight."

"Underestimate you?" I cry. "Never." But all the same, I wonder what she's thinking.

"The thing I can't ignore is that you, with your yachts, and jets, and power suits and money deals, you are the embodiment of the stories I've heard from my mom, from the clinic. My attraction to you feels like a betrayal of who I am, and a betrayal to all the people whose stories are buried deep in my heart like an ache that's always there."

I jolt, because she might as well have slapped me. She hates me because I remind her of all that is wrong, but she's attracted to me.

I can't win.

She stands, walks over to the balcony door and steps outside, gazing up at the night sky. I follow her. Stars twinkle like shiny orbs of light studded in a rich velvet sky. Below us, the hotel gardens are softly lit. I can make out the outline of the pool, and the curve of the stone pathway. A couple slow dances under a pergola.

Lucky people.

"But none of that explains why I still want you," she murmurs, as I stand by her side.

My heart explodes. Her words detonate something deep inside. She wants me. Maybe I'm not the only one who's been obsessed. Just like that, I forget what game we're playing.

"Look at it this way," I offer, wanting to lighten the mood. "We have more in common than not."

"How so?" Her eyes narrow on me.

"We enjoy a nice drink at the bar. We care for our mothers who were let down by abominable men. We have fathers who failed us. We have Dex and Dani in common. And we both just enjoyed a good game of strip poker."

Her lips curl in something akin to amusement. "Typical Knight, reducing life events to single bulleted points in a bid to move things on."

"Move things on?" It takes a few seconds for me to realize. "Princesa, I'm not racing to get you in bed."

"You don't want me in your bed?" She pouts so provocatively, I fight the urge to kiss her.

I was only half-joking. But the look in Raquel's eyes tells me she isn't entirely sure I'm kidding either. She turns her head away from me, taking in the view spread out before us from the balcony, lost in thought.

A strained silence falls. I touch her arm, wanting her attention, needing her eyes on me. She turns slowly, her dark, penetrative gaze stripping me down. She looks, really looks.

"You'd think I'd have an aversion to sexy, suit-wearing overly-confident assholes by now, yet, I'm confounded by this. By *you*, Knight. By how irrationally I want you."'

I rest my palm against the side of her face, and to my complete shock and relief, she doesn't move away. My heart skips a beat when she lifts her head, looking up at me. Our lips are only an inch apart, and her hands skate slowly up my chest. Her touch is warm, and soft, like her breath, and when her fingers skitter over my heated skin, I lean in and claim her mouth, my tongue sliding into her mouth and dueling with hers. She makes a little noise. One of those delicious fucking little mewls that tells me she's feeling it.

I'm feeling it bigtime. Especially when her arms go around my neck and she clings to me like she never wants to let go. Pressing her sexy body against mine, teasing me. Giving me the mother of all boners. My hands around her waist, and I reel her closer.

"Oh." She pulls back.

She felt it. My boner against her stomach.

"Must be painful," she murmurs, her hot breath on my face.

"You have no idea." My hands slide down, under her dress. She moves her face away a little, and my hands still, as if I'm asking for permission. She nods, and I slide my hands over her skin, my cock stiffening as I find the warm globes of her bottom.

Hot damn.

I blow out a sharp breath. She feels like sin. Like a rush of wind that makes it hard to breathe. I can't wait to feel her all over, not just with my fingers, but with my tongue.

She makes those noises again that let me know how much she's loving this. We get into it, touching, feeling, kissing, bodies pressed tight like we fit just right. Then her cell phone buzzes. "I bet that's my boss," she hisses. "I was supposed to send him something." She pulls away and disappears back inside. I follow her.

"It was him." She swipes a hand over her neck, looks at her desk, her expression tightening. She's gone from being so chill, to be so flustered.

"What does he want?" I hate this guy already.

"I have to work."

"Want me to leave?" I ask, because I'm a gentleman.

"You can stay."

"Stay? But you said—"

"Stay."

I start to undo the zipper to my pants, then look at her. "It's painful."

She shifts her weight, one hand gripping the back of the chair, like she needs something to hold onto, something to keep her grounded. Her eyes fill with want.

That's all I need.

I strip out of my pants in one smooth motion. Now I'm shirtless and in my boxers. Looking down, I see a small patch of pre-cum on the front.

"I can go," I offer. It doesn't make sense for me to stay here, especially if all she's going to be doing is working. And yet it also doesn't make sense for me to strip down to my boxers and offer to leave.

"This shouldn't take too long." Her voice is a breathless whisper. She sits down at her desk and I settle down on her bed. She really doesn't want me to leave, and I've given her enough chances to let me go.

"And then?" I ask. "Do we keep playing?

She shrugs. "Why not?" Her eyes fall to my tented briefs. "I wish I could take care of that for you." Then, she deliberately slides her tongue out, and licks all around her lips. It's the most suggestive thing I've seen in a while.

"I wish you would," I manage to rasp, adjusting my cock in my boxers.

"And you look like a big boy, too."

"You have an appreciation for these things."

This woman is exactly who I've been looking for my entire life. Beauty and brains, and a wit that is so sharp, she'll give most people whiplash. And she's up for it. Doesn't want me gone. Wants me here. Maybe this night will end well.

She raises a brow. "Wait for me."

These are the three most glorious words she could have said to me.

CHAPTER THREE

RAQUEL

It's hard trying to concentrate on my work. It's too complex. Requires too much of my focus, and that's the last thing I have.

I glance over at my bed where Rio is lying. A fine figure of a man awaits me in my bed and a shiver runs through me just gaping at him like the horny teenager I become around him. He's got his earbuds in. Said he's listening to music while I work.

Eyes closed and shirtless, he's wearing only his boxers. He didn't need to take them off but, *if only he had.*

Heat coils low in my belly as my gaze inches over the hard, sculpted lines of his body, his wide chest, the mix of muscle, heat and pure masculinity on display. When I see his strained boxer briefs, my thighs clench, and my pulse races into overdrive.

Must be painful.

I could take care of that.

I *would* love to take care of that.

Pressing my thighs tighter together, I drag my gaze back to my desk and to the report in front of me. My body slumps with dismay. I need to finish this tonight but the kiss we shared, has left me feeling hot and sticky. I'm lit up like a firework ready to explode.

It's still not too late and caution has flown out of the window. Rio is a Knight, and Dani just married a Knight. They can't all be bad, can they?

I shake my head, losing this battle and get back to the report. The quicker I get this done... maybe, *maybe* we can continue from where we left off.

Although, glancing at my watch, I see that we don't have much time.

I YAWN. IT'S ONLY WHEN I NEXT LOOK AT MY WATCH I REALIZE hours have passed.

I stop typing, pinch the space between my brows where the tension builds.

I've had enough. Closing my laptop, I get up and have a good stretch, then walk over to the bed. Rio's lying sprawled out, the tiny white AirPods case tossed on the nightstand beside him. My gaze naturally falls to his crotch and I can see that his boner has abated.

Pity. I was so tempted to see him. To see *all* of him. To have him. To *be* with him. He looks so peaceful, and irresistible. When he peeled off his shirt, I tried not to gawk. Tried not to let my eyes linger too long. Tried not to let him see the way he was affecting me. But now, I take my sweet time, my gaze inching over every ridge and valley of him, the taut lines of his abs, the curve of his waist, the deep grooves where muscle meets bone.

Every inch of him is sculped and real, and mine for the taking. I don't want to wake him up, and yet I should, because the night is not quite over.

But it would be cruel. It was a long day, what with the wedding and reception, and I'm exhausted.

Rio must be as well.

I didn't tell him I had an early morning flight and now I only have a few hours. I'm too tired to try anything. So I decide to let him sleep and take a shower. If he hears the water running and wakes up, well and good.

And if he doesn't, I'll catch some sleep, then slip away in the early hours and fly back to Miami without waking the sleeping prince.

RIO

My eyes snap open, and I stare at the ceiling. It's a different ceiling. Then I remember where I am.

In São Paulo. Then I remember *where* I am. In Raquel's hotel room. I bolt upright in bed and look around. My phone is beside me, and my earbuds in their case. The space next to me is untouched.

No sign of Raquel.

"Raquel?" I leap out of bed, and walk around.

The room looks tidy. *Too* tidy. The balcony doors are closed. There's nothing on the desk. No laptop, no legal yellow pad, no pens. Just a few sheets of scrap. The clock blinks 12:00, and my stomach twists, not with dread, but with sharp, rising anger.

"Raquel?" I quickly check the bathroom.

Empty.

I open the closets.

Empty.

There's not even her makeup, lotions and perfume on the countertop in the bathroom. I swipe a hand through my hair. So, she upped and left without waking me, huh? I check my phone, but there are no messages. She slipped away quietly, but how the hell did I not hear a thing?

Then I remember something.

Fuck.

I'm supposed to be at Dani's parents' house for a breakfast brunch, but I'm already late. Maybe that's where Raquel is? Surely she wouldn't go without me? She would've woken me up.

I walk over to the desk again, and look at the papers scattered on it. It's her itinerary. She's already on a plane out of São Paulo. There's a sheet ripped in two. I piece it together and read the letterhead. Tovey & Roth. A law company in Miami. I assume this is who she works for.

Oh, well.

I flop back onto the bed, a wave of disappointment washing over me. What a night it would have been. The sizzling chemistry, the strip poker game, the kiss we shared on the balcony. We were supposed to carry on from that but it's over.

She missed out. Poor princesa.

She feels something for me. She knows I feel something for her. She's different. Not shy. Not in awe of me. She's defiant and headstrong, and special.

I don't gush about women, and I don't dwell on them either. Never have. But Raquel. Hell. She's been in my head since that first drink we shared as strangers. One evening. One conversation, and she's still there, taking up space I never meant to give.

Maybe I'm lonely and in need of company, and that's why she's consuming so much of my head space. I don't do hookups like Dex. I don't want just sex. I want something deeper. Something meaningful. Something real.

I'm not talking long-term, particularly, and while I don't have one-night stands, I want something more. Something fulfilling. I've never yet gotten too close or too attached to form anything real.

Or lasting.

And lately, I've been more closed off than usual when it comes to relationships. I'm not the type of guy to flit from woman to woman. I prefer to take my time and I like to choose my partners carefully.

We need to fit. It's not just about sex. There has to be trust, honesty, and understanding. The things that are important, for her, for me, for *us*, these things take time. I wasn't looking for anyone when Raquel swept into my life like the hurricane that she is, wild and free, ripping through my indifference and rearranging my carefully guarded persona. Now she's left me, all twisted up and standing in the wreckage, wondering how I ever lived in calmer weather.

Even Dex knows something is off, but I've not talked about Raquel before, and I sure as hell won't be saying anything now.

What is there to say? That dude is busy with Dani. Good luck to him and that marriage of convenience. No idea how he's going to pull that off. He likes sex, loves his hookups, and I can't see how he's going to survive a month, let alone a year, living like a monk with Dani floating around his apartment.

Dani caught my eye that night the old man lured my brothers and I into a soiree. I'm ashamed of myself when I think back to how awe-struck I was. Even before that, when I sneaked Dani's photograph out of the old man's apartment, and had it in my place.

Only for Dex to find it.

I shake my head just thinking about how pathetic I was. I quickly forgot about Dani when I realized there was no chase. It's Raquel who piques my interest in a way I don't fully understand. Her telling me about her childhood, and not knowing who her father was, and growing up in a favela— that's all sorts of interesting. I now have a better idea of who she is, and I want to know more about her than ever.

Me and her getting together? We'd set the bed on fire. But instead, I'm now lying here, pissed off by her sudden disappearance. That's never happened to me before. If I'm in a room with a woman, sex is what happens.

Raquel's worth chasing, for sure, and the horny devil I'm feeling right now, I'm in the mood to catch her. She can't stay hidden for long. Her bestie has just married my brother and this gives me hope.

I reach down behind, me, and pull out the panties she'd taken off. Bringing the flimsy, teensy black strip of fabric to my nose, I take a deep inhale.

At once, she's there, her heady strong perfume making every cell in my body dance in readiness. My cock stands thick, and dripping. With her panties wrapped around my hand, I reach down and give it a gentle tug.

CHAPTER FOUR

Two months later …

RAQUEL

"I can't wait to see you," Dani squeals.

"I can't wait, either. See you soon!" I hang up.

While I love talking to Dani, it brings back the ghost of Rio, and trying to forget him is a battle I've been mostly winning these days. Rich men like Rio—charming and smooth and best avoided—are my worst nightmare.

In my legal career I've seen how the system protects the wealthy while crushing everyone else, so I've known that these are not my people. He is everything I hate, yet for the life of me, I don't understand why I'm still so drawn to him.

Sure, I've approached men in bars before. It's how I know they're not afraid of a strong woman. Of a woman who may possibly earn more than them, or be in a higher position than them. I like to know these things upfront.

Rio was charming, smooth and sexy. He was flirty and fun. We are similar in some ways, and that surprised me most of all. Dani told me about the two sets of brothers, about the secret mistress, about Paul Knights's wife, about the suicide. I didn't know that about him the first time I met him, but by the time of Dani's wedding, when I invited him into my hotel room that night, I knew his childhood trauma and story.

This man isn't just a stud or a player. He has heart and his outer shell is at odds with the deeper, wounded, quietly loyal man underneath. Dani says he loves his mom. He'd do anything for her and I believe her, because that night Rio spoke of her lovingly.

He makes me feel things I haven't felt in years and he also makes me feel reckless, a little dangerous, a little too eager to do things that are out of my comfort zone. I feel like he could wreck me in the best and worst ways.

It took me a while to stop thinking about him after that night in São Paulo. A month later, I got a traumatic phone call from Dani, crying and sobbing, and telling me what Paul Knight had done.

She confessed to everything. Her and Dexter's marriage of convenience, and why she'd done it.

I knew it.

I knew something was off, though at the wedding reception, they seemed to be so much in love. Then she told me about Paul Knight and the dirty trick he played on Uncle Arminio, Dani's father, wresting control of AO Electronica away from him.

I was raging with fury after that phone call. Dani didn't stop crying. In between sobs she told me she'd had enough, that she was sick of the Knights. I offered to look over all the contracts Paul Knight had given her and her father, and that was when I saw how dirty these Knights can play.

I should have flown out to be by her side, and to take care of her but Pierce kept me busy. I was stressed, overworked, exhausted, and still wrestling with that sleazy man, and the guilt at hearing Dani sob over the phone, knowing I needed to be there, ate away at me.

I was furious, because I was right.

She'd married into the worst, most dysfunctional family around.

Filthy rich bastards.

I did the right thing to have walked away from Rio Knight.

After that, I helped her through it. Told her she needed to go to the Dominican Republic if she wanted to get a quickie divorce. I had no idea she was thinking about marrying Oscar Ramos. If I had, I would have flown out and physically restrained her from doing such a thing. I just assumed she needed the divorce to be free of the Knights.

Now she's coming to visit me next weekend, with Dexter. I've been meaning to meet her in person to figure out what's going on with her. To find out what the hell she's doing with her life, because she's now back with Dexter Knight. I've been too busy, and so has she, so this weekend will be great for a catch-up.

Life for my bestie has been nothing but a roller coaster life ever since Dexter Knight landed in it. She sounds genuinely happy. I even called her parents, on another pretext, and they assured me that this is real. That Dex saved Dani. My head naturally spins at the story but I'll get it all out of her soon.

Talking to her brings back thoughts of Rio even now, months later. There's too much drama around the Knights. I don't know what to make of it. Dani, in love. I don't know what Dex does to her, but she's still with him.

That part, I don't understand.

What a crazy family. What a crazy father. I did my best to

avoid Rio but it wasn't easy when he kept calling and texting me. I only contacted him the one time, when I was helping Dani, and I told him that she'd left Dex and was getting a divorce.

Then I ghosted him again. I considered blocking him, but that would have been childish and petty. His texts suddenly stopped and the hectic pace of my job kept me distracted, though at night, I'd lie in bed thinking of him more than I should have, trying to analyze why he'd stopped texting.

Had he found someone?

Why did I care?

I consoled myself by saying it was for the best.

It's after 9 p.m. and the office is deserted. The only sign of life is the glow of my screen. My inbox is overflowing. My back aches, and I've read the same contract clause three times, but I don't want to leave yet. An empty apartment doesn't appeal, but next weekend will be different. I'm excited but apprehensive about my friends coming.

My eyes land on the folder that Pierce left on my desk, telling me to give it a quick look. I open it and start reading.

SUBJECT: NGO Pro Bono Request – Blue Star Eco Resort Construction Dispute (Belize)

Attached are more documents from EcoGuardians International, a nonprofit we've partnered with before, but not the Belize office. I continue reading. They're requesting "early-stage legal review" of a land dispute involving a new luxury development, the Blue Star Eco Resort. The community claims environmental damage—mangrove destruction, reef contamination and contaminated drinking water among other issues.

The phrasing in the documents is cautious. They're worried,

and I'm assuming it's because they've been burned before. There's mention of questionable permits, a shell developer, and locals losing access to their only clean water source. My heart begins to hammer in my chest.

I love projects like this. Passion projects which fuel me and give me a sense of doing something good for the planet and the people who are affected. This is something I can get my sharp teeth into. A resort that calls itself eco-friendly while poisoning the coastline? I can't wait to dive in, though I'm surprised Pierce wants me to look at it. He hates me doing pro bono work, and prefers paid clients, whereas I like pro bono work. Justice shouldn't depend on the size of someone's wallet, and many environmental and indigenous communities can't afford top tier legal representation. I like that I can give them a voice. Pro bono work lets me fight for what I truly believe in—saving ecosystems, protecting marginalized communities, and holding corporations accountable. I've seen how money dictates outcomes and how it buys silence or wins dirty.

"I knew I'd find you here."

I jolt. Pierce's voice oozes into the room like cheap cologne. I set the papers down, bracing myself.

He steps inside without invitation, leaning against my doorframe, tie loosened like he's attempting nonchalance. He's in his early sixties, self-assured, smug, and trying his hardest to look at least a decade younger. This man has a year-round tan, and the kind of perfectly manicured hands that have never known hard work. His hair has been a work in progress. It's been thinning at the crown for years, giving glimpses of scalp showing under harsh office lighting. A few months ago, he turned up at the office with a surprisingly dense head of hair. Hair plugs, probably. Maybe he hadn't gone for a weekend in the Hamptons as he'd alleged, but made a visit to Hollywood's finest surgeons because it wasn't the only change I noticed. His jawline was tighter than I remembered and those slight jowls he once had, had miraculously vanished. Even the familiar lines on his brow were gone. Now he has a perpetually wide-awake look of a someone who is always surprised.

"You're here late. Don't you have anything better to do? Anyone to see?"

I hate his nosiness.

"I'm looking at the eco resort case from the NGO in Belize."

"Ah, yes. Locals are upset. Whining about the luxury resort. Something about mangroves and coral reef damage."

"They have every right to be outraged," I snap. "They need a voice. Someone who will step into the boxing ring and take on this fight. Someone like me".

He makes a sound between a laugh and a sigh. "It's pro bono, and you're too smart for charity."

"They flagged it as an environmental justice concern," I say, evenly. "There may be a violation of the Indigenous Land Rights Act—if the permits were pushed through the way they're suggesting—"

"You sound so passionate about these things." His smile tightens.

"Because this is what fuels me. I enjoy taking on greedy corporations and making them accountable."

He shrugs, giving off mixed signals again. "Why did you want me to look at this?"

"They asked for an early-stage legal review. That's usually in-house work, but they want an outside perspective." He shrugs. "They probably want someone idealistic to give them a pat on the back. I thought of you."

I frown. "Why?"

He pauses for longer than is comfortable, before offering an oily smile. "Because I need to keep you sweet. Give you the occasional carrot to get you to stay." Another slippery smile that make my stomach turn. He's not holding back. Maybe he can tell I'm getting itchy feet.

"Do you want me to pursue this or not, because I'm already buried in the Santos arbitration and if we don't push back hard this week, our client risks defaulting on a multi-million-dollar federal contract. I can't just drop it to fly to Belize and babysit some NGO land dispute."

"Skim through it, but don't spend all weekend buried in it."

"I'll skim through it," I say, returning to the papers.

I wish he'd vanish into the night, but he hesitates, watching me like he's about to say something else, and I fear that its going to make my skin crawl.

But he doesn't go there. Instead, he says, "These kinds of cases eat up your time and spit you out with nothing to show for it. You're better than that, Raquel."

This only confuses me further. On one hand he wants me to look it over, and then with the other, he's slightly pissed that I will.

"Thanks for the concern."

"I'm always concerned about you." His snakish smile creeps back in. "You've got a great future here, but only if you stay focused."

I shuffle my papers, pretending to read, but he's staring at me. I feel his dirty gaze raking over me, and I freeze.

You're the reason I need a future somewhere else.

"Any plans for this weekend?" he asks, "Or are you just sitting alone in your apartment?"

Always fishing for personal information.

His words make my flesh crawl like an army of ants over me. I look straight at him, not smiling, and shrug. "The usual. Female serial killer documentary and ice-cream."

He heads towards the door, mumbling, "I'll uh-leave you to it then."

I wait five seconds then exhale through gritted teeth. My gut says something's off but the papers on my desk say opportunity. And right now, I need one. I continue reading through them again. There's something here, I can feel it. I'd rather lose a case fighting for something real than win one that helps a billionaire dodge accountability.

More than anything, I want to build a career based on impact, not income, and I don't care about money as much as I care about leaving behind a reputation for standing up to power, inspiring other women, and changing lives. That's the kind of lawyer I want to be.

CHAPTER FIVE

RIO

"Come on in." Dex opens the door wider and gestures for me to come in.

"All clear?" I look around his apartment, needing to be sure that Dani has left. I haven't opened up to him about Raquel before. There was too much chaos going on, what with Dani leaving and the old man being up to his dirty tricks again.

"So, you and Dani got engaged for real, huh?" They announced it yesterday at Jett's place, when Jett and Cari invited us over for dinner. It was a Knight family dinner, a real one. Not the torturous ones we have to endure with the old man.

"We sure did." He hands me a bottle of beer.

"Congratulations, dude. Really happy for you."

Dex nods, but his face has been softer, and even though he's trying not to smile so much, I can tell he's happy, like ecstatic, way deep down to his core. I've never seen him this calm before. Like he has an inner knowing and happiness, and a strong sense of purpose in his life. Before he was slightly reckless, slightly crazy. A guy who liked his hookups and casual flings. Now, he's completely different. Dani is his north star. His perfect match and the woman who tamed him. I'm happy for the dude.

"Have you told the old man about you and Dani?" The old man wasn't invited.

"I will do." He doesn't seem to be in a rush.

"I heard Dani say you're both going to visit Raquel in Miami." My ears perked up when I caught that snippet from Cari and Dani's conversation. The mention of that name—a name I've been trying hard to forget for the past two months—brings up all sorts of feelings inside me.

I've called and messaged and emailed that woman, and she completely ghosted me. I didn't understand it. We were getting on like a house on fire. She liked me. She felt the attraction. She's the one who wanted to play strip poker. She's the one who told me to stay when I offered to leave her hotel room that night of Dex and Dani's wedding.

And then we made out on the balcony after a blistering session of playing a card game. I didn't think I could have so much fun while keeping my clothes on. She told me to stay— because she had work to do—so I stayed, but when I woke up, she'd gone. Despite my attempts to get in touch, she ignored me like I didn't exist. Like I didn't matter.

Maybe, in the cold light of day, she probably rethought everything about me. Decided the Knights weren't worth getting close to.

Decided to put me in the enemy-zone.

I only heard from her when all hell broke loose, when Dani left Dex, and he fell apart. Dani obviously confided in her best friend and told her everything, because it was soon after that

Raquel texted to let me know that Dani was getting a divorce in the Dominican Republic.

I still remember her text:

> Dani has left your brother.

> You Knights ... 😠

> She's gone to the Dominican Republic to get a divorce.

> She should never have married a Knight 😠

I was so ecstatic to hear from her, and I quickly replied, telling her how I was sorry, I needed to explain, but it was good to hear from her. How was she?

She sent another text:

> I knew I was right to stay away from you.

But when I replied, she ghosted me again.

I've never heard from her since, and it's been over a month. This all feels so strange to me. I'm not one to sit and mope over a woman. I chase, catch, then see how it goes. Mostly, we have a few months of fun, but that's all.

This woman has me upside down and back to front. We haven't had sex. Kissing, and playing a game of strip poker is as far as we've gotten.

I need to see her, to kiss her, to touch her to prove to myself that she isn't as unique and captivating as I remember. I need to know if I've simply built it all up in my mind, since I last saw her. I need to prove that once I've had her, I can walk away unscathed, because if I can't, and seeing her again proves the opposite, I'm done for.

This woman unmoors me. She's the first one to ghost me this way, and she gives me so much grief, instead of kissing my ass. She hates my last name, and she whips my butt because of it.

"Daniela wants to tell Raquel in person, and I'm pretty sure she wants to tell her in detail about everything that went down. It's been mad, and Raquel doesn't know the half of it. Hell, she doesn't even know that I proposed to Daniela, and that this time it's for real."

I force a laugh, remembering the first time I met Raquel, and how Dex and Dani were interrogated by her. The woman I'm crazy about is smart. She needed convincing that Dex and Dani really were together. So now, after everything that's happened, I'm not surprised she wants details.

And no wonder she hates me.

The Knight name is poison to her.

"Why are you asking?" Dex looks at me quizzically, breaking me out of my thoughts.

I shrug. I'm having a tough time as it is, and all we shared was a scorching hot kiss on an unforgettable night in her hotel room. I've tried to forget her, but it's impossible, and because she's Dani's best friend, and Dani's now engaged to my brother, our lives will be inextricably intertwined. There's a high chance that I'll run into her again. There will be weddings and babies and birthdays and other anniversaries.

"You said you don't feel anything for her," Dex counters, slowly, trying to piece it all together—my interest in this woman, when I've not spoken at great length about her.

"I just haven't said anything about her to you, dude." I don't know how I feel about her. It's all hot and cold. There's fun and sizzle when we connect, and then long dry spells where we don't meet.

"You want to tell me something, brother? Just say it. It's not like you to get tongue-tied about a woman."

I pretend to laugh. "I don't think so."

He nods, slowly, knowingly. Then, "You said she'd been conquered and ditched."

"We had a few moments," I say, cryptically.

"A few moments? Brother, I've asked you about this before, when you didn't make the flight back with the rest of us after the wedding."

That was the day after the strip poker evening. I've been vague about it all since then. Not that Dex cared to delve deeper. I guess he was busy navigating through the surprise honeymoon the old man gave them, then he had to adjust to living with Dani in his apartment.

I left them to it, and I was too busy trying to get Raquel out of my head to worry him.

"We played strip poker."

Dex whistles low, leaning back. "Jeez, bro."

"It was a hot, *hot* night …"

"Did you …?"

"No. I'm sure we would have. That woman is dynamite. Kissing her? *Electric*. She …" I think about how she dangled her panties from her fingers, and how I almost shot my load. She was such a beautiful tease. Not taking off her dress, but her *panties*.

I swallow, and decide not to tell all. "I fell asleep, and she had work to do."

Dex roars with laughter. "Fell asleep? That's not like you."

"Biggest boner I've ever had in my life." I remember it clearly. I still think about that night every night. And I have her panties, unwashed, somewhere in my drawers.

Dex stops, mid-pour, the whiskey bottle in one hand, his empty glass in the other. "Jeez, bro. Too much information." He finishes pouring the drink, takes a sip.

"I was hoping I could come along to Miami with you guys." I throw it out there.

Dex's reaction is what I expected, what I feared. "I don't think that's a good idea," he says slowly.

"Why not?" I'm always ready to be his wing man at a moment's notice, and I expected him to be the same. No questions asked, just a readiness to dive in and do it.

Maybe being with Dani has made him go all soft.

Is that a bad thing?

"After everything that happened, Raquel hates the Knights more than ever. Daniela told me."

"Even now?" Rio asks. "After what you did, helping to get the company back?"

"With your help. I couldn't have done it alone," Dex adds. He's quiet for a beat. "You really like her?"

"Can't stop thinking about her. She won't reply to my messages. The only time I heard from her was when she told me Dani was going to the Dominican Republic, for the divorce, and that's when I told you."

He scratches his jaw. "I don't know, bro. I don't know. Maybe she'll come around and see you for the charming, sexy, nice guy you are." He flashes a grin at me. "It depends how she feels about you."

"That night at the hotel, she didn't have to ask me in, and she didn't have to suggest we play strip poker. I just wanted to make sure she got back to her hotel safely."

"That's all you wanted?"

"She's different."

His eyes widen. "And is she as captivated by you?"

"I'm not sure. She blows hot and cold. That's why I want to crash your weekend, just one evening, see if I can get her to talk."

"She might come around, she might not. She might hate you more than ever."

"She might."

Not that that's a bad thing. Raquel and I, we have a love-hate thing going on. Not love, per se, because we don't really know one another deeply, but we definitely have a hate thing.

I'm captivated by her. Entranced by her beauty. Mesmerised by her wit and intelligence. I also wouldn't mind having her in my bed, in any position she likes. Doing what the hell she likes. I'll be up for it, she only has to say.

I like that she isn't fooled by my name, wealth or status. She's the biggest challenge of my life, and the more she turns ice queen on me, the more I want to melt her and prove how fiery we could be together.

Dex narrows his eyes. "Sounds to me like you like the challenge."

"I always did. You know that."

"This woman sounds like a Rubik's cube level challenge."

"She's more than that. I need to know if she really hates me, or if she's playing hard to get."

"You did say you liked the chase."

"This woman has me doing marathons."

He chortles. "Maybe she's finding it hard to forget you."

"It's possible. I'm unforgettable. Comes with the charm package." I flash him a grin. "Some people call it arrogance. I call it a public service."

Dex rolls his eyes. "Then, *come*. Show up as a surprise."

"That's what I was aiming to do, like she did at your date with Dani, remember that, dude?"

"Often." He grins. "And based on *that* event, and where we are today, miracles are possible, brother. They're possible. So, yeah. Come along, but act surprised when you see us. Make out like you happened to be there by chance."

"Why?"

"Because I'm not sure Dani would think it's a good idea either."

I can't believe how smitten this dude is. He obviously doesn't want to be in Dani's bad books. "Don't worry. I won't land you in it." But secretly I'm thrilled, bordering on ecstatic.

I'm going to Miami, to meet the woman I haven't been able to forget. I thrive on the thrill, the quest, the race to conquer, and no woman has ever denied me like Raquel has.

CHAPTER SIX

RAQUEL

AFTER AN AWFUL DAY IN THE OFFICE WITH THAT SCUMBAG WHO passes for my boss, I'm looking forward to seeing Dani tonight.

Dex, too, I suppose. Though I'm still a little uneasy about them being back together again. I'm hoping this weekend sheds some light on what's going on with them.

They're staying at one of the top hotels in Miami—of course they would. I'm surprised the Knights don't have a holiday home here. They're going to take me to a fancy new restaurant for dinner.

We've arranged to meet at the restaurant , and I go there straight after work. As soon as I walk in, I see them. Dani is hard to miss. She always looks like a movie star in a crowd of people, and the best thing? She's so modest.

They've got one of the best tables, by the window. Dani gets up as soon as she sees me, and waves me over. I rush towards her and we throw our arms around one another and hug. I hold her for longer than normal, because I've been worried about her. Because I'm so happy to see her. Because a weekend with my bestie drowns out all the work and Pierce headaches.

Last night we met a client over dinner, and even after the client left, Pierce wouldn't let me go. Said he wanted to talk about my career goals. I hated every moment of sitting across a table from him, counting the minutes and the seconds, wondering how I could escape from him.

"You look good, hon," I whisper.

"I'm so happy to see you!"

We're still hugging. "Tell me you're happy, Like *really* happy?" I whisper. "Wink, if you're here under duress."

She roars with laughter. We pull away, hands on each other's arms, examining one another.

"Duress? Hon, you have the most vivid imagination. You think Dex is holding a knife to my back?"

I have to say, she looks magnificent. She always does, but there's an inner glow this time. She's bubbling with happiness. She hugs me again, arms going around my neck as she clings to me. Then I see Dex standing behind her.

"Anything is possible with these Knights," I murmur, before flashing a false smile at Dex. He stands there. Hands in his pockets, looking nonchalant and relaxed. Giving me and my girl our own space. But I can't forget what his family did to Dani. I can't forgive what his father put Uncle Arminio through. And now I'm supposed to forget all of that and accept this happy-ever-after?

Not so quickly this time.

"You're hilarious, hon, but I know you mean it." Dani dismisses my concerns easily. "That's why I needed to come and see you, to make you understand that we're good."

"I'm so happy that you're here." I shake hands with Dex.

It's cold and clinical. Like I'm meeting a new client. This man has to win back my trust and respect.

"Sit," Dani insists. She's super excited. Effervescent. I wonder if she's had too many cocktails.

"Let's get some champagne," Dex suggests. "And, dinner tonight is on me."

"Thank you." I smile sweetly as I peruse the drinks menu, then select the most expensive bottle of champagne. "Are we celebrating something?" It feels like it.

"Dex wants to make amends," Dani enthuses. She's fizzing with excitement. I start to worry and I wonder if he's drugged her and brought her here to allay any suspicions he thinks I might have.

You can never trust the Knights. Dex might have duped Dani, but he can't dupe me. None of them can.

Dex chortles. "You've only seen the bad side of the Knights, Raquel, and I want to put things right. My father's actions don't reflect how the rest of us feel, or operate."

I cock my head, my gaze ping-ponging between them. Something hangs in the air, with the way these two are looking at each other, and the way they're looking at me. Expectantly.

"What is it?" I ask slowly, because honestly, I'm expecting more drama. Dani's with a Knight. It's expected.

Dani smiles at Dex. He smiles back. I feel like a third wheel. Then she holds out her hand.

"We're engaged!" she squeals. My gaze falls to sparkling emerald ring, and I slump back in my chair, the weight of her words a punch to my gut.

"You were engaged before," I say, trying to sound more enthusiastic than I feel. That is a nice ring. So much better than the other one.

"We were, but this time it's for real." Dani's eyes shine like diamonds. She's insanely excited and deliriously happy. Almost as if she's lost her mind.

"For *real* real?" I'm watching their faces, trying to look for clues, for *what* this is. For *why* this is. She divorced him recently, and they hadn't even been married that long. I fear that my best friend has lost her mind.

"For real, this time," Dex says. They both hold hands on the table.

"But you divorced him. You went to the Dominican—"

"I know, I know! This is why I wanted to come and tell you in person. It's been a crazy few months, and I've got so much to tell you."

"I can imagine," I murmur under my breath, because Dani looks so happy. So ridiculously, over-the-moon happy. But my in-built warning system alerts me, and never lets me forget what's happened. Or the family Dex comes from.

She starts telling me, both of them talking and finishing each other's sentences. I find it so aggravating. They tell me the entire story. I've heard bits of it before. How Dex followed Dani to Brazil. How he discovered she had plans to marry Oscar Ramos, and how he was so thankful he got there just in time to stop her from going through with her crazy idea.

"Then I went and got my girl back," Dex says, looking at Dani lovingly.

"We've been inseparable since. Dexter loves me, and I love him."

"She's the only one for me," says Dex.

I don't know how I'm going to survive this evening. It's not like the girlie dinners Dani and I have. With Dex in the mix, it's something else entirely. "A marriage born from a fake marriage of convenience," I say flatly.

They gaze at one another, and I seriously consider getting up and leaving them to enjoy their intimate dinner for two.

"Don't be like that, hon." Dani seems desperate for me to like Dex, and she's probably wondering why I'm not more excited about her news.

"I get it," Dex says carefully. "Raquel has every right to be cautious."

I wonder if he knows about me and Rio. I wonder if Rio has told him.

"No, no," I say quickly, putting a hand to my chest, trying to push through the tangled mess of feelings. "I *am* happy, it's just, so *unexpected*." Dani's earlier exuberance fades. She's not silly. She knows me, and her excitement fizzles out at my reaction.

Now I feel bad.

"Dani." I get up from my seat and move to her. She stands up and I give her a great big hug. "Congratulations. "I'm so thrilled for you. I want you to be truly happy." I read her eyes, trying to extract clues from them, like I need proof of her happiness. "You're happy, aren't you?"

"Raquel!" She hugs me again, laughing as though I've delivered the funniest one liner. "I'm so hopelessly, ridiculously, madly in love and so so so happy. This time it's for real."

Okay. I believe her, but I'm still going to watch her like a hawk.

Then I move over to Dex and shake his hand again. The burn of Dani's gaze guilt trips me. I should be more excited. Be more receptive, hug him or something, but I can't. "If you hurt my best friend at all, in any capacity, I'll make your life a living hell," I say, with a forced smile, trying to pass my words off as a joke.

Dex nods, his gaze locked on mine. "Understood. Also, if I hurt her, I'd already be in hell."

Caraca. Those words and the way Dex looks at Dani, the depth of emotion in his eyes, tells me he would die for her. My heart flutters inside my chest. He really means it. I clasp a hand to my sternum, so utterly moved, and wondering if I will ever experience that kind of love. I move in for a hug, brushing off my emotions. Maybe it is possible that Dexter Knight is not the type of Knight I'd run a mile from.

As I pull away, he places his hand on my arm. "I don't blame you for hating my family, but we're not all that bad. We're not. I hope my actions, once we get to know each other, will make you see that there's good in some of us. Most of us. Us brothers, we're not all like our father."

Where have I heard that before? This might have thawed my feelings towards Dex a little, but my distrust of the Knights isn't going anywhere.

I quickly sit down again, feeling a pinch of sadness. I'm suddenly overcome by emotion. I'm happy for Dani, or, trying to be, and I make a mental note to keep an eye on her closer than ever now, but Dex's words, *"I'm not like my father"*, remind me of Rio.

I've barely heard from him but every now and then, he slides back into my thoughts again, and that night in São Paulo looms vibrantly in my imagination, feeling so real sometimes, it hurts. I try to focus on the present. That it's the weekend, there's no work and that my best friend is here. Tomorrow we have a girlie day to ourselves. There's so much cause for celebration.

"I'm sure that's what you all say." I soften my words with a smile.

Dex's brow furrows. "I get that you need time, that we have to prove ourselves."

"We?" Dani looks at me. "I don't have to prove anything to Raquel."

"He doesn't mean you," I say to Dani. I know who he's referring to. Something in my gut tells me he and Rio have talked. I feel it in my bones. Just like I sometimes remember the weight of Rio's gaze on me, his lips on mine, the fast and flirty banter that we shared that night.

"You'll have to earn it, all over again," I say, opening the food menu. "Shall we order?"

I'm hungry, and I need to process everything. Not just this, Dani and Dex engaged, but the ghost of Rio that has now come back to haunt me.

DANI HAS BROUGHT ME UP TO DATE ON WHY SHE GOT BACK with Dex, and why she believes he's nothing like his father. With the happy wonder of a child, she told me how Dex proposed, and I made all the appropriate excited sounds and comments as I drove to the spa center where we're spending a few indulgent hours getting pampered like the queens that we are.

Last night wasn't the right time to find out all the details of Paul Knight's trickery, not in front of Dex. And after dinner, they were tired and so was I, so we all went home.

But, I've interrogated Dani and I now know everything that went on, in detail. Maybe Paul Knight is a monster, and maybe his sons are different, but Dex will have to prove himself.

Getting AO Electronica back for Dani's father, with the help of the other brothers, is all well and good, and noble, but time will tell if I can trust Dex to be the type of partner my friend deserves. Once a Knight, always a Knight. I've known about this family and their business practices long before the Knights became a part of Dani's life.

I try not to think about them as we walk into the light and airy spa. The gardenia-infused air inspires a soothing calm that I don't fully feel.

We settle into the plush black velvet chairs, ready for our manicure and pedicure. I'm treating Dani and I'm determined that this will be our time. Pure girlie time with talk of no billionaires or family drama. Just two best friends catching up in style.

I miss her like crazy, and I miss our little catch-up sessions. When we studied together at Georgetown, it was one of the best years of my life. We're more than best friends; we're like sisters and spending time together always guarantees fun and laughter.

We haven't been here long and I feel lighter already. She's the only person I can let my guard down with even though I may not tell her everything, and she might not tell me.

The technicians start on h our pedicures.

"I didn't realize how much I needed this." Dani sighs in contentment and sits back in her chair.

"I did."

I clink my glass gently against hers. "To fabulous skin, juicy gossip, and getting taken care of by people who won't judge you."

Dani laughs, leaning her head back and closing her yes. "Only you would toast to exfoliation."

She sips her champagne. This is going to be a regular thing for her, in exotic locations all around the world, when she vacations. She'll have a jet-set life being engaged and eventually married to a billionaire.

"I've missed you so much, hon," I tell her.

"I've missed you."

We sit a while in an appreciative silence. The mood is light and easy, but my mind drifts. There's something I've been meaning to ask. Something that's been sticking in the back of my throat while I digest everything she told me.

"So…" I take another sip and lower my voice, "what does your future father-in-law think about your engagement?"

Dani opens one eye, turns and gives me a look. "Dex said that when he told him, his father just nodded and said he wasn't surprised."

Typical.

"He's pissed, Dexter says. After everything that happened, him tricking my father, and Rio and his brothers helping Dexter get the company back ..."

Paul Knight sounds dangerous and vile. I shudder with dread to think of Dani having him for a father-in-law one day. When I think of the family secret, the affair Paul had, of his wife's suicide, and the two sets of brothers, it's the stuff of soap operas. It doesn't seem real. But it is, and that's the sad thing. Two families were affected. Two women, who both loved a man. And six little boys.

Now that I know, I see the similarity between them, though it still surprises me that Rio and Dex are only half-brothers, because they seem so much like real brothers so strong is their resemblance, save for the hair, and Rio's olive complexion.

"Dexter told his father at work. He just walked into his office, told him we were engaged, for real, and that was it."

It doesn't surprise me, but it's so messed up. "Did his father congratulate you?"

Dani scoffs. "I haven't seen him since the Knight family dinner, at his penthouse, when Dexter told him that he'd been outplayed. Jett threw us a dinner last week, and it was such a wonderful evening."

"Wonderful?" She makes it sound like he did something amazing.

"It was informal, and Paul wasn't invited, and we all got on. It felt so relaxed, compared to the Knight family dinner. It was like being at home, when we have our cousins and aunts and uncles over. Usually there's no warmth with the Knights, but this was different. It's hard to explain. They don't know how to be a family." She looks at me, apologetically.

"They're dysfunctional."

"Yes, but that night, at Jett and Cari's dinner, it felt like we were all part of one family."

"You *are* all part of one family," I quip.

"But they don't act like it. If you saw them together, you'd see the divide. Rio, Matteo and Enzo versus Jett, Dex and Zach. Dexter said it used to be so obvious. But then he and Rio started hanging out, and discovered that they have a lot in common, and then they had to keep their friendship a secret from the others. That's crazy, don't you think?"

"They're a crazy family," I mutter. "You don't have to marry into it." I quirk a smile, but a part of me is being serious.

The technician starts on her other foot, around the same time that mine does. "You're wary, and you have the sense of a bloodhound and I love you for it, but you'll see, the more you get to know Dexter, that he's nothing like his father. None of them are."

"None of them?" My heart flips, and I anticipate hearing about the others.

"It was so sweet. Jett apologized to me for being so cold towards me, and I appreciate it. It means a lot coming from him."

"Why? Does he have a God-complex or something?" I roll my eyes. They think they're more important than they are. They think having all that wealth elevates them. I have so much disdain for these people.

She laughs. "No. He's just … more intense, more … brooding."

I glance sideways at her, trying to play it cool. "And the others?"

"They're interesting characters. Each of them are so different."

"How?"

"Zach is like the youngest. It's Jett, Dex and then him, and he seems to care more for their father. He doesn't dislike him as much as they all do. Rio and Dex are close. Matteo is cool, a bit indifferent. Keeps himself to himself. Enzo is a dark horse."

"Is he?"

"I think so. He's the quietest one, and the youngest of that set of brothers, but I think he's smarter and more savvy than he lets on."

We fall silent, and the soft music fills the air. I take a sip of my champagne, letting the bubbles fizz over my tongue. As casually as I can, I ask, "What about Rio?" She didn't say much about him.

"Rio?" She hesitates, as if she's searching for words. "Rio's complicated."

"That's one word for him."

She turns to me. "How would you know?"

I swirl my champagne, feigning nonchalance. "It's a gut feeling."

I can see that she doesn't buy it, but she lets it go. I lean back, letting the tech paint my nails. "When's the wedding?"

Dani snorts. "Hon, we just got engaged. We're not rushing. We're taking it slow this time."

I raise an eyebrow. "Hopefully there'll be no more drama."

"Not this time. Why would there be? I told you why we had an arranged marriage."

She did. I had no idea that AO Eletronica wasn't doing so well. Hopefully things will get better now. Uncle Arminio has been such an inspiration and so many have looked up at him.

"Did I ever tell you about me and Rio?" she asks, casually, like she's asking me what nail color I like the best.

"You and Rio?" I feel like I've been punched.

"He was awestruck when he first saw me. Remember I told you about the social evening Paul Knight held at his penthouse, where all the Knight boys turned up?"

I nod. She told me about that. She never told me about her and Rio. She sits back and holds up her hand, admiring her nails as the technician moves on to her other hand. She has no idea that her words gnaw away at my insides.

"What about you and Rio?" I ask, in a voice I don't recognize as mine.

She laughs, her green eyes twinkling like this is an amusing story. For her maybe. "He was so mesmerised he could barely speak. "

I force a laugh, and think back to the smooth talking, confident man who sets me on fire each time we're in the same room, and I can't reconcile him with this awe-struck, speechless version Dani's telling me about.

"I can't imagine that," I manage to say.

She goes on to tell me how much he liked her, how later on, Dex told her that Rio had a photo of her in his apartment. That he was smitten by her. Every word she says, every image my mind builds, is like a hook reaching into my gut and ripping my heart to shreds. It feels so sharp. So painful, and it surprises me that I feel this. I've never been jealous of Dani. We both had lots of admirers in college, but this news about Rio cuts in a way I'm not prepared for.

"But I chose Dexter instead," she says, with a giggle.

I find the idea of Rio being in awe of Dani extremely unsettling. She and I are both capable of turning heads wherever we go, but she has a lushness, a voluptuousness, and those twinkling bright green eyes, not to mention her height—something I don't have.

"Why Dex?" I ask, relieved that she did.

"Because he didn't fall at my feet," she answers, innocently, oblivious to the tsunami of emotions sweeping over me. I feel hollow to my core. "He barely spoke to me."

I dread to think what might have happened if he had. If Dani had chosen Rio. If she and Rio had gotten married. And I don't like thinking about that.

"Are you still working nonstop?" she asks.

I groan. "Yes. I've got a new case coming up— environmental justice stuff. Something messy down in Belize. Corporate corruption, deforestation, the works."

"That sounds intense. You must be loving that."

"I do. It sounds meaty, and you know how much I love fighting for our planet, and how much I hate these big corporations pissing all over the small people. Pierce is giving me mixed signals about it. He wants me to look at it, but he's not too keen on my going out." I can't get a read on him for this one, but I don't want to think about him or work for now.

"Is your boss still... you know, repugnant?" Dani makes a pained face.

I wrinkle my nose in disgust. "He's insufferable. I need to leave. I've been saying that for months but I really need to make it happen."

CHAPTER SEVEN

RIO

Dex and I met earlier in the day, in a bar at the hotel where I'm staying. That dude was all wrapped up in guilt. I could immediately tell that he feels bad for hiding my visit from Dani.

I get it.

These two lovebirds don't want any secrets between them. Totally understandable. Dex feels bad for the all the trickery Dani endured, on account of the old man. Raquel probably hates my guts even more, if that is possible.

That is, if she's even thinking about me.

I was starting to wonder if my surprise visit was such a good idea, but a few Negronis was all it took to convince me that it was. Dex said the girls were having a spa day, and then he told me about how the meal went last night, when they announced their engagement to Raquel.

I chuckled when he described her reaction.

"Not exactly happy," is what Dex said.

No shit. I'm sure Raquel wants nothing to do with the Knights, after seeing how the old man screwed Dani's father over.

Raquel's treating them to a celebratory dinner, and I can't screw this up. Dex isn't thrilled about sneaking me into their little engagement celebration, but he claims he understands why I need to crash it. He said he doesn't want to lie, so I'm the one who has to come up with a good reason for turning up unexpectedly.

I'll do it.

I'll do whatever I have to. Still, my stomach twists as I walk into the restaurant where Dex told me they'd be. The hostess leads me through the dimly lit dining room. This is good, Raquel won't see me coming.

It will be a complete surprise.

The ambiance is intimate. Soft candlelight and art deco chandeliers. People talking in hushed tones, making polite conversation. Charmed laughter.

That's when I see her. The woman who's taken up permanent residence inside my head.

Raquel.

Everything crawls to slow motion. My insides turn light and floaty, like I've just dropped from a great height in a rollercoaster. She has her hair pinned back, off her face, twisted into something elegant. No wild curls tumbling down. She looks sleek, and polished. She's always glamourous. Always eye-catching and beautiful. I long to trace my fingers along the delicate curve of her neck, to cup her face and admire those sharp cheekbones, to just stare at her dark Bambi eyes.

Even in the dimmed light, I can make out satin red stain on her lips. My heart jolts, and my pants start to feel tight again.

This woman doesn't even have to touch me to have an effect on me. I watch in wonder as a champagne glass dangles from her fingertips. It immediately reminds me of the panties she once dangled. I head towards them. She's mid-laugh, head tilted back, Dani leaning into her like a conspirator, and Dex sitting opposite them looking like he's an extra who wandered into the wrong scene.

She still hasn't seen me, and I get a few moments to stare freely. This woman is a hit of adrenaline and something more dangerous. She's the type of woman you remember months and years later. She's in my blood, but I'm not sure if that's addiction or poison. All I know is that it's annoying, and I just need to get her out of my system, so I can get on with my life. I adjust my jacket before stepping into the spotlight.

"Well, this is a surprise. What the hell are you all doing here?"

Three heads turn. Dani gasps. Dex tries to look surprised. Raquel freezes, the glass halfway to her lips as her smile vanishes before my eyes.

Dani's the first to recover. "Rio?" Her tone is warm, but confused. "What are you doing here?"

"Business." I lie smoothly, sliding into the booth next to Dex. A muscle tenses along Dex's jaw. Like he's thinking,

"Wrong move, brother. Don't make yourself too comfortable." Dex wants this to look purely coincidental. Raquel is sharp. Too sharp. He doesn't want her, or Dani, suspecting anything.

"Sorry. It just felt like old times." I immediately get back up again. "I won't stay long. Didn't mean to interrupt."

Raquel is still silent, her mouth open. Her eyes curious, as if she doesn't know what to make of this.

"This is a surprise." Dani lets out a nervous laugh. I find it odd that she's doing all the talking.

"Had a few important meetings that couldn't wait, I thought I saw you guys walking in so here I am."

"Are you stalking us? Is this planned? Are you trying to pretend that this is unexpected?" Raquel snaps. This woman. Her interrogative skills seem to be a permanent part of her personality.

"Why, hello there, *Judge*." I drop a nod, and try hard not to fixate on her lips, or her smoky eyes—charcoal liner blended with warm bronze. Damn if she doesn't look irresistibly seductive. My heart thumps inside my rib cage, and my nerves begin to fray, a feeling as unfamiliar as failure. My cocksure charm and easy banter abandons me and I'm uncharacteristically at a loss for words.

Luckily, Dex comes to my rescue. "Can I get you a drink, brother?"

"Thanks, but no. I was having drinks with the guys from the meeting, across the road." I vaguely wave in the direction of the street.

"You had a meeting here, in Miami, the same time that Dex and Dani are here, on a weekend?" Raquel's champagne flute still dangles from her hands. I keep an eye on it, in case she wants to throw it at me, such is the hatred flowing out of her gaze.

"You think I'm making this up?" I chuckle, running a hand across my beard. I catch the way she stares, the way she examines my face. Inch. By. Inch.

She's missing me. I know it. "Oh, princesa." I whip out a business card from my pocket. "Andre Berloni. The guy I had a meeting with. He and a few others are still there. Call him."

I venture a glance at Dex, who looks wide-eyed. I bet he's thinking, "What the fuck?"

"Sit down, Rio. Don't be a stranger." Dani seems to have bought my ruse, but Raquel snatches the card from my fingers, whips out her cell phone, and calls the number. I ease into the booth, next to Dex, watching her directly opposite me.

I know this woman. *So well.*

She gives me a let's-see-how-you-wrangle-your-way out-of this look. "Andre?"

I smile.

Her gaze fixes on me. "This is going to sound insanely crazy, but, did you have drinks with someone just now? A business meeting?" She's clever. She doesn't give him the name.

Dex looks like he's seen a ghost. Dani looks perplexed. I casually adjust the sleeves of my jacket, biding my time. I know Raquel. I know she doesn't trust or believe. I came prepared.

"You did? Uh-huh. Oh. It was? Thank you." She hangs up, resentment oozing off her. "Andre sends his regards."

I chuckle. "You had to check, huh, princesa?"

Dani laughs. "Raquel, give the man a break."

Dex is silent, but his eyes fill with a million questions.

That was the best use of a hundred dollars ever.

"I left the guys early, and figured I'd swing by and toast the happy couple, again." I glance at Dex who is still silent, but he lifts one brow, probably wondering what trick I'll come up with next.

Raquel picks up her glass, murmurs, "How convenient," and drains it dry. Her voice is satin and silk. Smooth as honey, sweet as molasses. The looks she's giving me though, are anything but.

"You look well," I say, giving her an easy smile.

"And you look ... the same. Still allergic to reading the room, I see."

I'm loving this. I miss the way we spark and converse with each other. "Ouch. No warm welcome?"

Those lips I adore press into a tight line.

"I'm glad to see that you're well," I say carefully. "I got worried, especially when you didn't text back all those times."

"I did text you," she retorts. "To tell you how right I was to stay away from you."

"I was thrilled to hear from you at long last, despite sending you million messages and getting cold-shouldered." I lean towards her slightly, see her eyes flash, and her mouth twitch. She's trying not to get riled up, but the fact that I can rile her up, feels good.

I yearn for another night of strip poker.

Dani cuts in. "This champagne really hits, huh?"

Dex clears his throat. "We, uh... should probably give you two a moment."

"No need," Raquel says, eyes still locked on mine. "We're great. Totally fine."

"Fine is such a subjective word," I counter.

Dex stands. "How about we get our dessert outside, Daniela?"

Dani hesitates. "Raquel?"

Raquel waves her off. "I'm good. I'll try not to kill him."

I smile, warming up to her. "You'd do anything to get your hands on me."

"Chokehold or a headlock?" she asks, eyes narrowed. Dex and Dani leave quickly, and then it's only the two of us. The air tightens around us instantly.

"That's not a good move for a lawyer." I wave the server over and order a Negroni.

"And I'll get the bill, please," Raquel tells him.

"You're leaving already?" I'm shocked. I didn't expect her to rush off this fast. I expected more time, more banter, more flirting. Now I'm doubting myself for coming here. Maybe she's in a relationship?

"You came all the way here to... what? Ambush me with banter and pretend it's business?"

"Who says I'm pretending, princesa? You spoke to Andre, didn't you?"

"Please." She scoffs, folding her arms. "I've met you, remember? I know you Knights have answers for everything. You people are good at covering your tracks."

"Want to go over and meet Andre?" I glance at my watch, but don't note the time. "We can go and have a drink with him. Maybe he can tell you all about our meeting."

"Nothing for me, thank you," she says, when the server asks if she'd like dessert.

"You're not asking me?"

"Absolutely nothing for him. My guests are outside, if you'd like to take their order."

"Certainly, ma'am." The server nods and disappears.

I relax back against my chair. "You're being rather strict on me, and we're not even a couple yet. Afraid I'll put on weight, or is it diabetes you're trying to save me from?" I flash her another one of my charming smiles I know she hates.

"You can overdose on all the sugar you want."

Ouch. She really is mad at me. Still, I don't want to waste this opportunity. "I came here to talk, princesa. To get the conversation going. I didn't take you for a coward, so why are you running away?"

Eyes blazing she glares at me. "I'm not scared of you, Knight. I'm being sensible."

"Tell me you don't think about that night."

Her eyes flash. I see something wild and defiant, like she's daring me to see exactly what she's thinking.

"I waited for you," I remind her. "You told me to. You had work to do, but even though I offered to leave, you told me to stay."

"I took pity on you," she snaps.

I lean forward more and touch her arm. Her skin is warm,

and prickly now. Every touch, every look, every whisper, it affects us both. Not only me.

"So much pity that you asked me in and then suggested a game of strip poker." I grab my drink from the server.

"It seemed like the polite thing to do, after all, you left your brother's wedding reception to walk me back."

"There's nothing polite about playing strip poker."

She shifts in her seat.

"Don't deny that you feel something for me, princesa."

"You should forget that night ever happened."

"Hard to forget when you vanish without saying goodbye."

"I thought my silence would speak volumes."

"It did," I say softly. "But I still kept listening, waiting for you to break."

"Break?"

"From your stubbornness, and give in."

She looks away, jaw clenched. I take in the gold earrings, the neckline of her dress, the thick black satin line extenuating her eyes. But still my gaze goes to her lips. Red, thick and plump, I want to ravage that mouth.

She's furious, and still so beautiful even when her face twists with anger. "Let's go outside," I suggest. She hesitates, but seems to be thinking about it. "You can shout at me out there. You can even slap me, if it'll make you feel better."

A smile tugs at her lips. "You give me permission to do that?"

"Princesa, I give you permission to do *whatever* you want to me."

She doesn't speak for a few seconds, and I can almost hear the hum of whatever's sparking between us. If the thoughts going through her head are anything like mine, I bet she's already molten heat between her thighs.

Raquel and I are fire on fire.

No retreat, no surrender, just heat building until something explodes.

"I'd want to know why you'd want to slap me," I say, all cocky charm, trying to coax a smile from her. But it's not forthcoming.

"You gave me permission. There doesn't have to have a reason."

I push my luck, say what's on my mind, give her honesty. "I think of your panties dangling on your fingers."

"I never did find them."

I can't contain my grin. "That's because I have them."

She blinks, her thick and curly lashes framing her eyelids perfectly. Her pupils grow larger until the deep brown of her irises is just a mere ring around them. I love that she's trying to make sense of what I just said. That she's trying so hard to not be shocked. I wonder if she's secretly thrilled.

"I kept them. I've used those panties, and kept them, unwashed, in my drawers. They have your scent on them."

"You kept them for what?"

I cock my head. She's even sexier when she plays naive. "With them wrapped around my hand, I've fisted myself more times than I can count."

She lets out a gasp. It's a sexy little rasp. The kind of rasp I imagine she lets out when she's coming down from an orgasm. What I wouldn't give to find out for sure.

"Tell me you don't think about that night?" I whisper close to her ear. I'm pushing, but I know this woman. I know what she'll take, and what she won't.

"It's getting hot in here." She flaps a napkin near her face. She's heating, my princesa, and I have no doubt that she's hot and wet, for me.

"Let's get some fresh air," I suggest, and this time she gets up. We walk outside, along the restaurant's side terrace, along a cobblestone path studded with lights and weaving around a lush garden.

The oppressive heat clings to me like Saran wrap, and I immediately feel oppressed by the weight of it. But Raquel? She seems to handle it. She looks as cool as a cucumber, even if there's a dewy sheen over her skin which suggests otherwise.

"Why are you here, Knight?" She folds her arms and leans back against the wall, surveying me.

All I want to do is put my mouth to hers and claim her. Then I want to take her back to my hotel room, and see where the night will lead us. But neither of these things are happening. It's not why I'm here, but the idea fixes in my head and refuses to leave, probably because my cock is getting harder by the minute.

"I wanted to talk to you. I woke up and you were gone. Vanished into the night."

"I had an early morning flight back to Miami. I was working a case."

"You told me to wait up. I did."

Silence falls thick and heavy. I place a hand on the wall above her head, moving into her space. She can push me away if she wants, but she doesn't.

"It was a mistake to let you in."

"Into your heart, or into your room?" I'm not letting her wriggle out of this.

She makes a disapproving noise with her lips. "You wish."

I'm not giving up. "We spent a night together, playing a game where we have to remove items of clothing, and then you had me waiting for you in your bed. And now you expect me to believe that it was a mistake. "

"I was working."

"I was ready to leave. Do the gentlemanly thing, but you told me to stay."

"You were wearing boxers."

"That's a poor argument, and you know it."

She folds her arms even more tightly. I lower my head, can see her guardrails softening.

I whisper into her ear. "You liked what you saw of me in my boxers." I inhale her scent. It's not sweet, or soft or flowery. It's sharp, like spice paired with heat. I want to tickle her earlobe with my tongue, drop tiny kisses along her neck, make my way to her lips and kiss her deeply.

She lets out a sound, and I can't decipher it. But it wasn't a denial. "You and I have so much in common. I find you intriguing, the most interesting woman I've ever met. Tell me you don't want me, princesa."

She exhales slowly, her chest rising and falling, like she's trying to get control of her breathing.

"You can't say it, can you?" I feel like I've done an interrogation of my own, and won the case.

She stares at me through thick lashes. "You think you're untouchable, and invincible. That the world should just bend to please you. People like you always want more than you're willing to give."

"Try me," I urge. Our faces are inches apart.

"I've been burned by your kind before."

"I'm not your past."

"No," she snaps. "But unlike Dani, I'm not willing to pay the price to find out."

My hand fists in my pocket.

"I think you want me, Raquel, because I sure as hell want you. I can't stop thinking about you and …" I pause, because I've said way too much.

"You want me?" she asks, the tease that she is.

"Damn right. I want you to let me in. I want you to give me the chance to get to know you, and if you don't want that, tell me to give up."

She looks at me, but her gaze falls to my lips.

She wants me.

She absolutely does.

"You can't, can you?" Wild courage boosts my confidence. "You want me," I whisper in her ear. She shivers, and I feel it.

"Then that's your mistake." She tilts her face up, her eyes falling to my lips. All I see are her red lips, the lips I yearn for. And just like that, we're kissing, falling into one another, bodies flush. She mewls and moans against my mouth, her hands tangling in my hair. Our kisses are hot and feverish, a letting go of all the frustration of everything we held back.

Finally, we break apart, gasping for air. Her lips are moist, her eyes shiny. "You do want me," I rasp.

"I wanted to prove that I don't. And I just did."

Her flawed logic makes no sense. I peer at her in disbelief. Her lipstick is a little smudged, on one corner. Not enough. But her hair is wild, pupils large, her chest rising and falling with each breath. She might say she doesn't want me, but the evidence suggests otherwise. Still, I'm shocked by her words, shocked that even now she's pushing me away when all I can think about is kissing her some more.

She steps back. "This can't happen. I won't let it." And just like that, she walks back inside. I stay behind, staring out at the Miami skyline, chest tight, hands itching to reach for her.

I think back to our earlier conversation, about where she grew up and how she'd sit in the corner while her mother helped out at the legal clinic at the favela, listening to stories of people being destroyed by the system.

That would be enough to make her wary of a man like me.

I scare her. The Knight world scares her. She fights people like us in court, and it frightens her to want me. But she can't deny the passion between us. The longing. The heat. Maybe she knows how good we can be together. Whatever it is, I can't push or pressure her. She has to come to terms with everything herself. She has to come to me on her own terms.

Enemies, then. If that's what she needs. That's what it will be. This time, it's best if I walk away, because it's over before it's really begun.

CHAPTER EIGHT

RAQUEL

I NEED A LOBOTOMY. THAT'S WHAT IT'S GOING TO TAKE TO GET that man out of my head. I haven't been able to focus since the weekend and I've struggled at work. Pierce can see I'm not on my A-game, and I need to be.

Dex and Dani's visit should've been a welcome distraction, and it was, for most part. Dani seemed happy. Dex was charming, sharp as ever.

But then he showed up.

The other Knight.

The bane of my life.

Uninvited, unexpected, and still impossibly charming and smug.

I wish I had more control. I usually do. I command, and lead. I decide if something happens or not, and as much as I tried not to give in to Rio Knight, I couldn't.

This kiss was even hotter than the first one; the one I've been trying to forget for months. Only now I have something more vibrant, new and electric, imprinted on my mind and body, and I doubt I'll ever forget it.

Or him.

Damn that man for knowing exactly how to unravel me without even trying. The way his voice dropped when he said my name. The way he looked at me like he still wants more.

I know I do. I was so sure this was a setup, him walking into the restaurant like it was unexpected. I was so sure of it, but he called my bluff. Turns out, he really was here for a meeting, even if it comes across as being too neat, too orchestrated.

Those Knights know how to do these things. They play 5D chess, while everyone else is playing checkers. I shouldn't have stepped out of the restaurant with him. Dex and Dani shouldn't have left us alone.

You didn't have to go outside with him.

I thought I was strong. I thought I could convince myself, and him, that I didn't want anything from him, but I can't push him away.

Rio is like a storm that wreaks havoc in my carefully structured life. He uproots it, creating chaos and leaving wreckage in his wake. He chews up head and heart and spits it out.

We didn't even talk for long.

Just enough to cause cracks in the walls I've built up around me.

Just enough to let him in and kiss him like I've never kissed anyone before.

By the time I walked back into the restaurant, I was shaking all over. I couldn't think straight. Dex and Dani returned from the garden, smiling like nothing had happened. They asked where Rio had gone. I lied and told them he called it an early night. They didn't press.

We had brunch the next morning before their flight. Part of me—the stupid part—half-expected Rio to show up again. He didn't.

And now, here I am, back at the office. Pretending to work. Staring at a file I've already read ten times but can't absorb because all I see is him. All I feel is him. All I want is him.

The Blue Star Eco Resort case.

The more I dig into it, the more it infuriates me because I've seen this before. The permits. The land acquisition. The way the local voices have been buried under layers of corporate silence. It stinks of money and power and unchecked arrogance. The kind of case that calls to my soul. No wonder I can't let it go.

Pierce wanted me to skim through it, but the NGO, the non-governmental organization in Belize, known as EcoGuardians, are expecting someone to fly out and do a legal review of the situation. Skimming through a file isn't enough.

I head into Pierce's office, ready for a fight, my sharp heels clicking against the wooden floor. It's only when I step in to his office that I realize, too late, that I took off my cropped blazer and left it dangling my chair. Now I'm standing in front of him in my navy-blue sleeveless sheath dress which hugs my figure more closely than I feel comfortable with. I hug the EcoGuardians folder to my chest, like a shield.

"I've skimmed through this. They want someone to do a legal review of the site."

He doesn't seem to be listening. His attention is on my appearance, his gaze roving over me slowly. "Then you should go and do a legal review," he says, his eyes finally lifting to meet mine.

This was not the answer I expected. "You want *me* to go?" This is a dream case, but I'm already working on the Santos arbitration and it's highly billable, complex, and time-sensitive. Panic grips me at the thought that he might be flying out with me, and that's the only reason why he's pushing for me to do this. I'll resign if that's the case.

"They mentioned your name."

"Who?"

"EcoGuardians want you, so I'm sending you."

"Just me?" I ask, my breath hitching.

"You're more than capable of handling this.." He adjusts the cuffs of his shirts. "You're one of the firm's brightest stars. Is it so wrong for me to let you sink your teeth into the kind of case that lights you up?"

I can't believe my ears.

"You're okay to let me go to Belize?"

"Yes."

I almost float on air as I leave his office. Getting out of the shadows of men like Pierce, even if it's only temporary, feels like I'm won a dream prize. But I'm not just escaping from him. I also need to get away from memories of *him*.

Rio Knight.

And Belize suddenly feels like an escape.

RIO

I NEVER SHOULD'VE GONE TO MIAMI.

I made a mistake thinking I could talk things over with Raquel. Thinking I could fix things. But I've made things worse since that night when we collided again.

This woman is fire and thorns in a sexy dress, and I walked right into the thick of it, thinking I could handle her as easily as I can most women.

But Raquel is not a like most women, and she can't be handled. She just is. She's wild, and free. And as sharp as a pin.

I kissed her, and she kissed me back. It was everything I knew it would be. Hot, and feverish, and all consuming. I could come from just kissing her. No sex involved. Sure, I had to fist myself to release so that I could fall asleep, but Raquel's face, her scent, the feel of her, everything I should be trying to forget, is now stronger than ever in my thoughts.

She and I, we're like boxers in a ring, circling one another with wary eyes, throwing insults, joking and teasing, but deep down inside, we hunger for one another. It felt like her entire body missed me, because she seemed as desperate for it as I was. And after? She shoved me away like I was nothing.

I thought I was going to Miami to find answers and maybe get some closure, but what I got was no respite, and my head filled with thoughts of her more potent than ever.

We parted on bad terms again and I'm not any wiser. She pushed me away with her words, and yet her eyes, her body, and the way she moved when I reached for her hand ... say otherwise.

Here I am, more conflicted than before I left for Miami, but one thing is crystal clear—I need to stay the hell away from her. It's best for me, for her, for everyone.

When my father calls me in for a meeting, I'm little distracted. I brace myself as I walk into his office and find him at his desk, flipping through a messy pile of newspapers and shareholder briefs. He doesn't look up until he's good and ready.

It's always a classic power play with him.

"Come in. Sit," he says flatly.

There's a folded paper on top of the stack. I catch a glimpse of a photo—me, Dex, Dani... and Raquel. Taken outside a restaurant in Miami.

My gut tenses. I hate the intrusion by the paparazzi. That picture of the four of us must piss him off. Me and Dex, with women, on what looks like a date, looking happy. Yeah, he won't like that.

"Good weekend?" he asks, pretending to skim a letter as I sit down hoping this will be over soon. But I instinctively know that something's up. The old man doesn't ask about weekends unless he's hunting for leverage. Or sniffing.

"Not bad. You?"

He doesn't answer, and lets the silence hang for a few seconds, before sliding a file across the desk.

"I have something I need you to handle."

"I'm about to fly to Verona, to meet with Nico Cazale. You recall the Cazale hotel empire I was telling you about?"

He dismisses my comment with a blink. Verona isn't far from Soave, the place where we grew up. The place the old man knows too well. I was planning to visit Mama at the same time.

"Verona can wait."

"What can't wait?" It's something pressing. Something he needs taken care of. I wonder what fire I'm about to put out now.

"We've got a situation in Belize, with the new eco resort."

"The Blue Star?" This is my area. Hotels and real estate. I overlap with Enzo on the real estate. "It's about to open within the month. What's the problem?"

"It won't open if this mess isn't cleared up."

He nods at the file. "Legal threats. Locals protesting. Rumors of environmental violations. We've been contacted by a non-governmental organization there, a pain in the butt group claiming water pollution, displacement, the usual activist drivel. If this hits the press, we're screwed, so I need you to contain it, and fast. I need you to work your charm."

"Containment and charm," I repeat, voice dry. "I can do

that." But at the same time, something niggles me. What's caused this? Did we do something wrong? Funny how the old man is all about cleaning up the mess, but what if we're the ones responsible for the mess?

"I need this buried, and quietly. I don't want any headlines, or courtroom drama. This could blow up in our face, so just deal with it."

I glance down at the file. "This isn't a Knight Enterprises internal project."

"It's tied to one of our subsidiaries and naturally, if they have a problem, we have a problem. But we have more to lose. I don't need that heat. The resort will be an absolute showpiece. This is where luxury meets sustainability. I plan to open more resorts like this in Costa Rica, Guatemala, and as many far-flung destinations as we can. But if this turns into a PR mess, it'll ruin everything. It won't open on time, and that's millions down the drain."

My jaw tightens. "Are we legit on this?" I find myself paying attention to Raquel's words and all the ethical problems she always accuses Knight Enterprises of.

The old man leans back. "Legally, yes. Ethically... we've seen better days. But that's not your concern. The case is baseless. Politically motivated. You're going down there to smooth it over and make it go away. Quietly."

That right there tells me it's not squeaky clean. Which means I'm going to have to rely on the people on the ground at the site in Belize.

I hear Raquel's voice in my head. I hear her accusations; about the damage we're doing. I'm starting to take note. I never listened. Never wanted to. But now I can't help wondering, just like I wonder why we stay and put up with the old man's bullshit. What he did with Jett, what he did with Dex, that shit with Dani's father, it's not normal.

I stay because the Knight legacy is worth billions. Because Knight Enterprises isn't just a company. It's a global, multibillion-dollar empire. Walking away isn't like quitting a job. It's walking away from the chance to inherit serious power, wealth, and global influence. We're not fighting to be loved. We're fighting to be the last man standing when the old man falls.

So, I nod. "Fine. When do I leave?"

"As soon as you can."

CHAPTER NINE

RAQUEL

I ARRIVE IN BELIZE, FULL OF EXPECTATION AND HOPING THAT this is more like a vacation than a fact-finding trip.

I'm expecting the work to be light. I still can't figure out why Pierce agreed to this, but maybe it's true. Maybe he senses my growing desire to flee Tovey & Roth.

At least this will be like a little break from my workplace.

The connection from the main airport to Placencia Airstrip was short but bumpy, and the small Tropic Air plane hummed like a tin toy as it skimmed over a patchwork of glittering turquoise shallows, winding rivers and jungle green.

The oppressive heat blankets me the moment I step off the plane. But something else takes my attention; the scent of salt, and something sweet and overripe floats in the air. The humidity is thick, clinging to my skin like an extra layer of sweat.

I walk out from the tiny customs area, my gaze darting around the small crowd, trying to match the mental image I have of Alma Flores. When she told me she'd be waiting for me, I was surprised. She's the head of the NGO, EcoGuardians, and I would have expected someone else to be here, not the head.

A flash of lettering catches my eye and I see EcoGuardians printed in neat black on a hand-painted sign. Holding it is an older woman with white hair pulled into a tidy bun and deep brown skin creased into a face that probably smiles a lot. She's hard to miss in her loose cotton dress patterned with bright flowers. Her posture is straight but unhurried, and she's wearing sensible sandals,. Everything about her signals that she's probably never rushed for anything.

Her eyes catch mine, warm and assessing all at once, and before I've even reached her, I feel like she already knows exactly who I am. It's a relief to have someone in the office who I don't have to dodge. Feeling relaxed, I walk up to her. "Alma, hi, I'm Raquel, from—"

"Ah, yes, Raquel. We meet at last. Welcome."

"Thank you. Nice to meet you."

She has the warmest of smiles as she shakes my hand. Her dark brown eyes are ringed with grey and fanlike wrinkles spread out from the corners.

"Did you have a pleasant flight?"

"I did, thank you." She is all warmth and softness, and I like her instantly. She's a breath of fresh air compared to Pierce.

"Are you hungry? I can pick up some wraps, or some sushi food along the way, before we head to the office."

"I'm fine, Alma. Thank you." I'm not hungry. The flight was under five hours, and I want to get on with the work.

We get in her car, and set off. It's only a short drive she tells me, then adds that she wasn't sure how much luggage I might have, hence why she drove here.

"Would you like to rest up first?" she offers. "I can take you straight to the office or wherever you're staying."

"I'm happy to dive right into the work." I don't have many days to wrap this up. A week at most.

"That's what I was hoping to hear."

I look out of the window in awe. Clusters of brightly colored hibiscus bloom vibrantly everywhere. "Your country is beautiful."

"Thank you. We'd like to keep it that way. It's why we do what we do. Unfortunately, big corporations don't see it that way."

I understand completely. Breaking a sigh, I tell her. "That's why *I* love what *I* do."

She glances at me. "We've had new evidence come in. New photos and local testimony which shows urgent and ongoing damage. All of this natural beauty, it can't be preserved if big corporations keep interfering. We need more people like you, Raquel. Companies like to set up their hotels and their eco resorts under the guise that they're good for the environment." Alma hurrumps her disapproval. "They want their money. They want their profits. They might start off with good intentions, maybe, but when it comes to damaging protected ecosystems, coral reef destruction, illegal deforestation, displacing indigenous communities, violating international environmental agreements … the list is endless, as you know."

"I'm well aware of the damage, most of it irreversible."

"They prefer to disregard these things in their thirst for more money. These big corporations will do whatever it takes to protect their profits."

I nod, agreeing with everything she said. "It makes me so angry. I'm sorry this is happening to you," I tell her. I despair sometimes, but despair won't fix anything. I've seen it happen before, how a lush environment, with its inhabitants going about peacefully in their normal lives have their world upended by wealthy, foreign companies. "Money is everything to them," I continue, getting more riled up. "Greed motivates them. Runs their life. Directs every thought and action they take." I think of Paul Knight and his cunning, devious ways.

And then I remember Rio.

Not good. Why can't I get that man out of my head? I came here to get away not just from work and Pierce, but from Rio and from Miami which, for now, is tainted with his memory.

"We think alike, Raquel. You remind me of a younger me."

"I do?"

"You have that air of determination about you. I like it. I get the feeling that you don't trust people easily."

She's right. I don't. "Are you psychic?" I ask, her words making me uneasy. This makes her smile.

"I have sixty-eight years on me, and by that time, you learn to read people and situations easier the older you get."

"Not everyone does." I'm reminded of Paul Knight again.

"Am I right?" she asks. "That you don't trust?"

"You are. Frighteningly so."

I like that Alma is calm and insightful, and she's not afraid to call things as she sees them.

"How long have you been with EcoGuardians?" I ask.

"About twenty years. I was put in charge to head it up, a few years after I joined."

"You have branches in other countries. I've heard of you before."

"Big money and big corporations are everywhere, doing damage. We need to be everywhere to match them. To do what we can."

"How much longer do you intend to carry on working?"

Alma chuckles softly. "You mean because I'm a grandmother?"

"No. *Are* you a grandmother?"

Her face softens, and I instantly know she is, and that she loves it. "I have three grandchildren," she says, pride and love infusing her voice. "Two boys and a girl. The youngest just turned four last week. Smart as a whip, and already bossing her brothers around. Her older brothers are five, soon to be six, and the oldest is eight." She goes on to tell me that she's been married for forty-four years to Samuel, the love of her life who she met in school when they were thirteen. He carried her books home every day. "He said it was because my bag looked heavy, but I knew it was because he liked me. It took him three years to work up the courage to hold my hand, and by then, I had already decided he was the one."

I listen to her with the biggest smile on my face, imagining the thirteen-year-old Alma and her Samuel, walking home from school, to grow older decades later and leave a legacy behind them. She tells me how they built their house themselves, on a small plot of land his father gave them. "I want to keep this planet for my children to grow up in, and I want their grandchildren to enjoy it too."

I like her so much.

"How about you? Do you have anyone important in your life?"

I let out an exhale. I dislike personal questions, but I don't mind opening up to her.

"Not really." I wish I'd said "No." I hate that I've left myself open to more questioning.

She pauses, for a beat in which I pray she doesn't probe.

"You work in Miami, for a law firm and as a lawyer I am assuming that you lead a very hectic life. We've never used your law firm before, but we were told that you're good."

"I don't recall personally working on anything for EcoGuardians before," I tell her.

"Somebody recommended you. I can't remember who."

"Hmmmm." We have a global newsletter where lawyers and successful cases are highlighted. Maybe that's how the recommendation came about.

"Your reputation precedes you." Alma looks at me as if I am the one. "As I mentioned, we have branches all over the world, and we are constantly fighting for our planet, and for people's rights. It can be exhausting."

"I'm sure it is, but we're fighting the good fight, you and me, and I'm glad to be here."

"Are you up to speed with the Blue Star Eco Resort?"

"I am." It made for light reading on the plane.

"Two years under construction," she says, her voice tight, like she's trying to stay calm. "They're selling it as though it will help us, as though it will be good for our environment and our people. As though they're doing us a favor by building it here. In an ideal world it would be true, perhaps. But this isn't an ideal world, is it? And this eco resort is built for rich tourists from abroad. There is nothing in it for the locals. Lot of low-paying jobs, of course." She gives a dry laugh. "The mangroves are already thinning, fish numbers dropping, and the community is not happy." She glances toward the horizon and shakes her head. "All this beauty … it won't last if big corporations keep carving it up."

"I hate it when that happens. I've seen this before, numerous times. It makes my blood boil."

We fall silent for a while. I feel a sense of moral righteousness, and feel blessed that I'm doing the job I am.

"You were born and raised in Miami?" she asks.

"I work in Miami, but I'm from Brazil, from São Paulo."

"Ah," her voice warms to me even more.

I tell her about how I got my law degree in Brazil, then spent a year at college in Washington.

"My boss," I say, "he doesn't like me doing this work."

"No?"

"He thinks I should be back at the law firm, doing expensive billable work, instead of pro bono work. I shouldn't have told you that." I don't know why the words tumbled out so easily. She's a client and it's wrong, but there's something about Alma which makes me feel like I'm talking to a friend.

"More of that capitalist greed," she murmurs.

We turn down a sandy lane, along a row of little bungalows all painted in different colors. There are different shades of blue, sunny yellows and corals, mint greens and different shades of pink, all brightening the already vibrant landscape.

She brings the car to a stop before killing the engine.

"Are we here?" I look around at what seems to be a residential street.

"Welcome to our HQ."

"HQ?"

"Our headquarters. It's not an office, but a residential home which serves as our base. I'll show you around, and later I'll take you to wherever you're staying."

I decide to leave my luggage in the car and follow her into what looks like a modest bungalow.

"This is nice. Very homely." I look around to see a large table full of paperwork, with two smaller tables facing the window. A handful of people are working conscientiously. They don't even notice us walk in.

"We don't spend money on corporate buildings and headquarters. This is more than enough for us."

"It feels like home." I nod as she introduces me as "Raquel from the Miami law firm" to the handful of people there. They turn around and we nod and acknowledge one another.

"Take a look at these." She walks over to the large table, where everything is spread out and arranged just so, for me.

"This is what I was telling you about—the evidence that's come in."

I take a seat, then look through photos and the documents that are spread across the table. Exhibits that are painful to look at. Pictures of uprooted mangroves, their twisted roots piled like rubbish at the edge of the construction zone.

I'm haunted by the photo of a young child holding a bucket of water so murky it looks like oil. Test results showed it wasn't just undrinkable, it was toxic. My throat constricts, as I gaze at the next photo. This shows fragments of dead coral washed ashore and bleached a deathly white. This so-called "eco resort" pushed through permits fast. It would be laughable, if it weren't deadly. My insides shake with rage because the people paying the price aren't the ones signing the deals. They won't benefit one iota.

It's not the first time I've seen this. The damage is the same, but it's a different country. Another paradise that is desecrated. And behind it? Another greedy corporation who thinks it can get away with it.

"I'd like to take you to the coastline later so you can see the damage for yourself," Alma says, pushing her thick, black framed spectacles up. "I need to tell you something." She pauses.

"Tell me what?" A jolt of panic shoots through me because I know that look, and I know it's not something I'm going to like.

"Initially we said this was going to be a fact-finding trip. A legal review, but we actually want to pursue an injunction."

My heart sinks. "An injunction?" This is not good. Not good at all. I can hear Pierce's disapproval already.

"We've decided."

"I thought you wanted some legal advisory help." I run a hand over the back of my neck, feeling the heat and sweat, but my temperature just went up a few degrees.

"We did initially, but the damage is too much. It's too far gone, Raquel. These companies don't learn. We want to make a scapegoat of this one. Delport Realty. They're the people behind the eco resort. We believe an injunction is necessary."

I try to find the right thing to say, or why I don't recommend this course of action, but it's not the right thing to do. My gaze falls on the photos in front of me again and I know that I need to fight for these people. I can't walk away. Pierce can find someone else to take care of the Santos arbitration. It isn't ideal, but neither would walking away from this case be. I'd hate myself. "This does look bad," I agree. "And I ... I understand your concerns. I'll need to go out and inspect the damage."

"We can do that tomorrow, and you'll see with your own eyes."

I let out a sigh, bracing myself for the repercussions back in Miami. "The resort is due to open in a month, am I right?" I pull out my documents from my leather satchel.

"Yes."

"This could raise plausibility concerns. Why now?"

"We didn't have enough evidence before, but satellite images from last week show dead fish washing up, and the water samples prove irreparable harm. We have a case now, where we didn't before. This might work better. It will teach them a better lesson."

My thoughts are all over the place. "A better lesson?"

"The closer they are to opening, the more it will cost them to stop. We have leverage, Raquel. That's pressure."

"You should have been a lawyer, Alma." She's tactically savvy, and she's making it harder for me to find fault with the injunction.

"That's why you're here." She pushes her spectacles up again, before sitting back in her chair, watching me closely. "I sense that you're having an internal battle with yourself, and I know you weren't expecting this. Are you worried about your boss?" She always seems to tune into my thoughts and can read me like an X-ray machine.

I try to sidestep the question. "I'm thinking of how that changes things. The scope of the work, and of course, I'll have to let Pierce, my boss, know."

"We're putting our trust in you, Raquel."

I shift on the hard wooden chair, feeling unsure. This isn't what I agreed to do. Pierce won't approve. He won't like this one bit. But my conscience won't let me walk away. Filing an injunction would be an act of courage. It would be the right thing to do. I agree with everything Alma has said, and looking at these photos only cements that thought.

"I wish you'd told me upfront."

"I'm sorry for telling you this now, but we only made this decision yesterday. We do need to act now. The damage is happening faster than we thought and construction of this eco resort has already damaged the local ecosystem. Delaying the injunction could make the harm irreversible.."

"I understand your reasons." I run the scenario through my mind. I was supposed to observe and maybe write a summary.

"Sometimes doing the right thing is the hardest thing to do. If you can't do this, I completely understand." Alma's eyes, wise and all-knowing, stare back at me. Walking away now would be an act of weakness.

"This matters to me, but, Pierce ... he might need convincing." I don't want to say anything negative about my boss or the law firm.

"Let me ask you plainly, Raquel. Are you a lawyer who cares about this, or someone who just wants to put it on her résumé?"

This woman reminds me of every reason I became a lawyer

in the first place. Clearly, this is no longer some basic environmental due diligence. Now, I'm going to have to build a solid legal case with urgency, precision, and verifiable data. I'm going to need evidence of damage, declarations and affidavits from affected parties.

"We have a lot of the information you'll need," she says, reading my mind. "We've been putting it together, preparing for the worst. All you have to do is put it all together."

I'll still need to verify everything. I'll still need to carry out interviews, visit the construction site, and venture out to inspect the damage. It's still so much more work than I planned for. Not that I'm afraid of hard work.

I inhale a deep breath. "Okay. Let's do this."

"You're fully on board?"

I don't blame her for needing to doublecheck.

"I am." Even though I'm caught off guard and didn't come mentally prepared for litigation. I feel guilty, because I came here thinking it would be a short break and already can tell that it's going to be nothing of the sort.

CHAPTER TEN

RIO

I'M ALREADY IN BELIZE. LANDED LAST NIGHT.

I'm sitting in the hotel lobby, sipping a rich cup of coffee fresh from the restaurant. It tastes different. Richer. Fresher. The weather here is warm and tropical. A pleasant contrast from the chilly, overcast and damp New York I've left behind.

I need to make a start on the day, even though the glittering pool beckons again. I checked into the best hotel here, at the Peninsula. I wasn't expecting it to be *this* good, and my mouth fell open when I walked in.

I have a suite, like always, but I didn't expect to have one here. Belize isn't Turks & Caicos, so I'm pleasantly surprised. The hotel is sleek and opulent; all glass walls and white marble with limestone floors. The full-length windows along one side offer breathtaking views. I imagine the sunsets from here will be spectacular. There's also a balcony that looks out onto a shimmering turquoise sea.

A balcony.

Just the thought of that takes me back to Raquel's balcony in São Paulo.

Damn it.

I shake my head.

I came here to forget her.

Air-conditioning and room service. It has a fully stocked wet bar. Perfect. And I've had a refreshing night's sleep in the super-king-sized bed. Crisp white linen. Fresh orchids in the vases.

My kind of luxury.

I had a quiet dinner by myself, some drinks too. Met Tomas Carrillo for drinks in the bar. He's my contact here and the on-site logistics coordinator for Delport Realty, the company behind the eco resort. He's a rugged guy in his fifties. A local and a family man with grandkids. He's humble. Easy-going, with a weathered face. He knows the terrain, the people, and knows how to get things done.

Over rum and quiet conversation, we talked about the eco resort and the noise caused by EcoGuardians who have now mobilized the support of the locals. I need to find out their concerns, deal with them and put them to bed.

He started to hint at things. Off the record stuff. Warnings. The kind that suggest the resort's promises come with a price, not just to the budget, but to the land and the people. Though he works on the project, he's deeply rooted in the local community, and over rum and quiet conversation, he said a few things that made me wonder whose side he was on. There's something about him; a quiet authority, some kind of moral compass he's trying to keep hidden under all the logistics talk.

It got me wondering if everything is as clear cut as the old man said it was. This is still very much a construction site, with the final touches being made. As far as I'm aware, there should be no problem with it being ready to open in a month.

After Tomas left, I went through some papers, then got an early night. This morning, I woke up and swam a few laps in the hotel pool. Had a long, lazy breakfast with strong coffee and a view of the ocean. I'm not in a rush. I've got ten days. Plenty of time to fix this mess.

I'm meeting Tomas at the construction site today and later there are a handful of local government officials I need to meet with. Should be an easy day.

I check my phone and see an email from the old man. Short and sharp:

Don't let this get out of hand.

As if I need a reminder. I know what needs to be done. Check on the construction site, see what trouble the NGO are causing. Maybe set up a meeting with a journalist or get the community together at the town hall and smooth over the local anger.

Simple.

This is going to be more of a vacation than anything else. If there's evidence of wrong-doing, then I'll have to deal with it. I know what the old man is like. I know he's never above board with anything, especially business dealings.

Just look at Dani's father, but luckily we fixed that injustice. Still, this isn't a project we're directly involved in. Delport Realty is, and maybe they have more morals than Knight Enterprises.

RAQUEL

. . .

I'M FEELING MORE ENERGIZED AFTER THE DEBRIEF AT HQ AND A light lunch, but I'm still hot and sweaty. Time is of the essence and I don't want to waste a second.

We're off to see the eco resort. We have temporary access to speak with the on-site workers and observe conditions firsthand, but Alma warns me that it's still a construction site.

We set off, but decide to stop off at the coastline first. She takes me on a short tour, and I see the destruction up close. Mangroves gutted. Trees fallen. Scarred land where once there was forest. The breeze off the water can't cool the heat in my chest.

She points out the damage as we go. I see everything and it makes me physically sick. Now I understand the quiet anger burning behind Alma's eyes. If I had children, if I lived on a paradise island and outside companies run by people who don't even live here—people with only money and capital at stake—started building their monstrosities, my blood would boil, too.

When I've seen enough, I tell her I need to see the eco resort, so we head there. As soon as we get to the site, I'm ready to interview the workers, observe the conditions, and get a sense of the project firsthand.

Two men approach us, with apprehension. Alma points out that one is the new foreman, and the other a logistics coordinator. She introduces them both. The foreman, a man called Orlando, seems busy, and distracted, but the other man, Tomas, starts chatting away to Alma. They seem to know one another, and he offers to take us around the site. From the outside, the resort looks nice enough, but it's clearly not finished. There's machinery and equipment lying around and the whole place needs cleaning and polish before it could ever pass for the luxury paradise in the brochures.

But we're here to throw a wrench in that dream.

"See that?" Alma says, her voice full of disapproval. She

points toward the shoreline where the afternoon light catches on a cloud of silt bleeding into the turquoise water, stirred up by dredging equipment that shouldn't be running this close to the reef.

A flash of anger shoots through me. I know that plume. I've seen it too many times in places that don't make the travel magazines. It's the beginning of the end for the life under that water. My hands fist, my nails slicing into my palms, and for a second, I'm taken back to the favela, to the smell of the oil-slicked river near us, and I hear my neighbors shouting at the men who came to take what little we had left.

After I landed here, as Alma drove me to HQ, I saw the sea and greenery from a distance. This place was paradise, but now that I've been up close and inspected the damage, anger wells inside me.

"We're going to halt this soon enough," I whisper to Alama, indignation seething out of my pores.

The deep growl of an engine interrupts us, causing us all to turn. A black, shiny Jeep, a monster of an automobile, pulls up right outside the entrance to the eco resort. The door swings open and out steps a man looking like trouble. He's wearing Aviators and a grin that is all arrogance and mischief, like he just won something. Tall and broad-shouldered, he's in a crisp white linen shirt, sleeves rolled up to the elbow, with the sun catching the dark tan of his forearms. He's wearing charcoal trousers that fit like they were made for him, and boots that send dust curling in late-afternoon light.

"Caraca," I groan. Because … what are the chances?

I know that man.

At the same time, Tomas informs us, "He's from the parent company and he's overseeing launch logistics."

I stop breathing.

Rio Knight. Overseeing *launch* logistics.

My mind whirs furiously, because I don't recall seeing the name of Knight Enterprises anywhere.

The man I was hoping to never run into again now stares in our direction. I can't move. Then he starts walking towards me, with that cocky swagger, looking straight at me, even though I can't see his eyes.

"Meu Deus," I hiss, louder than I intend. *My God.*

"Do you know him?" Alma's voice is suddenly cautious.

He takes off his dark shades, and our eyes lock.

He smiles.

That cheesy, annoying, sexy smile of his, the one where just the corners of his lips turn up. His beard is newly trimmed. He looks fresh and clean and my body begins to sweat more profusely than ever whereas he looks like he stepped out of a cologne ad.

"I don't believe this," I murmur, a knot of indignation choking my throat.

Rio walks up to me. His lips upturned at the corners, looking too smug for words.

He hangs his shades on the neck of his white T. "Don't tell me they let you in here legally." That voice, smooth as satin, reverberates deep in my core.

I can't help myself. "Don't tell me Daddy called and had you running off to do his bidding again?"

"You two know each other?" Tomas asks.

"Who is this?" Alma asks quietly.

Rio's fury comes off him like heat from a wildfire. We don't answer, and our eyes are fixed on each other, untrusting and cold.

"Well, well." This time Rio flashes me a full smile that reveals his perfect white teeth. "The climate crusader is on a crusade. Are you behind the noise?"

My nostrils flare. "If I'd known you were the one behind this mess, I wouldn't have wasted sunscreen."

Our eyes are on fire. Our voices stay cool.

"Meu Deus, just when I thought today couldn't get more colonial," I toss at him.

"Meu Deus?" His eyes twinkle with mischief, and he puts his hands on his hips. "I'm not God, though you might be forgiven for thinking so."

"Why are you here?" I hiss, poking a finger into his chest.

"I could ask the same." He takes hold of my finger, his eyes burning, his jaw locked. His touch is like fire. It always is. I flinch.

Tomas steps in. "We should get a move on, boss."

It's only then that I realize how close we are to one another. Rio drops my finger like I burned him.

I'm not the only one who felt the fire.

But Rio ignores the man and stays put, folding his arms as my gaze falls to the faint outline of his biceps under that T. His black and gold designer watch glints under the sun.

"Are you people behind Delport Realty?" My heart is racing, and I'm hoping to wake up from this nightmare. It wouldn't be the first time I've had a dream about this man.

He doesn't answer.

We're like two bulls, facing each other, ready to lock horns.

"Tomas?" Alma turns to him. So do I.

"Tomas." I look him in the eye. "Is Delport Realty a subsidiary of Knight Enterprises?"

He shrugs. "I'm sorry, I don't know."

"What does it matter if it is?" Rio asks.

I'm still trying to process this very unlikely event and start to wonder if he's stalking me. "You people… you people infect everything you touch."

"Not everything." His gaze dips lower, to my lips, then

lower. I know, I just *know*, he's talking about whatever is going on between us. He's already there. Bringing our personal matters to the fore.

"Was Daddy not available to escort you to this fight?"

He shakes his head slowly, showering me with disapproval. "Always fighting talk with you, huh, prin—" He cuts off, remembers where he is, who he is and what he's representing. But, at the same time, clearly, he's remembering what went down between us. He clears his throat. "I'm here to monitor and protect legitimate investments."

Meu Deus.

It *is* all owned by Knight Enterprises.

"You people manage to get your claws and your hooks into every decent part of the world," I snap. "Into anything and everything that you can make money off."

"We should look around the site," Tomas tells him, glancing at his watch, "If we're to meet the—"

"I'd love to stay and make small talk with you," Rio interjects, making me wonder what Tomas was going to say that he didn't want me to hear. "But I have meetings to attend, things to do."

I close my eyes, and take a moment after Rio disappears out of sight.

"You do know each other," Alma says softly. "The way you just lit up. It was like fire was burning inside you."

I wince. This is not what I needed. This man is a complication wrapped in temptation. He's dangerous in every way that matters. I came here to have a much-needed break, from Pierce, from work.

But also from this man.

Because I remember everything. The heat of his mouth, the way he looked at me like I was a dare he couldn't resist. A single glance from him still gets under my skin. He makes me feel reckless, like the girl who once dreamed of escape, not the lawyer who fights for it now. And beneath all that is the bigger truth, and problem. This resort, this damage, this fight, it's all tied to Knight Enterprises. To them. That family. "Did you know they were behind it?" I ask her, ignoring her question.

"Who?"

I'm not sure Alma would know. Thoughts run rampant in my chaotic mind as I try to process this. Rio being here, Knight Enterprises being behind the eco resort and the injunction Alma wants me to file. I am in utter shock. "We need to go back. We need to confirm who is behind Delport Realty. I need to do some more digging."

Alma can see I'm wound up, because she doesn't press me for any answers. She takes me back to HQ, and I look through the paperwork, both hers and mine, and check online.

Just as I suspected, it all leads back to Knight Enterprises. No wonder I didn't know at first, when I decided to take this on. The Knights are hiding behind a shady shell company. Typical trickery.

I really shouldn't be surprised.

CHAPTER ELEVEN

RAQUEL

I'M IN MY ROOM NOW AND I IMAGINE IT'S DIFFERENT FROM where Rio is staying. Daddy's credit card will have expensed the very best.

It's been a long day, but my emotions are further frayed by running into Rio Knight. I wonder why he's here. What connection he has to the eco resort. These Knights seem to get their dirty little paws everywhere.

A big part of coming here was to do the work I love, but equally, it was also to get away from Rio. I'm still trying to recover after the last weekend where he showed up unexpectedly in Miami. Now, my situation just became a million times worse, because not only is he here, but he's involved in the very case I'm working on.

It's my worst nightmare. He's my enemy, and one I lust after when my thoughts are adrift. I'll have to work even harder to focus, though he did look pretty fine in his shades and T.

It's too much of a coincidence and it doesn't add up, that of all the places in the entire world, he showed up *here.*

Naturally, my mind starts working overtime. Did he follow me here? I shouldn't be too presumptuous. He's not here because of *me.* He's here because Knight Enterprises have business interests all over the world, and while this is eerily freaky, crazier things have happened. Such as Dani marrying a Knight.

It's humid in this room, even though I have the AC cranked up high. It looks old, like it could do with a replacement, and every now and then it sputters, like it's going to die on me. I swipe a hand across my neck, my sticky, clammy skin feels uncomfortable. I'm tempted to take a cold shower but I need to work. I glance at the papers strewn across the desk and the bed, and sigh. I have so much work to do and I'm not sure it's possible within the week Pierce has given me. I might need to stay longer.

But I've lost focus. Concentrating has become harder. Things might have been different had I not run into that man, had he not been here, but now he is, my thoughts are as scattered as the documents showing the eco damage. Somehow I'm supposed to put everything together into one big cohesive report that clearly shows the construction is not above board. It means long days, working on this around the clock.

My laptop buzzes and an email from Pierce pops up. "How's the eco vacation?"

"Not a vacation," I whisper to myself. I don't even click the email. I don't want to read it. This is meant to be a break from Pierce as well. But I'm going to have to tell him soon about EcoGuardians changing their position. That's one conversation I'm not looking forward to. I click away from my email, feeling more conflicted than ever. This wasn't supposed to be a case. I wasn't supposed to get involved like this. I was supposed to walk around, take notes, maybe snap a few photos for the firm's newsletter—"CEO's firm supports the planet"—then fly back and bury myself in Pierce's work.

But now?

Now there's a village losing its water. Mangroves are dying. And a woman I look up to looks at me as if I'm the only one who can help them.

The sounds of distant waves and chirping birds distract me and I pad across the floor to look out of the window. I could have said "No" to this. Maybe before I went to see the coastline, a part of me was thinking it wasn't going to be so bad. That I could still walk away. Tell myself it isn't smart, that I need to think of my career.

I wanted to have something worthy to put on my résumé, and now I have it: a possible fight with a subsidiary of the Knights. I've always loved a good fight.

I pull my hair up and fix it with a crocodile clip, the way I always do when I'm getting ready for battle. I need to start documenting the land and water damage. Alma's anxious that we file soon. I get nervous just thinking about it. Pierce needs to know, but I can't bring myself to call him just yet. What I want to do is bury my head.

I'm drowning in so much stress, not just career stress but personal stress.

Rio Knight stress.

He's the last person I expected to see. The last person I *wanted* to see, even if I do lie awake at night thinking about him more than I should.

———

RIO

. . .

I set down my emptied third glass of tequila when the old man calls and demands an update on the situation.

I wonder if he's heard something.

"Everything's fine," I assure him, even though it's absolutely fucking not. Raquel Monteiro is everything that's wrong.

I've been trying to piece it all together. The NGO's been causing some noise, sure, but they're moving pretty quickly if they've been talks with a law firm in the US. I could ask the old man if he's heard any rumblings, but if I do, he'll know something is up. He'll think I can't handle things over here, and I don't want that. So I remain quiet on that front. Maybe Raquel can give me answers. I'm sure she'd love throwing her facts at me. She likes one-upping me, and I quite like it, too.

"And the resort? How's it coming along?" he asks.

I tell him that it looks great. It's exactly what the brochures said it would be. Low, airy, buildings with thatched roofs, and timber walkways raised over golden sand. Villas dotted around, far enough apart for privacy. Lush, native plants lining the paths, while the rooftops glitter with solar panels. The reception area is open-sided, catching the sea breeze. Even the furniture is made from reclaimed wood and dyed fabrics.

It looks inviting and full of promise. The perfect vacation for people who want to save the planet and have a good time.

"I might go and check out the coastline tomorrow," I tell him. "I need to see if for myself."

"What for"? he snaps. Then, without giving me a chance to reply, "Stick to what I told you."

I run a hand over my beard. "I need to be seen looking at their complaints. Just paying lip-duty."

"If you're after environmental data, we've got some, up to date, from the consultants. Want me to send it to you?"

"Sure. Anything that helps."

I hang up.

Today was a full-on day at the construction site. That was enough for one day. I saw the layout. Talked to the site team. Met with some local officials. Assessed timelines, took notes. Nothing stood out—on the surface.

But the biggest fucking deal of the day?

Seeing *her*.

It knocked my concentration. Made my heartrate rocket. It was like a kick in the stomach. And a stroke of my cock.

Raquel has that effect on me. It riled me up, because of how she left me last weekend, and it also sent my pulse soaring. My heart does that soft, stupid flutter whenever I see her. And she leaves me hard and aching, but it's not just lust and desire. It goes way deeper. It's more than familiarity. It's like we have a connection that transcends time and space. It sounds crazy, and it's not something I'd tell Dex, but this is what it is.

She wasn't wearing that red lipstick that's imprinted on my mind forever. Today she was fresh faced, and still as beautiful as ever. Still as feisty as ever. I like that more about her each time I see her.

The woman is fire. The way she and I play off one another, the way we hate and loathe each other, it's impossible to get her out of my mind.

Coming out here was meant to be a break for me. It was supposed to help me forget her. Now, she's not only here, she's working for the NGO. Now, I not only remember how we kissed outside that restaurant in Miami, but I'm also remembering that night in São Paulo. My cock is so hard, I'll have to fist myself to release later. The way I've had to do a lot of times. Getting off to a visual of Raquel in my head.

Wait until I tell Dex who I ran into here.

Then it hits me, I can't tell Dex, because if I do, word will get back to the old man, somehow. I don't want anything personal getting back to him.

About Raquel.

Or me.

As if anything is going to happen.

This is the stuff of my dreams, right? Me and Raquel, on an exotic island. It's work related, granted, and neither of us knew the other would be here, but it feels like destiny. Feels like this what meant to be. I knew it wouldn't be easy to walk away from her, but when the old man sent me to Belize it seemed like the perfect distraction.

But she's here. And somehow, it feels like divine intervention. Fate or not, she's in front of me again and I'm losing my ability to focus.

I'll check out the coastline tomorrow since Tomas keeps bugging me about it. When I asked him why, he said, "Because you need to see. You need to know more than what you're being told."

He sounds cagey. Careful with his words. I asked him whose side he was on, ours or the NGO's?

He said he wants me to see both sides. It gets me thinking as something gnaws in the pit of my stomach. Do I believe my old man? Or do I believe Tomas?

I know what type of man Paul Knight is. He's not known for speaking truth, or for his philanthropic ways. Hell, he'll easily lie to us. He lied to my mom, and to Dex's mom, his wife. There is no bottom when it comes to him.

But now some things are starting to get under my skin. Suspicion rears its ugly head, and I can't shake it away. The old man is shady, but do I trust Tomas? And what about Orlando, the foreman? Tomas told me that he only joined last month, around the time EcoGuardians started to make noise.

Who do I trust? Who do I believe?

And just like that, I know. There is someone I can go to for answers, even if its unethical. Even if she enjoys slicing my balls and wouldn't hesitate to serve them to me on a platter.

One person who has no compunction over telling the truth.

Raquel.

She'll give me the answers, whether I'll like what she has to say or not.

CHAPTER TWELVE

RAQUEL

"I FEEL BAD FOR PUTTING YOU UNDER SO MUCH PRESSURE," Alma says. It's been a long day at the HQ.

I look up at her slowly, breaking focus from the document I'm reading through. "It's my job, Alma. No need to apologize. I like the distraction. When I get into something, that's all my mind can focus on."

"I noticed." She shuts down her PC and nods at my messy desk. "Work is over for today."

I frown. "I just have to—"

"There's a cultural food festival tonight. Lots of tasty Belizean food. Time to unwind." I heard Vilma and Edwin, two of EcoGuardians' employees who are helping me, talking about it earlier. "I should get back to my—"

Alma's brow lifts, nudging higher above her reading glasses. "You can do that tomorrow. You've been sitting in that chair all day."

"But the injunction—"

"Tomorrow is another day," she says, looking like she's not going to let me wriggle out of this. There's no point in protesting.

"There'll be lots of good food," Vilma says. "Lots of tamales, conch fritters and fried jacks. Rum punch, too," she adds, her face brightening into a smile.

"Do we have to drag you there, Raquel?" Alma says, in the voice I imagine she uses for her one of her grandchildren if they've been naughty. "This will be the perfect opportunity for you to meet and relax with the people of Belize. It will show you a different side of Belize, instead of the walls of your room at the guest house or this office."

That does it.

"Come on," Vilma says, smiling. "You'll love it, Raquel. You were at work before me."

They've convinced me. The reason I was so early is because the AC at the guesthouse is playing up, and the room was hot and humid when I woke up. I switch my computer off and grab my bag. "Where is it?" I ask following them out.

Alma locks up. "Not far at all. You'll see."

But as soon as we step outside, the aroma of food wafts in the air, and I hear reggae blasting out. Maybe a night out is exactly what I need. Alma tells me she'll only come for a little while. I'll leave when she does, because as nice as this is, the pressure of work weighs heavily on me, and I tell her I only intend to stay for a short while.

The sidewalk is peppered with food stalls. Fairy lights are strung up between the trees. There are portable stages, and there's a DJ booth. Music blares from the speakers. Tourists and locals mingle. Children run around, happy and excited, their cries filling the air. But it's the aroma of freshly made food that permeates the air and makes my mouth water. The entire street is lively and vibrant with color. I walk through it, breathing in the sweet, smoky and humid air, listening to the music as the slight breeze blows through my hair.

It seems that my white summer dress and sandals were the perfect outfit for today. We walk past tables piled high with food and Alma points out the various dishes to me. There's stewed chicken and rice and beans, and conch fritters, which Alma says are so delicious, it would be a sin not to try them.

"Conch fritters?" I ask, because Vilma mentioned these earlier.

"Dunked in sauce, nice and chewy and so flavorsome. My granddaughter loves them."

I go ahead and buy some when a loud bang makes me jump.

"Fireworks," says Alma. "They'll be going off through the evening."

"What are they celebrating?"

"Nothing. No reason. Just good food, good music. People having fun."

Simple pleasures.

A small group of men sit under a banyan tree playing dominoes. Vilma points out another vendor store where the table is filled with roasted plantains and fried fish. I still have my plate of conch fritters. They all buy something. Vilma points to one of the tables over by the beach for us to sit down at.

"Everyone want rum punch?" Edwin asks. There's a collective chorus of agreement. He leaves as we head towards the tables. I kick off my sandals and sit down, letting my feet sink into the sand which feels like powder between my toes.

I take a bite of my conch fritter. It's chewy, and fishy, like a scallop, and it's so delicious. I pop the little nugget into my mouth, then devour the next three. When I've finished, I sit back and sigh in contentment. "Thanks for dragging me out. I would've gone straight to the hotel and worked some more, while sweating away."

"You don't have AC?" Vilma asks.

"That's with the AC on."

Alma's fork stops inches from her mouth. "Do you ever stop working?"

"Not really."

To my surprise, she doesn't question me further, but watches silently.

"Rum punch." Edwin brings over a glass pitcher of rum punch and some paper cups. He pours the drink for us all.

"Isn't this the life?" Edwin takes a swig of his rum and sinks his head back against the chair. The sun warms my shoulders, the perfect breeze ruffles my hair. I hear children laughing, music playing, and somewhere the rhythm of drums and the bright notes of a steel pan. I'm tempted to get some more conch fritters. I sip my rum. It's smooth with a hint of spice, and it slides down my throat like liquid heat, leaving a sweet burn that lingers.

This is perfect. It's a world away from Tovey & Roth. A world I could get used to. A way of life, a pace of life, that is gentle and fuels my soul.

"This is the life," I murmur.

We sit in silence, eating and drinking, basking in the warm summer evening. No one talks. There is no need to. We're all savoring the ambiance, the food, the surroundings. After a while Alma announces that she's heading back.

I sit up, suddenly. "So soon?" I was just beginning to unwind.

"I need to be in the office early, but you look the most relaxed I've seen you. You stay." Alma's voice is almost schoolmarmish. "You enjoy the rest of the evening. I doubt Vilma and Edwin will be heading off anytime soon."

Vilma nods. "We're staying a while. Stick with us, and you'll be fine."

We bid goodbye to Alma, and I stick with the youngsters, though, as I soon discover, they're only a few years younger than me.

Edwin gets up to play football with some young children.

"What made you work for EcoGuardians?" I ask Vilma.

"It seemed like the only way I could do something," she says, sipping her rum punch. "When I was fifteen, the reef near our house started dying. My brother used to take me snorkeling out there, and it used to be so colorful. So many colors; bright pinks, reds, and golden yellows. My favorite were the blue and purple. It was magical seeing that flash of color in the water with fish darting around. Then, one day, it wasn't there. It didn't happen overnight. It was gradual. The colors fading slowly. Not more vibrant and bright oranges, reds and yellows. They became paler, washed out, then turned bone white, like a skeleton. Their beauty wiped away."

I glance at her somber face.

"I felt helpless. My brother felt angry. I couldn't sit back and watch it happen and not do anything. I wanted it all to come back, that vibrancy, that beautiful, magical flash of colors that captivated me. That's why I'm here. I'm not a scientist, or a lawyer. I wish I could be like you..." She looks at me in awe, like I'm Wonder Woman, someone who's going to save the world. "I wish I could be a lawyer, but ... it costs money and ..." She shrugs. "But I can do this, and working for EcoGuardians has taught me so much. I'm doing something good here."

"You are, Vilma. You are doing good, and on the ground, right here where help is needed. You have such passion, such conviction, in your voice, and EcoGuardians are lucky to have you. All of you." She has the most gorgeous sun-kissed bronze skin, and wears her hair in a thick braid down her back. She's so passionate about protecting her community's land and water, that I sometimes see a bit of me in her. .

Hearing my compliment, she fills up with happiness.

"Never forget the power you have to make a change. You don't have to be a lawyer to do that."

Her smile widens, like I've given her the biggest compliment. Being here, I feel part of something. Unlike Tovey & Roth. I love what I do, but being here, in the same office and the others, fills my soul.

"This is so nice." I take a big sip of the rum punch and sit back in my chair.

"You like it?"

"All of it. The food, the rum, the music, this ..." I gesture with my hand, waving my paper cup around. "Having this just outside your place of work. Pure magic."

I forget the stress. The injunction, the eco resort and unexpected shock of Rio Knight being here, in Belize, at the same time as me. Just as the thought of him settles on me like a fading picture, I see him again. Rather, I *feel* him first, as goosebumps pop up all over my skin. He's leaning against the trunk of a tree, dressed in a white linen shirt, sleeves rolled up at the forearms, his top buttons undone, and trousers.

He looks out of place here. Too clean. Too perfect. Too photoshopped, amidst all this joyful, colorful chaos weaving around him.

Our eyes meet. He doesn't move, but even with the short distance between us, I can tell that something in his expression shifts. I don't know how long he's been watching me or if he's just as surprised to see me, but now that our eyes are locked, time seems to stop.

I look away first. It feels like I've been holding my breath and I need a big, desperate intake of air to fill my lungs. I dare not look at him again, but force myself to watch Edwin play football.

I'm suddenly conscious of the powder soft sand under my feet, and the rays of the sun on my skin. I take a shaky sip of rum. Still feeling conscious and still wondering if he's looking my way. I'm barefoot, and wearing a sundress—not my usual work clothes. Maybe that's what he sees that's different.

Vilma laughs, then jumps up and joins the football game. I turn to look at Rio again, but he's gone, and a tidal wave of disappointment washes over me. But then he reappears in front of me, looking entirely comfortable in a chair that isn't his.

Just like he did at the Miami restaurant.

"Let me guess, you had a meeting across the street and you happened to see me."

"The world doesn't revolve around you." He gives me a cheesy grin. "But you still remember that night, huh?"

"It's like a nightmare I can't wake up from."

He slides out his long legs, making himself even more comfortable than he has any right to be. Edwin and Vilma come back, hot and breathless after their game of football. I don't bother to make introductions, but he does.

"Rio." He offers his hand. "I'm a friend of Raquel's."

Edwin and Vilma introduce themselves and sit down, reaching for their paper cups.

"I didn't think this was your scene," Rio says to me.

"This?" I wave my hand around. "Friends, food, drinks, gorgeous scenery. It's very much my scene. Shame you had to crash it, *again.*"

"This is a small place, and my hotel isn't far from here. I'm staying on the Placencia Peninsula."

"You're staying there?" Vilma asks.

Edwin looks impressed. "Nice string of hotels along there."

I can't help myself. "Only the best for—" I'm about to spurt off something when I stop. Edwin and Vilma don't know who he is. They don't know that he's on the other side. I shouldn't be seen with him. I need to be professional and keep my distance as much as I can. "I didn't think street stalls and fairy lights was your scene," I say, instead.

"It's not so bad." His eyes rove over my sundress. "You don't look very lawyerly today." His gaze burns into my skin and I take another long sip of my rum punch. The music pushes up a notch, and Edwin and Vilma get up and join a group of people who have also suddenly jumped up and started dancing.

"Why don't you show us your moves?" I dare Rio.

He sits back into the chair, crosses his ankles, and laces his hands behind his head. "I can't dance on sand. I'd rather just sit here and admire the view."

"Come on." Vilma holds out her hand for me to get up. The rum has loosened me up, and I don't feel like it's the end of a normal working day. It feels more like being on vacation. With a dash of daring, I get up. The vibe, the crowd, the music, it pulls me, but the way Rio watches me is what tips me over the edge. His gaze slides over me, and suddenly, I want him to see me like this, unapologetically wild and free. The shackles of my usual work day restraint undone.

I jump up, accepting Vilma's request. The rum has gotten to my head, because I wouldn't be so eager to get up and dance on the sand otherwise. It's not easy, but the rum punch courses through my veins, and with the sun starting to dip seemingly into the sea, my carefully constructed guardrails fall away. Buoyed up by being a million miles away from Pierce, and being with people who are easy to get along with, where I don't need to dodge comments rife with sexual innuendo, I'm swept up in a wave of gratitude.

I'm basking under Rio's intense, watchful gaze. Something about me and him, running into each other unexpectedly, on so many occasions, feels strange, and yet familiar. I can't get a handle on it, but it's there, an invisible force that connects us and becomes stronger with each meeting. Building, to what, I don't know.

I start to dance, swaying my hips, moving my arms, feeling unashamedly free. laughing and feeling free. Dancing with abandon. Vilma and Edwin are letting loose beside me, their smiles wide and unfiltered. The crowd is alive, pulsing with heat and rhythm. There's a buzz in the air—maybe it's the rum punch, or the beauty of the setting sun, or just the pure joy of being barefoot on the sand, surrounded by strangers who feel like friends.

A group of young guys join us. Loud and raucous, they look like tourists. Someone grabs my hand, reeling me towards him. I don't like it, and wrench my hand free. He puts his hands up, in a surrender pose, and steps back. He's cute, too young for me, and now he looks genuinely alarmed that he might have offended me.

"Sorry," he shouts, over the music. "Feels like a carnival, ya know." His twangy accent makes me think he could be Australian. I nod, and continue dancing. He doesn't reach for my hand again, and maintains the distance between us.

But in the next moment, Rio steps in. His face is like thunder. He eyeballs the other guy, scaring him off until he's forced to turn his back to us, and move back to his friends.

"Thought you didn't dance, Tarzan," I shout, while still dancing. Rio cups his hand to his ear, like he can't hear. I lean forward. Without my killer heels I have to tiptoe to reach his ear. "I thought zht you didn't dance, Tarzan."

"I'm not dancing." He stands there, arms folded, territorial and possessive, like I'm his property, and he's watching over me. Ordinarily, this would set off alarm bells. Piss me off, but it's Rio. We have a history now, sort of. And I like him being possessive, even though it goes against my grain. Everything about this man goes against my values, and yet, I find myself drawn to him in ways I can't explain.

He doesn't even attempt to dance and stands there, arms still crossed, like he's immune to the music thumping through the crowd.

"You just going to stand there like a statue?" I shout in his ear again, the beat thudding in my chest. I accidentally bump into him, and his arm wraps around me like a reflex as if he's scared I was going to fall.

"Steady there," he murmurs, his voice low, his breath grazing my cheek as he loosens his hold on me.

But the touch has already left an imprint during those few seconds that our bodies brushed. A current rips through me and my heart somersaults inside my ribcage. Heat curls low in my belly, fanning out slowly, electrifying every cell in my body.

My body remembers.

It misses him.

I play devil's advocate. "You got rid of my dancing partner. Why did you go and do that?"

This time he leans down, and into my ear. "Why do you think?"

Fire flashes through his eyes. In this moment, the music and surroundings blur into the background. In this moment, it's just me, and him. My heart beats furiously, and a trail of heat licks my skin, warming my body as it moves south. A throbbing begins between my legs.

He likes me.

He wants me.

Every ounce of resolve I had, to keep this man at a distance, has vanished.

The music pauses for a bit. Edwin and Vilma tell me that they're going to get more food and ask if I want to come along.

I shake my head. The crowd breaks up and Rio and I stand there, facing one another, unsure, and hungry for something, but it's not for food.

"Walk with me," he says. I can't read his expression. I can't tell if's he annoyed, or calm, or bored. We slip away from the crowd, and along the shoreline, moving further away from the crowd, leaving the colorful array of vendors and DJs and lights behind us. It's quieter here. The sand cooler, slightly damp beneath our feet. The sun dips low, almost sinking into the ocean, its hues of gold and orange looking resplendent as it touches the horizon. The balmy air is a mix of salt, and rum, and the aroma of grilled food.

We walk side by side, not speaking, yet it doesn't feel uncomfortable. It feels … normal. There are no barbs, no digs, no sarcasm. Only me and him, and the sound of waves lapping against the shore as we leave footprints in the sand.

He seems pensive, and the adrenaline rushing through me is finally calming down.

"He came onto you. I didn't like that," he says, finally.

It takes me a moment to figure out what he's talking about.

"Why?" I ask. A hundred thoughts run through my head. Who are we? What are we? We're not seeing one another. We're not even friends. We're just two people who keep running into each other. Two people who are attracted to one another.

"I just didn't."

No explanation. But I understand it. I'd feel the same if some young beautiful woman made a move on him. I wouldn't like to stand by and watch that.

"I came here to get away from you," he says. "But everywhere I go, I see you."

"I came here to get away from you," I say. "And everywhere *I* go, I see *you*."

"And yet, here we are."

"Here we are."

He stops. "Are you drunk? You're repeating everything I say."

"I'm a little tipsy. I'm mostly having fun, though. You don't though. You don't look like you're having fun." I don't recall him eating any food, or having any punch. He didn't dance. He stood by me. "What were you doing here?"

"I saw some fliers at the hotel. Thought I'd check it out."

"And there's me thinking you came out here looking for me." I look up at him, feeling flirty.

"That was the real reason I came out here." His expression is so deadpan, I can't tell if he's joking or not.

I swallow. "Did you really?"

He looks at me in something that looks like disbelief.

Caraca.

He played me.

"I didn't, but it was a nice surprise, seeing you, once I got over the shock of it."

He's saying that to make me feel better. My heart pounds and I try desperately to say something witty and clever. And I fail.

"We have unfinished business," he says.

That's when I remember something I've been wanting to ask him. "I heard that you were smitten by Dani. Couldn't take your eyes off her at the special evening your father hosted."

He opens his mouth, and his eyes start to widen, just a little. Just enough for me to know he's feeling uneasy because he hasn't uttered a word .

"You even had a photo of her in your apartment," I add, watching his reaction like a hawk.

He swipes a hand across his beard. "I was wondering when

you might ask me about that. I guess there are no secrets between you and Dani."

"It's true, then?"

"Oh, princesa, you weren't sure?"

"I was sure. Dani wouldn't lie to me."

"You jealous?" he asks. And for the first time tonight, I feel a little of how he must have felt when that guy wanted me to dance.

I am jealous. Or, I *was*. I'm not now. I'm thankful, more than anything. I'm thankful that he didn't pick Dani. That his interest was only short lived.

"I wonder what your babies would look like, yours and Dani's." What a stupid thing to say. I immediately regret it. He recoils in disgust, then gently wraps his fingers around my wrists.

"Dani is in love with Dex, and he's completely in love with her. Me, princesa? I like the thrill of the hunt. I like the chase. I like the flirtatious phase that comes before I fuck the only woman I have eyes for. Our babies, yours and mine, if you ever give me the chance, will be beautiful and bold, charming and fearless."

My mouth hangs open, my heart thumping, and my breaths quicken, shallow and uneven. Heat spirals low in my belly as the rough promise of his words spark a hunger I'm trying so hard to resist.

He loosens his grip but doesn't completely let go. Instead, his thumbs stroke the insides of my wrists. It's one of my erogenous zones and I'm already feeling clammy between my legs.

"That time in Miami," he says, his voice husky and low, making my insides heat, "that time when I showed up in the restaurant, allegedly unexpectedly …"

"You *planned* it?" I murmur. Each lazy brush of his thumb

on my skin makes sparks shoot up my arms. My body betrays me each time this man is near me. I shouldn't want him this much, and yet, I always do.

"I sure did. I wanted to see you."

"And so you ... you had a meeting in order to—"

"No meeting. I just paid a guy in the bar across the street to say we did."

I sink back into myself. The levels of manipulation on these Knights is astounding. Yet, I'm oddly touched, that he went to such lengths, just to see me. A warmth unfurls in my chest, sneaky and uninvited, and I hate that it makes me smile. This man is dangerous, and I know better, but the happiness bubbling up is impossible to ignore. I can't deny that I feel something for him. I'd be lying to myself if I did. I want him, and he, it seems, wants me. He'd go to any lengths to see me. If I'm honest with myself, that terrifies me, too.

"We should head back," I say, wondering if he's going to make a move. He lets go of my wrists, and I miss the touch of his fingers. The flickering fairy lights look like fireflies in the distance and night is falling. I don't want to walk barefoot in the dark. He starts to walk. I guess we are heading back.

When we return to our chairs, Vilma and Edwin are standing in a group of people.

"We're going to the lagoon. Why don't you come?" Vilma asks.

"You're going where?" Rio asks.

"To the Anderson Lagoon."

"What for?" He sounds cautious.

"To swim. It's known for its bioluminescence. It'll be fun," Edwin says, starting to clear our plates from the table. I help him. Vilma picks up the empty paper cups.

"There's a group of us going," she says. "It's the secret spot. Nice to go for a late-night swim under the stars."

Edwin takes the trash from us and walks away to dispose of it. Rio looks at me and I have a feeling he isn't keen on going. The crowd is mainly youngsters, early twenties. Maybe he's feeling a little old. I've never swum in a lagoon before, and especially not one that is bioluminescent. "I'm game. You?" I turn to Rio.

"How are you getting there?" he asks.

"Luis has a truck," Vilma replies, then, sensing his concern, "It's safe. I know these guys. Luis's an experienced tour guide. He does tours like this all the time. This isn't a tour. It's just a chance for us to have a dip in the lagoon."

Rio doesn't look convinced, but I want to go. I don't care what time it is, or that I have so much work to do. When will I ever get the chance to swim in a lagoon that lights up?

"Come along," Vilma says. "You'll like it. It's so pretty."

But it's not the prettiness I'm thinking about. It's about being in a lagoon, with Rio Knight, under the stars.

CHAPTER THIRTEEN

RIO

I DON'T LIKE THIS IDEA. DRIVING LATE AT NIGHT, ON ROADS I don't know, in a truck I'm not even driving. It's a young guy behind the wheel, and I'm worried he's drunk too much. No way do I want him behind the steering wheel.

I'm about to go and question him when Raquel tugs my sleeve. "You're not the boss here," she reminds me, her voice warm with amusement. "They want to have fun. You should let them be."

"That's all good, but you want to make it home alive, don't you?"

"Just go with the flow, Knight. Loosen up, You might like it."

She smiles, looking more relaxed than I've ever seen her. Her curls are wild from dancing, and her skin glows in the moonlight. This version of Raquel is reckless, radiant, and maybe a little tipsy—and I can't look away. I don't want to look away. I want her to be safe, and get back in one piece.

I won't like it. Driving out this late, to go to a lagoon, where who knows what creatures might be hiding, is not a good idea. But I'm not about to let Raquel go alone, even if her friends are with her. I'd hate for anything to happen to her. So I go along, trying not to ask a million questions is hard though, but I somehow manage it.

We all pile into an old Toyota truck. It's the kind of pickup that looks like it belongs in a dumpster. The cab fills up first, and the rest of us cram into the open bed at the back. Bodies wedged together, legs dangling, arms bracing as the trucks jolts along the dirt road. Someone starts singing, too loud, and not too great, but everyone joins in. Except me and Raquel. We grin at one another.

It feels chaotic. Alive and dangerous. I like it more than I want to admit.

After what feels like forever, the truck grinds to a halt. Darkness covers everything, except the faint outline of trees and a narrow dock leading out over still water. comes to a stop and we're told to get into a boat.

"Out," someone shouts. "Get onto the boat. Slow and easy."

I help Raquel off the truck and eye up the small, flat-bottomed boat nearby, my stomach filling with dread.

"Seriously?" I mutter, glaring at the guy who is leading us all like a pack of sheep to the wolves.

He grins and pats me on the shoulder. "It will be worth it, boss."

"Why are you doing this?" I ask. "Are you charging money for this?" I don't understand why anyone would do anything like this for free.

Vilma seems annoyed by my questions. "He works here. He wants to give us, the locals, a chance to do what tourists like you pay to do. He's allowed to, no?"

"Try not to offend anyone, Knight," Raquel whisper-hisses.

"I hope we don't drown." This is incredibly reckless, incredibly unnecessary, and here we are. Setting off late at night, in darkness, to swim in a lagoon. I dread to think what creatures could be lying in wait for us.

I'm almost thirty, and these kids look like they're in their early twenties. Is that the difference between reckless stupidity and knowing exactly how fast things can go wrong? I give in. Raquel wants to go, so we are going. There's no way I'm letting her do this alone.

We all get into the boat. As I look up, I see stars that take my breath away. Not just a few dotted around, but hundreds of them, sparkling brightly in the clear night sky. Beautiful. I've not seen a night sky like this before.

"Wow," Raquel gasps, looking up. We're sitting crushed up against one another, both staring up in awe. It is majestic. Utterly breathtaking.

"This is so beautiful," she murmurs, her voice thick with awe. I have to agree. The construction site, the meetings, the noise the locals are making, all seem so far away. This is something I would never have experienced had I not begrudgingly come along. Now I'm glad I did.

The boat drifts to a slow stop in the middle of the lagoon, and the guy who's in charge, cuts the engine. We float in near-silence. He expects us to jump into that, from this?

Alarm bells set off in my head. This is so irresponsible. There could be all sorts of creatures lying in water in the still, inky black water. I try not to think about crocodiles. Or snakes. Or whatever the hell else lurks here.

"You look scared, boss." The main guy prods me in the ribs. "It's safe."

"You willing to bet your life on that?"

"It's safe. I trust him." The guy, Edwin, says.

There's no dock. No shoreline to wade in from. Just still, black water stretching all around us, and a quiet that hums beneath the surface.

"This is it," someone says. "Jump in."

Around us, people are stripping down to their underwear and jumping in from the boat.

"I trust him. He's a tour operator," Vilma says. I turn my back to her, because she starts to undress.

"I didn't have you down for being a scaredy cat, Knight," Raquel says, shimmying out of her dress.

I catch my breath. She's in her bra and panties, and she looks sexy as sin, the moonlight illuminating her body, giving her an almost ethereal glow. The swell of her hips. The line of her collarbone. Long, strong legs, the kind that look like they were made to wrap around someone's waist.

Hot damn.

"I'm not a scaredy cat. I just like being in control."

I hate unexpected shocks and surprises. I'm bearing the scars of the shock which ripped through our family all those decades ago, and I decided then that I like my life to be controlled and orderly.

Everyone has peeled off shirts and shorts, laughing and tossing clothes onto the benches. One by one, they jump in.

Splash!

The water explodes in glowing blue light. Trails of neon shimmer in the dark, like stardust. It's otherworldly, and unreal. It's magical. Almost as magical as the night sky with its myriads of stars. I start to slowly, reluctantly undress.

"Look at that!" Raquel cries. The water glows when people swim or move, every movement leaving a trail of electric blue light, illuminating the movement, like stardust suspended in the water, leaving a trail of suspended stardust in their wake. She gasps, bending over gripping the side of the boat. "It's like they're swimming through stardust." She watches, mesmerized … but she doesn't move. Not yet.

"You okay?" I ask, stepping closer.

She turns, lips parted, her eyes wide as she sees me in my boxers. "You brave enough to jump in?"

"I'm not scared. Just careful."

She straightens her spine, and steps up onto the edge of the boat, pausing for a heartbeat, before diving in. The water explodes around her in glowing blue. Her body becomes a comet—blazing through the water, blue and beautiful, as she swims away.

I dive in after her and swim towards her.

"This is insane," she murmurs, swiping her hands over her hair as she smooths it back off her face. Everyone has jumped in, and the once silent lagoon is a flurry of noise and light. It's magical. Like swimming through the stars and the galaxy.

Raquel glides up beside me. "Aren't you glad you came?"

I nod. "You look like you're all lit up from the inside out."

She circles me slowly, sending shimmering halos through the water with her every move. I tread water, kicking off a wave of light with my movements as I watch her, the way her hair floats around her shoulders, the moonlight catching the droplets on her skin, her smile wide and unguarded. The kind of smile that steals my breath. The kind of smile in a moment I'll remember forever. This isn't the intense lawyer who incinerates her opponents in court. The woman in the sharp and sleek pressed business suits, with armor to match. This is Raquel, raw, soft and vulnerable. I think I like this version even more.

The others are in the middle of the lagoon, and Raquel and I have somehow drifted to one side.

"You look the happiest I've ever seen you," I say.

"Being away from work does that."

"You really hate it where you work?"

"With every moral fiber in my body."

"Work consumes you." It seems to, she's intense and focused, and such a justice warrior, I wonder if she ever makes time for fun. It took her coming out here to relax.

"I see it more as a vocation."

We swim around one another. Treading water, swimming a few strokes, staying in our own secret orbit.

"You like to be in control?" she asks.

"Always."

"You like to be on top?"

A rush of heat hits me and my mind flashes to picture what that would look like. What it would *feel* like. It's enough to get my cock swelling. I circle her, close enough to catch the faint glow of bioluminescence trailing off her skin, and she mirrors my movement.

"I'll let you go on top occasionally."

"I'm sure you'd like that." Her voice is soft, and it turns my cock even harder. We stop, treading water, getting into deeper water with our innuendo.

"I would *love* that." I struggle to keep my voice level. The words conjure up a picture of her doing just that, head tipped back, breasts thrust out, glowing like a damn goddess in this electric blue water. My cock cheers me on. I know what she wants, she wants to make serious conversation, but stripped down to our underwear in a bioluminescent lagoon is not the place for serious confessions.

She floats closer to me, her hair fanned out in the water, her eyes, dark and intense, locked on mine. "I very much like being on top," she whispers so close to me that her lips brush my ear. Her body brushes mine, for a few seconds.

Fuck me, if she doesn't leave me speechless and with a boner that's going to hurt all the way home.

"I'll let you do that, one day, princesa." My voice turns hoarse.

"One day?"

"You decide, princesa. Totally up to you. I showed you my cards, told you some things. Now it's up to you."

She treads water, facing me, her movement keeping the water all lit up wherever she's been. I move nearer, and she doesn't move away. Instead, she floats nearer, the slight undercurrent maybe pushing us closer together. Our bodies bump together, bare skin on bare skin. The water lights up between us, slithers of glowing blue swirling around us.

I brush a lock of wet hair from her face, feel the wet softness of her skin. She tilts her head, we move closer, and soon we're almost bumping legs. Our faces close now. Close enough that we could kiss. I don't move but when she splays a hand on my chest, the movement sets off tiny grenades inside me.

"I do like you, Knight," she murmurs.

"Yeah?"

She nods.

We're making fucking progress.

"So, what are we going to do about it?" I ask.

My insides feel hot and tight, like a tightly coiled up spring, needing release. She's waiting for me, but I'm in awe. Suspended like this, with the water blue and magical and magnificent around us. This feels like a moment suspended in time. She dips her head towards me, and I mirror the movement. Our lips brush. Soft and wet. Her body brushes against mine again. I'm pretty sure my boner's grazed her skin, but hot damn if this doesn't feel amazing.

"Time to head back!" someone shouts.

We stay still. Lips brushing again. The kiss eluding us,

again. We breathe each other's air in, poised in time, waiting with want.

She floats away. "It's always the timing with us."

No shit. It's always the damn timing. "Another time," I say, watching her with admiration. And wondering how the hell I'm going to climb back on board, hiding a humungous hardon.

CHAPTER FOURTEEN

RAQUEL

I GOT INTO WORK SURPRISINGLY EARLIER THAN I EXPECTED, given that it was just after two in the morning when I got back to my guesthouse.

What a night.

Rio drove us all back, even Vilma and Edwin.

This morning, I'm determined to focus, but every now and then my thoughts drift to last night, and Rio, and the lagoon. Us almost kissing. My body brushing against his and feeling his excitement for me. I keep going over his confession, about how he fabricated events to run into me at the restaurant with Dex and Dani. Secretly, I'm thrilled, and excited, but nothing can happen.

We can't forget our roles. He's on their side, not ours. I can't be seen to be fraternizing with him. So now, I have my head down back at HQ, documenting the environmental damage. Alma is getting everything arranged for me in chronological order.

I'm determined not to venture outside. It makes it easier to stay out of Rio Knight's way. I'm also trying to get enough information together before I talk to Pierce.

Vilma taps me lightly on my shoulder. I stop typing. "It's your friend again, from last night. He doesn't want to come in."

"Oh." My heart fills with joy, and then deflates as quickly, because I'm torn. I don't know why he's here, and I don't know how to be around him.

Alma looks at me, but says nothing. I huff out a sigh, because my fingers were flying and I was in the zone, getting lots done. As I head towards the door, I see him taking up the doorway, hands placed on the sides of the door jamb like he owns the place.

"Good morning, princesa." Dark shades cover his eyes, and a smile tugs at the corner of his mouth. He lifts his hand and removes his shades, revealing eyes full of mischief.

"Hi." I feel shy. A little off kilter. A little blindsided. I was hiding here, hoping to cut off all possibility of running into him, and now he comes to me. "To what do I owe this pleasure?"

"I was getting ready to go to work and I thought I'd pass by. Didn't expect you to be up and working so soon. Thought you might sleep till noon, what with needing your beauty sleep and all that." He's back to being obnoxious again.

"I've been here since seven."

He makes a face like he's been injured. "Seven? I was still in bed having sweet dreams at that time. I couldn't get out of bed, I was dreaming so much."

His words make me blush, because they sound intimate, direct, like he knows he'll get me thinking.

"The escort you hired must have been good." It's a low blow, jokey, but with a sting, giving him a dose of his own medicine, but I'm not prepared for his reaction.

He looks shocked. Like I've made a blatantly unjust

accusation. "I'm not that guy. You must have me confused with someone else." His tone is cutting, and I'm curious as to why he's so hurt.

"I ... I ..." I shrug, because words fail me.

"You still think badly of me, princesa? You should know that loyalty is something I don't fuck with." He leans a little closer, voice low and intimate. "Once someone catches my attention, that's it. Game over. No backup plans. No wandering eyes. Just one very unlucky woman stuck with all of me. Even if she likes to bust my balls every chance she gets."

"Unlucky..." I mutter. "That'd be right. Why are you here?" I ask, part annoyed, part frustrated. I'm trying to maintain my distance from him, but he's come to my place of work. I don't want to give Vilma or Edwin something to talk about, and I really don't want to give Alma cause for alarm.

"Can we talk? Off the record?" He straightens up. I can't tell if it's because of what I said, or if he wants to discuss something serious. Or if this is about last night. If so, the timing couldn't be worse. He keeps saying it's fate that keeps bringing us together, but I'm going to get fired if I'm not careful.

"Off the record?" I'm about to make another quip, but stop myself. "I don't have long, Knight. Some of us have to work for a living."

"Just a few moments. Out here. My Jeep's parked across the street."

I glare at him, needing him to lead the way. Instead he moves slightly sideways, beckoning for me to go first. I walk past him, but unfortunately end up brushing against him. It feels like I've touched a live wire. The scent of his cologne, rich, masculine and just this side of sinful, hits the moment he steps closer.

I manage to keep my composure as he overtakes me, leading the way across the street. He stops by his Jeep, and opens the door for me. I hop in and he enters from the driver's side.

"What do you want?" I ask, feeling a little weary. "Is this about last night?"

He lets out a labored breath. "What are you doing here?"

Now I'm confused. "I'm working. You know I'm working."

"But why are you *really* here?"

Did he get out the wrong side of his bed? What is this? I don't reply.

He waits, in silence.

"It's pro bono," I say finally, my voice clipped. I don't want to tell him we're going to file an injunction. I want the satisfaction of seeing his face when he finds out about it. And now I wish we hadn't met last night. I wish I hadn't gone to the food festival because then one thing wouldn't have led to another. We wouldn't have ended up almost naked in a lagoon, almost about to kiss.

What am I doing?

"EcoGuardians want me to gather information." Which, technically, they do, so I'm not lying.

"A high-flying lawyer like you? Here, to gather information? Surely they could have sent an intern to do the job."

He sounds like he doesn't believe me.

"Why the shady company? Why a subsidiary?" I ask, deflecting.

"It's not illegal. This is how business is done."

I narrow my eyes. "So you can hide behind lots of different layers?"

"It's a common practice." But the way he says it sounds more like a warning than a fact. Like he wants me to back off. "Blue Star is doing good here—"

"Says who?"

"It will offer jobs. It's going to put a lot back into the community."

"Have you seen the coastline?"

"Not yet."

"Why not? Afraid of what you might find?"

"I'm going there later. I've been busy with matters at the resort."

"Just because you decide to put a monstrosity in the middle of a green space doesn't mean the surrounding areas are untouched. In fact, you're doing the opposite. You need to open your eyes, Knight. Stop blindly accepting whatever Daddy spoon-feeds you."

He clenches his jaw. Doesn't like what I've said. "You're making a lot of assumptions."

"I have facts and data on my side, what do you have?"

He scratches his beard. "Do you know something I don't?"

"It's not for me to tell you. Do your own homework."

"Okay." He pulls out a folder. "I have some information if you want it. Environmental data. I figured it might help you."

I stare at it with suspicion. He's been so oddly, subtly hostile with his questioning, so hot and cold, I don't know if I can trust him. "Thanks, but I can draw my own conclusions. I've got eyes and ears."

He hangs on to the folder. "I'm not forcing it on you. If you don't want it, that's fine, too." A moment of silence passes.

"This must be a nice vacation for you," I say.

"You think all we do is play, princesa?" His words are light, but his tone is ice. It makes me wonder if my earlier comment about hiring an escort offended him that much. He taps his fingers on the folder lying on his lap. "You don't have to take this. I just thought it might help, that's all. Not all Knight moves are underhanded."

I frown and wonder if he's talking about last night, then I

force myself to focus on the task at hand. I can't have any romantic daydreams about us. As for this folder, he's not pushing me to have it, and I guess it won't do me any harm if I take a peek. I'm curious to see what their angle is "Why do you want me to have this?"

"I don't want you to do anything. I thought it might help, that's all. It was carried out by third-party consultants. We've got nothing to hide."

"I don't know. Everything with you guys always feels so ... calculated."

"What feels calculated? Me handing you this file? You don't have to take it, princesa."

"Can't you stop calling me that?"

"Make me."

I peer at him, almost laugh out loud. "How old are you?"

"You want my deets? My date of birth, my measurements? My length, my girth?"

I screw up my face, glaring at him. "Once again, how old are you?" I notice that we've both crossed our arms.

He brings out the warrior in me. He makes me want to slap him and kiss him with equal measure. He's infuriating, and charmingly annoying at the same time. Here I am, in Belize, thousands of miles from home, and I run into him.

What are the chances?

I'm hot and bothered, and this time, it's not even due to the weather. It's because of him. Heat rolls off his skin like a slow-burning fire. He's wearing a black T-shirt that clings a little too well to his chest, his bronzed forearms now resting on the steering wheel. Even sitting with him here in his Jeep makes me start to sweat like I'm in trouble.

And maybe, I am.

"You're very Jekyll and Hyde," I say, waving a hand between us. "Last night you were different and today—"

"Last night you were different, too. I know you're a true professional. I'm trying to be mindful."

Oh.

I appreciate that.

"You have a bad impression of the old man," he continues. "That's warranted. I'm assuming Dani has told you everything. Just remember that we're not like that. *I'm* not like that."

I'm trying to figure out his angle, on why he's really here this morning. The man had a hardon when I last saw him. Did he sleep? Did he take care of himself? Like I had to so that I could sleep?

I put out my hand, nod at the folder resting on his lap. "I might glance at it. See what your independant consultant has to say."

He shrugs as he hands it to me. I rest it on my lap, not even bothering to open it or flick through it.

"No 'thank you', princesa?"

I grit my teeth together. Fake a smile. "Thank you."

"One more thing. Just a heads up. We're having a meeting at the community hall later this evening. Your boss might already know about it."

"She mentioned it. Why are you being so nice and helpful?"

"Can't I be?"

"But why? You didn't answer my question."

"Are you always so suspicious of people being nice to you, princesa?"

"Rich people, yes. I'm always worried that they're ten steps ahead, buying their way out of a mess."

He shakes his head. I climb out of the Jeep and walk away without looking back. But a swirling feeling in my gut tells me he's probably watching me. I go back inside the bungalow and sit down at the table again. Alma watches me intently.

"What's that?" she asks, as I set the folder on the table.

"He asked me to meet off the record. Said I could take a look at this."

"He gave you some information? Is that wise?" She raises an eyebrow. "You remember whose side you're on, don't you?"

"I do. It's environmental data, done by a third-party."

"Who?"

"I don't know." And that's my warning bell. My thinking brain isn't fully engaged, because if it was, knowing what I'm here for, what we're about to do, and what the Knights are, I wouldn't have taken those documents from Rio. "I want to see what angle they're coming from," I tell Alma, but I feel like I've already let her down.

CHAPTER FIFTEEN

RIO

It's so hot in here, I feel like I'm melting with every passing second.

I run my finger around the collar of my shirt. I wasn't going to wear a business suit today. I didn't relish the idea of melting in this heat, but dressing the part might help gain respect.

Plastic chairs scrape along the floor and loud murmurs fill the air. Ceiling fans spin above our heads. The community hall is packed, rife with the smell of body odour from the stifling heat. It's starting to feel claustrophobic.

After talking to the local government officials and ministry reps, discussing the public fallout over the resort, I was advised that it would be better to call a meeting, to talk to the people, in order to avoid protests and media spotlight. Now we're here, sitting in chairs facing the crowd.

A massive image of the eco resort hangs behind us, showing it in its fine glory; solar panels, palm trees, blue sea. It's an image. Not an actual photo, and I'm worried that people might ask why we have this instead of an actual photo of the place.

I've just seen Raquel in the audience, with her boss. They're in the first row, and to my right. They're sitting close enough that I can see the dewy sheen on Raquel's face. She must have gone back to her hotel and gotten changed, just like I did, because she was in a casual dress earlier today. Now she's dressed smartly. Lawyered up, wearing a business suit and killer shoes with pencil points for heels. I like her like this, but I liked her more in her white sundress, and barefoot.

Focus.

I look away, feel my shirt sticking to my skin. A trickle of sweat meanders down my back. I glance at Raquel again. She's on her phone. Her skin is glowing, and she swipes a hand across her neck. I'm sure she's overheating too. Lucky for me, I get to watch her as she takes off her blazer. And now my mind freezes, seeing her in a beige-colored satin blouse. It's an elegant blouse, with a V-neck that dips down at her cleavage. An image of her in her bra and panties from last night flashes across my eyes. Raquel about to dive into the lagoon and leave a trail of neon blue behind her. We almost kissed. Our bodies touched, giving me a taste of what it could be like to hold her, to be close to her.

I snap back to reality. Fuck. I'm going to have a hard time getting through this evening. Sitting between Tomas and Orlando, I force myself to focus. I'm only here as a liaison for Knight Enterprises and I'm interested to see what the locals have to say. I'm going to keep quiet and let Orlando talk. He can take the heat for Delport, even though he was only recently hired, late in the project, a fact that I find odd, and a little suspicious. No one can give me a reason why the other guy left. Not even Tomas.

The reports and data I've been looking at tell me

everything's above board, but as I look around me and see the packed hall, I wonder if there's more here than I'm being led to believe. Needing to get information from Delport, I've been in meetings most of the time, but I really do need to get out and see the damage for myself—the mangroves they claim are untouched, the coral reefs they swear are thriving, the drinking water they say is clean. I'm not taking their word for it. I need to see it with my own eyes.

My old man sent me here to hush everything up. I see that clearer than ever now, and I need to be absolutely certain that this construction site is fully compliant with every environmental law and regulation. No loopholes. No shortcuts.

There's something that's been needling me. Raquel is smart, and passionate. She doesn't care about money. She's here for a reason. Delport says everything is fine at their end, but the NGO are saying otherwise. Both of us can't be right.

My shirt sticks to my skin and I feel another trickle of sweat meandering down my back. Tomas points out the journalists here, sitting in the second row along with local leaders and a bunch of people from Delport Realty.

"See there?" Tomas talks in a hushed tone, his gaze directed at a group towards the back. "They're the fishermen, concerned about reef destruction, and behind them are the farmers. They're worried about water contamination and land loss."

"But the reports all say—"

"Listen to the people," Tomas urges. "Listen to *their* stories."

He says it with such finality. I realize that it's not only what Tomas says that I need to heed, but what he doesn't say. I know things aren't going to go well when Orlando pushes me to get up first and make an introduction.

CHAPTER SIXTEEN

RAQUEL

I want to see how the charming Knight heir performs when he hasn't bought the audience.

In the sweltering heat of the community town hall, Rio sits at the front, facing the crowd, along with some people I recognize from the construction site. They huddle together, and it seems like they're trying to decide who gets up first.

Then, Rio gets up. He looks reluctant, but in a split second, his demeanor changes, and he's polished and confident.

He walks up to the front and stands to face the audiences. He's wearing a white shirt and tie, dark trousers, and carries plenty of attitude. No blazer, but his signature shades dangle from the pocket of his shirt. Hands on hips, he welcomes everyone and thanks them for being here. Then he makes a joke about the sweltering heat.

I don't expect anyone to laugh, but to my complete shock, some people do. Looking around, I'm not surprised to find that it's mainly the female contingent. The moms and grandmas who are here.

Caraca.

I was hoping they wouldn't be taken in by his good looks and charm, like I was, unfortunately. I blame the rum punch for that.

"I'm Rio Knight, here on behalf of Knight Enterprises, Delport Realty's parent company. I'm not a spokesperson. I'm here to listen."

He's about to return to the side, when I stand up. I'm not going to let him get away with that.

"As the parent company, can you enlighten us as to your mission for the eco resort?"

He blinks, before giving me the death stare. I press my lips together, to stop them from flashing a smug smile.

"And, who are you?" he asks.

He's playing that game, is he? "Raquel Monteiro here, with Alma Flores, to record testimony. Let's stay on track, Mr. Knight. I'm still waiting for an answer."

He shoots me a what-the-fuck look. Like he can't believe I've had the balls to stand up and ask him. I almost didn't. I almost stayed seated, but maybe that's what he wants. Maybe he's trying his best to quieten me, and using his good looks and charm to do it. It's not going to work. I mean business, even if, deep down inside, I feel he's doing his best to make this difficult for me.

Last night was a bad mistake. I'm starting to believe that he engineered it, right from the start when he turned up, leaning against the tree looking like someone out of a Condé Nast magazine. These Knights play dirty. I must never forget that.

"Speaking on behalf of Delport Realty, we believe that sustainability and progress can exist together. We're bringing jobs, infrastructure, and eco-conscious tourism to a region that deserves visibility and investment."

I give him a pointed stare. Did I hear correctly? Visibility and investment? Is that what they're calling mangrove destruction these days? To my dismay I note that a few people are nodding in agreement. A journalist next to me scribbles in her notebook. No one questions a word he's saying.

"Are you planning to disclose that the resort sits on land previously designated as being protected under the 2008 Coastal Conservation Agreement?" I throw back. Sweat trickles down my neck as all eyes turn to me.

To my satisfaction, I notice his Adam's apple bobbing, as a hush descends. The only sound I hear is that of the whirring fans. Rio's eyes lock with mine. "The agreement expired in 2018 and was renegotiated in 2019. Those terms were reviewed by the Ministry of Natural Resources."

"Renegotiated? How convenient." He's implying that nothing shady happened, but he's also not denying it either. A vein along his forehead pops. He slicks his hair back, and my attention fixates on that bold, brash watch of his. How cool, smug and self-assured he is. It's a trait baked into the Knight DNA.

"I can assure you that all of our permits are above board, and we followed every legal procedure."

"Hmmmm." I put on my most serious face, and nod, as if I'm thinking about something. "But legal doesn't always mean it's ethical, Mr. Knight."

"And unethical doesn't always mean illegal, Ms. Monteiro." His tone is sharp again, like he's been wounded. Like when I mentioned him having an escort.

Something hits hard and my spine stiffens. This man isn't only defending the eco resort; he's defending himself.

My blood boils. "A resort, an *eco resort*, no less, built over bulldozed coastline, a waterway blocked, mangrove trees destroyed. Communities affected. You call this *sustainable?*"

The crowd's murmur turns louder. Someone stands behind me. I turn to see a local elder. "They promised we would have better access to water, but they lied! We're forced to buy bottled or get sick."

The silence is deafening, and only the scrape of a chair breaks it. The men from the construction site, sitting next to Rio look sheepish. One of them, the foreman, stares down at his shoes. I wonder if he's wishing the floor would swallow him up. Tomas, the guy Alma knows, nods in approval.

My eyes fix on Rio. "Do you still insist on calling this sustainable?"

His jaw flexes. I've put him in a tight spot and he doesn't like it. "We're working on it, Ms. Monteiro. I didn't design this resort, I didn't approve the plans, but I'm here now, representing the parent company, and aiming to put things right."

A couple of people get up and take photos of us. We're only a few feet away from each other, in a fiery standoff. Faces twisted in anger, nothing like how we were last night in the lagoon.

Alma gives a discreet tug of my skirt. "Calm down," she whispers. "Not like this."

I should have backed off, but I wanted to dig the knife in. Still, I don't regret it. I sit down.

Rio looks at the elder. "If the resort caused this, I'll make it right. But I want facts—not rumors."

A roar of disapproval erupts.

"These aren't rumors. They are facts." Another elderly man stands up.

"That's all I said I wanted. I will check it out and I will make it right," Rio says smoothly. The crowd murmurs quietly.

People are nodding. They seem to like him. They're being duped by what they think is his honesty. His charm.

Maybe I was, too, last night.

I should know better. I know the Knights, these people don't.

Rio mutters something about handing it over to the foreman for questions about marine safety or environmental compliance. The man sitting beside him gets up. He looks awkward and clears his throat, looking at the audience in trepidation. Then he starts talking about responsible development and coastal monitoring. Sounds to me like he learned that little spiel off by heart.

"What about the reef? It's already turning white. My son can't even fish where we used to," someone from the audience shouts out.

He stammers, says something about "future impact assessments" but disapproval flows around the crowd like a wave.

Then Tomas gets up. I like him. I feel he's more trustworthy than the others, even if he works for the other side. He looks calm, and assured.

"I've lived here all my life. I was born here, raised here, and I will die here. I know this land. I know the ocean. Growing up I've seen the changes. Yes, the reef is hurting. Yes, the mangroves are thinner. We'd be lying if we said otherwise."

This catches everyone's attention. The crowd sit taller, necks craned, eyes on Tomas. The mood in the room shifts. Everyone waits for him to continue.

"But screaming at each other won't fix this. Neither will ignoring it. We need accountability, and not just empty promises. I've seen the site plans. I've worked with the engineers. I know exactly what's being built, and what's already been lost." His scans the crowd, his voice turning lower, graver.

"But the project isn't yet finished. There's still time to make it better—"

"It opens in a month!" someone shouts.

"It does, and there is still some time to fix things, to make improvements. I don't have the power to make promises, but I'll keep pushing from the inside, because I live here, too, and it matters to me, to my children, and to my grandchildren, and it does for most of you here."

The last line skims like a stone on water. It hits hard, causing ripples of a promise fan outward. It seems to quieten the crowd. He's good. He's better than the foreman.

More questions follow, about the opening, and expected tourist numbers, about jobs for the locals and expected revenue. My thoughts turn inward, flitting between last night, and the distraction, and temptation that Rio Knight is, and the job at hand.

As soon as the meeting ends, I rush outside to get some air. The humidity hits me like a wall and I'm halfway down the steps when I hear footsteps behind me.

"Raquel."

I stop and turn, even though a warning in my head tells me not to. Rio catches up, his tone low and controlled.

"You could've come to me first."

"What? *Why?* This was a community hall, you called the meeting. I turned up and asked questions."

"Like this?" He looks at me in disbelief. "You put me on the spot back there." He's standing on the same step as me, so close that I feel the heat rolling off him in waves. Doesn't help that every last detail from last night floods back in vibrant technicolor.

"I asked questions. I'm here for a reason." My attempt to make this professional, instead of personal only results in pissing him off.

"It satisfied you, making me look small?"

I make to move, but he grabs my wrist. Heat engulfs me as his fingers wrap around my skin, gently, though. His thumb sweeps across my pulse point, eliciting a wave of something warm and fluttering inside me. Something which could easily turn weightier, heated. Something that could lead to …

I blink, needing to snap out of it. He knows my weakness. He knows how to play me and manipulate me. I won't allow it. I can't afford to mess up. I can't let down my guard, something I seem to do each time this man is near me. I try to calm my reaction. Try to calm my breathing, before wrenching my hand away.

"I didn't make you look small. Maybe it was your conscience, assuming you have one."

He looks flummoxed. "Jekyll and Hyde," he murmurs, like he's trying to reconcile two versions of me.

I feel the same. "I could say that about you." We blow hot and cold. Too much. Too often. Like we're both afraid to let go. Let loose. Be vulnerable in front of each other.

He pinches the bridge of his nose. "Why didn't you come up to me and ask me these questions in person, especially after last night?"

Especially after last night. I cock my head, my gaze bouncing from his eyes. I'm still trying to determine if last night was a strategy, and not just a cultural food festival. "Did you set it all up? Running into me at the food festival? Going with me to the lagoon? Is that the Knight way?"

He swipes a hand over his face. "Damn it, Raquel. I'm not playing you. Last night wasn't a setup. Last night was real."

Last night was real.

My insides hollow out at the realization that he's possibly, maybe, shown me his vulnerability. I want to believe him, but I'm not sure I can. "You have a problem being held accountable in front of the very people you're supposed to be look out for. People on whose land you're building your eco-monstrosity."

"It is not a monstrosity. Did you hear what I said? About last night?"

"I'm here on legal grounds. I can't forget that."

He nods. Doesn't push anymore. Doesn't blur the lines between personal and professional. "I still don't understand why you felt the need to make a show of things just now."

"You have a fragile ego, Knight. You called a community hall. What did you expect? To be wrapped up in cotton wool, and not have to answer hard questions?"

"Forget it."

His jaw is tight and he looks furious. I'm wondering if he's just pissed that I did this publicly. Like his ego took more of a bruising than he expected. Also, he likes to be in control. Maybe that's the thing he can't handle. Not being able to dictate how things turn out.

I turn to leave, and he lets me. But as I go down the stairs, I know he's right. It was personal. I could have stopped. Like Alma said, I didn't have to go so hard. I was trying to get us back on a professional footing, because last night, we were swimming in dangerous territory.

But tonight, I have an injunction to prep. I can't let EcoGuardians down and I won't disappoint Alma.

They're the ones who deserve my focus.

Not Rio Knight.

RIO

THIS WAS PERSONAL.

I could see it on Raquel's face, the joy she got out of questioning me. And now, the weight of everything she said sits on my chest.

Legal doesn't mean ethical.

Unethical doesn't mean illegal.

She came at me like I was a proxy for every land grab, every corrupt corporation, every broken promise ever made to this place. She hates the Knights, but she's taking all that pent-up hatred and frustration, whatever quest she's on, to get revenge for Dani's father—she's taking it all out on me. If ever there was confirmation that this woman detests me, I had it just now.

The air feels heavy. It smells like salt and sweat and something sour. Raquel intended to show me up, and I think she succeeded. Tomas comes up behind me.

"That went well."

I shoot him a look. He shrugs, like he's too old and too tired to care about boardroom pleasantries.

"She's not wrong," he continues.

"I didn't ask for your opinion."

"You didn't have to."

I swipe a hand over my face, feeling tired. Feeling frustrated. Feeling defeated. What happened just now, not just what Raquel said, but the others, the elder man and the people complaining about the reef, and Orlando not being able to hold his own, tells me something doesn't fit. Tomas also hinted at these things.

I rub the back of my neck, look out at the dirt road winding away from the hall. It's lined with low houses, banana trees, kids kicking a ball barefoot in the distance. This place doesn't need glossy images of an eco resort. It needs clean water and protection.

I hate that I'm starting to see it. I hate that Raquel is maybe right.

"The mangroves are thinner?" I ask Tomas.

"Yes."

"The reef is damaged?"

"Yes."

"Is the water undrinkable?"

"Yes. Ever since they rerouted the drainage for the foundation."

"Then why are the reports not showing that?"

He looks ahead of him, nods. Seems to be weighing something internally. "It's time you looked at the evidence with your own eyes, instead of relying on what you've been told."

I groan. A hall full of people can't be wrong. Tomas knows more than he's letting on. He's too careful with his words. I need to get out there soon, but tomorrow the old man's got me locked into back-to-back meetings with government reps, environmental consultants, and a parade of so-called project managers. The kind of people who'll smile, show me charts, and spin the story he wants me to hear.

Listening to what Raquel said, even if she delivered her words in a brutal way, there is some truth I need to look out for. She was amazing back there, even if she put me on the defensive. I see now that she's passionate, and fights fiercely. I'm beginning to understand her more, and see who she is behind all those thorny brambles and high walls she puts up around her.

She's only trying to do her job, and she thinks I'm trying to get into her panties. Not true.

Well, not entirely.

CHAPTER SEVENTEEN

RAQUEL

I NEED TO SHOWER AND COOL DOWN BUT I NEED TO PREPARE the brief. Alma wants to file tomorrow and I have a lot of work to do tonight even though I've been working flat out.

I quickly change out of my work clothes and slip on a tank top and shorts. Then I put my hair up into a bun, but I feel sticky and sweaty all over. Sweat clings to the back of my neck, my temples, and runs down my cleavage. But I sit myself down and get into work mode.

Only, there's an important phone call I need to make. One I should have made a few days ago, but I've been avoiding it. Avoiding *him*. Maybe because I've left it until the very last moment. Maybe because part of me doesn't want to deal with the fallout.

It's not professional. It's borderline insubordination. Pierce will rip me to shreds, no matter how solid the case is.

He picks up on the second ring. "Raquel. I thought you'd gotten lost in the jungle."

I release a shaky breath. "I've been busy. Pierce, there's something I need to tell you."

"You're having too much fun and you don't want to come back," he replies, joking.

"Everything's changed. EcoGuardians want to file an injunction."

"What? When?" His tone is low and he's pissed at me already.

"Alma told me as soon as I got here."

"Who?"

"Alma Flores, the woman heading up EcoGuardians. She said this wasn't just a fact-finding mission anymore. They wanted me to file."

"You're not there to file, and why the fuck am I hearing about it only *now?*"

"I've been busy. They don't want to waste time. They want it done fast." I try to keep my voice level. "There's serious immediate damage being caused here. I've seen it with my own eyes."

"No. *NO*. That's not why we sent you." His voice sharpens. "You were meant to smile, gather info, look serious and come back with a folder we could shred."

"I can't ignore this. If you saw the damage—"

"I need you back by the weekend," he growls.

I refuse to be bullied. "If you saw the damage, you would realize we can't walk away from this. It would reflect badly on us."

"You can ignore it, Raquel. You *will* ignore it. You're on my payroll and, last I checked, we bill clients, not tree frogs."

He doesn't understand the gravity of the situation. "But—"

He cuts me off. "This little eco-crusade was never supposed to take up much of your time. It was more a PR gamble for us. I let you go because someone recommended you, and because you're into all this environmental, activist crap."

"It's not crap. It's *important*."

I hear his outbreath and imagine his face turning red with fury. I'm so glad I'm not in the Miami office right now.

"You're smart and talented, and I have invested too much time in you to have you throw it away on mudslides and mangroves."

"I took an oath. If I see something wrong, I act. I'd have to be blind not to see the damage. "

"Be blind. Think of your future. Someone like you: beautiful, smart, clever. We need you here. I need you here. If you play your cards right, you could be a partner here, someday, not a whistleblower."

I recoil at his words. The shift in his tone, that subtle innuendo, the polished charm slapped over something that grimy, makes me uncomfortable and I'm reminded of why I want to leave.

"Then maybe I don't belong here."

"Don't you dare make this personal." His tone cuts like a blade. "This is business. You're needed on the Santos case—"

"I thought you had Mila working on that?"

"She doesn't have your expertise. You wrap this up and get back to Miami. *Now.* You're not being fired, *yet*, and it's in your interest to wise up."

Was that a subtle threat? He could fire or demote me. I could be blacklisted in certain corporate legal circles. I risk facing accusations of acting outside my brief. Pierce could make sure I never make partner. Going against him, and against the firm will make my life difficult, but only until I find another job. I'm going to file, anyway, because it's the right thing to do.

I didn't become a lawyer to bill hours for people like Pierce while the world burns down.

"Legally, I'm bound to follow my client's instructions."

He says nothing, because it's the truth but I can feel his fury over the airwaves. I take my chance.

"Listen to me, Pierce ..." There's a wobble" in my voice. "Just listen. We held a community meeting earlier, and they're desperate. There's real damage here and this could be a strong case. I've seen the coastline myself. The reef's already showing signs of destruction." I pause, then go for it. "Did you know Knight Enterprises is behind this? They're hiding—"

"Knight Enterprises?"

"Yes. They're hiding behind a subsidiary. Delport Realty is a front used to distance Knight Enterprises from direct liability."

"Jesus. Fucking. Hell, Raquel. Do you have any idea who you're going up against?"

"I'm aware."

"This firm is *not* going to war with the Knights over some sea turtles and reef damage."

"It's much more than that. Also, why not?"

"Because we don't pick fights we can't win. The Knights are *dangerous*. You don't just serve them papers and expect it to end happily ever after."

"This isn't optional, Pierce. I'm here now—"

"I told you to just do a fucking legal review," he hisses.

"And that's what I thought but EcoGuardians changed their mind and now they want to file. I have no choice but to act. I'm serving the injunction tomorrow."

"You will do no such thing. You'll come back. *Now*."

"But—"

"Do you hear me?"

I stare at the phone, heart pounding. "How can I walk away now?"

"I'll send one of the juniors. You've done enough."

"They'll be eaten alive out here," I snap. "EcoGuardians will lose the injunction."

A few seconds pass in silence. Finally, "I don't like this," he hisses. "I don't like this one fucking bit."

"But you sent me here."

"It wasn't supposed to take this long."

A labored sigh falls from his lips. He's struggling with something. I don't know what's happened to him. Work pressure? Maybe the Santos case is veering off course.

"I should never have …" He stops.

"Never have what?"

He doesn't answer, and I can sense him battling to make a decision. "Must you file tomorrow?"

"Time is critical. Alma insists. She was worried they might try to clean up their mess before inspection and we all saw how smooth Rio Knight was at the community meeting. We don't want to lose the window."

"Wait. Stand by. I need to check something."

I'm puzzled. This has never happened before. What is Pierce doing? Who is he consulting? My thoughts are interrupted when he calls be back a few minutes later.

"You'd better make sure you have an airtight case. If the opposing lawyers get whiff of sloppiness, they'll gut this injunction in five minutes."

He changed his tune pretty fast. I wonder who he called. "You're happy for me to file?"

"Happy isn't the word I would use."

"I've been working flat out. I didn't have much time to get everything together, but I'm almost done."

"Don't fuck this up and make it any worse than it is," he snarls.

"I won't." I hang up and glance at the file Rio gave me and consider that I might need to look through it. Pierce seemed shaken and I need to ensure I have a watertight case. Seeing what evidence the other side has might give me an insight into their case.

I get to work immediately, pulling my hair up into a messy bun again. I'm sweating as I type. My fingers move across the keys, but everything slows me down. The soft whine of the air conditioner sputters, then dies mid-sentence. I get up and press the button but it doesn't come on. Annoyed, knowing I have to soldier on, I return to my desk, but a few seconds later, the Wi-Fi signal disappears from my screen.

"No, no, no, no, no!" I peer at my screen, as if I have some magical power to turn it back on. I've saved a copy, but I still need Internet access because I'm pulling documents from online sources. I have enough for now, and hopefully the generator will kick in again soon. I begin to type again as more sweat trickles down the back of my neck, the sides of my face, and down my cleavage. Its starting to feel like a sauna. I persist, working on. It feels like I've been at it for a while, but to my dismay, when I glance at the clock, it's barely been ten minutes. I can't work like this. Not in this heat. Not without a fan. Without AC. Without a connection.

I pick up my phone to call the small reception desk—just as someone knocks at the door. I open it to find the same young man who manned the desk when I checked in. He's smiling way too brightly for my liking.

"I'm sorry, Ms. Monteiro. We're experiencing a temporary generator overload. The power should be back soon."

"Soon?"

"An hour, maybe."

"An hour?"

"Maybe more."

"More?" My body slumps with disappointment.

He gives me an apologetic smile. "It could be less than that ... but ..." He's trying to be optimistic and failing.

I think we're talking hours, realistically. Maybe all night. That won't do. That can't happen. I wonder if Rio orchestrated this. Then I wonder if the heat is making me paranoid.

"I'm sorry." The young man smiles nervously. Clearly, relaying this news hasn't been easy on him and my amateur theatrics are only making him feel more guilty. It's not his fault, and I shouldn't be venting my frustration on him. "It's not your fault."

"There is a storm coming. It happens sometimes. I'm sorry. If you need anything, we'll try to assist. But the backup generators have also failed. Just a few hours, ma'am. We're trying to get it together."

"I'll be fine," I say, with a determination I don't feel. Meu Deus. This poor boy must think I'm a monster. I close the door and walk back to my desk, deciding that I will work through this no matter what. There's another knock at the door.

"It's really quite alright ..." The words peter out. It's not the apologetic concierge.

It's *him.*

"It's really *not* quite alright. You're staying here, princesa? This place should be shut down." He looks around in disbelief.

"How did they let you up here?"

"Small establishment. "They don't have much security or care about your privacy." He folds his arms across that broad chest, forcing me to gawk at his biceps that stretch the sleeve of his T. His stance is all dominance and quiet challenge, as if he can't decide whether to throw me over his shoulder and haul me out of here.

"What do you want, Knight?" My tankini clings to me, patches of it still damp from the heat.

"You look like you just stepped out of the shower," he remarks.

"I've been working."

"You're wet."

His skill for innuendo is unmatched. I feel a throbbing between my legs. It happens so easily. He says something and my body reacts. Now I really will be wet, with arousal, and desire, for this cocky man who yet again, lives to distract me.

"May I come in?" His gaze runs over me, slow and deliberate. I cross my arms, suddenly aware of how little I'm wearing. In answer, I step out of the way, still curious as to why he's here. Why, suddenly, I'm seeing him everywhere, all the time, all at once. He walks in, looming large in the small stuffy little room.

"If you're hoping to replay the strip poker night, it's not happening," I tell him.

"If you're hot and sweaty and not fresh out of a shower," he says, "then strip poker is the last thing on my mind."

"What are you doing here? I've seen enough of you today."

"We didn't finish our conversation, at the end of the community hall."

"We did."

"I didn't like how we left it. I want to talk about it away from prying ears and eyes."

"In my hotel room?"

He looks at me like he doesn't understand. "You're here, melting by the second, I might add. I needed to see you."

"To say what?"

"You didn't have to go so hard on me, princesa."

Meu Deus. Can't he let it go? "Your ego was really battered in there, huh? I'm sorry if your feelings were hurt, can't have been easy standing up there trying to look like a stud, only to get shot down again."

"You think I looked like a stud?" That infuriating grin is back. Caraca. This man thinks I'm paying him a compliment. I don't even dignify that with a reply.

"I'm here, in Belize, for a reason," I retort. "Not a vacation. It's a fact-finding mission and people like you need to be held accountable."

"The eco resort will be good for the region. It will bring jobs and—"

"Have you even been to the coastline?" I snap. "I've got evidence. I've seen the damage. Have you?"

"Have you looked through the environmental data I gave you?" I note that he doesn't answer my question.

"Not yet." I wipe the back of my neck. My hand comes away clammy.

"You're melting, princesa. Maybe you should take a shower. I'll wait."

"Good try, but it's not happening."

"Do you like sweating? Why isn't your AC on?" He looks around the room, his nose wrinkling in disgust.

I explain the whole backup-generator failure to him.

"I need to finish this work," I say, rubbing my temples.

His gaze lingers on my hands, my arms, my shoulders, dipping down before he catches himself and looks me in the eye again. I recall last night in the water, how we almost kissed. How our bodies touched. How I wished we could have seen that through. Maybe that's why he's here.

He shoots me a look. "Your plan is to melt into a puddle while you wait for the electricity to come back?"

"The generator will come on soon," I say defiantly, while at the same time silently praying.

"We don't have problems like this where I'm staying. I'm in the Peninsula. Not too far away."

So he keeps reminding me. "Are you done now?"

"I don't like us being at odds with each other."

"We're not on the same side, Knight. Don't you realize that?"

"I thought we were friends."

"Is that what last night was for? Was that your plan to soften me?"

He shakes his head, half in surprise, half in annoyance. "You think I would go to those lengths?"

"Your father did."

"I am not my father." He grits his teeth together, nostrils flaring.

"Tell me the truth, for once. Are you covering up for Delport Realty? Or are they covering up for you? Does Knight Enterprises always hide behind subsidiary companies?" He stiffens, so I press harder. "I've seen this kind of behavior from your people before. You're known for it."

He cocks his head. "As far as I'm aware, we do things by the book."

"And what about your father and what he did to Uncle Arminio, Dani's father?"

He doesn't respond. Because he knows I'm right.

"What makes you think he plays by the rules when it comes to anything else? If he can ride roughshod over Uncle Arminio, do you think he gives a damn about the people in Belize? Or in any other country? People who are poorer, more vulnerable? Do you think he cares about them?"

Rio looks at me—really looks. As if something I said finally lands and hits him hard. "I'm going to look into this," he says softly.

"You're already so late. It should have been one of your first tasks."

"I'm always in meetings, with planners, reps, consultants, project managers."

"Then make the time to do your own investigation."

"You're not the first person who's said that." He sighs. Swipes a hand across his neck again. "I can take you to my hotel, if it would help. I've got the Jeep, and we'll be there in a few minutes. You'll be able to get your work done. You'll die here."

"You're worried about my health and safety all of a sudden?"

He opens his mouth, a strange expression in his eyes. I chuckle, more to fill the silence, than anything else. I'm starting to feel uneasy at what he might say. "I thought you might have orchestrated the generator failure," I add. "Just like you did the surprise meeting at the restaurant in Miami."

He gasps. Blinking furiously. "You think I'm that manipulative? You think me and my brothers control people and events for our benefit?"

"You said you like being in control."

He looks away. "Of *my* life. I don't want to control others."

I feel like I've touched a sore point, so I stay silent, watching him.

"You still have no idea of who I am," he murmurs.

A moment passes.

"I'm not here on a vacation—" I start to say.

"Neither am I."

"I have to work. I have lots to do."

"My suite is a lot nicer. It's cool, and big, and I promise not to strip off and lie on the bed waiting for you." His cocky charm is back, and that veil of sadness I just saw slips away.

Something about his words sets me on fire again. I'm melting in this heat. I'm sweating, exhausted, feeling gross and agitated. Having access to AC and working Wi-Fi is too good an opportunity to pass up, even if it's the devil offering me those things. Before I know it, I'm gathering my belongings and my laptop and following him outside to his Jeep.

We drive in silence broken only by the sound of the cicadas chirping. The sun dips below the trees, and night falls fast. I hate that I've already wasted so much time and I'm going to be up all night.

A déjà vu moment of São Paulo suddenly flashes through my mind and I see Rio in his boxers. His *tented* boxers. If I'd have joined him in bed, we would have ended up ...

I force myself to focus on something else. How ridiculous is it that soon I'll be in his hotel room, prepping an injunction he doesn't even know is coming?

When he opens the door to his suite, I step in then stop dead in my tracks, my mouth hanging open. "Meu Deus," I whisper. "This place is enormous. It's *gorgeous*."

"Glad you like it. Make yourself at home."

<h1 style="text-align:center">CHAPTER EIGHTEEN</h1>

RIO

I OPEN THE DOOR WIDE AND LET RAQUEL PASS THROUGH. SHE walks in, looking uncertain, her skin dewy, her vest sticking to her like a second skin, making it impossible to not think about what's underneath.

She looks way too sexy and desirable in her frayed denim shorts. I already know that this evening is going to be trouble. It's going to be torture and I'll willingly endure it because there's something about this woman that makes it impossible for me to walk away.

"I'll only need an hour, if that." She drops her laptop bag on the sofa as she surveys my suite.

She kicks off her sneakers, then starts untying her bun, and long, wavy hair cascades down her back like a waterfall.

"No need to strip on my behalf, princesa. You're here to work, remember?" I can't help but grin. She's ice cold and professional in front of people, and she was in her element at the community hall, doing what she does best. But now, here, just me and her, she softens, like she did last night at the lagoon. That's the real Raquel, without her high walls and armor wrapped around her like a defense shield.

"It's hot," she says. I turn the AC up to max.

"If you need to shower, knock yourself out." I gesture in the direction of my glass-walled, slate-tiled and oversized walk-in shower.

She bunches her hair back into a bun. "This isn't that night, Knight."

"It can be anything you want, princesa." I raise a brow, watching her. She's perfection, she's everything, and she's here. I wish we could quit this pretence and admit how we feel, instead of dancing around one another, treading water like we did in the lagoon. I wish we could get down and dirty in the trenches. Fuck like feral animals.

And just like that, my cock twitches.

"Don't flatter yourself," she shoots back. "I'm only here because you have Wi-Fi and AC, and I need to work."

"There's my desk." I head towards it and move my papers and laptop out of the way. "Take as long as you want."

"I won't need it for too long. I'll be out of your hair in no time."

"I like having you in my hair." I waggle my brows. She looks away hastily. Because she's feeling something.

"What's the password?" She opens her laptop.

I walk up behind her, and lean over her, my arms bracketing her on either side, my cheek almost pressed against hers as I slowly start to type. I feel the warmth of her skin, even without touching her. I smell the fresh fruity smell of her shampoo. Or maybe it's her shower gel. An image of her lathering herself all over under the shower circles around my addled brain, and it's no wonder I mess up my password. It takes me three tries to get it right.

"Just write it down," she protests, albeit weakly, shifting in the seat.

"It's Knightalwayswins," I say, as casually as I can, while the blood in my body shoots south, rendering my brain ineffective.

"Y-you should have just written i-it down."

"It's a combination of numbers and letters." I've finished typing, but I can't bring myself to move away.

"Knight always wins. Seriously?" she cries, but her protest, like her laugh, feels a little forced.

I slowly straighten and move away. "It's the truth, isn't it?"

She says nothing, but whips out her folders and documents, and sets to work. I leave her to it, but first I grab a cold bottle of water out of the mini-fridge and place it next to her.

"Thank you," she murmurs, her eyes flitting from her document to the screen. She types fast, her fingers flying across the keyboard, and I watch as I move away. Raquel sitting at my desk, in my hotel room, feels soothing, feels right.

She belongs here.

I wish our interactions weren't only about work. I wish we could move on to other things, more important things.

Us things.

The things she's denying.

I leave her to it, before she looks up and thinks I'm a freak, watching her, so I decide to have a shower. I was fresh and cool when I left here, but after being in her hotel room, I'm disgustingly sweaty again, despite the AC in my room cooling me down.

I need a shower, like I need air to breathe. I'm all coiled up with need, hard as steel, and I need to take care of it.

RAQUEL

It's cool in here. The AC is working perfectly. I have Wi-Fi, but I still can't concentrate.

Despite the cool temperature, there is so much heat around me, in the space Rio left. My body vibrates and hums with need, and now that I'm feeling cooler, now that I'm not melting, I realize that this was a bad mistake.

Terrible.

Catastrophic.

I can't concentrate because all I can think of is *him*.

It felt like forever when he typed in the Wi-Fi password, and then he hovered around, watching me. I could have won an Oscar with the acting I did, pretending to type, pretending to get on with my work.

I was typing gibberish and my thoughts were all over the place, but then he left, and I was relieved. I hear the sprinkling of water and wonder why he needs to have a shower now of all times. This leads to a different kind of frustration. One which has me pressing my thighs together hard. And then, naturally, it lands; the thought and the image of Rio in the shower, butt naked, only a few feet away from me.

I stop typing. The hard-won zen like feeling escapes as quickly as it came and blood courses through me, pooling south below my belly. I imagine joining him, standing under the showerhead, embroiled in a kiss as rivulets of water spurt down on us. Closing my eyes, I picture his mouth dropping to my breast. He starts to suck, one hand reaching between my legs, making me squirm in my chair.

I hear a noise. It sounded more like a grunt. And then I think I hear my name. Can't be. I'm imagining it. But another grunt follows. Curious, I get up and walk over to the bathroom door, wishing I could see inside. Pressing my ear to the door, I relish the coolness of it, but a second later, I hear my name again, on Rio's tongue. My insides jolt and I shrink back from the door, like it's on fire.

I know *exactly* what he's doing in there.

I'm so flustered and so aroused. The images were already in my head, but hearing my name, and those deeply feral groans, knowing what he's doing, makes me ache in places I shouldn't. My skin tightens, my breath turns shallow, and every nerve ending is heightened and tuned to the sound of the water hitting tile. Heat pools between my thighs, knowing what he's stroking. Suddenly, I long to stroke him, too.

I stand there, paralyzed. Knowing that only a wooden door separates us both. He's naked, and wet, and sated now. What I wouldn't give to ...

The water stops running, and I quickly tiptoe back to the chair, and pretend to be hard at work. But what I'm really doing is trying to steady my breathing. To throw imaginary cold water over my arousal. I hear the door open, so I start typing, breathing in and out slowly. Hoping he won't notice.

"That's better."

I turn around, because, how could I not? My willpower is shot. Always is around this man.

The devil who's trying to kill me by torture quickly grabs a shirt from his suitcase, but he doesn't put it on. He's wearing only lounge shorts, and he's barefoot. Damp chest, damp hair. Shiny rivulets of water runs down his pecs. A smattering of dark hairs leads from his navel downwards into the delicious V shape at his lower region.

He's holding his t-shirt and now he walks over to me, trying to torture me with his scent, his heat, his body. All I can think about is what he was doing in that bathroom, and how badly I wanted to be there with him.

"You hot?" He's about to roll the white T over his head, and I wish he'd hurry up and do it.

"What?" I try to act nonchalant.

"You look flustered."

I swipe a hand across my back, feel my breasts turn heavy, my panties soaked. I rub my temple. "This is impossible." I stare at the blameless screen and pour fault on it.

"What is?"

"Work," I manage to say, as he rolls the t-shirt down, then swipes his hands through his long hair, slicking it back. It falls with a middle parting, framing his face. I feel a slickness in my panties.

"Need some more water?" he asks, then sees that the bottle is still half-full. He saunters over to the mini-bar, while I take this opportunity to admire him from behind. He grabs a bottle of water and slowly returns, twisting the plastic top and taking a big gulp.

That's when I notice his pants are starting to tent again. I bite back a gasp as he puts the lid back on the bottle, and sets it on the desk, He leans on the edge, too close again and I'm caught in a thrum of desire. A magic spell weaves around me, reeling me in, and the air becomes charged with something prickly.

Our eyes lock.

"Do you believe in fate?" he asks, smiling softly. Not the usual smug tug of his lips. No joking around. He's refreshingly honest and bare in this moment.

I'm a fly caught in a web of lust. "Maybe."

"Have you noticed how we keep running into one another? You keep pushing me away, and I keep trying to forget you, and then I run into you again."

I try to swallow, but my throat constricts. "It's a coincidence."

"I don't believe in coincidences."

"Then, what are you saying?"

This isn't about the resort, or the community meeting. It's about him and me. I realize in that moment that Rio isn't the sharp, slick, mafia-like personality who has no heart.

Rio is all heart.

He feels.

He cares.

And he's looking at me like I'm the answer to his prayers.

"You care about this work," he says quietly, nodding at my documents.

"I care passionately about people who get trampled on. For people who can't fight for themselves. For me, I see law as a weapon for the voiceless."

He nods. "I like that about you. I admire you for it."

"Unfortunately, many times, you're the problem. You and your family and the companies you hide behind."

"I'm not my father."

"I don't believe you are."

He says it so many times. It's like he's afraid he might turn into him. I stand up, and make to move away. Where to, I don't know. Maybe I'll go to the washroom. He grabs my arm.

"Don't. Don't run away like you always do, Raquel. I don't bite."

But this is too close for comfort, and he's right, I do run. I run because Rio is everything I should walk away from, but can't. He's everything I shouldn't want, and everything I can't resist. Danger wrapped in charm. Sinful temptation dressed in a perfect T. This man lowers my guard as easily as heat melts ice. I don't trust myself around him.

"We keep meeting. São Paulo, New York, and now here. Every time I try to forget you, every time I go someplace to empty my mind, you turn up." His voice is raspy, filled with desperation.

His words reverberate in my chest. I shift from one foot to the next. He's still perched on the edge of the desk, and I'm standing awkwardly to the side of his thigh. But he hasn't let go of my arm.

"I wouldn't read too much into it," I say.

"Once, sure. Twice, maybe, but three times?"

"Why are we talking about this?"

"Because I didn't want the first time you were in my room to be about air conditioning and Wi-Fi."

My breath catches. We're inches apart now, my heart thudding in my ears. His eyes fall to my mouth.

"It's high time we talked about it, don't you think? Tell me you've never thought about me, and I won't bring this up again, but last night was special." His voice is barely a whisper.

I think back to the lagoon, to us swimming around one another. To the streams of neon blue we left in our wake. "It was."

"I dream about you, Raquel. I think about you. After Miami, I came here wanting to forget all about you, so imagine my shock and surprise to find you here."

The mood changes. From heavy with unspoken words, to honesty, and lightness. If he kissed me now, I'd let him. He tugs me towards him, guiding me between his thighs. His palm strokes along my arm, before sliding up to cup my face. I lean in, instinctively, and our bodies brushing, breath mingling.

Our first kiss is tentative, like we're tasting the idea of each other. But when I press closer and feeling the hard length of him through the fabric, something in both of us snaps. His hand drifts down to palm my breast through my vest, stroking the underside with his thumb. He holds me there like he's weighing me, assessing every curve, memorizing my shape.

A slickness dampens my panties, and we kiss again, deeper now, hungrier. My fingers slide down, slowly, unsure, but when he murmurs against my lips, "Touch me, princesa," I wrap my fingers around him, tracing his length through his pants. He thickens in my hand, heat surging, and I press flush against him, greedily taking more of that closeness.

His hands roam lower, finding the waistband of my shorts, his thumbs brushing my skin. He fumbles at the button, impatient, while I grind against him, needing friction. We kiss again, deeper, longer, tongues sliding, breathing each other in, until his groan rumbles against my mouth, raw and wanting.

I need more. I need him. Naked, skin to skin. And then, my phone rings. It's happening again. Just when we're about to get close, my stupid phone rings. I bet it's Pierce, again. The man is a parasite, a constant shadow I can't shake. He drains me, frustrate me, suffocates me. Every interaction which him feels like a chain tightening around me, squeezing the life out of me. I can't live like this.

I make to move away but Rio pulls me closer. "Let it go." His thumb circles my nipple, but I force myself to reach for my phone.

"The generator is working now, ma'am. All of the amenities are now available again."

I say "thank you," but I doubt he heard me. Excitement shoots through me, thick and heavy, and I know how this night will end, if I let it. With great determination, I pull away from Rio. "I have to go." It's automatic, how my words tumble out. Ignoring my heart. My wants. My desire.

His lips brush against mine. "We're only getting started, princesa." His hardness pokes me, and I'm reminded of him showering, of the way my name fell from his lips.

"The generator's working," I manage to say, as his lips tease mine, and his hand kneads my breast. I want to stroke him again, but it will lead to more. Things I desperately need, but the injunction weighs heavy on me. "I need to finish this."

"Finish? We haven't even started, princesa."

"My work," I wail. "Please don't make it any harder for me," I beg. "I won't get any work done," I protest, weakly. If I stay here, the injunction would be the last thing on my mind, and it's imperative I get it done. I'm only halfway through. The realization shakes me to reality. I have a long way to go. I'm going to barely get any sleep. I move away.

He lets me go.

I don't want to leave, I would much rather stay here all night kissing Rio, seeing where this leads.

But … the injunction.

"Running away again, princesa?" The weight of his disappointment is as heavy as the outline of his magnificent cock. I bite a lip, trying not to think of him inside me.

"Sorry." I start gathering my things together.

"I'll drop you back," he offers, just as I catch him adjusting himself in his pants.

"That's not necessary. I can get a taxi."

"I'll take you."

I laugh. "A taxi will take me back."

"I'll take you back. I need to know that you're back safely."

My safety. He's always concerned about my safety, and that makes me feel cherished in a way I didn't know I craved.

CHAPTER NINETEEN

RAQUEL

RIO DROPS ME BACK AT MY HOTEL, BUT WE BARELY EXCHANGE A look. He waits outside in the Jeep until I make it through the lobby doors.

My heart races. It feels light and fluttery, and me? I feel wicked, sinful and dirty. After that scorching hot time in his hotel room, I'm thankful to be in my own space. Away from a man I'm deeply attracted to, but a man whose values I abhor. A man who comes from an empire I abhor.

That man does things to me, he's in my mind, under my skin, imprinted everywhere he's touched me. It feels impossible that I'll ever get him out of my system.

I was torn. My body had other ideas, but my mind was fixated on that damn injunction.

He kept talking about it not being a coincidence, how we keep meeting in different countries. It's almost as if life is trying to tell us something.

I flip on the air conditioning. The place is already hot and sweltering, adding to the heat simmering under my skin. But it's late, too late, and I don't have much time. Alma wants the injunction served tomorrow.

I take a cold shower—because I need one. Then I get to work.

———

It's two in the morning and I'm rechecking my notes, making sure I have enough photos, enough written statements, enough evidence. Then I panic, Pierce's words echoing in my head. Make sure this is watertight.

That's when I see the folder Rio gave me. I skim through it. It's detailed with more figures and data. It's solid information. This is good. *Really good.* I wish I'd looked at it earlier. I probably would have but the constant interaction with that man during my short time here has fried my brain.

After tonight, after we kissed, and touched, and fondled, and wished we could do more, my brain was even more frazzled than ever. I struggled to get this done, but now that I have his report in my hands, maybe I can use parts of it. He's trying to help. Maybe he's doing what he can—as a representative for Knight Enterprises, sent here by his father—to do the right thing.

I'm doing what I do best. Speaking up for the people who don't have a voice. I pull what I need from his file, and at four a.m, I crash out on the bed, completely exhausted.

The next morning, I'm up at eight, and I tell Alma that I need a few more hours to work on this. A little after noon, I'm ready. I head to HQ, to meet Alma and we set off for the construction site. When we get there we're told by one of the workers that Orlando isn't around. He gives us the name of a small café off the roadside, where

Orlando's having lunch with some of his colleagues. We head there.

"That must be them," Alma says, pulling up on the side of the road. I see Rio, and immediately freeze. I was hoping he wouldn't be here. I don't want to do this in front of him, even though he'll find out soon enough. I feel like a coward, because after last night this also feels like betrayal.

I inhale a breath, remind myself of why I'm here, and get out of the car. I walk toward them with purpose, the injunction folder tucked under my arm. No heels today—just sneakers. Dirt roads make wearing heels impossible.

The men are seated at a shaded café table, laughing over cold beers and grilled fish. As I get nearer, my gaze falls on Rio's broad, muscular back under a casual white T-shirt. His dark hair is slicked back. Thankfully he's not facing me and won't see me coming. I try to push aside the memory of his kiss. Of how he looked at me. Of how he wanted to talk last night.

Tomas leans back in his chair, looking cautious, not entirely at ease. Beside him sits Orlando, the foreman. He was the one who fumbled his answers at the community meeting. I step into the shade of their umbrella. Alma stays close. I've asked her to record me handing over the injunction. Tomas is the first to look up, squinting.

"Can I help you?"

Rio takes off his shades, and stares at me his eyes widening in disbelief. His bronzed forearms on the table suddenly flex. "What are you doing here?" His voice is like ice.

I don't answer him. Instead I face Orlando. Voice steady. "Orlando Rivero, you're the site foreman for Delport Realty?"

The man's eyes narrow. "You know who I am. What can I do for you?"

"Raquel Monteiro. I'm legal counsel for EcoGuardians," I

say clearly. "I'm here to serve you with an injunction regarding the continued development of your beachfront property—Blue Star Eco Resort. Effective immediately, all construction, excavation, and marine work must cease until further notice, pending legal review."

The table quiets.

"What?" Rio snaps, sitting up suddenly. Tomas slumps back in his chair, watching in silence. The foreman rises.

"What is this? What the hell is this?" He grabs the folder, flipping through it fast.

Rio glares at me, shock all over his face. "You didn't say a word about this."

I face him, trying not to flinch under his hard stare. The foreman mutters, "This is an emergency injunction filed with the Belizean Environmental Court?"

"It is indeed. You'll find all relevant documentation inside —including aerial images, reef samples, and sworn community testimony."

Rio leans back, hands laced and behind his head. Looking defeated, and pissed. "You have got to be kidding."

"Does this mean what I think it means?" the foreman asks.

"You're seriously doing this?" Rio asks. "You're shutting us down?"

Tomas still hasn't said a word.

I nod. "We are."

"But we're close to finishing. The place needs to open next month," the foreman cries.

The expression on Tomas's face is still unreadable. Then Rio stands slowly, pushing his chair back. We're almost eye-level now, heat rising between us like steam from an electric kettle.

"Raquel," he says tightly, "what are you playing at?"

He so did not see this coming.

I turn to Alma. "Did you get the recording?"

She nods and puts her cell phone away.

Rio's voice lowers. "A word in private?"

We step away from the table.

"Again, you could have come to me about this. No notice. No warning."

"We're not on the same side," I remind him.

He shakes his head. "You blindsided me."

"You work for a company that blindsides entire ecosystems."

"You should've told me."

"That I was going to serve you with an injunction? Why?" I throw back.

"Because then I wouldn't have kissed you."

"I tried to keep away from you."

A line forms on his brow. For a few seconds he's speechless. Then he scrubs a hand across his beard. "This, after everything. I didn't even see this coming."

I round on him. "Did you even pay attention at the community meeting? Did you hear the man who needs to buy bottled water now because of your site runoff? You said you'd make it right. Have you even been back to check?"

"I haven't had time," he murmurs, a vein throbbing across his temple. "The old man keeps me so busy, I haven't managed to even get out."

"That should tell you something."

His expression is undecipherable. I don't know what he's thinking. He's silent, examining me like I'm an oddball. Someone he'll never understand.

"Must you completely halt construction?"

"We're stopping construction because you're illegally operating without proper environmental clearance. Because your machinery is already causing damage," I continue, seething with a rage that builds the more I talk, and the more that contemptuous look on his face grows. "You tried to fast-track permits through people who don't speak English and you hoped no one would notice!"

"We did no such thing."

"Do you even know what was done when your back was turned?" I'm shaking with anger at his ignorance.

Around us, locals watch from shaded stalls. I hear whispers in a language I don't understand. Glancing at the table, Tomas flips through the folder. The foreman's already on the phone.

Rio drags a hand through his hair, furious. "You didn't have to do it like this."

"I did," I say quietly. "Because doing it *any other way* would've meant backing down. You always worry about the optics. That's not what's important here. Doing the right thing is all that matters, and the sad thing is, you don't even know what the right thing is."

He stares at me for a long moment. Then he lets out a sharp, humorless breath.

I've seen and heard enough.

CHAPTER TWENTY

RIO

I glare at Raquel as she gets into the car with that old woman, and they drive away.

I don't fucking believe it. After everything between us, she hits me with a fucking injunction. My insides burn with fury because I didn't see it coming. I always knew she had balls bigger than a bull, and I let myself fall under her charm again.

Now this.

But when I calm down, and sit back, thinking it over, I realize I'm mad at myself. For being blind to something that's going on. Raquel wouldn't file an injunction if there wasn't a good reason for it. The old man has kept me mired in meetings. I shouldn't be sitting here having lunch. I should be out there, examining the mangroves, and the reef, and talking to villagers. I should be out there talking to the elder who said he had to buy bottled water. I should be checking the claims made by the people at the community hall instead of blindly accepting everything I've been told.

"What are we supposed to do?" the foreman asks.

"We have to stop construction," Tomas says.

The old man's going to freak out. He'll think I've failed and he'll accuse me of screwing this up like he always does. I was sent here to smooth things over, make everything look clean again. But he has no idea that I'm up against one of the smartest damn lawyers I've ever encountered. Someone who knows exactly where to hit us where it hurts.

I rake a hand through my hair, feeling panicked. The injunction isn't only a legal move, it's a statement, and I was caught flat-footed. That pisses me off more than anything.

I have a lot to do. Also, I need to let the old man know we've been served. That construction is frozen. Halted. Nothing happens until this is resolved. He's going to be pissed so badly that we can't open on time.

"What are you thinking?" Tomas asks, his eyes wise, knowing. Like he's giving me a chance to do the decent thing.

He's said just enough over the last few days to get under my skin. A few offhand comments about corrosion on the water tanks. He hesitated when I asked about the foreman before Orlando. No one seems to have a real answer for that, but it's what Tomas *hasn't* said that's starting to eat at me.

I haven't seen the reef. I haven't walked the far end of the mangrove basin. I've been too damn busy in meetings and reading polished reports from Delport and smooth-talking execs, no doubt handpicked by the old man.

Which is exactly how he wanted it.

"I'm thinking we sit tight, for a few hours." Because once the old man finds out, all hell will break loose. I get up and walk away, heart pounding, and when I'm out of earshot, I call him. He picks up immediately.

"Tell me everything's fine and you're about to come back," he says. He already knows something's wrong. I can hear it in his smug and oily tone, like he's been waiting for my call.

"I just wanted to give you a heads-up. We got served."

"What?"

"An injunction. EcoGuardians filed it. We've been ordered to halt construction effective immediately."

"How the fuck did this happen?" he thunders. "You were supposed to use your fucking charm and get this fixed."

"I tried." I clear my throat and brace myself. "There's more going on here than we were told."

"I trust Delport to handle things."

"I don't think Delport are being transparent."

"You don't need to worry about Delport," he says, smoothly. "Just leave that to me."

"But you sent me here to get a handle on the situation."

"And you haven't, have you?" he snaps. "Now we'll have lawyers crawling all over the site soon, and headlines waiting to explode. You should have had this locked down by now. Fix it."

I grit my teeth. What the fuck does he expect me to do? "I'm not going to overlook an injunction."

"You'll do what needs to be done."

"There could be real damage out here," I push. "People are upset. Locals at the community hall are talking. No one can tell me what happened to the last foreman."

"Don't worry about him."

"This whole thing smells off."

The old man is silent for a beat. Then he says, low and lethal, "If there's a problem, we'll bury it. Just like we always do."

A pain slices through my chest. "Bury it?"

"You're too close to it, boy. That's your problem. You're letting that lawyer cloud your judgment."

I resent him talking about Raquel.

"The eco resort needs to open on time, boy. You make sure it does."

He hangs up before I can respond.

And now I'm in a real fucking mess, because now I'm more certain than ever that something isn't right here.

CHAPTER TWENTY-ONE

RAQUEL

I haven't slept well at all, for the second night. I feel groggy and tired having tossed and turned all night.

My muscles feel tight, and I feel restless, maybe it's sheer exhaustion from insomnia, or maybe it's guilt because I feel like I betrayed Rio when I handed the foreman the injunction yesterday. I shouldn't feel guilty. I was just doing my job, but somehow, I do.

I'm relieved that it's the start of the weekend. I'm supposed to be taking a small boat to go further along the coastline and get more evidence. Pierce's words haunt me, and I need to make sure we have a watertight case. .

But lying in bed, it's Rio's face I see. The way he looked at me, his face twisting with shock and anger. I wasn't prepared for that reaction. That's when I understood. He thinks I used him. He thinks I planned this. He thinks I worked him over just to beat him down again. That's the worst part, because there's something real and raw between us, and beneath his fury, he feels something for me, just like I feel it for him.

Maybe he'll even throw that in my face next time we talk. I'm playing with fire, getting involved with him, but he was the one who came to my hotel room. He was the one who suggested I go to his.

It's all getting so complicated. So messy. We should have stayed away from each other, but we couldn't, and now things are spiralling out of control.

I should never have sat next to Rio Knight at that bar in Manhattan.

I should never have bought him a drink.

But, maybe our paths would have intertwined later down the line, given that my best friend is engaged to his brother. She's already been bitten, and I'm hoping that this time around things will work out just fine.

It's best for me, for my career, to stay away, even though Delport Realty is the company behind the Eco resort, it's the Knights who are really running this operation. They're just hiding out of plain sight.

As I lie in my bed, ruminating, my phone rings and my heart jolts with anticipation, then quickly deflates when I see Alma's name on the caller display.

"How are you, Raquel?" she asks. "I wanted to check in on you."

"Check in, why?" I let out a small, nervous laugh.

"Because of the injunction."

"That's just work. It had to be done." I'm trying to figure out her angle, what it is that she's worried about.

"Your friend didn't seem to take it too well. Is he your friend?"

"He's someone I know from back home. You don't need to worry about him, Alma."

There's a long pause. She doesn't say anything. She doesn't need to. I feel her judging me. I suspect she knows Rio and I are involved, in some strange capacity, and she probably knows it's wrong for me to be mixed up with someone from the other side—but I'm not involved with Rio. We just got carried away the other night, like we always seem to do whenever we're around one another. I blame it on the scorching off-the-charts chemistry between us. I've never had it with anyone else, and I'm finding it harder to fight each time we meet. I sense he's also struggling to keep things purely professional.

"Why don't you come with me, if you're free today? My daughter's having a barbecue for my grandson's birthday, and I'd like you to meet my family. You'll get to have some of the tastiest home-cooked Belizean food."

I'm taken aback by her inviting me to meet her family. "That's so kind of you, Alma, I would love to but I had plans to go further along the coast to get some more evidence."

"Evidence? For what? We already served the injunction."

"I just want to make sure that it's watertight. You saw the way Rio Knight reacted."

"It was hard to miss," she agrees. "The foreman wasn't too happy either, but we already have evidence. We've got pictures and satellite images and—"

"My boss cautioned me, now that Knight Enterprises is behind Delport, he wants me to make sure their lawyers can't gut this case. I want to put my mind at ease. The Knights have deep pockets and they'll hire the best lawyers. They'll gut this injunction if we're not careful."

"Shouldn't we have gotten that additional data before?"

"We didn't have time, Alma," I remind her gently. "You wanted to file immediately, remember?"

"Are you sure you want to do that today? Ordinarily I'd come with you—"

"It's the weekend, and you have plans. You can't miss your grandson's birthday."

"I'll send someone from the team."

"Not necessary. It's the weekend," I echo again. "I'm sure we already have enough evidence but this is for my own peace of mind. I was going to have a quick look at Caye Encanto. I won't take too long."

"Be careful, Raquel," she warns me. "The roads up there are bad. Must you go?"

"I would like to."

"Then take a small boat, and be quick." She doesn't want me to go, but I'll be so quick. Pierce has it in for me, I can tell, and I need to have this locked in.

"Don't worry about me. You enjoy your grandson's birthday."

"Don't go too far," Alma warns. "I hate the thought of you being out there all alone. The weather can turn in a minute and the sea can get dangerously choppy."

"I'll be back before you know it."

I make my way to the place where I can hire a boat. I've seen the little rowboats with the outboard engine. Easy enough for me to handle. I've ridden jet skis and quad bikes before. This should be easier by comparison.

A FEW HOURS LATER I HEAD DOWN TO THE DOCK AND HIRE A small motorboat. It rattles a tiny bit when it idles, but I'm not going too far. Setting my backpack down, I check the bearings on the GPS on the dash, then enter the location of Caye Encanto.

Even though we've filed, it's prudent to get more documentation, especially if I'm already out here. I've looked at the map. The caye is a narrow stretch of coastline, about thirty minutes by boat. It's a place tourists don't see. It's undeveloped, a tiny fringe of jungle and I'm curious to see if the damage reached that far.

Alma has her suspicions. She's thinks Delport Knight bulldozed through mangroves but they also violated marine protection zones too.

I tie my hair up into a knot, wipe my hands on the back of my shorts, and slide my phone into my backpack. The battery's dying. I didn't charge it last night. I was too tired, too wired, too *everything* after that confrontation with Rio.

There I go, inviting more thoughts of him in. I can't seem to help myself.

I push the boat off the dock and start the engine. It's a lovely day. The sun's shining and the sea is calm and shimmering. It's a perfect day for sunbathing, and for reading and having cocktails. For relaxing. Maybe I'll do that later when I get back. I might even go for a dip in the sea.

I'm two miles along the coastline when I see the caye. Slowing the engine down, I ease the boat into the shallows where I toss the small anchor overboard. It's light enough for me to pull back up on my own, but sturdy enough to keep the boat from drifting. I wade through the warm, knee-deep water, and pull the boat slightly onto the sand, just to be safe. Then I tie the rope around a thick mangrove root at the water's edge so I can climb back in later.

I climb out of the boat and walk around the edge of the caye. It's quiet here. Very peaceful. Very still. Maybe a little *too* still. A little too eerie.

The narrow strip of land is hemmed in by mangroves, but some of the trees look unhealthy. Off-browning leaves, exposed roots, dark water swirling at their bases. A powdery gray film clings to the trunks and floats in the shallows. I've read about this. It's a telltale sign of sediment runoff. The roots are getting choked, thereby starving the plants of oxygen. This is what happens when construction runoff isn't contained. When concrete washout and chemicals spill into coastal ecosystems. It's a slow and quiet killer.

I shake my head in dismay. Caye Encanto is anything but enchanted. It's looks damaged beyond repair.

Taking out my phone I start snapping photos—wide angles and close-ups of the damage I see. It's so pronounced here. The discolored water, the broken roots. I quickly jot down field notes, then feel a breeze brush my skin. I rub my arms because it felt a little chilly. I snap a few more photos as I make my way along the narrow strip of land.

I see a small hut further up. The roof is a mixture of tin and weathered corrugated iron. I walk up to it, knock on the door, but the door pushes open. I gingerly step inside. It's small inside. Small, and wooden, and dilapidated. The walls are thin, and uneven, with holes. They're patched in places with rusty sheets of corrugated metal, and palm fronds stuffed into the cracks like plugs, to keep the wind at bay.

A small wooden bench runs along one side. I can't work out if it's to sit on or sleep on. At one end of it is a little hurricane lamp and a box of matches. There's a rickety table, two chairs, but one is broken. On the far wall is what looks like a crooked little window. It looks more like a hole covered with a rusted shutter barely hanging on. Battered crates are stacked in the corner, with a pile of old tattered newspapers lying on top. A sagging fishing net is draped over a hook.

A musty smell of decay and salt and iron fills the air. I step back out, closing the door behind me and continuing with my investigation. I wander a little father along the shoreline, on the lookout for any other signs; chemical sheen on the water, floating debris, a break in the vegetation where equipment might have been dragged ashore.

Anything that will support my case.

Anything we can use.

Suddenly, a gust of the wind tears at me. Trees begin to sway and bend slightly. The air shifts.

I look up. The sky starts to darken; a flicker of fear lances through me. I'm almost done. I look up and the sky darkens in an instant. Feels like a storms coming. The clouds are thick, like heavy clumps of dark and foreboding matter, bruising to a garish violet.

I try to head towards the boat, but the wind is so strong, I can't take a step forward. It feels like I'm fighting with an invisible monster. The wind slaps into me, the trees swaying and bending like strings. I'm enveloped in danger, and suddenly, I feel afraid because it's all happened in an instant, and I never truly believed it could turn so fast.

I try harder to move towards my boat, but it's like wading through tar. Buckets of rain crash over me. Like the heavens cracked wide open and emptied. I'm soaked through in seconds, caught by surprise. That's when I see my little boat bobbing up and down, tossed around like a dog chew.

I can't get into that. I turn around, with great difficulty, getting drenched by the second, in my shorts and spaghetti-strap tank which seemed perfect this morning. Now they're my worst mistake, second only to coming out here alone.

I should have listened to Alma. I suddenly hanker for a young child's birthday celebration. A barbecue. To be safe, surrounded by people, laughter and dry clothes. Instead, I'm battling the elements, and so badly ill-equipped for it.

I manage to reach the hut just as the sky opens, like a round of firecrackers erupting. Once inside, I close the door behind me, leaning against its flimsy frame, my soaked backpack sliding off my shoulder and falling to the floor in a sodden heap.

A sharp crack of thunder shatters the silence, and lightning flashes outside.

It's too close for comfort.

I freeze. The tin roof? Not good.

I could die in here.

I could die outside.

I sink to the floor, not caring that it's dirty. Not caring that I'm soaked and scared and very much alone.

I don't want to die. I'm too young, and my mom has only me.

I can't die. It would break her. Heart thudding, I tell myself it will be fine. This will pass. I'll wait it out.

Somehow, I'll get back to safety.

CHAPTER TWENTY-TWO

RIO

I'm on a mission to find Raquel and ask her what the hell she's playing at.

How could she do that to me, after everything? Not only do I have to deal with the shitstorm of this injunction, served by Raquel herself, I've also got my old man breathing down my neck.

He's ordered me to make sure the resort opens on time. It can't. I can't and won't ignore an injunction. I see what Raquel means now. We, the Knights, make deals in the finest establishments. We give contracts and put things in place, but there's an element of manipulation that takes place.

But when it comes to the law? I adhere to it, most of the time. Sounds like the old man doesn't.

Now the whole situation is fucked. This was supposed to be simple. A clear-cut PR stunt to smooth things over. I didn't think Delport had done anything shady because everything I've seen so far—everything in that folder, a copy of which I gave Raquel—suggested that the evidence is solid.

But I've seen and heard enough of other things to not sleep easy. Tomas makes subtle gripes under his breath and keeps going on about me needing to see the coastline with my own eyes, but I've been busy trying to charm the officials.

Or maybe, the old man's been keeping me too busy to have the time to go and investigate. The community meeting was exhausting, but I need to take a look.

Before that, I need to talk to Raquel.

I call her. No answer. Just like the last three times I tried. I'm sitting in the hotel restaurant having my breakfast; some fruit and yoghurt and grapefruit juice after a grueling workout in the gym, followed by a few lengths in the pool.

I call her again. Still no answer. I consider heading over to her guesthouse, but decide to drive straight to where EcoGuardians are based. When I knock on the door, Vilma answers.

She smiles. I smile back. The lagoon night seems eons away. She tells me that Alma's not here, because it's the weekend.

"I'm not after Alma. I need to speak to Raquel."

"Raquel?"

"She's not here." That voice comes from behind me. I turn around, startled to find Alma standing behind me. She's holding two helium balloons and a stack of decorations, and she looks surprised to see me.

"I came to pick up something," she says carefully. "What are *you* doing here?"

"I was after Raquel."

"Why?" Her eyes narrow with suspicion. "I hope you're not thinking you can convince her to withdraw the injunction, Mr. Knight."

That's what she thinks of me? I smile. "I wouldn't dream of it. I don't interfere with legal affairs. I just want to talk to her." The way she's looking at me, I feel like I need to make a case for my honesty and intentions. "Though the injunction causes a serious problem for us. It means a serious loss of income for—"

Alma cuts me off. "There's a reason for that."

Maybe I should have kept my mouth shut. "Where is she?" I ask. "I've called her a few times but she's not answering.

Alma's expression shifts and she looks suddenly worried. "She was going to head further along the coastline."

"Why?"

"To get more ..." The old woman stops talking.

To get more evidence? If so, it tells me she doesn't have a watertight case. She filed too early. Probably because this woman told her to. "How far up the coastline? Do you know?"

"She was heading over to the Caye Encanto, the small caye east of the main developments."

I wonder what possessed her to go there now. But I know why. At least, I have an idea. I might have come on too strong yesterday. She knows my moods, just like I'm getting to know hers. I swipe a hand over my brow. She went digging for more evidence, to make sure she had enough, because I threw a tantrum. She probably thinks I'll go running to the old man and there'll be serious pushback.

"She was going to take one of the small boats," the old woman says.

"Small boats?"

"I told her not to go, but she said she'd be quick."

"I heard on the radio that there are reports of a storm coming," Vilma announces. She glances up at the sky. We all do. It's darkening fast.

"When did you hear that?" her boss asks.

"Just a few minutes ago. I was going to close and head home."

I glance at my watch, heart thundering. Fuck. Raquel is out there, in a boat, looking for evidence that I probably pushed her into getting. She could be in serious, life-threatening danger. Out alone in the sea, in a small boat, with a storm coming. Everything around me falls away, and my thoughts narrow and fix on Raquel. Rules and consequences vanish. I'm going after her, because if something happens to her, I won't be able to take it.

I make to move. "I'm going after her."

"Please hurry." The old woman doesn't try to stop me. "Everything can change in an instant."

I make to leave.

"Wait!" She calls out, then disappears, reappearing a few seconds later with a large satchel she shoves at me. "You will need this." She hands me a small bag.

"Of supplies you might need."

I grab the bag. "Thank you." Then jump into my Jeep, type the location into the maps app on my phone and drive like a fiend. My journey starts off easy enough, despite the relentless rain and strong gusts of wind. But then I hit a narrow dirt road that winds through the jungle. It's dark here, and the road isn't so clearly delineated. Rain lashes down but I have a little cover under the thick foliage. Above me, palm fronds bend and thrash in the wind. To my right is the ocean. Surf hurtles against the rocks, a salty spray making my windscreen even blurrier.

All I think about is Raquel, being out in this.

What was she thinking?

What did I drive her to?

It's all overgrown jungle, and what can barely be called a road. There's no signage. No markers. I keep going in the direction the map last pointed before my connection cuts out.

"Fuck."

The storm fully unleashes. Wind tearing through the trees like an invisible deathly predator ripping its prey. Rain slices sideways. The jungle feels oppressive. A dark and wet prison that's impossible to escape from. Something catches my eye. A boat violently bobs up and down. It's the only sign of life out here. I swerve off the road, the Jeep's tires skidding in the mud. I pull off to the side, kill the engine and open the door, but the storm smacks me full on, making me buckle up. Somehow I manage to push forward and get out, pushing through the tangled mess of roots and wet brush, my boots slipping and sliding in the mud as I fight my way toward the shore.

The sea is no longer a glistening blue. It's angry, and violent, churning black and violet as it crashes against the coastline like a frenzied beast. The boat is empty, but rocking wildly, the rope tied to a mangrove branch. That must be the boat Raquel came in.

I look around, desperately scanning the waterline, the trees, the stretch of wild land. Rain hits my face, hard and heavy as golf balls. My eyes sting, my hair and face, are drenched, my clothes are soaked through. I struggle to move forward in the muddy, slushy mess.

"Raquel!" I call, but the wind shrieks, and the rain buckets down. "Raquel!"

What if she slipped and hit her head on a rock? What if she got pulled under? What if she drowned?

For a moment fear paralyses me. I lose the ability to think. But then I see her face, hear her laughter, and I refuse to accept these scenarios.

This woman is determined. She's pigheaded and stubborn. She's likely chasing more evidence because she's worried. Is it because of me? Panic courses through my veins. "Raquel!" I yell, scanning the coastline. I scan for any sign of movement. For Raquel.

Still nothing.

An angry gust of wind almost knocks me sideways. I still, bracing myself, under the deluge of the downpour, under the weight of the wind, planting my feet as wide as I can. The wind tears through the trees, screaming like a wraith.

Where the hell is she? I look out at the sea again, my eyes sweeping the coastline, then the tree line. That's when I see it. A small hut, tucked to the side of some trees, barely visible through the downpour.

With newfound strength, I rush toward it, reaching the door and pushing it open. "Raquel?"

There she is. Cold and shivering, huddled on the floor, arms around her knees. She looks up. She's wearing nothing but a soaked skimpy little strappy top and denim shorts.

And she's cold.

But she's alive.

"What the hell?" I bark. "Are you out of your mind going out alone like this?" But it's relief, masked with anger.

Fuck. I'm so happy that she's alive.

RAQUEL

THE DOOR BLOWS OPEN, AND I SEE HIM.

The flickering flame from the hurricane lamp I managed to light illuminates him. It's just as well, otherwise I would have been terrified in the dark, not knowing who it was.

Rio Knight, stands there, hulking at the door, face twisted, looking mad as hell, glaring down at me where I'm huddled up on the floor, trying to block out the noise of the storm.

He yells something at me, while the wind whistles and billows around him and the rain lashes down in sheets. I got soaked, but this man is getting drenched. His shirt clings to him in a way that sets my heart aflutter. Open at the collar, it's plastered to his chest, and his longish hair flops forward, falling in wet curtains over his eyes. He swipes his hands through it, slicking it back, and briefly resembling some storm-drenched, furious Jesus figure.

I stand up slowly. "I was working," I reply, defensively. He walks inside, shuts the door behind him, and the sound dims.

"Your phone doesn't work and your boat," he snarls, "I assume that's your boat, looks like it's going to let loose any second. Have you seen the sea?"

"I have."

"You could've gotten yourself killed!"

"It was nice and peaceful when I set out."

He shakes his head, causing water droplets to fall off. He's soaked through. "You could have drowned."

"But I didn't. I lived to have the pleasure of your company again."

"What the hell are you doing here?" he growls. "Couldn't you just have a cocktail by the beach?"

"I'm a working woman, besides, I could ask you the same. What are *you* doing here?"

"I came for you." He pulls his T-shirt away from his chest.

"Why? I didn't ask you to." I fold my arms, because if he thinks I'm going to be grateful and thank him forever for this, he's sorely mistaken.

The silence between us turns thick and heavy, just like my shorts. His face twists, and I guess I do sound ungrateful. He smooths his hair back again, jaw clenched. The storm still rages outside, and the amber glow from the lamp still throws long shadows against the run-down walls. The wind sneaks in through the gaps, and the light flickers, barely, because the oil is low and it's not going to last long enough. Not all night, which is what I've prepared myself for.

Water droplets dribble down his face and he flaps his arms, trying to shake the water off. This is my worst nightmare. Being trapped in here, just the two of us.

No, your worst nightmare would be to be here alone.

"You always think you know best," he snaps.

"And you always think people owe you answers."

He glares at me, and my insides turn to steel. I waggle my finger at him. "I don't want to hear a word about the injunction, if that's the reason you came looking for me."

"I needed to talk to you about the way you went about it."

I wipe a hand over my face. "You can't. We shouldn't even be in the same room together."

"And yet somehow that's how we end up."

I'm curious and puzzled. "You should have called me, Knight. Saved yourself the journey here. How did you get here?"

"I drove."

"But the roads are bad!"

"A road. One, narrow, windy, dirt road."

And he came anyway. For me, to make sure I was safe, and he put himself in danger. The hardness in my chest loosens. This man who was filled with wrath yesterday, put his life on the line to come and find me. The walls I've kept steadfast and fixed around me, to keep him out, start to crack a little. I'm so pathetic at this. Constantly running into Rio has softened my resolve.

"You should've come to me," he says.

"My generator was working just fine this morning," I quip.

I can't help myself. I resort to sarcasm when things start to feel too serious.

He steps closer, and I almost step back, needing space between us. But I hold my ground, refusing to be intimidated.

"Why are you out here, still chasing evidence? Still trying to make sure your case actually holds?"

I laugh out loud. Not only because it's absurd and the last thing I expected him to come out with, but because he's *so wrong*.

"How did you know I'd be here?" I demand.

"Alma. She hinted that you were trying to get something. Is it more evidence?"

"Might be, but not for the reasons you think." I cross my arms, and try my hardest not to let my gaze wander to the way his shirt sticks to his chest. "I have more than a watertight case."

"Bullshit."

"A lot of this damage is caused by the construction. *Your* construction."

"Did you look at the folder I gave you?"

"I did." I added some notes from it, but I'm not about to tell him that, although, now I'm starting to wonder if that was wise, because the data looked too clean. Too sanitized. Images of mangrove roots mysteriously healthy after supposed clear-cutting. Photos that looked staged, of "replanted" trees. Environmental impact reports saying that the resort will "boost biodiversity" when it's not what I see with my own eyes. I didn't include too much of what he gave me, and now that I've been here, I'm glad I didn't.

He looks around the hut, moving the flickering lamp to shine a light on something lying on the crates. He picks it up. It's a flashlight. He flicks a switch and the light comes on. He shoves it into his pocket. "You find whatever it was you were looking for?"

"I did. I've seen enough. I'm shocked you don't see it."

We're barely inches apart now, and I brace myself for his cocky rebuttal.

"I believe you."

"I want to protect this island," I snap. "Wait, *what?*" That's the last thing I expected him to say.

"You heard." Thunder rolls. Lightning strikes again, and the roof of the hut shudders. I jump, startled.

He looks up. "This isn't safe."

"I know." It's barely a whisper.

"It's no safer outside." He glances at the door.

I wish I hadn't come here. Was it worth it? Maybe. But I want to make it out alive.

"Now we're stuck here," he says, taking his shirt off until he's standing in front of me, his muscles and abs rippling under a sheen of dampness. I suddenly feel hotter. Forcing myself to look away, I stare at a gap in the wall.

"I didn't ask you to come looking for me. I'm not a damsel in distress. I can take of myself."

"You think so?" He shoots me a look that makes my stomach wither. "Look where we are. And it's a tin roof." He gestures around the battered living space.

I hear him, and I'm all too aware of the danger. But I wish he'd put that shirt back on. Instead he spreads it out over a rickety chair, and he looks as sexy as sin, distracting as hell, and as infuriating as only a Knight knows how.

"Again, I didn't ask you to come looking for me." I slap a hand across my slick neck. My tank top sticks to me, and I'm certain I look like a mess. My frayed denim shorts feel heavy and uncomfortable, and if I didn't have a visitor, I would have taken them off.

"I'm not going to argue with you about this now. I'm here, and I'm going to do my damndest to make sure we're safe."

"I hope Daddy Knight doesn't sue me to death, if anything happens to his beloved son."

A muscle ticks along the side of his jaw. He frowns, like he's about to say something, and I feel the weight of his stare. Wish I'd kept my mouth shut, because he must think I'm such an ungrateful woman. I clear my throat.

"You said you believe me. So, have you stopped believing the lies you're being fed?"

"I came here to smooth things. To calm things down. I wasn't aware of what was going on, but now I believe something definitely is going on, and I'm going to get to the bottom of it."

"It's not hard to do. You should try using your eyes. Didn't you see the dying mangroves?"

He turns silent. His brows pushing together like he's thinking about it. "You hate the Knights."

That's his rebuttal?

"I have good reason to."

"You hate us because your warped sense of belief tells you we're the bad guys. That we're out to damage the world and take everything from people less fortunate than us."

"But that's exactly what you're doing."

He shakes his head, looking as perplexed by my stance as I am about his.

"Don't you see the damage?" I snap. "Didn't you hear the people at the community hall? You'd have to be blind and deaf, or willingly callous, not to."

He lets out a loud sigh, hands on hips, rain still dripping off him. "We try to be ethical, most of the time. Sometimes, it's not possible, and we do the best we can, for the land and the people."

"That's what you tell yourself," I snarl. "Why are you dumping construction runoff near protected mangroves? You might think you're He-Man, fighting the elements to come and find me, but when the storm calms down, I invite you to come out here again and take a good look with wide open eyes. See for yourself. I'm shocked that you still haven't managed an inspection."

"My old man says the indigenous communities exaggerate damage to get leverage, and sometimes to extort corporations. That it's climate change, not Delport, or Knight Enterprises, ruining the coastline."

I can't believe my ears. "Do you seriously believe that?"

"It's what he says but, the truth is, I don't know what to believe anymore." He pauses, looking more conflicted than ever. "But I'm not ignoring it now."

The wind howls like a banshee, causing the roof of the hut to shake again. I look up, feel suddenly scared that it could cave in. Wind whistles through a gap in the wall, cooling my skin, and I become more afraid with each passing minute.

I'm glad Rio is here. I wouldn't want to spend the night alone. He's right. I could have been in extreme danger. I probably still am, and I've also now put him in danger.

The light of the lamp flickers as if it's on its last few breaths before dying. The light in the huts dims, and soon we'll be in utter darkness.

"I'm not as bad as you think," he says, quietly.

He's not. I have to hand it to him. "I'm glad you're here. I wouldn't have wanted to spend the night alone."

The lamp flickers suddenly then dies, leaving us in darkness. It feels suffocating in here. Outside, the storm rages like a demon possessed, wild and violent. In between pauses, I hear Rio's breathing. Maybe he hears mine, tight and shallow, like I'm afraid to draw a deep breath, like I'm playing small, and safe, and invisible.

I feel scared. Not scared of the dark, but scared of how tonight could end, of what being trapped in here with the one man I can't resist might do to me.

"We can't stay like this all night," he says, his voice moving away. I hear an "Ouch," then a "fuck," and some noise as objects clatter.

"What are you doing?" I put my arms out, feeling around me as I take a few careful small steps forward the sound of his voice.

He shines a light, in the air, illuminating us. "Your boss gave me a bag of supplies, but I left it in the Jeep. I'm going to get it."

"Don't be so stupid—"

But he opens the door to leave. The noise is deafening. The wind gusts inside and sends a few things flying. Then, the door shuts and he's gone. Leaving me in the pitch blackness, in utter silence. He's outside in this, all because of me.

CHAPTER TWENTY-THREE

RAQUEL

I STAND IN THE PITCH-BLACK DARKNESS, LISTENING TO THE wind howling, rattling the flimsy little hut which is all that stands between me and the wildness outside. The clattering roof is a constant reminder of the fragility of my refuge.

Rio ran out into the storm to get the supply bag Alma gave him. *For me.* He put his life at risk. *For me.* He cares. He's nothing like his father. We bicker and flirt each time we're together, and yet there's a hum, a spark, a zap of electricity zinging between us.

I move to the hole in the wall that doubles as a window, and lift a rusted shutter slat. The trees are hunched over, swaying like they might snap any moment. I'm suddenly fearful for Rio, that he could get blown away out there.

What was he thinking?

He was thinking of me.

Were it not for him, I'd be trapped in here, in the dark, all night, living in fear that the hut could collapse on me at any time, or that I could be struck by lightning. It could still happen.

"Rio," I murmur, feeling at a loss. Feeling hopeless, feeling scared. It would kill me if something happened to him. I begin to fret. What if he gets swept up by the wind? What if a falling tree hits him on the head?

I can't just stand here. But I can't go out either. I don't even know where his Jeep is. I don't know in which direction he went, and it's so dark, it would be fatal. He had a flashlight. I have nothing. But I feel useless standing here doing nothing, while he's battling the elements and is in danger.

I can't let him die because of me.

I told you he was a good man, Raquel.

Daniela's voice is in my head. I suddenly miss her, and long to be with her, having another catchup over cocktails and a spa treatment. Daniela said Rio was nice. That the Knights aren't as bad as I think they are. That the boys aren't like their father. Maybe I should heed her words.

I move to the door. He's been gone too long, and I can't stand around waiting. I nudge the door open a little and immediately get shoved back by a vicious gust of wind. For a second I can barely move. I try again, taking a step forward, only to walk into *him*.

"What are you doing?" he yells, pushing me back inside, slamming the door shut.

"I was worried about you!" I yell right back. He shines the light towards me, not directly at my face, but close enough to give us light.

"You were concerned for *me?*" The corners of his lips turn up in that smug, sardonic way that is so uniquely him.

"You were gone for so long!" I can't help myself, relief floods me and I throw my arms around him. "I'm so glad you're okay."

"I'm back now, princesa." He sets the bag down and puts his arms around me. "You okay? Or do I need to check for signs of amnesia? This isn't like you."

Typical.

I move away and we peer at one another. Something has shifted in the time he left and now. I'm still wary, but less suspicious of him.

"Shine this on me so I can see." He hands me the flashlight which I spotlight on him, then watch as he pulls out a lamp from the supplies bag.

"You had the foresight to bring that?" I'm impressed.

"I didn't. Thank your boss."

"Alma is a legend."

He starts taking things out of the bag and setting it on top of the crates. "This is going to save us," he says, rubbing the dirt off his hands. There's a rolled-up poncho, a tightly wrapped up emergency blanket, a tin of sardines, a pocket knife, a ziplock bag of matches. A small med kit, a packet of dried mango slices, and three bottles of water.

"That should keep us going for a day," he announces.

"All thanks to Alma," I say proudly. "She knows this land like the back of her hand. She doesn't take any chances."

"Just as well that I ran into her." He opens a bottle of water and hands it to me, before taking one for himself. After guzzling a third of it, he sets it back down, alongside my empty one. I look up at him guiltily. "I should have made that last, huh?"

"You were seriously going to go out there looking for me?" he asks.

I wipe my mouth. "You were gone forever."

"I was gone for …" He glances at his watch. "For fifteen minutes. The Jeep is parked nearby."

"It felt like forever."

"What did you think I was going to do? Vanish into the sea?"

"I don't know. I thought you might be dead."

He smiles, leans back, assessing me as if I'm someone he doesn't recognize. "You were worried about me?"

"Don't push it."

He takes a step towards me, and I inch back. He raises an eyebrow. Challenging, daring, then takes another step. I inch back further until my back is against the tinny wall. It's rough surface grazes my heated skin.

"What did you think would happen to me, princesa?" he whispers.

"I-I don't know."

We're so close now, I feel his breath on my lips. He brackets the wall on either side of me with his hands, caging me in. I'm worried that his strength and weight might cause the flimsy structure to collapse, but the thought instantly vanishes. He's all I see. All I sense. And he smells like storm, and heat and adrenaline. My heart begins to pound and an ache spreads low in my belly.

Whatever fears I had being stuck in here, disappear, as heat rolls off his body, heating mine. His hair's plastered to his forehead and he's drenched again, water running down his skin. All I can think about is licking up every single drop.

"But you were worried?" He doesn't let this go.

"Yes."

He leans in, our lips brushing. "Good," he murmurs. "Now we're even."

My chest heaves and heat pools between my damp panties. His hand brushes my skin, his fingers resting along my jaw, as his thumb traces around my lips. He looks at me like he's daring me to push him away.

But I don't.

I won't.

I can't.

His eyes burn into me, causing my body to combust under his touch. His hand slides gently onto my shoulder, then slowly trails to my waist. My back arches with anticipation, with yearning, with memory.

"Raquel." His hands cup my face and soon his lips are on mine, a fevered collision. Our mouths claiming, bruising, wild and hungry, as unrelenting and as inevitable, as the storm outside.

Our tongues duel for dominance, and our kiss deepens, turning urgent, hot and frenzied, like we only have a few seconds. He devours my mouth, tilting my face up, angling his head to deepen the kiss, like he's drinking from me. I melt into him, pressing my body against him, feeling pressure building low in my belly. The hut fills with the sounds of harsh breathing and my soft mewls as I kiss him back, greedy for more, my fingers running up the bare skin of his chest.

"You went out shirtless," I breathe against his mouth.

"Should I have worn a tux?"

There's a pause. Then he pulls away, moves the lamp to the edge of the table, so that more of the light falls onto me. The soft glow fills the hut, flickering against the scratched up walls. I look at him—really look at him. His chest is bare, soaked, perfect. Drops of rain still slide down the ridges of muscle like water over carved stone. His eyes drop to my tank top. His voice is low.

"I've made you wet again."

"I've been wet a long time."

Before I can say anything, we're kissing again. Harder. Hotter. Desperate with need. Hands everywhere. His hard body presses against me, but I feel something harder poking at my stomach.

"You like this, huh, princesa?" His hand cups my breast gently. In answer, I suck his tongue, grinding against him, every inch of me screaming for his touch. I'm greedy and needy, and desperate for more.

———

RIO

I'M HARD AS STEEL, AND WHEN RAQUEL GRINDS AGAINST ME, I have to fight not to lose it.

This woman tests my restraint, and it takes all of me to resist her. I kiss her hard, fucking her mouth with my tongue, trying to eke out my pleasure, and taking what I can without going too far.

Raquel isn't a wallflower. She takes, consumes, gets her satisfaction, and I'm more than happy to let her.

The air between us crackles, not just because of the heat between us, but because of the friction that comes from unspoken words.

"Touch me," she begs, splaying her hands against my chest.

I tilt my head, wondering exactly where and how she wants me to do that. I have no problem obliging, but I don't want to mess anything up, assume too much, especially when my cock is driving this, not so much my brain.

Her hands glide slowly all over me, from my pecs, my shoulders, my biceps, down my abs, like she's trying to memorize every inch. I can't wait for her to get familiar with every part of me, just like I dream about doing the same with her. Every inch, every crevice, every dip, every nook, every fold.

"Wait." Miraculously, I have enough clarity of mind to think about comfort. There's nowhere to sit. There's only one chair. Another one that's broken. There's no bed, or anywhere to lie down. Just a wooden slat that looks like a low hanging shelf. I take the heap of newspapers from the corner and tile a patch on the floor, then spread the emergency blanket over them. I spread the thin poncho over that, trying to make a comfy area.

I move the lamp higher, onto the table where it no longer spotlights the dirt and mess, but shines on Raquel, on her long hair, cascading over her in waves, and her big brown eyes which stare back at me.

"Let's sit," I suggest. We do, fumbling for space on the little safe area I've created, but it's uncomfortable. She adjusts her position, trying different variations.

She groans. "I can't get comfortable.

I try not to gawk at the way her nipples poke against the fabric of her top. All I want to do is clamp my mouth around them and suck hard. I'm not comfortable, either, but at least I can bring my knees up. Sitting like this, we're so close together, I feel the warmth of her body, and her hair brushes my shoulder when she adjusts her posture again and tries to sit with her legs tucked under her. Finally, she kneels, sitting back on her heels, her hands on her thighs.

That doesn't look comfortable either. "Your shorts look tight," I remark, though my voice sounds oddly weird.

"I was going to take them off, before you showed up."

"Go ahead, princesa. Don't let me stop you."

Her eyes flash, not with anger, but excitement. Like I've dared her to do something and she's not going to back down. Eyes fixed on me, she rises slowly. The view from the ground up is tantalizing. Like the tease she is, she slowly undoes the top button of her shorts, before peeling down the zipper.

As if that weren't a call to my cock, she then tries to wriggle out of them. But it's not easy because they're stuck to her. Each inch she wriggles them down, her panties get pulled down as well. It turns into a balancing act; her trying to keep her panties on, while trying to get her shorts off.

"Want some help?" I offer, swallowing hard and wondering what possessed me to make the suggestion.

"With what?" Her eyes pin mine, as if she's challenging me to make the next move.

"Y-you're trying to take off your shorts," I point out, my voice hoarse, "without pulling your panties down at the same time." Her nipples strain against her vest, and I begin to salivate. With my cock straining against my boxer briefs, my shorts feel even tighter.

"How will you help?" she asks, ever the interrogator, even in moments like this.

"I-I could hold onto your panties so that they stay up, while you pull down your ..." I swallow, my mouth suddenly parched.

"Or I could do both in one smooth move." She rolls her shorts down with her panties. My mouth hangs open. She's almost bare, neatly shaved, except for a perfect one-inch wide landing strip. I see everything. The delicate bud that screams to be sucked.

What the hell, Raquel?

I feel like I could be the first man to die from sheer temptation. She's left me speechless. I want nothing more than to fuck Raquel's brains out, and the way she's looking at me, I get the feeling she'd like that, too.

But I'm a gentleman, and I need to be one hundred percent sure, because I could never exploit this situation.

Also, I don't have a condom on me.

She steps out of her garments, picks them up and drops them over my shirt, on the chair, as if it's the most normal thing to do. I don't mind. I won't ever mind. Her scent all over my shirt is something I can live with.

She's completely oblivious to the hurricane of emotions hurtling through me, to the way my heart and cock battle with my brain to do the decent thing. But what is the decent thing in this situation?

"All done." She stands before me, teasing, fully aware of the effect she has on me. I still haven't closed my mouth, and I pray I don't drool because I'm salivating so much. And I can't stop staring. I've been with a lot of women before, but none has ever stood so confidently, with her bare pussy merely inches from my face, before.

"You look like you've never seen this before."

Hot damn.

She stands, proud, and not the slightest bit shy. Nor does she make to turn away. Instead, she lets me gawk like a pubescent teen. My eyes move to meets hers. They're dark, and hooded, her smoldering eyes waiting to see what I'll do next.

I never expected that from her, but also, I'm not surprised. This is Raquel, after all. She's confident and ballsy, and knows exactly what she wants. What surprises me more is that she's finally given in to this heat between us.

"What exactly do you need me to do now?" I need clarification, though I would willingly shove my head between her legs and happily eat her out.

"That's so much better." She fans her face with her hand and she sits back on the floor, letting out a huge, contented sigh. She's still kneeling though, and I get the merest peek of her landing strip.

"It was good of you, brave of you, to come and find me. But why would you do something like that?" she asks, matter-of-factly, like taking her panties off and sitting back down to make conversation is the most natural thing in the world.

It takes a while from my brain to switch gears. For me to ignore the throbbing of my cock, and to keep my eyes on her face. "I know how stubborn you are, and I couldn't live with myself if something happened to you."

Her laugh is soft, almost disbelieving. "You hate me."

"You know I don't hate you. After everything that's happened here, between us, in the lagoon, at the food festival, after everything I've told you, you know the truth. I haven't lied to you about anything."

Flashes of lightning illuminate her profile, and her wet curls cling to her body. Suddenly it feels stifling hot in here. If I leaned towards her, just a few inches, I could taste the salt on her lips. I could kiss her, and one thing would lead to another. But, would that be the thing to do?

Instead, I murmur, "You exhaust me, Raquel."

"And you infuriate me, Knight."

"You ever think of calling me by my first name?"

"Not yet."

Another flash of lightning sparks up and I see the hunger in her eyes. I know one thing, if this storm continues through the night, we won't survive it unchanged.

"You're naked from the waist down," I remark.

"I am."

I peer at her, trying to work her out.

"At least now I'm comfortable," she adds.

"I'm not. My pants are way too tight." Sitting propped up with my hands behind me, and my knees bent is not comfortable.

"Then take them off."

That's a dare if ever I heard one.

CHAPTER TWENTY-FOUR

RAQUEL

I STRIPPED DOWN, AND I'M ONLY WEARING MY BRA AND TANK, in front of Rio. I'm completely naked from the waist down.

A part of it is me needing to push the boundaries. I want to see how far he goes, because we both want this. We're stuck together tonight, and the truth is, I was uncomfortable in my shorts and I would have taken them off had he not turned up. I held out as long as I could, but I saw the hunger in his eyes as he looked at me and now that fate has thrown us together again, maybe I should heed what it's trying to tell me.

I'm a woman with a healthy appetite; it's my inability to trust that causes problems and makes me hold back. But when there's something I want, I go for it.

With Rio I've held back because it scares me just how perfect he could be for me, despite who he is. Now he's here. He came looking for me, and he probably saved my life.

Maybe this was meant to be. I don't know if we'll ever get

another chance like this again, and we've had a fair few already.

So I decided to make the first move. Even though he's charming, flirtatious and cocky, and he gives off dangerous vibes with the way he struts around, he's a gentleman at heart. He'd never make the first move.

So, I had to.

I peeled off my shorts and my panties because I was desperate for him to see me, and when he looked tortured enough, I knelt back on the floor so he couldn't see much. Just enough to tease him. Sure enough, he announces that his pants are feeling tight on him too.

I tell him to take them off.

It's like we're daring each other slowly. Inching forward in this slow tango of ours that started on that hot night in São Paulo. He kicks off his sneakers, then takes off his shorts, and then his boxer briefs.

I let out a small moan. The flickering lamplight illuminates his breathlessly large cock, which promptly springs to attention now that it's free. I reach for him, my thumb stroking his slick tip, as I watch his face contort in pleasure.

A shiver darts through me. I feel a slickness between my legs.

All I want to do is take him in my mouth and suck long and hard, the way I've dreamt about for months. He met my challenge. He's completely naked now, as he sits down beside me.

"It's always a stripping game with us, isn't it, princesa?"

"Seems to be."

"And yet you're still wearing something," he murmurs.

That's all it takes.

Lifting my arms, I peel off my tank top, then, with my eyes fixed on him, I unhook my bra from behind. The instant relief makes me sigh. Rio lunges forward, his mouth closing over my breast like he's been starving for it. He groans as he sucks greedily.

The first pull of his mouth makes my breath hitch, and when a low, greedy rasp rumbles from him, vibrating against my skin, heat surges through me. My fingers tangle in the thick, dark tufts of his hair, and I grip just enough to tell him I like this. That I want more.

The more he sucks, the wetter, hotter, more undone I feel.

He shifts, his free hand sliding up to my other breast. His palm curves over it, full and warm, kneading gently before teasing my nipple between his fingers. They're full, perfectly rounded, and high; I've always been proud of them, but seeing the way his eyes darken—seeing the way he worships them, makes me desperate for more. I need all of him.

"Fuck, I needed that." He doesn't even look up at me, he's so mesmerized, and then he latches onto my other breast and sucks—teasing my nipple over his teeth, biting just enough to make me gasp.

I arch into him, tugging his hair, desperate for him to take more, to claim more. I'm so hot, so turned on, and have been for so long now, that when his hand slides between my legs, a low, primal noise rumbles from deep in his chest, like a man about to go wild on me.

"Raquel …" I love the way he says my name, like he needs me, like he's desperate for me. He's working both his hands; one tweak my nipple while the other slides over my folds. He sucks hungrily at my breast, and it's the most exquisite sensation, being taken care of like this. Pleasure shoots through my veins, and I let out a low moan. I'm so wet, dripping with want. I reach for his cock, and give it a gentle tug before sliding my thumb around the wet tip. He shudders in approval, stiffening some more, then he groans, low and feral. He's loving this. He's loving this *a lot*. My fingers wrap around him, and I stroke his cock, stopping every now and then to slide my thumb along his wet tip. He jerks involuntarily. I love that I can make him feel this.

We stay like that, giving and receiving pleasure simultaneously, but when his fingers hook inside me, a wave of pleasure darts me and I stop, letting it pulse, while I pant slowly, trying to not come undone so fast. I've been so wound up with frustration over this man, and now I'm so close to coming, embarrassingly so.

"So soon, princesa?" His teasing voice is a whisper in my ear.

"More," I gasp.

He slides in another finger, and I cry out, bucking against his hand. I'm so slippery, and there isn't the friction I so desperately crave.

"I want to … come," I pant, trying not to fall apart so quickly. The floor is hard. We're on our knees, him slightly bent over, his mouth suctioned to my breast while he fingers me beautifully.

His tongue slides over my lips, and I gasp, wanting more. It's slow, and lazy, yet heat flames my skin, and I want more than just this. His cock pokes into my stomach, tempting and teasing, as if it's trying to find its way to my wetness. In this position, I could so easily have him slide inside me. Make him lie down so I could straddle him and ride him, but the floor is dirty and hard. His gaze locks onto mine. It's like we're both thinking the same thing.

"I don't have a condom."

"Oh." Disappointment crushes me.

"But there are plenty of other things we can do."

"Oh."

He guides me down, so that we're lying on our sides,

propped up on our elbows, facing one another. I barely have time to adjust and slide my hand over his chest when his greedy fingers slide over my folds and slip back inside me. I shiver involuntarily, before reaching for his cock.

We kiss again. It feels perfect. His fingers inside me, while mine are wrapped around his length. Inside this hut, we're lost in something deep and sensual, while outside a storm rips around us. We're cocooned in our lust hazed heaven. Deep in a kiss, he murmurs against my mouth. I sigh appreciatively, my body amped high, savoring the ways his fingers slide in and out of me, but something is missing. I need more than his fingers to give me the pleasure I so desperately crave.

"Sit on my face," he says suddenly. His directness shocks me, and I blink. He looks pleased, probably because he's managed to shock me. Without giving me time to think about it, he stretches out on the floor. The blanket isn't big enough to accommodate his body and from the knees down, he's touching the floor.

"You don't feel comfortable?" he asks, sensing my hesitation. His fingers tweak my nipple, causing a ripple of pleasure to shoot through me. "Have I shocked you?"

"Not shocked," I reply, sitting up, twisting towards him, staring at the temptation that is his glistening, throbbing cock. I lick my lower lip and consider bending over and sliding it slowly into my mouth.

"Don't even think about it," he warns. "I want to bury my face in your pussy."

The thought of him doing *that* makes me want it even more.

"Turn around, on all fours, over me," he commands.

When I hesitate, he tells me how to move and position myself exactly as he wants me.

"That's it, princesa." His hands skate over my bottom,

appreciatively, examining, feeling, almost like he's holding a peach and trying to assess its taste.

I feel vulnerable, like he can see me from an angle that exposes everything. I'm grateful for the subdued lighting.

"That's perfect." His voice turns gravelly, like he's consumed by a hunger that needs to be sated. "Down a bit." He gently adjusts my hips, and my pussy is exposed and wide open for him, just inches above his face.

He's lying down and, with my head lowered, I'm inches from his glistening, engorged cock. Burning with need, every nerve buzzing with desire. I don't care the floor is dirty, that the storm is unleashing Armageddon outside. I don't even care that the tin roof could cave in.

My mouth waters for a taste of him, and I lower my face, sliding my lips over his glistening engorged cock, and swallowing him slowly.

As I begin to savor the feel and taste of him, something soft and wet laps at my folds. He moans, starts guzzling like he's drinking nectar, adjusting me, angling my hips as he buries his face deeper.

His face buries deeper, making noises that tell me he's enjoying this. Like he's feasting on something delicious and satisfying. "You taste so fucking good," he rasps, taking a breather before diving lapping up my arousal again.

I groan loudly as the pleasure hits, as his tongue laves over me, as he sucks my clit. I jerk, feeling on edge, ready to lose myself completely. It takes a few seconds before I start to suck him slowly again, giving him my complete attention.

This is bliss. I'm being taken care of while I'm taking care of him. The lamp casts long shadows over us. It's quiet, except our sounds and sighs. He speeds up, sliding in another finger, thrusting hard, such a contrast to when his soft tongue latches to my pussy. He's good, so skilled, and he knows exactly where to touch me and how. He's gentle, and rough, and I have never experienced so much pleasure, and so much feeling, like this before. I throw my head back, unable to contain the wave of pleasure I'm caught up on. He doesn't let me go, his mouth still latched on to me, tweaking my clit, making me jerk and shudder as my orgasm rips through me. My ragged breath is all I hear. I lower my head again as I remember that I haven't finished taking care of him.

He's still hard when my mouth slides over him again. I suck him harder, and it doesn't take long. In fact, he takes me by surprise, how quickly he comes in my mouth. I swallow it all.

For a few minutes, we stay like that, our bodies pulsing, hearts thumping. Slowly, I move off him, wiping my mouth as I turn around to look at him.

"Was that good, princesa?"

Was that good? He's fishing for a compliment. "It'll do, for now."

His eyes widen. His lips part. "I'll see what I can do next time."

I smile then, because I feel ridiculously happy. Then I do something even more risqué. I lie down beside him, snuggling up against him, tucking myself into his chest, as he wraps his arm around me.

We lie our breaths slowly calming down, naked and hot, on the uncomfortable floor, listening to the storm wreaking havoc outside.

CHAPTER TWENTY-FIVE

RIO

I open my eyes, and everything looks unfamiliar. Then I remember.

The lamp's gone out. The hut is quiet, and dim, with enough light coming through the rickety old window. I feel my arms around someone, warm and soft. When I turn to look, Raquel is staring up at me.

"I was waiting for you to wake up." She looks unsure, even though we're lying tangled up in each other and neither of us moves apart.

"You should have woken me."

"You were sleeping like a baby, I didn't want to disturb you."

This is sweet. I was worried things would be awkward in the morning, that Raquel would turn back into the feisty lawyer, but she's not like that. She's sweet, and a little vulnerable, and she still likes me. I like this version of her.

"Sleep well?" I ask, because I sure did. Too well, given where we are.

"On and off. The floor's hard. I couldn't get used to it." She presses a kiss into my chest, and when she presses another one, I settle back, smiling lazily, like a contented lion. I could get used to this. "Don't stop."

She makes a dreamy sound. "I've been drawing little invisible circles all over your chest."

I like that even more. I bask in how wonderful and natural this feels, me and Raquel, lying like this, after a night of intimacy, is even better.

Who is this creature?

"I know someone who has a nice big, soft, comfortable bed, and AC, and Wi-Fi, and the most incredible shower," I murmur softly.

"The most incredible shower?" she cries, quickly moving to a sitting position. "I could do with a good shower."

I sit up and place my hand on her bare back. Her skin is warm to touch, soft, like satin. I lean in and rain kisses along her shoulders and neck.

She squirms and giggles. "Ticklish."

My hand stays on her back, sliding down along her spine, to her base. I quiver at the thought that's she still naked. That I'm with her. That maybe we can carry on from where we left off.

"This doesn't change what I'm doing," she says, pulling on her bra. My insides freeze. The old Raquel is back—interrogator, judge, lawyer, attorney.

"I don't expect it to." She's got clear boundaries, and last night she blurred them. I try to find the words to win her back. To make her think with her heart instead of her brain.

"The storm's gone," she states, sliding her tank over her head and pulling it down. "Alma will be worried. I couldn't text her to let her know I was okay."

I reach for my phone, but my battery is also now dead. "Even if I'd had the presence of mind to give it to you last night, I didn't have a signal."

She stands up, and rolls on her panties, then her shorts. Casual, yet cold. It feels like a dream, how intimate we were only a few hours ago.

"She'll be worried," she says. "I need to let her know I'm okay."

I don't like how quickly she's reverting to the other Raquel.

"She might even have sent out a rescue party," I add, wondering how to get the conversation back around to us. Not work. Not the eco resort. Not business. I'm not ready to leave yet, and I want for us to talk. To say something, about what happened last night and what happens next. I try to get my cue from Raquel but she's sliding her sneakers back on.

It's suddenly become awkward.

I get up and get dressed.

She watches me shyly—so uncharacteristic of her—as if the night we shared wasn't hot and steamy and everything I've wanted more of. Unfazed, I reach out and touch her face. "I don't want this to be the only night I have with you."

"I didn't expect this to happen."

"But it did. You can't deny that," I insist.

She pauses, like she's trying to work out if I mean it or not.

"I'm glad it happened." That elicits a frown from her, but I mean it with all my heart. "If all I get is one night, I'll take it. But I'm not giving up, Raquel."

Her expression softens. Then, "You mean, you didn't just conquer and ditch me?"

Fuck. It was a comment I made to Dex once, when he was snooping around, trying to find out what had happened between me and Raquel.

How the hell does she know that? And probably out of

context, too, if I know Dex. I'm horrified. "Shit. I'm sorry. I did say that. Does Dani tell you everything that goes on in the Knight household?"

"No. Mostly only the stuff that pertains to me."

"I didn't mean that. I was trying to deflect attention away from you," I protest. I can't fucking believe that Dex would relay that conversation to Dani of all people. It was meant to be only between us. Now, when I feel I'm getting somewhere with Raquel, my words have come back to bite me. "I'm going to strangle Dex when I next see him. He wanted to know why you and I missed the breakfast brunch Dani's parents put on the day after the wedding. It was a casual comment. I didn't want him on our trail. Not that we had a trail …"

She nods, then. "Did you mean what you said?"

I take her face in my hands, focusing on her beautiful brown eyes, needing her to believe me. "You weren't conquered, and I can't see any way that I'd ever let go of you, were I ever lucky enough to have you in the first place."

She relaxes in an instant. The hardness, the walls, the armor that she was putting back on, suddenly melts. I realize then, that Raquel is all about protecting herself. Her mind, her heart, her body.

Growing up in a favela, she must have learned early on that trust is a currency you spend sparingly, that you keep your soft spots hidden, because once someone finds them, they can use them against you. She's had to guard herself against men who wanted to take, against a world that doesn't give second chances, against anything that could hurt her or make her feel small.

"I meant the other bit. The part where you said you're not giving up."

I thumb her jaw. "Yeah, I meant it."

She looks pensive. "I wasn't sure what to make of you.

You're a Knight, and I already have my reservations about your family."

"But I am not my father." I feel like that's becoming my mantra.

"That's what Dani said, and I'm starting to see that you're not."

I must thank Dani the next time I see her.

"So …" I say, gingerly, rubbing my thumb over her lower lip, and taking my chance, fully aware that Raquel is always the first one to walk. "I want more with you. More time, more conversation, more intimacy. We're not done. This is just the beginning. So how about you take a chance on me?"

She looks like I've asked her to skin a cat.

"I don't want to get hurt, Rio."

I squeeze her hands, and as much as I want to hold her and kiss her, I hold back and restrain myself. "I won't hurt you. I promise."

"You really do have a nice big bed." She looks up at me.

"You could get a good night's sleep in it." I nod, my cock twitching already. As if I have any intention of letting her get any sleep.

"A good night's sleep is exactly what I need." She tilts her head up, her luscious lips reminding me of how perfectly they were wrapped around my cock last night.

"It's still the weekend," I remind her, trying hard not to remember the rest of last night. Of my face buried in her pussy. "You don't have to work today. You can recharge and take a nice shower, recharge your phone …"

"I should let Alma know I'm okay."

"What will you tell her? She knows I went looking for you."

"I'll keep it vague."

"What do you want to do?" I ask.

"You do have the nicer hotel suite. It's not a room, Rio. It's a suite."

"For you, princesa, it can be whatever you want. We can get room service all night long."

"There's something else we can do all night long too," she says.

That's my girl.

CHAPTER TWENTY-SIX

RAQUEL

I start charging my phone as we drive back in Rio's jeep.

As soon as my phone has enough charge, the messages and emails come flooding back, and I see Pierce's email. He wants me back, quickly, to work on the Santos case. He says there's no point me hanging around here now that we've filed. He's ordered me to fly back tomorrow.

My heart sinks, and I push work related stuff far from my mind. I don't want to tell Rio just yet.

No sooner do we get back to his hotel, we barely make it through the door when our mouths crash together, and he presses against me, hands framing my face as his mouth devours mine.

"Fuck," he growls, in between reigning kisses along my jaw, my neck, along my sternum.

My fingers tug at his hair as his lips slide over me. My tankini is dirt, just like his clothes are. We're both dipped in sinful sweat, and I need to shower. He peels my clothes off me with expert ease, while I claw at his T, trying to get it off him. His hands move all over my bare skin, feeling, touching, sliding, tweaking. I struggle with his shorts, but he's pushed me against the wall, and is peeling the clothing from me.

"Shower," I murmur. "Need to clean up." He falls to his knees, ready to sink his face between my legs again. "No." My hand tugs his hair, lifting his face so that he looks at me.

"We said we'd shower."

"I want to fuck. I'm ready, aren't you?"

He moves to standing, and his cock is wide awake and ready again.

Caraca.

My mouth hangs slack. Here, in bright, unfiltered, strong light, I see it in all its raw, unfiltered beauty. This man is so insanely hot. His cock, so ridiculously, beautiful, and big, jutting out against his dark pubic hair.

My body jumpstarts into arousal overdrive, and a slickness dampens the space between my thighs. His fingers slip between my folds, and he nods. "Drenched, princesa. I want to slide right in and fuck."

Just like that, so do I. Thoughts of cleanliness fall as easily as my clothes did.

This man, inside me, now?

Oh, yes.

He grabs my hand, drags me to his enormous bed, its white bedding so virginal and pure.

I climb onto it, on all fours, trying to get to the middle, when he grabs my ankle and yanks me. I turn around, and he's on me, straddling my hips, a condom wrapper in his hands. He watches me watch him sheath himself, and when I sigh with want, with longing, he bends down, pressing a kiss to my lips while his big, hard hands shackle my wrists.

"I love your calluses," I murmur.

He grunts in response, his tongue sweeping inside my mouth and taking my breath away. He lines up against my opening, and I arch my back in sweet expectation.

He slides inside me in one swift, smooth motion that fills all of me. I cry out, feeling the stinging stretch. Then he pauses, stills inside me. He's heat, and steel, and I feel a few seconds of pain which quickly vanishes as I succumb to his size, and accommodate him.

His face inches from mine, he swipes his tongue over my lip. "You okay, princesa?" He drops a soft kiss at the corner of my mouth.

I feel full. My nerve endings jangling. My erogenous zones filling with blood, my senses heightened.

Our eyes lock, as he begins to thrust in and out, the room fills with wet sloppy noises as our bodies connect. I jolt each time he thrusts in, my body jerking with each push. We move together. It becomes faster, messy, needy. Hands clutching everywhere. Mouths everywhere. Hips grinding like we're fusing together. A riptide of pleasure surges through me. I feel so close, and when his mouth latches onto my breast, first one then the other, I close my eyes, pressing my head into the mattress, tilting my head back, unable to take any more.

This is more than just sex. More than just a connection. Being with him feels like on another level. Like being in another dimension. Like I'm having an out of body experience.

His hands hook under my thighs, and he lifts my hips, angling them so he can thrust deeper. Just as I'm loving this new position, he grabs my ankle and moves my leg over his shoulder, diving deeper inside me. He hits the spot, and I dig my nails into his back, spurring him on.

The air turns hot and salty, the scent of our heated bodies filling the already thick and heavy air. Our breaths are ragged, as he continues to drive into me, hard and fast, brutal, yet tender. I'm almost there when he slams so hard into me, my cries fill the air, and I don't care who hears us. My back lifts off the bed while he holds inside me. He watches me writhe and mewl and ride it out. When I'm done, when he's done watching me, he leans down and kisses me. "I love being inside you," he whispers.

I manage a lazy smile, through the haze, as my body still tries to come back down from the high. I've barely had time to recover, when he flips me over on my stomach, his hands bracketing my hips, and pulling me to all fours.

He ropes my hair into his hand, and slams into me from behind, tugging my head back. Shock knocks the wind from my lungs. Shock, and how fully he fills me again. Tiny ripples of delight spread out from my core. My legs feel like jelly, my breasts heavy, and tomorrow, I know I'm going to be sore down there, but in this moment, that doesn't matter. Rio fills me with so much pleasure, I can scarcely breath. He rides me hard, and deep, and I lean on my elbows, while we go at it again. The room fills with the slap of wet skin, his grunts and curses, my mewls and sighs.

"Are we together, princesa?" he asks, his balls slamming into me.

I'm not coherent enough to process what he's asking. "Huh?"

"You and me? Are we together, or still playing games?"

"Not … a … game," I pant, in between his thrusts.

"*This*. This is what I dreamed of, princesa."

"Me too. Ever since the ...the … Manhattan ... Blue .... bell ..." I manage to say, as the pleasure builds, all over again, and again.

I'M LYING IN RIO'S BED.

It's something I've dreamed of, but I could never see happening. After all the bickering between us, letting go and giving in feels right.

The injunction is filed and the case will proceed. I keep telling myself that this, what we have between us, is private. It's nothing to do with the law. We hated each other so much, and we believed in different things, but he's coming around. He's starting to believe me, and doubt his father more than ever.

I just have to leave him to figure things out. I can't be seen to be involved in that. But as I lie in his arms, I feel content, and happier than ever. This feels right. And the silence, it feels comfortable.

"This will complicate things," I murmur. Never one to completely let go of my working brain.

Rio presses a kiss on the top of my head. "I should have known better. Money is the only thing that matters to the old man. A part of me had suspicions that things were shady. I didn't realize they were shady on this level."

"Drinking water contaminated with construction runoff. Locals getting skin rashes from their own wells. Coral reefs dying because Delport rushed the permits and dumped rubble straight into the bay."

His hand reaches down and tweaks my nipple. "We fucked up, but I swear I didn't know about it before."

"Slapping the word "eco" on a resort doesn't give anyone the right to bulldoze mangroves and poison a village, Rio."

"It doesn't. I'll look into it and I will find a way to fix it." His fingers get to work again, kneading my breast, tweaking my nipple.

"I hate that the villagers are drinking bottled water and swimming in filth."

"I hate that, too. I'm going to find that elder, the one at the community hall, and I'm going to look into his concerns."

"You've been here how long? And you still haven't gone out to investigate?" I should let it go. I need to. This isn't the time or place to keep talking about work, but a part of me wants to pin him down. To say "I told you!" That's the competitive streak in me.

"My old man kept me busy, I told you. And you were right. It was part of the process."

"What's in this for him?"

His hand stills again. "Money, the usual."

"At any cost? That's not … that's not good, or human, Rio."

"You don't know how twisted he can be."

"I think I do now."I lace my hand through his.

"I love my mom," he says, lifting our entwined hands up, like he's examining how they fit together so perfectly. "She's suffered a lot and I just want to make things perfect for her."

I wait with bated breath. He's sharing something deeply personal and I want to hear more.

"She fell in love with this businessman, thinking he was her prince. She fell fast, and hard for *him*."

"Didn't she ever want to marry him?"

"She did, but he kept coming up with excuses, and she was so smitten, she didn't push him. It didn't go down well with her parents, but she loved him so much."

I snuggle against him some more, wanting to hear anything, and everything he's willing to share about his past, and his family, and his upbringing. Anything I can get so that I can understand him better. But he doesn't say anything more.

I intertwine my fingers in his, feel the roughness against my skin. "I thought you'd have baby soft skin."

"I box regularly. Not just for fitness, but control and discipline. These calluses are from sparring and using the gym."

I kiss his hand. "I think we found a great way to get fit just now."

"Babe, I hope we can make that fitness a regular thing." He slides lower, and we end up kissing again. In the deep recesses of my mind, I know I need to shower, and that I've served an injunction, and that Rio and I being in bed isn't a smart thing. "You believe me now?" I ask him. "That there's been a cover up?"

He groans. "Did you have to bring up work?"

"I need to know."

He props himself up on his side. "I believe you, even though Delport Realty claims what's happening is because of climate change."

"So they acknowledge that there are problems?"

"Only minor ones."

"They would," I snarl. "I hope you dig deeper and uncover everything."

"I need to go back to the coastline," he says. "Didn't see much because of the storm."

I skate my fingers over his bare chest. This feels so right. So perfect. Lying in bed with him, talking about work. A conversation I need to let go, but can't.

"I see you're passionate about this, Raquel."

His fingers skate over my thigh, causing my breath to hitch. My body knows what's coming. Blood pools south, and I get ready for more. Seems like I can't get enough of this man.

"Do you trust your father?" I know what Paul Knight is capable of, and I'm not even a member of that family.

"No."

His hand slides under the covers, and between my legs again. His father is the last thing on his mind, and let Rio do what he wants. I let him explore, and touch, feel my insides flutter and go loose when his fingers slide in. When he hooks them inside me, hitting the right spot, the pleasure is so intense my back arches off the bed. He's so masterful, that it doesn't take long for me to fall apart before his eyes again. He watches, intently. I know it turns him on, because he starts tugging his cock.

"I love watching you come," he murmurs, stroking his cock again.

"You planning on keeping me here all night?"

"I'm planning on never letting you go, princesa."

That reminds me. Pierce's email pinches me back to reality. I make a face, preparing Rio for the news.

"What?" he asks.

"Pierce has ordered me to come back quickly."

"When?"

"I fly out tomorrow."

He sits up. "Tomorrow?"

"The injunction was served. I've got something important to get back to. Something I left to come here for."

He lets out a groan. "The old man's not too happy either, but I have to stay behind. He thinks its to fix things, but I need to get to the bottom of this."

I feel happier that we're on the same side, even if we're not.

We fall silent.

"When will we see each other again?" I can't bear the thought of being away from him.

"As soon as I get back," he says without hesitation. "But I don't know when that will be. I want answers, and I'm going to figure out what's really going on with Delport."

This is what I needed to hear from him. It's never too late to fight the good fight. He's not the man I thought he was. And that's a good thing. I see him now, as he really is, and I like the man I've found him to be. Him coming after me in the storm was the moment I realized, but looking back now, Rio has always been there. In the gardens, at Dani's wedding reception, then in Miami. And now, here in Belize. But he didn't come here looking for me, he came here to work and I just happened to be here.

Maybe fate did bring us together, and maybe we're meant to be together. I've given him plenty of reasons not to stay, but he does. He's persistent, and he told me, he won't give up. I want more of him. I want everything he wants, and it's not just the physical, he wants it all. Me. A deep commitment. Something lasting.

We lie in bed, quietly for a while.

"You're in New York, and I'm in Miami," I say finally. I wonder how that will bode for us?

"Don't look so sad. It's not Pluto." He moves over me and gives me a long languorous kiss which makes my toes curl.

Maybe I won't head back to my hotel yet. I consider getting under the covers again, taking my fill of him again.

"You know what you said about fate? About how sometimes things are meant to be? We keep running into each other. But I never thought this would happen. I never thought I'd be rescued by you, or that we'd spend the night together in a hut."

"What a night it was." He surprises me as he climbs out of bed. "I say we take a shower." He holds out his hand, and I have a feeling that there will be more than a shower taking place in the bathroom.

Rio drops me off to my guesthouse early the next morning. I feel sad when he drives away because a part of me knows—he's the right one.

Even though he's a Knight. This man is solid.

Later, I return to the EcoGuardians bungalow. I texted Alma soon after we reached Rio's hotel room, and left a message, but it was vague. Too vague—because I didn't want to give her details.

"Raquel, could we speak in private please?" She stands as soon as she sees me, and leads me to the kitchen. "You spent the night with Rio Knight?" she asks the second she closes the kitchen door. Her tone isn't accusatory. I detect a hint of worry, and concern.

"We were trapped in the hut, Alma. He came looking for me. I didn't plan it. The storm hit faster than expected, and it was so wild. I was so scared. My phone died, and the sea was so choppy, I couldn't take the boat back. I hunkered down in this little hut I found, and Rio found me."

She doesn't say anything. Just watches me. So I keep going.

"And before you ask—no. I didn't trade anything. I didn't make deals. I listened." I swallow. Because I can't lie to her. I respect this woman too much, and I don't want to let her down.

"Why did he come looking for you?" she asks quietly.

"He ... he was annoyed about the injunction, more because he didn't see it coming." I don't want to land him in it. I hate lying to her, but I can't tell her that Rio suspects Delport are covering things up and wants to fix things. She can find that out when the time is right. I also know that I'm skating on ice so thin, pretty soon, if I'm not careful, I'll end up in ice cold water.

"He should have brought that up with me."

"But I filed on your behalf."

She takes her spectacles off, and blinks a few times, pinching the space between her eyebrows. "I'm worried that you'll get hurt. I don't want that for you."

She's justified in her worries. "I didn't give away anything about the case."

"It's not the case I'm worried about. It's *you*. Forgive me if

I'm overstepping my boundary, but I don't think you trust easily, Raquel. Or fall in love easily."

I laugh. "Love? Who's talking about love, Alma?"

She stares at me, quietly, as if she's contemplating something. Maybe she wants to ask me something, but doesn't want to hear a lie. Or maybe she's trying to trust me, but she's being careful. Very careful.

"Look," she says eventually, "you don't want to be in a difficult position if this escalates legally."

"I know I'm not co-counsel," I say. "But I'm going back today." I already prepared her for it when I called her earlier. "He's not counsel either. He's not negotiating, Alma. He's PR —damage control wrapped in a tailored shirt. Talking to him off the record is no different than interviewing the construction lead or a local official."

"With the injunction filed, I don't want any blowback."

"He was worried about me, when you told him I'd gone further along the coastline. And what with the storm and everything ..."

She nods slowly. "We trust you to do the right thing. We believe in you. Please be careful."

"I will," I promise. I look around me, at the cosy little bungalow that was my safe place of work. I will miss these people. "I'll miss you, Alma. I'll miss all of you." I look at Vilma and Edwin, and remember our night at the lagoon, and I try not to get too emotional. I'm doing a lot more of that these days. It's not like me.

"You better come back and visit," Alma says.

"I promise."

CHAPTER TWENTY-SEVEN

RAQUEL

I fly back to Miami with a heavy heart and return to my normal life—only this doesn't feel normal anymore, but being with Rio does. Talk about a strange turn of events.

I miss him already.

We text. We call. We email. But it doesn't feel the same, because he's not here. And what complicates things is that ethically, what we're doing, getting involved romantically, doesn't sit right with me.

I'm the type of lawyer who always does the right thing. I have boundaries. I know black from white. There's no grey with me.

But with Rio, I'm slipping into so many shades of grey.

My job in Belize was to investigate and compile evidence, and then I ended up filing an injunction at Alma's behest.

I tell myself that Rio and me being together is fine.

It's fine because I'm not negotiating with him. There's no coercion or bribery or manipulation. What we have is emotional. It's personal. It's not professional. We're not in a lawyer-client dynamic. And my law firm isn't representing Knight Enterprises. Nor is Rio personally a defendant or a client in my case.

I'm not compromising my legal stance. But I do feel guilty. And I do feel conflicted.

Now that the injunction has been filed, the court takes jurisdiction over the matter. I'm not a permanent in-country legal rep. I'm just a US-based lawyer, an NGO advocate and now I'm going back home while the local court begins its reviews. Anything that happens—any hearings, pauses, rulings —in the following weeks, I'll be notified of remotely.

When I check in at the office, Pierce's gaze slides down my body making my insides harden. I'd forgotten how stressful this working environment was.

"Back from paradise already?" he drawls. "Not only did you survive the jungle, but damn, that sun did you good."

I don't respond. I never do when he talks like this. *It wasn't just the sun*, I want to scream at him. I reluctantly take a seat in the chair opposite him.

His eyes linger. "You should wear that more often."

I grit my teeth and ignore the comment. "The court's reviewing the injunction. I'm keeping an eye out for updates. Alma's handling local follow-up."

"Good," he says. "In the meantime, you need to get back to the Santos case."

"Of course." I'm grateful for the distraction, even if I'm not fully ready to move on. I get up to leave. "Is that all?"

Pierce's eyes snake across my body with a slow and painful sweep that makes me itch. I miss Alma, and having this sleazeball for a boss is slowly poisoning my mental health. Being in the same office as him is a daily assault on my boundaries and well being.

I need to get out. And fast.

Still, I am grounded by the thought of the man I can't stop thinking about. I miss him. I need him and want him. Rio is such a perfect gentleman in contrast to this snake. He never once looked at me like I was a piece of meat. He wanted me, but the concern and care he showed me, is a stark contrast to this viper before me.

"You're tanned ..." He remarks, his voice low, and dirty. "All over, I imagine."

"It was hot out there." I glare at him, try to level my breathing. Try not to make my chest heave as his gaze dips there, unashamedly. He shrugs, his eyes settling on my chest.

"You look like you spent too much time by the poolside, slathering yourself in sunscreen."

My insides churn with nausea. I feel as if something rotten touched me. I taste bile in my mouth at the visual he's got in his head. I ignore the heat rising to my cheeks and try to focus on my escape from this law firm. I need to get out of here. I've put up with this man for too long.

I square my shoulders, unable to put up with this anymore. "If you ever comment on my body like that again, Pierce, I'll file a formal complaint."

His smug expression falters, only for a second.

"It's not a compliment. It's harassment," I add, my voice calm and cutting. "I'm not in the mood to be polite about it anymore. I've put up with your sleaziness for too long."

He stares at me, his expression tightening. He looks offended that I dared to say the word *harassment* out loud. Like it's an insult to *him*. He looks shocked that I've finally called him out.

I have zero fucks to give. I'm done tiptoeing around men like him. After Belize, after Rio, I can't unsee how toxic this place is.

CHAPTER TWENTY-EIGHT

RIO

I WENT BACK TO THE CAYE WHERE RAQUEL AND I GOT CAUGHT in the storm, and I looked at the mangrove basin. I saw exposed roots, the dirty, cloud water, yellowing and dead foliage, trash tangled in the roots.

It was bleak, and it was right under my nose, if I'd bothered to look sooner. If I hadn't taken the old man's orders blindly. It was hard to miss, just like Raquel said it was. What stared me in the face wasn't just deception and lies, but irreversible damage to the ecosystem.

I felt sick to the core. It would have been easier to stop there, and return to my hotel. To swim for an hour, and then have a couple of drinks at the bar. To call Raquel and see how she's doing. Any of those would have been a great distraction from facing the ugly truth, but I didn't take the easy way out. Instead I drove to a small fishing village near the eco resort and got a local fisherman to take me out. He didn't say much, in fact his silence spoke volumes, and I had sneaky suspicion that he recognized me from the community hall meeting.

When we reached the reef, I looked down at the murky water and didn't relish the thought of diving in, but I had to, in order to see for myself, firsthand.

I stripped off my shirt, took a deep breath, then dove in. The salt burned my eyes, and everything blurred for a few panicky seconds. I swam around in the cloudy water and saw it, what Delport did its best to hide.

I saw the coral reef, bleached a pale white and damaged beyond repair, nothing like the myriad of colors I was expecting. There was no sign of life here. I remember Tomas telling me these waters once teemed with schools of fish. Not anymore. There is no sign of life here, only silence and decay. What was supposed to be untouched marine paradise is no more.

It's what the locals said. What the people in the community hall said. What Raquel tried to tell me. But the reports didn't show this. The reports said the reef was thriving, and the photos I saw seemed to confirm it.

I finally understood. This whole coverup has been perpetuated by Delport, and indirectly by us, by me, by Knight Enterprises.

Fuck.

I gasped, coming back to the surface, my chest burning from the dive, but also from what I'd witnessed. The fisherman looked out, silently. A quiet dignity surrounds him, and he didn't look at me once. I was filled with shame and guilt, because I had a part in this. I might have been in the dark to begin with, but deep down, I had my suspicions and I chose to ignore them.

My eyes should have been wide open from the start, but I

kind of treated this trip like a much needed getaway; a little jaunt the old man sent me on. A PR stunt.

Turns out, people's lives are at stake, and I should have done better. Now I'm wrestling with my regret.

Delport blinded me with polished reports and touched up photos. The old man kept me busy in meetings with people who talked about issues other than the ones I was interested in. I stood at that community hall and pretended to listen to the people. Lied and told them I'd look into things.

I still didn't do a damn thing about it.

But Raquel did.

That woman doesn't need anyone's permission. She knows right from wrong. She knows what needs to be done, and like the justice warrior she is, she goes out and does something about it.

I was annoyed that she blindsided me with that injunction. But the truth is, she woke me the hell up. I've seen that Delport is hiding something. As for the old man? He's not just aware of everything that's going on here. He's counting on it.

It's been a long day, and I'm about to head to the village to meet with the elder who told us the villagers now had to drink bottled water.

Tomas said he'd meet me there, because I'm not sure how the locals will take to me turning up like this. Also, he can help with translation, if need be. With construction halted on the eco resort, the workers are tasked with minor things and Tomas was tasked with taking stock of equipment and materials on-site. No wonder he's offered to meet me here.

As I head towards the village, the Jeep slows down as the road turns to gravel. There are no signs or fences, just a narrow path between palms and half-flooded ditches. It smells like wet leaves and brine as I pull into a clearing.

I scan the area around me. Scattered around are a handful of homes on stilts, chickens wandering aimlessly, and children watching silently from under the porches.

Tomas is talking to a few people, but he stops and heads toward me as my Jeep pulls up.

"Hey, boss." He nods. When he asks about my earlier visits to the mangrove basin and the reef, I tell him the truth.

"You saw then, eh?"

"I saw, and I'm angry and ashamed."

He tilts his head, his eyes examining me. "It's good that you saw. It means you can do something."

I feel the pressure already, and know I have to make good. These people must hate us. I must have come across as such an awful douchebag at the community hall.

Then there's my old man to contend with. It's going to be a fucking nightmare.

"Let's see what we have here." We start to walk towards the area in front of the houses, where a few people have gathered.

"You told them I was coming?"

"Did you want to surprise them?" he asks. I feel like they're getting ready to attack.

"They've been asking for help for over a year," he says. "They've been sending emails, letters and reports to Delport, but they get nothing back."

This is the first I've heard of it. "Are you sure?"

"Yes boss. You know what they got back?"

I don't answer. I already know what they got back.

"Marketing brochures and bottled water," he says.

I have no words. What can I say that will make any of this better?

The local elder walks towards us. I recognize him. He's the same man from the community hall meeting.

"You came," he says, his heavily lined and tanned face, making me wonder about the life he's led.

"I told you I would." But I'm a liar. And a cheat. When I said that to him at the meeting, I had no intention of doing such a thing. It was PR. Easy words. I needed to look good, and convince the audience, but I never really had any intention of coming here.

It's being with Raquel that's made me look at myself. It's seeing what she's seen, at last, with my own eyes. It's opening my eyes, and letting the veil of lies disintegrate, that's led me to this place.

I feel like a phony, and this man is looking at me like I'm a saviour. The injustice, the lopsided scales of justice are all that these people have known, and people like me have benefitted from their misfortune.

We walk together. "Show me where you used to get your drinking water from."

He leads me behind the houses, and he tells me he used to draw water from the spring beyond the mangroves. But the spring is gone.

"It is not dry," he says. "It is blocked. It is buried." He motions for me to follow him as he goes behind the houses. Black plastic drums line the wall, catching rain. I peer closer and see that one drum has algae on the surface. He points to the drums. "This is what we have to drink now. It's why we have to buy bottled water."

My stomach churns, and I feel the urge to heave. I wouldn't give this to my pet—if I had one.

I remember the words of the Delport engineer I spoke to the one who told me that the impact would be minimal. I ask Tomas, and his eyes fill with contempt. "Maybe he said it and believed it. He didn't say it out of experience, because he's never lived here."

I grind my teeth together, feeling even more ashamed. I see a lot more during the visit, and it all fills me with loathing. The eco resort means death for the habitat, and a poor quality of life for the people who live here. The rich tourists will have a great time, but will they even know at what cost?

Raquel was right, and I feel like shit for doubting her. On the ride back, Tomas is silent and staring out of the window. I wonder if he's judging me. He has every reason to.

"My father told me the environmental audit came back clean," I finally say. "He said the reports were exaggerated. I was told that the mangroves were already degraded before we arrived."

"You believed him?"

"I had no reason not to."

"Maybe you believed it because it suited you."

"I was sent here not knowing the truth. I was sold a lie, and now my eyes are open."

"Then you understand why EcoGuardians did what they did."

That hits like a punch to my stomach. Even Tomas knows we're on the wrong side. I drop him off to his small raised wooden house. It's built on stilts to protect from floods. It's a world away from my hotel suite, and I feel even more guilty as I drive away, feeling sick to my stomach, wallowing in my wretchedness, with a dawning realization that Knight Enterprises is truly one of the bad guys.

I can't forget the algae drifting across the surface of the water drum, just like I can't forget the children's faces as they watched me walking around. It doesn't sit well with me that they'll grow up in this, while the guests at the eco resort enjoy a wonderful vacation. They'll leave without knowing the abject misery of the people who have suffered, people who will never experience what they did.

It's a good thing that Delport Realty has been forced to stop all building activity while we wait on the court's decision.

The old man was furious and wants me to fix it, but I can't overturn this decision. Nor do I have any intention of trying.

Delport Realty are scrambling to gather evidence—counterevidence, or at least something to reassess the permits. But this time, I'm here to fix what I think my family has caused—indirectly—through Delport.

I'm starting to see things as Raquel saw them.

CHAPTER TWENTY-NINE

RAQUEL

I READ DANI'S TEXT:

You've been quiet. Are you OK?

I should respond. This is the third one she's sent me, and I was so busy in Belize, first with the injunction, then with Rio, to reply. I don't want to let anything slip about me and Rio, so I text back and tell her I'm fine. I tell her that I've had a busy week in Belize working on a case.

Just as I set down my phone, an email pings through. It's from Alma. She says the court has paused enforcement of the injunction pending supplemental review of jurisdictional scope and site-specific evidence.

Hmmmm. Not what I wanted, but, this is normal. The Belize judiciary wants more evidence before making the injunction permanent. These things happen. It's a procedural issue. I feel confident we've done enough for now. At the same time Rio calls me, and my pulse races.

"Hey." His voice is slow and gravelly, and it excites me. I could talk all night to him. "The injunction has been paused."

"I know. Alma told me."

"What does this mean?"

"It's routine. These things happen. They need a few weeks to check a few things. It might be to do an independent verification of the submitted evidence."

"Well, I'm coming home," he says. "Back to New York."

"You are?" My heart flips in my chest.

"The old man says there's no point in me wasting time over here."

"When?" He'll be back in the US soon?

"Why, you miss me, baby?"

Baby. Ordinarily, I hate a man calling me that, but coming from Rio, it hits different. "You know I do."

"I want to see you again, too. I miss you." His words make my heart do another flip. I press my thighs together as the anticipation of seeing him again starts to build. Suddenly, the Santos project I'm working on falls to insignificance. It's been difficult getting back into work mode, not only because of Pierce, but because what Rio and I had in Belize was magical. I want to experience that all over again.

"I miss you." I smile, because it feels right, and it's true. I've been wondering what it would be like to make this man a permanent fixture in my life.

"Can you come here? Matteo and Enzo have gone to Italy to see my mom."

I jerk to attention. He doesn't talk much about his mom, or his childhood, and when he does, I take notice.

"I could fly over," I say, liking the idea the more I think about it.

"We'll have the entire apartment block to ourselves, and I will do unspeakable things to you in the pool and on the rooftop garden."

I love the sound of that. "You promise?"

"I promise."

"I'll come. I'll be there." I don't need a reason, or for him to beg.

"One more thing … it might be an idea to wear a disguise," he suggests. "Maybe a wig and shades—"

"A wig and shades!" I cry. "Am I acting out a dirty little fantasy of yours?"

I hear his low, filthy laugh. "Could be. You can act out any little fantasy you want. It's more in case Dex drives past and sees you."

"I'll be in disguise. Don't you worry."

I hang up, giggling as I think about the weekend. But at the same time, I'm racked with guilt.

I shouldn't be seeing Rio. We're not on the same side. But, my heart tells me that no one knows about us. I haven't broken any laws.

It still feels wrong. The injunction is paused, but I need to recuse, and I will, once the case becomes active again. I'll step down before the next hearing, but for now, I want to be kept in the loop, because once I recuse, I won't hear what's happening and I have a bad feeling that Pierce will make sure I don't have access to any updates.

He knows how passionately I feel about this and he's being deliberately difficult, especially after I threatened him with harassment the other day. He can be a petty little tyrant when he sets his mind to it.

I want to make sure EcoGuardians are on top of things. I promised, and owe, that much to Alma. I'll withdraw. I'll do it in time.

My thoughts drift to Rio again, and I sink back in my executive chair, my heart skipping a beat. I'm going to see him sooner than I expected.

I don't know how things between us will work out. Ethical complications notwithstanding, distance is also a problem. I'm in Miami. He's in New York.

Maybe I can do something about that.

CHAPTER THIRTY

RIO

I'M BACK IN NEW YORK, ABOUT TO HEAD INTO THE OLD MAN'S sterile and cold office. He told me to get my ass back home once news of the injunction being paused hit.

As I step inside, the air suddenly chills. Everything in this office is sharp and abstract, just like the old man sitting behind his huge desk. He's furious. I see it in those glacial grey-blue eyes which fix on me like the cross-hairs of a rifle.

"The injunction is a fucking mess," he says, quietly. It's his calmness, despite his words, that warns me of just how pissed he is.

"It's halted," I say carefully. "For various reasons. Might not be so bad for us."

"It was served by that lawyer woman. Daniela's friend. I remember her from the wedding." His words are sharp, and deliberate and my insides empty. This is not good. It's way too close for my liking.

"How would you know that?" I ask.

He shrugs. "Pictures get around." His vagueness rattles me. I have a dozen questions, but, deep down, he's right. He knows who filed the injunction.

He steeples his hands. "This isn't the result I wanted. You were sent there for a simple purpose."

He looks at me, with his how-the-fuck-did-you-mess-up expression on his face. His perfectly manicured hands are clasped together on the table as he leans forward, sucking the soul out of me with that look.

I can't work out if he's pissed about the pause, or about the actual injunction, but he's not going to like what I have to say, because I can't ignore what I saw. Delport's data doesn't match reality. The damage is real. The locals were telling the truth. I feel his fury, and suddenly understand something chilling.

He knew all along.

He knew Delport were at fault, and he sent me out blind and stupidly naive, to lie and cover it all up.

To do his dirty work.

I take a deep inhale, flex my fists. I've been quietly investigating—requesting internal data from Delport, looking through audits and environmental reports, and I've started comparing site plans with satellite data, rainfall patterns, erosion zones.

There's a pattern, and it stinks. Now that I'm no longer out there, I've started reviewing site plans and historical permit records. I'm piecing it all together. I prepare myself for the onslaught as I let it out. "I don't think a lot of the information you have—or that you've been given—is correct. I think Delport's hiding things. A lot of things."

The old man likely knows all of this. He's just not going to admit it.

I brace myself for the pushback, and denial. His lips curl up at the corners slightly, like he's about to hit the knock out punch.

"Of course they are. It's normal. This is how business works."

The weighted silence is deafening. I open my mouth to protest, then think better of it.

"Do you think I'd let the locals stop this construction with complaints of a few dead mangroves and some blurry photos of erosion?" the old man growls.

"There's much more evidence than that. Irrefutable evidence."

"You've spent too long in the mud, boy. You seem to forget who you are."

"This has nothing to do with who I am, but everything to do with justice and doing the right thing."

"I don't give a fuck about doing the right thing!" he rages.

I'm too shocked to move.

"You think those people are going to fix their coastline?" he rages. "Rebuild their village? They can't. They've got no infrastructure, no capital, no future. We're building something they can't. Something that will make money. Brings jobs. Progress. You think the world gets built on good intentions?"

"We can do the right thing. We can—"

"Progress is messy. Sacrifices have to be made. If a few reefs get wrecked, if some fishing communities lose their bay, if the drinking water isn't clear, it's unfortunate—"

"It's much more than that, the drinking water—"

He cuts me off again. "It's unfortunate, but it's reality. Do you think any of those people would even have a job without companies like ours pushing through the red tape?" His eyes narrow. "*We* are not the problem. We're the solution, and you need to remember that. We do good in the world. It might not look like that at first, but it is. We know. *I* know. And I won't have you torpedoing that with your goddamn newfound conscience."

I don't blink for a few seconds, my throat constricting with disgust.

So that's it? That's what he really thinks of the locals? Those poor people. Those poor children.

This is who we are?

Monsters.

The old man sees the destruction as a necessary inconvenience, the lawsuits as minor speed bumps, and human lives as irrelevant. Now that I'm sitting here, face-to-face with him, having heard those words from his mouth, I see him for what he is.

Not just ruthless.

Not just a monster.

But a force of evil that will keep going unless he's stopped.

I always knew who he was, but I thought he might change with age. With time. Become less evil. No fucking chance. He's warning me to keep my mouth shut, because it threatens his bottom line. But this time, I'm not going to sit back and let him dictate how this ends.

***

RAQUEL

RIO TOLD ME TO WEAR A DISGUISE.

He also said he'd pick me up, but I told him not to. I told him I'd get a taxi to his place. I want to surprise him.

I get ready in the washroom at the airport, then step out donning the blonde wig which looks odd against my olive skin and dark brows. I've painted my lips red because I know Rio likes it. I wear it for myself, but the way his eyes always fixate on my lips tells me he really digs it. I want to please him.

As I get out of the taxi outside his apartment, I catch my breath. This place looks impressive. It's everything I expected it to be. The concierge is expecting me and tells me to take the elevator to the top floor. I do, and when I get out, there's only one door. I knock on it.

I've come early, because I want to catch him off guard. He opens the door, wearing only shorts, looking like he stepped out of the shower, or the pool, which I see over his shoulder. My insides heat in preparation. His face lights up into the biggest smile. We've only been apart a week, but it feels like forever.

"Wow." He pulls me into his arms and drops a slow, lingering kiss on my lips. "You're early, I was taking a shower."

"Perfect. You're all nice and clean for me," I murmur, stepping inside his apartment as he drags my small luggage trolley inside and closes the door. It feels strange seeing him, and not being in Belize—with the sea salt, the breeze, the exotic haze surrounding us.

Once inside, we kiss again, hands all over each other, tongues dueling. It feels familiar and hot, and when his cock pokes into my hips, I'm even more desperate for him. We pull apart, and he gives me a slow once-over. "You came straight from work," he says, appreciatively, before fingering a lock of blond hair between his fingers. "I like it."

"You wanted me in a disguise." I splay my arms out, and do a twirl. "Ta-da!" I say, with a flourish.

"Cute." A playful smile dances on his lips and his eyes fill with fire. "But ..." He gently takes my wig off and sets it on top of my luggage trolley. "I think you're more perfect as my dark-haired princesa." He smoothes his hand over my hair, gaping at me like I'm a timeless painting from one of the masters.

He reaches for my hands. "You must be tired and hungry.

We can get takeout. I was going to cook something, but you surprised me by arriving early."

"Are you complaining?"

"No … no." He reels me in for another slow, lingering kiss that makes me tingle below my waist.

"I *am* hungry." I run my fingers slowly down his bare chest, before dropping them lower, and brushing them over his tented hardness. *This* is what I'm hungry for. This is what I've been thinking of on my flight over. I sink to my knees, my hand sliding into his shorts and freeing his big, beautiful cock. My fingers wrap around him, and my mouth moistens in anticipation.

"Oh, baby, you don't have to—" he starts, and then sighs as I finger his glossy tip.

"I've been thinking about this the whole time," I rasp, gaping up at him, watching him lean back against the door, watching me.

I keep my eyes on his face as I wrap my lips around him and slide my mouth over him.

He groans, still watching, but now his face is a picture of pleasure. I start to suck. The deeper I take him into my mouth, the more he groans, his fingers grabbing my hair, and tugging gently. He pushes himself further into my mouth, hitting the back of my throat. Then he lets loose, thrusting into my mouth with unbridled restraint. Fucking my mouth, setting his own pace. And I let him because I hear his low growls and I know how much he loves this. The more sounds he makes, the faster he thrusts. My eyes water, and I look up at him.

"*Princesa* … " His eyes are closed, his mouth open. Then he comes, letting out a primordial grunt, letting go, letting loose. Emptying himself. This big, tall, strong man is putty in my hands. Soft and boneless. Lost in his own world, muttering sweet endearments and curses as he slowly untangles. I love doing this to him; wielding a power that undoes him. I wipe my mouth. His eyes flicker open. "You blow my fucking mind."

"Yeah?" I stand up. "That's not all I blew."

That gets a chuckle from him, and he runs his thumb over my moist lips, back and forth, then with more force, like he's smudging it. I let him. His eyes don't leave my lips for a few seconds, and then they meet mine. He nods.

I'm pretty sure I look like a disheveled mess, and I'm pretty sure he likes it. I love that he does. My lips feel swollen, and my lipstick is smudged, my hair is all mussed up where Rio's fingers gripped it. I feel like a messy, wanton goddess, and when he looks at me like that, like he wants to fuck me all night long, in every position, I love it. I *so* love it.

He presses a kiss against my lips. "I love you being here."

"I love being here."

He wraps his arms around me and we stand like that, foreheads pressed together for a few quiet moments. "I'm not going to let you sleep tonight."

I move my head back a few inches. "Promise?"

He nods. "But first, let me order some takeout. What are you in the mood for?"

I shoot him a mischievous grin. "I just had what I was in the mood for."

This makes him smile. "You're fucking unbelievable, you know that?"

I raise an eyebrow. "So I've been told. Mind if I take a shower?"

"Sure. Let me give you a quick tour of the place."

He quickly shows me around his penthouse. I'm not in the slightest bit surprised that this man has a penthouse apartment with his own rooftop pool and garden. Everything about it, about the entire four-story building screams trendy and futuristic with its glass and steel structures.

I slip into a simple black dress after my shower and find Rio in the kitchen. He's made a chicken Caesar salad. We sit outside, drinking white wine and eating a very impressive salad, under the stars.

"The old man's pissed," he says, finally. "I didn't think he'd take it well, but he's furious. He thought everything would go his way."

Neither of us have mentioned the injunction, probably because neither of us wants to talk about the great big elephant sitting between us.

"Let's not talk about work." I feel conflicted about the case, and I need to recuse.

"Agreed. Let's not."

"Let's talk about how we're going to spend the weekend." Ever since we got together, work has slipped to the background.

"Are we getting out of bed?" He waggles his brows.

I stroke his cheek. "At some point, we should."

We make rough plans for the weekend. We want to hang out in the city, soak in the ambiance, go to Central Park, visit coffee shops and have brunch, or lunch, and make dinner back at his place, before I fly back late on Sunday evening.

"Should I wear a wig while we're out?"

"No. Matteo and Enzo are visiting Mama in Italy, so there's no danger of running into them here. I was more worried about Dani and Dex driving by. They visit me sometimes, but if we're out and about in the crowds, there's no danger of running into them."

"Do they visit often?" I think it's sweet. With five brothers, two of them living in this apartment block, I doubt this man is ever lonely.

"It happens more now. Dex and I used to meet in secret."

"What?"

He explains the rivalry between the two sets of brothers.

How Matteo and Enzo didn't know that he and Dex used to talk, neither did Jett and Zach, on Dex's side. I find this most bizarre and find myself sitting on the edge of my seat, needing to hear more about his past, and his family, and what made him who he is today.

"Do you guys visit your mom regularly?"

"As much as we can." He intertwines his fingers in mine as we sit back, gazing out at the skyline. He asks if I have any plans for the things I want to do tomorrow. Any places or tourist attractions I want to see.

I move my foot and place it strategically over his cock. Just as I expected, its hard as steel. "We had a night in a hut during a storm on a tropical island. New York pales in comparison to that. I don't need culture."

"Just another adventure, then?" He grins, shifting in his seat, enjoying the weight of my foot.

"Some fun." I press my big toe into him. His mouth falls open. Those dark, dangerous eyes meet mine. "What do you want?"

"Just you."

"Come and get me, then."

I jump up and walk towards the edge of the pool, where I shimmy out of my clothes, before diving into the pool. He strips off, too, and dives in. We splash around and laugh like kids. Something about being this high up, under cover of the night sky, imbues us with daring. Makes me feel invincible, capable of anything, with this man beside me. I love being in our own little bubble, where no one can touch us. Where his father, the injunction, and Pierce are a million miles away.

We kiss again, tongues tangling, just like our hands, all over each other, teasing and touching. He's hard again, and his fingers sink inside me again, but we pull apart, making it last, the torture of restraint.

After a while, we float on our backs, naked, staring at the stars studded in the inky night sky. Floating like this, without a care in the world, we discover precious nuggets of information about one another, all the mundane but captivating things that form the foundation of who we're becoming. Favorite colour. Favourite place to travel to. Favorite meal. Favorite film. It feels easy and natural, like we've known one another our entire lives.

Up here, on the rooftop, away from civilization, but closer to the stars, there are no more barriers between us.

CHAPTER THIRTY-ONE

RAQUEL

I STRETCH COMING OUT OF THE WATER, STARING AT THE morning sky. I'm still getting used to the idea that this man has a pool all to himself.

What different worlds we live in.

Rio's inside, making a fruit smoothie. I could get used to this. Not just a weekend break every now and then—this could be all our weekends. There's a small problem about distance, but I'm getting ahead of myself again and I remind myself to enjoy each moment, and not to dwell on what might be.

Later, we head out for a long walk through Central Park, stopping off for coffee and brunch. It feels exhilarating, but normal, being with him, like this. Holding hands, exploring the city like a tourist, giddy with life and love, and not the highly stressed lawyer that I usually am.

Being with Rio has enabled me to give in, to let down my guard, to become vulnerable, but being vulnerable with Rio feels safe. Later, He rents a rowboat without asking me first. I protest, naturally, as he grins when handing me an oar.

"You want control? Take it."

"Is this because of Belize? Does this remind you of how I ended up in that hut?"

"Oh, princesa, that was some night, huh?"

"I'll say." I remember stripping down, taking my shorts and panties off. I'll never forget the look on his face. Just like I'll never forget how we pleasured one another with our mouths.

"You scared the hell out of me," he says quietly.

"I wanted to get more evidence. I was worried that being up against the Knights, I needed ironclad evidence."

He's quiet for a while. "The old man is up to something."

"Isn't he always?"

"Let's not talk about all that stuff, not now, not today, while I have you."

I nod, smiling, because I agree. We drift across the lake's shiny surface, the city and crowd fade away. It's just us, and it's exciting, and exhilarating, and just perfect. I want all my weekends, all my free time, to be like this.

When we get back, we sink into the sofa, still holding hands like we can't bear to let go. We're just … resting. Doing nothing. Saying everything without having to say a word.

After a while, he reads the newspaper, says he has to see what's going on. Keep abreast of the news. I'm pretending to check emails on my phone, but mostly I'm just watching him. We're talking, low and easy. About life, art, stupid headlines. Random things.

I sigh loudly, seeing an email from Pierce pop up. He wants to know where I am with the Santos case. It just slips out. "Asshole," I murmur, not really meaning to say it out loud.

Rio's head snaps up. "Who?"

"Pierce."

"Is he still being a prick?" His voice goes hard in an instant.

"He hasn't changed, but I stood up for myself. I told him I'd report him for harassment and that shut him up."

Rio puts down his paper, cups my chin gently, forces me to look at him. "You said that to him?"

"I sure did. I was sick of him. Have been ever more disgusted with him since I got back. Something about leaving you in Belize and coming back to that douchebag, made something in me snap."

"I swear to God, I want to pull that man's eyeballs out."

I laugh a little, trying to lighten the mood. "Please don't commit murder on my behalf. Not yet. I'm biding my time and I don't plan to stay there for too long."

"I'm super proud of you for standing up to him, not that you should have to do it. I know you can protect yourself, but just remember that you're not alone. You have me now."

I nod, and he kisses me softly.

"I've started looking around at other law firms," I tell him.

"Yeah?"

I nod.

"Would you consider something *here*?" He holds my hand, intertwines his fingers in mine, like a lifeline.

Here?

I had. And I did, but hearing him say it, lights me up so that I feel like I'm glowing all over. "Maybe."

This brings a smile to his lips. I can't stop thinking how good this feels. How easy. How right. I like this. Us. What we're doing. The way we're slowly becoming something more. We walked around the city for hours, and now we're here. Just existing, together.

"I'm going to make you something," I say, pushing up from the couch. "Let's see what you've got in that fridge of yours."

He grins. "Good luck." But he heads into the kitchen with

me, opening drawers, pulling out ingredients, mushrooms, tomatoes and onions, when his phone buzzes.

"Hold on," he says. "It's Matteo. He's FaceTiming me." He picks up the call.

I listen as he paces a few steps away. I hear another male voice, probably, Enzo, and then a softer older female voice. Their mom. They're talking in Italian, fast, and furious. Rio's laughing, and I hear his voice, become softer. I hear "Mama," and then the sound of his mother laughing.

He glances at me, and he's so happy. I see another side to him. I shrink back, knowing I'm a secret, something he has to hide, for now. This little family unit, is touching, especially now that I know the tragic story behind it.

"Ciao, Mama."

I lean against the counter, arms bent behind me, listening to them all say their goodbyes. He's beaming as he walks towards me.

"Everything okay?" I ask. "I couldn't understand what you were saying, but it was sweet, the way you talked to your mom. Your voice went all soft and gooey."

"Soft and gooey?" His arms wrap around me.

"You were so sweet."

"My mom is amazing." His eyes shine. There's something endearing, about a grown man, someone like Rio, who loves his mother. He lifts a hand to my hair, runs his thumb across my brow, looking at me like I'm something precious. "So are you. I think she would love to meet you."

He's talking about me meeting his mom. Before I can start thinking about how my mom would like him, he grabs my face and kisses me again, hard and hungry. In an instant, the kiss ignites something explosive. All the tension, the denial and hurt, it combusts into heat. I grab his shirt, pulling him to me, gasping when his mouth claims mine with a desperation that borders on savage. We go from kissing to hands exploring everywhere. Tugging, gripping, exploring. He's already hard again, pressing against me like he wants to take me now. Like he can't hold back. The thought makes heat pulse through me. I'm so slick for him. I wish he would take me here. Take me now. He spins me around, his breath hot against my neck. He pushes up the hem of my dress. His fingers hook into the waistband of my leggings before yanking them down in one quick, eager motion, along with my panties. He leaves them rolled down around my ankles, so it feels like my legs are shackled together. The cold air cools my skin, and I bend over, elbows on the countertop, moving the vegetables away.

"Aren't we supposed to be cooking?" I ask, breathless, as his hands slide over my naked cheeks with gentle appreciation.

"The food can wait." His voice is thick with need, and I know what he wants. When he gently bends me over the countertop, so that my breasts are pressed against smooth surface, I wait with eager anticipation. Hearing the familiar rip of the foil packet makes my pussy throb with need.

"Ready, princesa?" he rasps.

"Alwa—"

He doesn't wait, but thrusts in rough and hard, filling me completely. I moan at the delicious friction. At how completely he fills me. He's been holding back all day and my heart swells with each beautiful hard thrust. He's everything I want, everything I need.

"Princesa ..." he moans. My pleasure builds with each thrust, and I steady myself each time he slams into me, then push back, when he's buried to the hilt. I try to extract every ounce of pleasure from him, just like he's taking from me. It's fast and furious, nothing soft and slow about the way we're rutting. He sets up a rhythm, and the pleasure builds and builds. I'm so near to coming, I feel like I'm going to combust. And then his fingers find my clit, and that does it. A final few thrusts, and I cry out in pleasure, my legs buckling. I grip the corners of the countertop, riding out the waves as he stills inside me. I feel my pussy contract around his length, hear his raspy growls as he empties. I go limp, my head falling onto the countertop. His face rests gently on my shoulder, his lean arms coming down on either side of me to support his weight. He rests for a few moments, gently leaning over me. Then he pulls out slowly, kissing my back, and pulling my dress down before helping me to straighten up. I turn around, to find him walking away. Taking care of the condom, probably. He reappears a few seconds later, eyes twinkling with mischief as he watches me roll up my panties and pantyhose.

"Want some help, princesa?"

I want his hands on me all the time. "We won't get any cooking done, if I accept your help," I tell him, marveling at this handsome creature who is all I ever think of now.

His arms slide around my waist and we kiss again, his tongue sweeping into my mouth and making me melt.

"I want to shower first." I'm still breathless as we pull apart. I can see us spending the rest of the evening like this, and all night, and tomorrow. But I will be sore, and we will be starving. "We can start cooking after that."

He tightens his hold around me. "So practical, princesa. How about we fill the tub up and see how things go?"

I look up at him, marveling at his stamina. "You have the energy?"

"For you, always." He tucks a lock of hair behind my ear. "We could take some wine and glasses in there?"

Before I can answer, he pulls out a bottle of red wine from the wine rack.

"Someone's in a hurry." I smooth down my hair, watching him get out two wine glasses out which he sets by the wine bottle. He taps his fingers on the countertop, watching me with amusement. "I'm not fully sated yet. That just now, that was only an appetizer."

In which case, I can't wait for the main course. Forget eating food. Rio's suggestion sounds like the perfect end to a perfect day. "Wine in the bathtub sounds like heaven."

A knock on his door makes us both freeze.

"Who the hell is that?" he growls, walking towards the door. "I'm not expecting anyone."

I sprint to the bedroom and wait, my heart thudding as I wait to see who our unwelcome visitor is.

RIO

WE HAD THE PERFECT EVENING MAPPED OUT, AND NOW someone's at my fucking door. Matteo and Enzo aren't even in town, so who the hell could that be?

I freeze as I open the door and find Dex and Dani standing there, wide grins on their faces. While I like their casual drop-ins, this interruption freaks me the hell out.

Do they know?

Did they see us?

Is *that* why they're here?

"Hey, dude." Dex steps in with Dani right behind him. "We just got back from watching a movie and thought we'd come check in on you. Figured you might be flying solo with your brothers gone."

"This is a surprise." I try not to sound as pissed as I feel.

"We were going to grab a bite," Dex adds. "Thought we'd

ask you to come along. You've been pretty quiet since you got back."

"We were about to—I mean, *I* was gonna cook something," I say, catching myself.

I head towards the kitchen area in a bid to lure them away from where Raquel is. I can't tell if they suspect something or if I'm just being paranoid.

"You're cooking?" Dex asks, seeing the ingredients Raquel and I had pulled out still lying untouched on the countertop.

"Was thinking about it." I scratch my jaw, feeling out of sorts.

"Two wine glasses. You entertaining, brother?" Dex picks up the bottle of Tignanellow.

Damn. How the hell do I explain this?

"Nice wine," he adds, setting the bottle back down.

"I was saving it for someone who'd actually appreciate it," I throw back.

"Who's the lucky woman?"

Before I can answer, Dani pipes up. "Are you expecting someone, Rio?" She glares at Dex, "I told you we should have checked with him first."

"When's she coming?" Dex asks.

"Uh … soon."

He frowns at the stilted replies I'm giving him. "You okay, brother? I haven't heard from you much since you got back."

"Back from where?" Dani asks, rearranging the vegetables we'd gotten out into a circular shape.

I hesitate.

"He was in Belize. Thought I told you," Dex answers.

She spins around. "Raquel said she was in Belize." Her eyes narrow. She's sharp. Pays attention. "When were you there?"

"Last week," I answer carefully, watching Dani like a hawk as she observes the room, as if looking for more clues.

I should've kept them outside. Should've offered them a drink at the pool, steered them toward the bar. But no—my post orgasm brain is hazy. I can't think straight. "Would you guys like a drink or something?" I force myself to be polite, even though I'm not feeling it. Then Dani marches over to the kitchen island and grabs something off it.

Fuck.

It's Raquel's Cartier watch. Dani's holding it up, dangling it like damning evidence. "I know who this belongs to. It's Raquel's. Where is she?" She looks around the apartment.

I chuckle, then stare at them in disbelief. "You don't think… me and Raquel?" But I'm failing miserably because they're not buying it.

Dex mutters something like, "The fuck, dude," but he's not mad. He sounds more amused than anything. He's happy for me. I can tell. But Dani glowers at me. "Where are you hiding her?"

There's no point in me pretending that the watch belongs to another woman with impeccable taste. I'm busted, and I might as well own up. "I am entertaining," I say with a shrug. "And I do have someone here."

"Raquel!" Dani calls out. "You can stop hiding now." To me, "I haven't been able to get a hold of her either. She's been lying suspiciously low for too long."

I give in. "Raquel, just come out, babe."

Within a few seconds, Raquel appears, looking sheepish as hell. Her cheeks are flushed, her hair a little mussed.

"I knew it!" Dani gasps. It's not anger, more like shock, surprise and disbelief all rolled into one. "Raquel," she whispers, eyes wide, mouth open. She looks at me, then at Raquel, then at me and then at Raquel again before lunging into a hug with her bestie.

Dex turns to me, arms crossed. "Really, brother? How long were you going to hide this from me?"

"Please don't make a scene," I say quietly. "It's our first weekend together."

"You were both in Belize," Dani says, folding her arms. "Huh." Her tone shifts. Her eyes narrow. "Funny how the tables have turned, don't you think?" she says to Dex.

"Oh yeah," he mutters. "Remember how they ganged up on us back at The Bluebell Manhattan?"

I do remember. Apparently, so do they. They're half-joking now, but Raquel and I are still standing there like statues, trying to figure out how this became an intervention. Our friends start firing off questions, fast and furious, and we slip our arms around each other's waists, taking their questions. How long? When did it start? Did anything happen at the wedding? Or did it begin in Belize?

We let little snippets out. That it started in Belize. Raquel gives a brief reason for her being there, and I tell them it was about the Blue Star eco resort.

"I heard about that," Dex says. "It's not opening yet, and the old man is pissed."

We haven't had a meeting about it, everyone's busy working on their own projects, but it's clearly the old man is pissed to have let this slip.

"Does the old man know about you two?" Dex asks.

"No. He doesn't. Let's keep it that way."

"Sure. Don't worry about that. We're not going to tell him anything," Dex says. More questions follow, especially when they discover this is our first weekend together, since we've returned.

"Oooohh!" Dani squeals, looking at Raquel for answers. "You have a lot of explaining to do."

Raquel folds her arms. "Hit me with it. I can answer

everything." They grab the bottle of wine and the glasses, and slope off outside to the pool.

Dex grins, his hands resting on the kitchen island. "Well, well, well. The secret is finally out. You look different, dude. Softer."

"She's good for me." I lean back against the countertop where we just fucked. "She's the one. No one else comes close."

Dex jolts to attention. "There was always something about you two. I couldn't put my finger on it, but I suspected something."

"Me and Raquel, we were fire and ice. Love and hate."

"And now?"

"Now I'm wondering how the hell I'll cope when she flies back tomorrow."

"Long distance relationship?"

"Maybe." I shrug, thinking about how today has been so full. So perfect. How I can't imagine having a day without Raquel in my life. How the thought of her in Miami with that sonofabitch boss makes my blood boil.

Dex gives me a look. "You don't think that's a little too convenient?"

"What?"

"You and Raquel, in Belize at the same time, dealing with the same issue?"

"Maybe," I shrug. "Or maybe it's fate." Because that's what I believe.

"Hmm." He rubs his jaw like he's mulling it over, and all I can think about is whether Raquel and I will get to have the perfect end to the perfect day.

CHAPTER THIRTY-TWO

RIO

RAQUEL GOES BACK TO MIAMI, LEAVING MY APARTMENT EMPTY
and a huge void in my life.

I can't wait to be with her again. We talked about how we
could make this work. Weekends here and in Miami. Taking
things slowly.

She said she needs to step away from the case, recuse
herself. I told her I was looking into things, finding ways to fix
it. I didn't tell her what the old man said. I figure the less she
hears about him, the better.

Dex hasn't stopped teasing me. First thing on Monday
morning he was in my office, leaning against the door with a
wide smile, trying to get more details from me. I'm not going to
tell him about the hut. Or how we were marooned on that island
overnight. He doesn't need to know everything. But he's
secretly happy for me. What's even cooler is that Dani and
Raquel are best friends.

He's talking like Raquel and I have a future and I want to

believe that. What she said about maybe looking for work here in New York, gave me hope, but she's career-driven, single-minded and focused. This could just be a fun distraction for her while she's working so hard.

I don't want to dream too much, or dare too much. I don't want to expect too much but I meant it when I told Dex that she's the woman for me.

So far only Dex and Dani know about us, and that's how I want to keep it. Even though they've now returned from Italy, I can't risk Matteo or Enzo finding out, because once they do, something always finds its way back to the old man.

This has to stay between us.

Dani won't leak anything, because she's loyal to her friend, and I trust Dex implicitly. I trust him like a blood brother—because that's what he is. It's time we stop pretending we're on different sides. Time to stop holding these differences like they matter more than loyalty.

Having Raquel with me feels right. Like something in my chest unlocked and I can breathe again. No wonder Dex thinks I'm softer now. Raquel's the one thing in my life that makes perfect sense when things around me are chaotic.

We didn't fix our weekends, or make plans to see one another every weekend. Raquel said it wasn't possible with her caseload. I'd make time for her. I'd put other things on hold for her, but she's focussed. That's what I worry about. Her career means so much to her.

I try to focus on my work, but a week passes, and I can't take it anymore. I need to see her. I have my assistant call her assistant, ask some casual questions, figure out when she's free. I discover she's got a meeting scheduled Thursday evening. Friday's booked too.

I fly to Miami early on Friday evening, and keep it quiet. I pull up in a black SUV across the street from her office. She strides out, looking polished and perfect, as ever. Exuding power and elegance in her heels and a fitted business suit. I climb out of the car and lean against it, my insides heating up at the sight of her. She's about to hail a taxi, so I call out her name. She stops, looks at me, and those sexy, sinful lips—not painted so rich red now, but nude—shape into a smile, and then she darts across the street, dodging traffic, making me panic for her safety. Briefcase swinging at her side, she charges at me, like she doesn't care who's watching.

Fuck. This woman. She lights up my entire world. My heart beats out of control, my grin tugging wider, and when she crashes into me, I catch her like I've been waiting my whole life to it. I hold her like I'll never let her go.

We don't even say anything. She looks up and I see it in her eyes. The way she looks at me, like she can't believe I'm real. Like I'm home. I'm hers. I see it all in her dark brown eyes, relief, adoration and happy surprise. A sharp, unmistakable flicker of love she hasn't said out loud yet. Words I'm biding my time to say to her. I drag her into my arms, and we kiss, hot and messy, like we've been starving for each other.

"Inside," I rasp, my voice as tight as my pants are now. I open the doors of the sleek black SUV I've hired, we make out like teenagers in the backseat, my hands all over her. She parts her legs, letting my fingers find their way to the silk of her panties. Sliding the flimsy fabric to the side, I sigh as I explore her slippery folds again. My cock hardens as the familiar contours of her body send urgent signals to mine.

She groans, jerking off the seat, nipping my ear as I pump my fingers inside her. I consider undoing her buttons, think about latching my lips to her breasts, when she murmurs, "I have a meeting I need to get to."

""I know. I checked." I watch her intently, as I finger fuck her, feel her legs part even more. We don't have much time, but we have enough for me to watch her come. "Don't worry. I'll drive you there," I murmur. "But I want to mess you up completely first."

She goes soft and boneless, flopping back against the seat. Her arousal paints my hand as I tweak and rub her clit. It takes all my restraint not to sink my head between her legs.

"The … meeting …" she pants.

"I know …" I slide another finger inside her, and she sinks lower against the backseat, her back arching off it. She throws her head back, her neck lengthening, my mouth watering at the expanse of bare skin. I consider giving her a hickey, branding her there, for all to see.

"Riooooooooooooo." She grinds against my hand desperate with need. "They brought it forward twenty minutes. I can't be late. Pierce will ..."

His name makes me move my hand away. The last thing I want is to put her career at risk. To give the fucker she works for a chance to be mad at her. I kiss her delectable mouth, my tongue finding hers. A rush of blood makes my cock swell. I want her all over again, and I kiss her, harder, framing her face with my hands, angling her mouth so I can kiss her deeper. She mewls against my mouth, her hand finding its way to my cock.

"Only took a few seconds," she chuckles.

Thoughts fill my mind. I consider fucking her like this, while she's sprawled so sensually across the seat. But I can't. It will have to wait until later. I pull back and admire her. She's such a beautiful sight for my eyes. And she's mine.

"I'll drive you there."

She adjusts herself, smoothing down her skirt and her hair. "This is a surprise." She curls her hand around the back of my neck, kissing me quickly. "How long do I have you for?"

"I'm at your disposal for the entire weekend, if you're not too busy."

She kisses me again. "Never too busy for you. We'll continue this later?"

"You bet."

She pulls out a mirror and checks her face and hair.

"Where to?" I ask, getting into the driver's seat, ready to be at her beck and call.

RAQUEL

THE MAN I LOVE IS THE BIGGEST TEASE. WHO WOULD HAVE thought I'd ever call Rio Knight the biggest Romeo? I cannot get enough of him.

Still smoothing down my skirt, I walk into the client meeting five minutes late. Pierce looks at me with contempt. I see cold hatred in his eyes too. Ever since I called him out on that sleazy comment, he's been distant. He completely blanks me. Doesn't even look my way. Barely speaks to me. I'm not sure if this patronizing, sneering down at me version of him is any better than the sleazy douchebag he was.

The meeting lasts for a painstaking hour. I force myself to focus, but it's almost impossible. My brain is here, but my heart and body are back in the SUV with Rio. I feel restless, itching to escape this meeting room, knowing that Rio is somewhere close, and waiting for me. Knowing that I have something I thought I'd never have. A man who loves me deeply, a man who cares, and a man who only wants the best for me.

It's knowing that there is more to my life than just my career. It's knowing that I have a home to go to, and not an empty apartment.

Rio stays for the weekend and we make love, and talk, even though we still dance around the case.

We even call Dex and Dani. It's good that they know because keeping this secret is getting harder. After we were forced to come out to them, Dani was so happy for me, but she hasn't stopped teasing me since.

"You're with a Knight?" she keeps saying, mock scandalized. "Don't you hate these people? You used to think say there were so despicable. Now you're telling me that this one actually got through to you?"

I have no defence, because Rio Knight did. I used to hate the Knights. I hated them before I even knew who they were. The name alone was enough to put me off them, and once I realized what they were like to have as family? I hated them even more.

But from the moment Rio walked into my life—or slouched lazily on a stool in an upscale Manhattan bar—I couldn't take my eyes off him.

"He was the man who broke me," I told Dani.

"They don't break us, Raquel," she replied. "They get lucky enough to keep us."

She's right.

Rio and I cook and stay in most of the weekend. Partly because I don't want to run into any work colleagues, especially Pierce, though mostly because we're still making love all over my apartment, and we've turned into hermits.

When we're not in bed, we cook, we watch TV, we talk about the future. I've started looking for jobs in New York, but I don't tell Rio that because I don't want to get his hopes up. Or mine.

But, I see him in my future. I need him in my future.

CHAPTER THIRTY-THREE

RAQUEL

THE FIRST I HEAR ABOUT IT IS WHEN ALMA CALLS ME, HER voice high and panicked. "Where did you get some of the data?" she demands.

My heart stops. "What data?"

"The data you used in the report, when you filed the injunction. "It's problematic."

"W-What do you mean it's problematic?" My insides hollow out and a heavy weight lands in my chest. Surely she's not talking about the file Rio gave me?

No. It can't be.

"It's false. It's falsified. The case has collapsed. They didn't just reject the injunction. They tore the whole case apart. We've lost credibility. The donors are panicking. We're withdrawing the case, Raquel. It's over."

"Over?" The word barely makes it out. The room tilts around me and I sink into my chair, as my legs begin to buckle.

"The court found inconsistencies in the data. They're

questioning the validity of your key evidence. The case has no legs to stand on." Alma's voice is grim.

I press a hand to my forehead, feeling dizzy. "They can't do that."

"They can, and they did."

I open my mouth but no words come out.

"Was this to do with Rio Knight? Did he play you?" Alma demands.

I clutch the phone tighter. "No. I-I ...I don't think so." That's just it. I'm not sure. But he wouldn't do this, would he? A dark, dark thought worms into existence. I'm still in shock, trying to process what she's telling me.

"He gave you a folder. You told me it was data by a third-party. Did you use it?"

"I-I ... I might have used a little of it."

I hear a loud exhale at the end of the phone. "You will have received an email from the Belizean court. Cross check the data specifically and get back to me."

My gut twists, and I'm wondering what it could be as I sink back into my chair. My heart slides further down my ribcage, like it's given up. Hands trembling, I pull up the file on my computer. It *could* be the data Rio gave me. I didn't intend to use any of it, but I did, because I was struggling to get the report together. I didn't use a lot of it. At least—I didn't think I did. But I think back to that night. It was late and I'd arrived at Rio's hotel room, where I'd gone only because the generator at my hotel failed.

That was my first mistake, going *there*.

And then one thing led to another, and another and we got carried away. I hadn't slept enough as it was, and with me and him making out, it's no wonder my mind was frazzled.

When I got back to my hotel, it was late. I was panicking, and rushing. I got sloppy, and I think I added more of the data than I intended to. I open my own records and pull up the same file I submitted last month. My fingers shake as I compare it line by line to what the court flagged.

I read through Section D. The part that refers to coral reef damage in the southern coast—it's not even consistent with the field notes I took on site. I never noticed. There are other consistencies throughout, all highlighted. A horrible thought creeps into my brain, sour and slow.

Rio did this to me. *Deliberately.* I was too trusting. Too reckless. And now the court's thrown it all out. It's rejected the injunction which means Delport Realty have won. Knight Enterprises have indirectly won. And the people of Belize have lost.

I feel wretched. Like someone's fisted me in my gut and winded me. I think back to the way he handed me that file. Confident and casual, like it wasn't a big deal. Like he expected me to trust him.

He even said I didn't need to take it. Made it sound so innocent.

I fell for it.

Was this to do with Rio Knight? Did he play you?

I can't get Alma's words out of my head. Because I think he did. He played me like a sad and sorry tune on a violin. I close the laptop slowly, like the truth might stop screaming at me if I just shut the lid.

Now I wonder, did he do this on purpose? I still can't believe it. He wouldn't. He couldn't. But then I think back to everything—his visits here, mine to New York. All those soft moments. All those silences. All those nights thick with heat and want. Wickedly wild and etched into my skin.

I sink further back into my chair, desk, hollow and stunned. I trusted him, emotionally and professionally. In doing so I forgot who he was. A Knight. Through and through. And this is what those people do. Rio has helped me to sabotage the case.

I call Alma back, my voice shaky, as I tell her it was the data from the file Rio gave me. I start to say I'm sorry, but she cuts me short. Tells me that the NGO has paused my work. They've launched an internal review.

"This was a betrayal. You let us down. You let me down, and you let yourself down. I trusted you to help us, but you've ruined everything."

I'm broken. My reputation is in tatters with the NGO, with the wonderful team at EcoGuardians, with Alma. She meant so much to me. Now she tells me that the case is damaged beyond repair. She doesn't have to tell me how betrayed she feels. I feel it in my bones.

My credibility is on the line and my future is hanging by a thread. I don't even want to know how Pierce will react. But I don't have to wait for long. As soon as I get off the phone from Alma, my office door slams wide open and Pierce storms in, his face twisted with fury, cheeks red, glaring at me in such a way I'm scared his eyeballs will pop out of his sockets.

"I got a call," he snaps. "Your documents were discredited. Your case has been officially thrown out."

I stare at him, cowering like a child, unable to formulate a word.

"What data did you use?" he cries. I look at him, cold and cornered. I tell him it was from a file passed to me by someone. "Who?" he barks. I know just how bad this looks.

"It came from a file. Passed to me by someone I trusted."

"Who?" he barks again.

I hesitate.

"I told you I didn't want you to file the injunction, but you went against my wishes. You submitted this mess. Don't make me ask you again. Where did the data come from?"

I pull open my drawer and hand him the folder. "I have it right here."

"Where the fuck is it from?" he bellows.

"Rio Knight gave it to me."

Silence.

"Rio. *Knight?*" His cutting tone slices through me, and I feel it shredding my gut into pieces. "You're fucking him," he states calmly, glaring at me. "I thought as much."

A warning bell goes off in my head. Before I can say another word, he beats me to it. "You have him running around after you, like some whipped billionaire lapdog, you ..." He screws his face up, like he's revolted by me. "Having his hands and mouth all over you, turning up at that meeting late, looking like a ..."

He saw.

He saw us together.

That night in the SUV, when Rio surprised me, when I climbed into his backseat and let him do what he wanted to with me.

He saw it, and the way he's looking at me? He's going to destroy me. I open my mouth but my throat closes. Something icy twists in my gut.

"This was before ... before anything happened between us," I say. Anything *major*, is what I mean to say, because up until then, I'd still crossed a line, albeit blurry.

Who am I kidding?

I can't defend myself. Everything points to me. Unethical, reckless, shameful behavior. I lost my head. That's what. Pierce laughs, and I wince. Because I know that prickly laugh well. It's a warning that something bad is coming my way.

"You know what the board's saying right now? That we've been compromised. That your relationship, personal or not, with a Knight has tainted this entire operation."

"Pierce—"

"You handed the court falsified evidence. You violated legal protocol. And you buried this organization's credibility in the process."

"I didn't know—"

"No," he snaps, "but you should have. Were you thinking, at all, while you were in Belize, or did one look at that Knight turn your brain to mush? You submitted evidence without verifying the source. That is negligence and that, is career-ending." He steps closer, drops his voice to a dangerous level. "The executive director is already calling for a full review. And if they ask me to make a recommendation?"

I already know what's coming.

"I'll say you breached protocol. That you compromised the mission. That your bias, your involvement, cost us one of the most important environmental cases we've ever brought to court."

That's what he's calling it now? He didn't think it was so important when it first dropped on his desk. I know what he's doing. He's going to paint me as the worst, humiliate me, and ruin me.

"You wanted to play the hero, but you've caused your own downfall. This is what happens when you mix business with bedtime."

"Please don't do this," I whisper.

But he's already walking away.

"Oh, I didn't do this. You did this to yourself," he says. "You handed them everything they needed to tear us apart."

The door slams shut behind him.

And I fall apart.

CHAPTER THIRTY-FOUR

RAQUEL

I GO HOME SOON AFTER THE CONFRONTATION WITH PIERCE.

I'm in pieces, barely treading water in the bad news swimming around me. It's too much to process; too many memories and conversations to sift through, to make sense of. I can't wrap my head around it all, and a part of me wishes this were just a big, bad dream I'm soon going to wake up from.

Here in my apartment, sitting on the couch, clutching a cushion, staring absently at the coffee table, nothing has changed. Time still marches on, and I still feel as lost and as hopeless as ever. I pinch the space between my eyes, hoping to relieve the tension, but restlessness takes a hold of me, leaving me feeling uneasy all over.

A montage flashes before my eyes, of my career, and everything I've worked so hard for. The sacrifices I've made. Unlike Dani, I don't come from wealth or power. I've had to earn my place and build my reputation. I built it inch by inch. One brick at a time.

And now it's gone. All because of a folder. Because I trusted. Because I was blindsided by a man I should have stayed away from.

Remembering Rio makes my stomach twist so hard, I brace myself as the nausea claws through me. Tears slide down my cheeks, hot, fast, and bitter. He said he believed in me. Said he respected the work I was doing. Said he cared. He made me feel like we belonged together.

How could he do this to me?

Why would he?

Is it possible that he didn't know?

No. He's far too smart to put himself at risk.

It's my fault, because I should have known better.

I need to hear his take on things. I grab my phone, my fingers wet and slippery, but have trouble hitting the call button. My hands shake so badly I can barely hold it to my ear. It rings once, twice, and then he answers.

"Princesa?" His voice is filled with joy. I imagine him smiling, getting ready to say something flirty, or dirty. Something familiar that would make me melt, only now it makes me want to retch.

"Don't call me that," I snap, my voice breaking. I hate that I'm falling apart so easily.

There's a pause. "What's wrong?" His tone changes, filling with concern, shock and worry.

I give a brittle laugh. "You gave me falsified data, Knight. You handed me a folder full of fabricated environmental evidence. The court threw out the injunction."

"What?" The shock is real. He's a damn good actor. I bet they're all trained for this. "Raquel, what are you talk—"

"You gave me the data," I say quietly, cutting his lies short. "The one you said was from a reliable source. You gave it to me saying it might help, but it helped throw the case out of court. You jeopardized me intentionally. I trusted you."

"No," he gasps. For a minute it sounds genuine. Then I remind myself of how good he is. How good they are, at coverups.

"I didn't know it was fake," he maintains.

"The hell you didn't. Where did you get it?" I demand. "Where was it from?"

There's a pause, and right there, his hesitation is the confirmation I need. He can't answer.

Because he's been caught.

I feel like the roof caved in on me. Like my life as I knew it, is over, because, in a way, I lived for my career, and that just ended.

"You used me," I say, voice wavering. "I trusted you. I used that data. I put my name on it and now everything I've worked for—everything—is gone."

"Raquel," he says again, but it's too late.

I hang up, but he calls me back straightaway. "Listen, just, please, listen," he begs. "Don't hang up." It's the desperate tone in his voice, the raw, almost unsteady pitch that cuts straight through my defenses. It makes me stay on the line.

"I had no idea. My old man told me about the data. He didn't tell me to give it to you. He didn't even know you were there. It was my idea, and the only reason I decided to give it to you was because … I wanted a reason to see you, and it seemed like the right thing to do."

I scoff. "I wish I hadn't met you out there. I wish you hadn't been sent there. I wish it had been someone else."

I hear a noise, something low, and undecipherable. "Please let me finish. You have every right to hate me, but I wish you would believe me. This is the first I've heard that the injunction request was denied. I thought the old man would have told me." He seems to mutter this to himself.

"They've withdrawn the case. My reputation is in tatters. Alma and EcoGuardians feel betrayed and let down. Pierce knows about us, and he's letting me go."

"What?"

"You people won. You and Delport, and your family. The eco resort wins. Congratulations. You can continue with construction and still open on time, if you bring in enough workers and pay them a pittance, while turning their water to poison. You should feel proud of yourself, because you got everything you wanted."

"I didn't want this." His words are strained, like he's fighting for survival. "I understand you not believing me, but I'm going to prove it to you that I had nothing to do with this. I love you, Raquel. Now's not the right time to say it, but it feels like you never want to see or hear from me again, but I'm not going to let you walk away. I love you. I'm madly in love and I have been, maybe I fell for you that night we played strip poker. It was nothing to do with the card game. It was all to do with you."

"Just … stop. Right there."

"This isn't the end of it, Raquel."

"You don't get to have a say in it, Knight."

I hang up, and switch my cell phone off.

CHAPTER THIRTY-FIVE

RIO

I CALL RAQUEL BACK WHEN SHE HANGS UP AGAIN, BECAUSE goddamnit, she doesn't believe me. But her cell phone goes straight to voice mail.

She doesn't want to talk to me and now I feel a piece of me start to fray, tearing at the seams. Raquel wants nothing to do with me. Only because she thinks I did this to her. That I set her up.

I sit at my desk staring at my phone like maybe if I hold it long enough, this will all go away. Like if I call her now, she'll pick up and say it was a joke. That she wanted to prank me. That the court didn't throw out the injunction, her name isn't ruined, and I didn't give her the very thing that destroyed her.

But it's not a joke, it's the truth.

The data I gave her, thinking it would help, the data I used as excuse just to see her again, is what broke us apart.

I didn't lie when I told her it came from a reliable source. I thought it did. I thought it had been thoroughly vetted, but I now see what I should have been smart enough to see then. It was too convenient. Too perfectly timed.

Just like Dex said.

Me being in Belize, the same time that Raquel was. Working on the same case. The old man knew. He always knows. He's like some cruel God who plays with people's lives. An all-seeing bastard who thrives on ruin.

I shove back from my desk, my mind spinning now that I suddenly see what I should have seen all along.

This wasn't fate. This was calculated. This was all him. He's capable of much more than I've ever led myself to believe.

I storm out of my office and down the hall, jaw clenched so tight I feel a molar crack. I don't even wait for his assistant. I shove the door open to find him sitting behind his desk, looking amused before he even sees my face.

He's been waiting for me, knowing about the injunction being thrown out. Funny how he still hasn't said a word to me.

"You gave me that data," I hiss, barely recognizing my own voice. "You said it was from a third-party. That it was verified and clean."

"I did, and it was," he says coolly.

I stare at him. "You knew it was falsified."

He says nothing, but his cold-as-ice eyes look back at me, his lips turn up at the corners. The fucker is smirking. "Something wrong?"

"You know perfectly well what's wrong." I stand across from him, fists buried deep in my pockets, shaking with restraint. Every cell in my body screaming to punch him as I struggle to contain my fury.

"You knew Raquel was on the case, didn't you? That's why you sent me to Belize."

"Knew?" He sits back in his chair. "The court needed a reason to throw it out. I gave them one."

"You used me."

"No," he says, almost gleeful now. "I handed you the match. You're the one who lit it."

My breath stutters. I want to hit something. Throw something. But I don't. Instead, I hear my own voice crack. "You wanted to destroy Raquel?"

"She was never the target. Not directly. She was just collateral."

"Then? *I* was the target?" I ask, in disbelief. Me, *his son*? "Why?"

"You needed to be taught a lesson. Helping Dex, ganging up on me with your brothers, fighting me, going against me. Me?" His voice lifts a little at the end, the only clue I have that he's barely keeping it together.

This is about AO Eletronica. It all clicks into place. He was pissed when we helped get control of that company back to its rightful owner.

I look at him then, and see past the polished suit and the cool façade. He's unraveling, too. We've all started to see it, ever since Jett stood up to him at the dinner, with Cari by his side. Then Dex followed suit, in his own way. It feels like the old man is scared of losing control, and he can't take it.

"How?" I snap.

"Bringing you both down a peg or three. Giving you enough rope to let your girlfriend hang herself with it."

"You fucking bastard." My fists almost fly out of my pockets, but I somehow manage to keep them there. "Raquel had nothing to do with AO Eletronica."

"But you did, and your brothers, and Dex."

What the fuck?

What the actual fuck is wrong with this man? Raquel's world has imploded and he's happy about her downfall. I still don't understand. "What the fuck has Raquel got to do with AO Eletronica?"

"She was instrumental in getting to you." He smooths his hand over his tie.

Bile rises in my throat, thick, bitter, and burning. "You thought we were an item?"

He pauses, searching my face. "Aren't you?"

I go cold.

He knows.

"You brought her down to get to me?"

I feel sick to my stomach that he knows so much. I had no clue about any of this. No point looking even more stupid than I already feel. No point in pretending she doesn't mean anything to me.

"How?" My stomach prepares to drop. I feel like I'm at the top of a rollercoaster, about to dive to my death.

"You're the one who handed her the folder," he says, low and quiet. "Not me. I never even met the girl, to talk to. I know she was there, at the wedding in São Paulo. I know you, Dex and Daniela met her in Miami."

The sly fox. "Did you have private investigators follow us?" Because it starts to make sense.

"Didn't need to. The wedding and the golden couple, your half-brother and his fake wife—"

"They got engaged recently, for real this time. They're in love."

"Love," he snarls, like the word is poison. "Those two seem to cause a stir wherever they go. The media did the rest. Photos of you and Raquel in Miami surfaced. I didn't have to do a thing."

"And yet, somehow you did, and you seem so fucking unbelievably proud of yourself."

"As far as the eco resort goes, yes. With no injunction,

construction resumes immediately. The bulldozers roll at sunrise."

"But this isn't about the eco resort, is it?" This is personal. This is about breaking the woman I love and punishing me. "You knew I cared about her."

The old man sighs. "Of course I did. That's why it worked."

An ugly silence stretches between us, heavy and final.

"How... how did you ensure she got the case?" I always was suspicious of Raquel and I being in Belize at the same time, but I wanted to believe in fate.

The old man huffs out a sigh, likes he's bored with having to explain to me. "When you've been around as long as I have, you have eyes and ears on the ground. People do what you tell them. It's easy."

The sonofabitch.

"I called an old golfing friend," he continues. "One of the people who founded the law firm in Miami. William Roth, a founding partner, long since retired. But very much aware of the skeletons in Pierce Tovey's closet. Sexual misconduct. Women leaving left and right. Interns. Associates."

A memory slams into me.

Raquel.

Telling me about how that asshole made her feel. "You blackmailed him."

"I offered him a choice. Give her the case, or deal with the fallout."

I stiffen, hatred seizing every inch of me. He's talking about her as if she's just another pawn. Another tool in his twisted game. "You bribed Roth, to put pressure on Tovey?"

"I did whatever it took for the case to end up on her desk. Her boss doesn't like her doing pro bono work, so I pulled some strings to make it happen."

My stomach turns as I try to get to grips with the scale of the old man's manipulation.

"I have people everywhere. People who can do things for me. When you have more money than you know what to do with, you can do anything, be anything, get anything. People will do as you command."

This man is dangerous. He's a fucking monster. For all his wealth and finesse, this man has morals no better than a barbarian.

"Once she was dealing with the case it was easy. Pierce thought it would be over after the legal review. It should have been, but the woman heading up the NGO is smart, and didn't let it go. She's like a territorial Doberman and she wanted to file an injunction. Pierce didn't want Raquel to have any skin in the fight. He needed her to come back. I placed pressure. Told Roth to let him see it through. Let Raquel do what she thought she could do. Give her enough rope to hang herself with, and she did."

I swallow, my insides are in upheaval, trying to absorb everything the old man is telling me, calmly and quietly, like a bedtime story, only, it's nothing that will let me sleep. This is the stuff of nightmares.

"You went to all that trouble?" My sarcasm is caustic.

"These things require attention to detail. They require finesse and strategy." He speaks with pride, as if manipulating people's lives is like a game of chess.

"And me?" I ask, hollow.

"You were supposed to go to Verona, something to do with the Cazale hotels, but I needed you in Belize. It all came together so easily. It was perfect. You deal with hotels and real estate, but if you hadn't, I would have found a way to put you in Belize."

The fucker would have. He absolutely would have. I feel

like we're all just puppets in his little show, and he's the grand master pulling our strings.

"And if I hadn't given her the file?" I demand. "If I hadn't played into your hands?"

The old man returns to his desk, and sits back down. "There were other failsafes. Other weak points. I never rely on one play. I could've planted a third-party study. Bribed land registry clerks. It's all about pressure. But your move was perfect. She trusted you. You were the fire." He chuckles to himself and leans forward, looking proud. "And it worked."

"What the fuck were you hoping to gain?"

He leans across the table. Eyes glinting like a serpent. His smile drops. "No one outplays me. Do you understand, boy?"

My stomach knots. My blood boils. I feel like I might explode. I suddenly get what this is all about.

"You gang up against me? You get Matteo and Enzo, and help Dex? Against me?" he says quietly. I would prefer it if he raised his voice, or showed some semblance of losing control, but he's still, and deathly quiet. Not losing his shit. He's an absolute fucking psycho.

The only thing that goes through my mind? How did Mama ever fall for him?

"I need you to understand," he says slowly, "that every time you fight me, you lose something more than you realize."

My breath catches. My pulse roars in my eyes. What. The. Fuck. He made it happen. He gave me the match, and I handed it to Raquel. This man didn't just sabotage Raquel's career—he burned it to the ground. Everything she was proud of, her name, standing up for marginalized communities. Everything that mattered to her, is gone.

And he used me to do it. This fucker was the architect of that. He lined up the dominoes and played the long game. He watched and waited. "You're sick." This was about revenge. About wanting to punish us, and make us get back in line.

He couldn't punish Dex, because Dex is in love and engaged, and doing his thing.

But he could punish me, and he did.

"I'm effective."

"Why are you telling me this?"

"So that you never forget what you're up against."

I almost stumble backward. The sheer audacity. The ice-cold menace in every word. He thinks this is over. That he's won.

"You think we're scared of you? Not just me, Matteo and Enzo, but Jett, Dex and Zach?"

He shrugs. "I think you like to pretend you're not. I'll let you dwell in your ignorance, but don't ever forget, you all rely on my empire. My money. My control. And I'm the one holding the reins."

And that's the awful truth. The reason why we stay. Why we don't walk away and find our peace. Because he's the puppet master of Knight Enterprises.

"Careful, *Father.*" My low voice is a warning. "All empires fall, eventually."

My pulse hammers in my throat as I turn to leave, jaw clenched, heartbeat racing like I've run the four-minute mile in three.

This man will pay for what he did to Raquel.

There will be consequences.

I'll make sure of it.

CHAPTER THIRTY-SIX

RIO

I STORM OUT OF MY FATHER'S OFFICE, MY JAW CLENCHED SO tight it aches.

My hands are fists, and my chest burns with rage I can barely contain as I process what he's revealed, and so proudly, too. He didn't even try to hide his manipulative actions. He seemed to brag about them. It unnerves me, how long he'd been sowing the seeds for his revenge.

Because that's exactly what this is. *Revenge.* To keep me in line, and by example, my brothers. To prevent us from working together.

I feel sick. He didn't just sabotage Raquel's life, he used her to get to me. He knew exactly how I felt about her. That's why he did it.

By the time I reach my office, I'm already pulling out my phone. I know she won't answer, but I call anyway.

It goes to voicemail. My insides enflame, heat surging through me like a fuse has been lit. She doesn't want to talk to me. She doesn't want to hear from me. I grip the cell phone so tightly my knuckles turn white. I've just destroyed her life. She's pissed at me, thinks I betrayed her. Every precious moment we had, is gone. She warned me. Tried to stay away from the Knights, but I convinced her otherwise.

Told her I was different. I wasn't him.

Now, with what's gone down, she must think I'm just like him. Nothing could be further from the truth. Maybe she's busy, with a client? I quickly call her office, and the call goes through to reception.

"Raquel Monteiro," I say, feeling hopeful. She can't escape me that easily.

"I'm sorry, sir, but Raquel Monteiro no longer works for the company." For a second, I'm sure I've misheard. "What?" I feel like I've been hacked in two. "What do you mean she no longer works for the company?" Fuck. It's worse than I thought. "Was she fired?" I ask, my voice cold enough to freeze the air between us.

"I'm sorry, sir, I can't divulge any information. Ms. Monteiro is no longer with us."

Hand shaking, I slam my cell phone onto my desk, hard. "Fuck this shit." My pulse roars in my ears.

He won.

The fucking old man won.

I can't believe this. The old man knew. He did this. He had a hand in Raquel's firing. Is this what he meant by getting to her through me?

The consequences of that stupid file reach so fucking deep. If it hadn't been that, it would have been something else. The old man has not only cost Raquel her reputation, shredded her case to bits, he's ruined her.

She lived for her work. She was proud of what she did. Granted, she hated where she was, but to be fired? I'm not surprised she never answered my call. I'm not staying here another damn second. I'm going to her.

And I'm taking the fucking private jet.

HOURS LATER, I'M OUTSIDE HER APARTMENT, MY HEARTBEAT A steady, punishing drumbeat. I need to see her. Tell her I'm going to fix it. I'm going to fight the old man, and play it dirty, like he does.

I knock. No answer.

"Raquel." I knock again. Still nothing.

She's not a coward. She'll face me. She has to. And if she doesn't…

"Raquel, it's me. I need to speak to you. I heard about the job." I knock again, and now I'm ready to break the damn door down. "

The door opens. The sight of her like this, something I've never seen, Raquel, broken, hits me like a punch to the chest. Her eyes are red-rimmed, her cheeks blotchy from crying. She looks like she's been through hell. I step in. She steps back, but she doesn't shut me out.

That's something. I close the door behind me, the click loud in the silence.

It's late. Sweat clings to me, my shirt sticks to my back. She looks so gaunt, it scares me.

She stares at me blankly. "Pierce fired me."

"I'm sorry. I heard. He's a fucking asshole." My gut twists. For someone like Raquel, who loves her job so fiercely, it must feel like she's lost some of her identity. All because of the old man, and me.

She's about to walk away, when I grab her wrist. "Don't walk away."

She wrenches her wrist free. "What is there to say? I can't even bring myself to look at you." She spits the words with such venom, I shirk back I shock. She hates me because she blames me for this.

"Don't do this. I came here so we could talk. Because it was important I see you face to face. I need you to believe me."

"Well, I *don't*." She yells so loudly, I startle, not recognizing the woman before me. I let in a shaky breath, because I won't give up. "I should never have believed you. I should never have trusted you."

"It's important. Please." The pleading in my voice must have had some effect, because she folds her arms and glares at me defiantly. At least I have her attention. "I was ten years old when I learned the man I trusted was a liar and a cheat. That same man is the one who's trying to break me now, by getting to you. By destroying you."

Her eyes widen, fear lancing through them. "What do you mean?"

"That's why I'm here, now. I'm begging you to listen, and I don't beg, Raquel. I've never begged in my life."

She takes a step back. "Then don't start now."

I step forward, because I'm not letting her get away. "I will. For you, I will." There's a desperation in my voice that is unfamiliar. "That monster who calls himself my father wants to break me, and he thinks he can by ruining you, by breaking us up."

"How does he even know we're together?"

"He has ways and means. Paparazzi photos. That's not important, what's important is that you listen to me. I had a meeting with him this morning. I wish I could've recorded it, but I didn't. I was too shocked. I didn't realize what I was walking into when he called me into his office.."

I pace around her living room. She doesn't sit down, just stands there, arms folded, watching me.

"He's such a Machiavellian bastard. He set you up. Belize was a real situation that he manipulated to set you up. Then he sat back and watched you fall."

She shakes her head in disbelief. I move towards her, almost reach out and touch her, and fight the need to do so. "It sounds incredulous, I know, but he manipulated the entire situation. He worked it so that you'd get this case. He said Pierce didn't want you to have it. That he doesn't like you working pro bono. He also knew about Tovey's sexual harassment of his employees—something else you mentioned to me. Turns out, William Roth knew, too, and he buried it. The old man and Roth know each other. They've played golf together, and the old man knew exactly what to threaten Roth with."

Her arms fall to her sides, her brow creasing. "Surely that's not … not possible?"

"It is, and it was, and it happened. He lined up all the dominoes, just for this to happen."

"For me to lose my job?"

"For all of it. It was to teach *me* a lesson, to teach us. Me and the other Knights, He didn't like that we were starting to band together, and that his divide and conquer strategy was waning. So he fought back hard, worked on way to get us back in line."

"It sounds too farfetched."

"I know." I reach out to cup her face, then slide my hand back into my pockets. This is so damn hard. She's hurting, and all I want is to hold her and make everything be right again for her. Not even being able to touch her, it's slicing a blade against my own skin. The restraint cuts sharp and deep, because every instinct in me screams to take her pain. "He got Roth to pressure Tovey to make sure you took the case. He manipulated us. It's no surprise to me, because I know what he's capable of, but he knew you'd be in Belize, and that's why he sent me there. He wanted this to happen, but he didn't expect Alma to file an injunction. That threw him. Another thing you need to know is if I hadn't offered you the data file, he would have found something else. He would have found another way to bring you down and he'd have pinned it on me anyway. That man is relentless. As for the data, I'm not a scientist. I didn't compile that report myself. I'm not detail-oriented like that, but more than that, I would never do this to you. This was never about the file. It was about taking us both down, because I care about you."

"But what does that achieve?"

"The only reason he wanted to hurt you was to punish me because of what I did with Dex, Matteo, and Enzo. When we got together to help Dani's father. I told you the old man forces us to attend family dinners, keeps us in different apartment blocks, keeps us divided. Us working together, shocked him. That's why he did this. He couldn't get to Dex, because Dex and Dani are strong, they love each other. He can't touch them. So he came for me. He wanted to teach me a lesson and make me the scapegoat, to warn the others."

I stop, and stare at her, needing a reaction, but she looks at me blankly. Her face is so pale. Her eyes dull. There is no spark, no vivacity. The fucker did destroy her. I step towards her, needing to hold her, and comfort her.

"Don't." She backs away, her voice a warning.

I stop, halted by her cutting tone. She doesn't want me anywhere near her. I understand, but I feel defeated, because she doesn't believe me. I unfurl my hands, only realizing now that I'd been fisting them tightly. I've failed to convince her.

"I just wanted to tell you, in person." I walk towards the door feeling like a failure. I flew here thinking she'd understand, but this all sounds so crazy, so unreal, she doesn't believe me.

How can she, because only a Knight would understand the depth of the old man's manipulation and deceit.

It's late, when I turn up outside Dex's apartment. He looks shocked to see me.

"Jesus. What the hell happened to you?"

I walk inside.

"You look like shit, bro. What's going on?"

Dani appears, and the way she looks at me, tells me I must look like death. I feel like it.

I head towards the mini-bar and pour myself a drink, then another one, and then I tell them both how my day went. The meeting with the old man, the visit to Raquel, peppering in just enough about the eco-resort and the injunction, and the data file, to explain everything.

"What the—brother, are you serious?" Dex gets up and stomps around, looking like he can't quite believe it. Dani sits on the couch, speechless. She lowers her head into her hands. "You saw Raquel?"

I nod.

"And your father planned all of this?" she asks, stunned.

"Your soon to be father-in-law," I clarify, not that I want her to have second thoughts about marrying Dex.

Dani looks worried. "How was Raquel?"

"She's not really talking to me."

Before I can even finish, she reaches for her phone and starts talking to Raquel. My hopes lift. Maybe Dani can comfort her. Make her feel better. Dani slips away from us, needing privacy. I understand it. Raquel won't want to talk if she knows I'm around.

Dex looks at me. "What are you going to do, brother?"

"Need to find a way to deal with him. Can you fucking believe this?"

"No." Dex's jaw clenches, and his body tenses like he's about to punch something. I sit back on the couch, contempt and revulsion simmering in my veins, wondering why the old man always fucks up our lives. "You'd think he'd stop trying to control us." It's something I've thought about a lot. "He knows he can keep us here. He has control of the money. The empire."

Dex blows out a breath. "I'm so tempted to walk the fuck away."

"Me too. Sometimes."

"Why don't we?"

"Because we're better together. Because we're family. And because... do we want him to get the better of us?"

Dex shrugs. "I don't want him to die, but sometimes ..."

"I don't care how he lives," I snap. "He ruined the lives of my mother. Your mother. This isn't a normal family. This is a crazy dysfunctional clan." I swipe a hand through my hair, pacing. I can't shake the image of what he's done. Of what we lost. "He destroyed Aurora, his wife, your mother, and he wrecked my mother's life. We were all so young. Just kids. We didn't understand. And now he's still trying to wreck our lives."

"He tries, but we don't let him," Dex says, his voice quiet. "We're pushing back."

"I need to fix things for Raquel. She wants nothing more to do with me. She's pissed."

"I understand why," Dex says. "I remember how it was when Dani got upset with me and left."

"We've got to work on something." I mutter. "I've got

people in and I'm already looking into things. It's not true. None of it's true."

"What's not true?" Dex asks slowly.

I tell him everything. About Belize and the eco resort, and how everyone pulled the wool over my eyes.

"These are standard business practices for a lot of corporates, bro."

"I know. That's what the old man says," I say quietly. "Doesn't have to be that way though, does it? Do we need to skimp on profit margins? Pay the workers so low? Cut corners?"

Dex sits back, watches me quietly.

"No, we fucking don't." I answer my own question.

"We need to be better," Dex offers. "We need to *do* better."

"Just because the old man says it's got to be done a certain way doesn't mean it has to stay that way. I don't want to be like him. I don't want to inherit his practices. I don't want Knight Enterprises to be a dirty, sleazy, greedy company that ruins everything in its wake." I pause. "He always talks about legacy. But maybe Knight Enterprises deserves a better legacy than the one the old man gives."

Dex places his ankle on the knee of his other leg. "Tell me whatever you need."

"I have an idea. For now, I need Dani to be there for Raquel."

"She will be. Don't you worry. Those girls are like sisters."

"Are we just one big family?" I say, almost smiling.

"You're getting cheesy on me, bro."

We sit quietly, drinking, contemplating. When Dani finishes her phone call, she walks back in. "I'm going to Miami, first thing tomorrow morning, to check in on Raquel."

"Thank you."

"She would have done the same for me," Dani replies.

I leave and head back home, mulling things over and trying to figure out what I'm going to do. Then I pick up the phone and call Tomas.

RAQUEL

DANI ARRIVES ON MY DOORSTEP FIRST THING THE NEXT morning.

I fall into her arms with relief. I'm all out of tears, but now they start up again.

"Hey, hey." She strokes my hair. "Come on, hon. You don't even have to tell me everything. You don't have to talk about it, until you're ready. I'm here for you, to cook for you, to listen to you, whatever you want, I'm here for you."

I saw my face in the mirror, just before I opened the door. My eyes are red-rimmed. I look a wreck. I've lost my job. Alma doesn't want to talk to me. And Rio turned up yesterday with the most ridiculous story. I already knew that Paul Knight was devious, but this level of calculation defies comprehension. And, for revenge? Against his *son?* This man has never known, or will ever know, the meaning of family.

Dani being here is true friendship. True sisterhood. True family. I love this girl with all my heart, and my life would be so much bleaker without her in it. We sit in my living room, Kleenex tissues all spread out over my couch, and I hastily try to tidy up. But she stops me.

"Just sit, and talk. I'll do the rest." She picks up my crumpled tissues, some soggy, others long dried out, and she doesn't balk in disgust. She simply gets on with it like its no big deal. And just like that it feels like such a big deal to me that she cares so much. Dani has always shown up for me. We're not bound by blood, but by choice, and whether I'm crying, heartbroken, raging, or worn out, she somehow knows and appears when I need her the most. She clears up the mess, picks it up, holds it, clears the space for me to feel whole again. She never lets me go through the bad times alone, in the same way that I would never let her. We've always been there for one another.

I've lost my job. My reputation is at risk of being maligned. I don't expect Pierce to go easy on me. Now I'm powerless. I feel foolish for letting myself believe that me and Rio could ever work, and Dani being here is a salve on the entire, bloody wound.

Rio talking about the meeting he'd had with the old man. He was angry and seething with hatred, and while it sounded so farfetched that at first I couldn't wrap my head around it, by the time he left, I started to believe everything he told me. But today, I don't know what to believe.

I'm shocked by the lengths that man will go to ruin his family. It makes no sense. But Paul Knight did this to his wife. He already had a wife, and a family, and he went and created another one. He's the type of man who takes, takes, takes.

Dani's sitting on the couch, which is now tissue-free.

"Want me to make you something to eat?" she asks.

I shake my head and instead tell her about the Rio's visit yesterday, only to discover that he went over to Dex's place late last night.

"He was a mess. He really was," she tells me. "I'm not telling you this to feel sorry for him, but he looked broken."

I saw it myself. I *heard* it in his voice. But my head is all over the place again and nothing seems solid. I feel fractured, and unsteady, like I'm unravelling at the seams and I don't know how to hold myself together. This state of weakness isn't something I'm familiar with.

Before Rio and I got close, and I abhorred the Knights, I was of the opinion that a man like Rio would learn his ways from the master of deception.

Paul Knight has inflicted so much damage to other people. I already knew that he was the worst. He's despicable, evil, and greedy. But Rio always told me it wasn't true. That he wasn't a monster. That it was all Paul. That he's nothing like his father.

He offered me the data file, but he didn't force it on me.

I was the one who took it. The decision was mine. But it was planted. Fed to me through him, and then it blew up and I got discredited because of it. I remember what Rio said. He said if his father hadn't done it this way, he would've found another way.

"I don't hate him," I say, "but I've questioned every conversation, every interaction we've had and I'm as confused as ever now because while I want to believe him, I'm too scared to trust him again. Do you ever worry that they have a part of their father in them?"

Dani looks at me. "I worried about it once, but I've come to know that Dex isn't like that at all. It's a valid concern, and I totally get why you're thinking it, but if you can find it in your heart to give Rio a chance, you'll see that he's not like that either."

I have a feeling she's right, but I'm too bruised by all that's happened. It's not only my personal life, but my professional life that has taken such a hit. Everything I lived for is gone. Alma, Vilma and Edwin—all the people at EcoGuardians—they must think I'm a fake and a phony and a cop-out and a sell-out.

My credibility is gone. And the man I trusted with my body, my career, my heart—somehow was the weapon that his father used to ruin me. I might've been manipulated. And Rio might've been a part of it. But he was an innocent bystander. He didn't know. If I was played, so was he.

What am I going to do? It doesn't matter. Because my bestie is here, and together we'll figure it out.

I haven't told my mom yet. I don't want her to worry about me. She worries as it is because she thinks I'm overworked. I haven't told her about Rio. We do have our regular weekly calls. She could tell something was wrong, but I didn't tell her. But she knows something is up.

"I gave Dex a chance," Dani says. "I was about to marry Oscar, and Dex came and saved me."

"Rio saved me."

"From what?"

I don't need to tell her all the details, but I think back to the night of the storm when he came looking for me.

I don't think I could have survived out there by myself. I would have survived somehow, sitting in that hut by myself, all alone and scared, but having Rio there was a lifeline.

He was my lifeline.

He put his life at risk to come looking for me.

He proved to me that night that he isn't his father, and while I want so much to think we could salvage what he had, my life is such a mess right now. Everything I worked for has fallen apart, and I need time to recover from this.

"Tell me what you need me to do," Dani says, resting her hand on my arm.

"I just need to be here, and I love that you came here for me."

"Like, you didn't come running for me," she says. "I remember how you've always been there for me, turning up out of the blue when I said to you I was marrying a stranger."

I sigh, remembering. ""That was the night I met Rio. Sitting at the bar, keeping an eye on you and Dex."

"Was it such a bad thing?" Dani asks, tentatively, "Being out there with him?"

"It was wonderful, how we slowly, came together, but when we got back, that's when I knew he was special."

"Special?" Dani lifts a brow.

I shrug. "I don't know. Sometimes when we're together, since we got back from Belize, Rio and I ... we've had such amazing weekends.

Being away from the case and the Eco resort. Forgetting that we're on opposing sites. It's been the best thing I've ever had."

She nods. "That's what it's like, with these boys. When I said to you they're lucky to have us, I meant it. I think it also brings out the best in them."

CHAPTER THIRTY-SEVEN

RIO

Dex and I have been working nonstop.

I didn't want to get the others involved, not when this is going to piss the old man off bigtime. I don't want him going after them the way he went after me, though after this, hopefully it will make him pause and think. If he's capable of such things.

Dani's been staying with Raquel and I've been hearing updates through Dex. Little slivers of information of how she's holding up.

I'm still so cut up about her being fired. That news devastated me. I know how deep that must hurt. And just as bad, EcoGuardians, the people she genuinely respected, feel let down by her. I know how much they meant to her, and how much she meant to them.

It fucking sucks, all of it. What sucks most of all is how much damage the old man causes for the sake of propping up his own ego. He doesn't care about anyone but himself, and he'd burn down someone's life so he could stand taller in the ashes of theirs.

Just so he can convince himself that we're all still dancing in the palm of his hand.

Well. Screw him.

I've called a board meeting, something that's never happened before, not for something like this. Maximum public stakes. Irreversible fallout. A corporate reckoning. Dex and I rehearsed it over and over again until every step, every word is firm in my muscle memory, but still, the weight of what I'm about to do weighs heavily.

You don't expose the old man and forget about it. But that's the only way I can think of to turn this around. Funny how life shifts. Not long ago, it was me and my brothers fighting alongside Dex, to help Dani's father.

Now it's me and Dex fighting to help Raquel.

This seems like the perfect opportunity to expose the old man for what he is. Up until now we've never done anything like this, but he seems to be getting worse. He's becoming more emboldened. Dude thinks he can manipulate us and bend us to his will.

He issued veiled threats and quiet warnings. Wanted me to turn a blind eye and shut the hell up. I can't do that. This Eco resort isn't just some glossy PR stunt. It's a lie. A front for environmental crimes and, worse than that, it was the catalyst to bring down the woman I love.

Tomas has been helping me from the ground in Belize. He's being brave, putting himself in danger, and I appreciate all he's doing.

He's tracked down internal emails, real evidence, showing that the old man ordered the falsified data. There are memos going back over a year, proving that Delport orchestrated an intentional cover-up.

We have documents detailing first-hand proof that directly contradicts the reports Raquel submitted.

She didn't fail. She was set up and I have everything I need to expose the old man and I plan to do it publicly—not over some torturous Knight family dinner where we smile through gritted teeth and try to force the food down.

This one gets resolved in a board meeting. The proper way.

Vilma reached out to me, via Tomas. She warned me that she was taking a big personal risk, but when she heard about Raquel, she was upset. She told me, "You didn't get this from me. I'm not doing this for you—I'm doing it for her. Raquel deserves better than silence. And if I lose my job over this, so be it."

She said she still believes in EcoGuardians, but Raquel didn't fail the NGO, they failed her. To keep her safe, I've asked her to act as a technical reviewer. That's all. I've asked her to verify environmental inconsistencies in the data that the old man via the third-party, submitted.

She's risking her job and reputation to do what's right. Just like Raquel did.

Now I'm going to defend Raquel in front of the entire board.I can't legally stream the board meeting live, because its a private and confidential, but I need to show Raquel that I did it. I stood up for her, and I stood up to the old man.

Dani's been working to bring Raquel to New York, to meet Cari. To have a change of scenery. Dani's arranged it so that the girls have a relaxing evening in, with wine and cheese and whatever the heck they want.

I'm going to publicly defend the woman I love and I don't care if it costs me my position in the company.

I need to vindicate her. I need to restore her career—or at least salvage her name. Maybe she doesn't want to go back to

Tovey & Roth. Maybe that chapter is closed. But her reputation deserves better than what the old man did to it.

She deserves to know that when I said I loved her, that I cared about her, that I wanted the best for her—that I meant it. It wasn't just empty words.

I want the old man's actions exposed and challenged in real time. I want the damage to be visible, but the fallout must be strategic, and calculated.

Knight Enterprises can't be burned to the ground, not while there's still so much tied to it.

We can't afford to walk away from it, and no way can we afford to ruin it. The old man's authority will be wounded, not destroyed. He'll be hit with something. Up to him how he weathers it. Personally, I don't care what this costs me. I want an apology to Raquel. I want her name cleared, her reputation restored. I want her life to be put back together again.

It's the only reason I'm doing this.

***

RAQUEL

"Come on." Dani grins, looping her arm through mine. "It's going to be fun."

We're having a girls' night out. Kind of. At Jett's apartment. It's a place I've *never* been to. I get to see where the others live —Jett, Dex and Zach.

We arrived in New York earlier today. Dani spent a week with me, and it's been wonderful. Exactly what I needed. I felt a little guilty, having her to myself, keeping her away from Dex, and from her work, though she worked online, often in the early morning, before I got up.

It's been weird. Going from having my every hour diarized, every minute accounted for and billed, to suddenly have *nothing* to do. It's been oddly freeing. But what saved me was having my bestie by my side, seeing me through the pain and taking care of me in my darkest hour. She had work and deadlines, and a life, but most days she stayed close. We watched rom-coms. Ate too much. Drank even more. I let myself fall apart in the safest place I know—next to her. A place Rio would once have had. Dani made me laugh when I didn't think I could. She helped me forget. She helped me *heal*.

My heart still hurts, but it's not quite as raw.

Occasionally, I'd overhear updates about Rio. Not from Dani directly—just things she'd let slip. He's so mad at his father, and he's working on something. Investigating. I didn't press, and she didn't offer much. But then one morning she looked at me and said, "Let's go to New York. You need a change of scenery. We need a girlie night, somewhere else, out of this apartment. Away from here. And, you need to meet Cari."

Cari.

Jett's girlfriend. I've only met her a few times; when all the Knights came to our home in São Paulo, the day before Dex and Dani's wedding, and then at the wedding. She seemed nice. Sweet. The perfect young mum to little Brooke.

I hesitated, because—well—Rio's in New York, but in the end, I agreed. I *did* need a change. When Dani told me Cari had offered to host us at Jett's apartment, in the afternoon, I didn't know what to expect.

"Doesn't she work?" I ask. I recall Dani telling me about Cari's flower shop.

"She's taking time off today."

"For me?"

"She's lovely." Dani tugs me toward the door. "We're

growing close. You'll always be my bestie, Raquel, but it's nice to have someone here too. Someone who gets it. Cari offered to host, and I thought—it's perfect."

I glance at the sleek apartment block as we approach. I've never been here. I've only ever seen the apartment block where Rio and his brothers live. This place also feels expensive.

I pause at the door. "What if Jett's home, with his brothers?" Though Rio likely won't be here. He and Dex are close.

Dani laughs. "Relax. They're still at work. There's no Jett. No Dex. No fancy black-tie dinner tonight, and that would be at their father's penthouse. That's not something we'd be willing to attend. Relax, hon. It's only the three of us, a couch, wine, and too many carbs."

"You promise?" I still feel nervous, and I don't understand why. I was fine, until we landed in New York. Somehow knowing that I could run into Rio, makes me feel anxious.

"I swear. Now get in there."

The door opens before we can knock. Cari stands there, smiling softly. "Hey, Raquel, welcome." To my surprise, she leans in and gives me a warm hug which I wasn't expecting.

"Thank you for inviting me over." I hold out a bag with chocolates, wine and a cuddly toy for Brooke.

"You shouldn't have, but thank you." She takes the bag, and she and Dani hug. "Thanks, for convincing her."

Convincing her? I'm not sure I heard right. I enter and look around the apartment Like Rio, Jett also has a penthouse. I can see a hot tub and a terrace outside. It's all sleek and modern, and I'd expect nothing less.

"Where's Brooke?" I ask. I want to see her face when she pulls out the cuddly elephant.

"She's at school, and after that she's going to her friend Eden's for a playdate. We have the entire evening to ourselves."

"I wasn't sure about this," I admit as we step inside. "But thank you for having me."

Cari smiles. "We all need our girlie me-time, especially when the world's been a little cruel." Her voice is warm and kind with no trace of judgement or tension. I can see why Dani likes her so much.

It's only early afternoon, which I find odd. I would have expected something like this in the evening, at the end of the working day.

The living room smells like freshly popped popcorn. There are bowls of M&Ms and pretzels, little platters of cheese and grapes, and three empty wine glasses.

"Red, white, rosé or champagne?" Cari asks.

"Champagne!" Dani cries.

"Let's start with some wine first, and then we can move onto the champagne?" Cari gives her a look which I can only describe as cryptic. I start to wonder what is going on.

"Rosé," Dani suggests, and Cari disappears into the kitchen, I presume.

I turn to Dani. "What is going on?"

"Nothing." It's when she smiles sweetly that I know I should be worried. Cari returns with the rosé and pours generously. "To healing, and new friendships."

I clink my glass against hers, then Dani's.

"To not being alone," I add quietly. I'm so passionate in defending others, but when it comes to me, I'm too hard on myself. Seeing their warm smiles, and the understanding in their eyes, I realize that it's okay to lean on people. That strength isn't always about standing alone, but sitting beside the ones who won't let you fall.

"Rom-com or breakup revenge?" I ask, feeling comfortable, and relaxed as I sink back into the oversized couch.

Cari looks at me. "You choose, and maybe we can watch that later."

"Later?"

"Hon." Dani turns to me. Here it comes. The hairs on the back of my neck stand up. I know when something isn't quite right.

"It's ready," Cari says, fiddling around with a laptop and cables. I have a feeling we're not about to watch something a rom-com.

CHAPTER THIRTY-EIGHT

RIO

Despite being full, the boardroom feels colder than usual.

Shiny glass water jugs and glasses abound neatly around the long, rectangular table polished walnut table. Men in suits sit around it looking somber. Dex sits next to me, his expression stern. On either side of us sit our respective brothers. The old man is at the head, looking like a victor. It secretly amuses me that he has no idea what's coming. He thinks this is me talking about the Eco resort, and other real estate deals I've been working on. The rest of the table is filled with legal counsel, PR heads, and two outside board investors.

I set the phone on the table and tap the screen. The red light blinks, telling me that we're live. I'm streaming the show.

"You sure, brother?" Dex asks, his voice still cautious, like he's not sure. He didn't want me to do this.

"I'm sure."

I considered recording it, and giving a copy to Raquel to

watch, but I changed my mind a few days ago. Dex couldn't talk me out of it. I'm breaking protocol but I don't give a damn. Raquel needs to see it happen live. They can come for my head later. I told Dani of my plan, and she was the one who suggested she bring Raquel to New York, and set up some sort of girlie event with Cari. I love how these women all have each other's back. It's puts us Knight boys to shame. Though we're learning. Decades of the old man's conditioning is slowly being stripped away. Shivers skate along my back and neck at the thought that, if all has gone according to plan, it's possible that Raquel might be watching this right now.

The old man's eyes narrow to slits. "What is that?" he asks, tone clipped, and cold.

I meet his gaze without flinching. "A live stream. For someone who deserves to hear the truth."

He leans forward. "This meeting is private. You're violating protocol."

A few board members shift uneasily in their seats. Their murmurs rush around the room like angry whispers.

"Then fire me." I shrug. "But first you'll listen to what I need to say."

It's slight. The tiniest flex in his facial muscles. I turn and speak directly to the camera. My mouth suddenly turns dry, like I've swallowed a bucket of sand.

Matteo leans forward, like this suddenly became interesting for him. Enzo is quiet and contained, giving nothing away as he watches the old man. Jett frowns. He has no clue what this is about. Good. That's exactly how me and Dex wanted this. As for Zach? Dex said it was about time the poor kid opened his eyes and saw the truth.

I take a deep breath. My insides twisting into knots. I'm scared as hell, but I've never been so sure of what I'm about to do. I drop the folder on the table. The old man doesn't flinch, though a few of the non-family board members do.

"Is this a dramatic gesture or is there substance?" the old man snaps.

"You fed me falsified environmental data," I say. "You told me it was clean and vetted. I handed it to Raquel Monteiro, the environmental attorney for Tovey & Roth. She used parts of it, and the court threw out her case. You know about this, *father,* we already discussed it."

Muted gasps ripple around the table.

"She submitted it," he says calmly. "You gave it to her. Don't look at me for the consequences."

"You knew it was wrong. You knew what would happen." I hold up the folder, and hand it to Dex, then encourage him to pass it around. "It's all in there. Internal memos and emails. Direct orders from Knight Enterprises, signed off by Delport. All traced back to him." I jab a finger toward the old man. "She was set up and used as a pawn. And I helped do it without knowing."

The old man jaw tightens. "I would caution you to stop before you do something that—"

I pin him with a stare. "I said you needed to listen to what I have to say. So, *listen.*" I smack down another document. "This proves you manipulated the entire situation. Got Raquel on the case, then sabotaged her credibility. You destroyed her name to protect your lies."

"You stop this, *boy.*" The old man hisses.

"We need to hear this," one of the board members says. A murmur of agreement flows around the table. I glance back at the camera. My voice softens. "I should have seen it sooner. I should have questioned why the numbers didn't match, why everything felt off, but I didn't. I was late getting out and doing my own investigation, but I've more than made up for it. I have a lot of data now. Data which, I hope, will vindicate the person you sought to destroy."

The room is dead silent.

"She trusted me," I say, eyes still on the camera. I want to say so much, but this is not the place to become personal. I still need to keep it professional. "But because of me she walked into a trap." I try to still the wobble in my voice. I can talk about work without emotion, but when it comes to Raquel, I go all soft and blubbery. "I'm not going to let that be the end of her story." I slowly look at everyone around the table, then rest my gaze on the old man.

"This company claims to stand for innovation, sustainability and transparency. I say we need to prove it. So, today, I'm putting it all on record. If you want me gone after this, fine. But I'm not going to let Raquel Monteiro take the fall for something we did." I lean forward, resting both palms on the table. "I won't stay silent while the man who calls himself my father ruins her just to feel powerful. This is proof of wrong doing, by someone who needed to soothe a pain point. One, I might add, he inflicted on himself."

If looks could kill, I'd be slumped over the table. But I hold firm, determined to see this through. "That folder being passed around is proof of misconduct, of planting false data, of deliberate sabotage. And for what?"

One of the external board members leans forward. "Mr. Knight—this could trigger legal exposure."

The PR officer chimes in. "If this leaks, it's reputational suicide."

The old man's jaw tightens. A strange thought flashes through my head. It wouldn't surprise me if he put a hit out on me after this. He killed his wife, indirectly, by breaking her heart, and he ruined so many lives. He doesn't care about family. I'm just his son.

"We're not here to destroy the company," I say. "This isn't about revenge."

"But there needs to be accountability," Jett adds. His face is hard, his eyes like blue ice. Sometimes, I wonder, out of all of us, if *he* would be the most like the old man, if crossed, if pushed hard enough, if betrayed.

Dex crosses his arms, glaring at the old man. "You went after someone innocent. That matters."

Matteo nods. "This was unethical. We can't look the other way."

Enzo's voice is soft but firm. "There have to be consequences."

"You want a pound of flesh?" the old man snaps.

"No," I say. "We want you to fix it."

He stares at me.

"You'll issue a formal apology to the Belizean Environmental Authority and EcoGuardians. You'll fund a restoration project. It will be independent, transparent, and monitored. I'll oversee that. I'll make sure you're not up to your old tricks. You'll donate a significant portion of the profits from the eco resort to support marine and community protection programs."

He scoffs, sitting back and smoothing his tie. "And if I don't?"

"You'll be voted down," Jett says. "The board will remove you as chairman and install a watchdog oversight committee."

He glares at all of us, his boys, who are speaking against him. Standing against him and holding firm. Not walking away. Not yet.

His nostrils flare. "Fine. You want a symbolic punishment, I'll let you have it."

The audacity of it. *I'll let you have it.* This man lives to control. It's in his blood. In his DNA.

"It's not symbolic," I say. "It's justice."

"For *her*?" he sneers.

"For all the people you hurt. For the land your actions damaged. For what this company was supposed to stand for."

The old man gets up, ready to speak, but I cut him off.

"This is your legacy. But you raised sons who'd rather burn your empire down than become you."

"You accept Rio's offer?" Jett asks the old man.

He nods once, but says nothing. This is killing him. Everything about him is tense. He's like a statue, carved out of stone hard and unyielding. It would have been brutal if I'd done this at a private Knight Family dinner. There would have been plenty of drama, and accusations. Screaming and swearing. He wouldn't have held back, and neither would I.

But doing this here, in front of board members. That's what he can't forgive. He despises me for it, and I know he'll never forget it. There will be a reckoning for me one day, and I'll have to brace myself for it.

Protect the ones I love, always.

I cut the live-stream, and boardroom empties, and it's just us. And him. My brothers crowd around me, all of them, including Jett, Dex and Zach.

"That must have taken guts," Jett says, gripping my hand hard. "Well done."

Zach gives me a look. "Did you have to do it like this?"

I see his soft spot for the old man. "Yes. I did."

Matteo fist bumps me. "Bold."

Enzo nods. "Wish you'd told us beforehand, but I understand why you didn't."

Dex slaps me on my back. "Well done, brother. We're celebrating tonight. No excuses."

The old man's voice cuts through the air like a blade.

"You're suspended, effective immediately. Hand over your

badge, your passcodes, everything. Security will escort you out."

Dex sniggers. "You waited until the board members left before saying this?"

Jett leans against the oak-panneled wall, arms folded. "Doing things underhandedly again, father?"

The old man's glare could incinerate a city. "I want this off the record. Expunged from the transcript. This was a breach of confidentiality, and anyone who sides with him will answer to me."

"No." I say, hands fisted deep in my pockets.

"You heard," Jett growls, stepping forward. "It won't be erased, and Rio isn't leaving alone."

The old man's nostrils flare. "You're siding with him?"

Jett's voice stays calm, but there's steel beneath it. "You know it's right. Just as you know what you did was wrong."

Dex shrugs. "I'm siding with the truth. And frankly, it's about time someone did."

"Truth." Matteo echoes, tilting his chin defiantly.

Zach hesitates, glancing around. "Can't we find another way to—"

"No." I cut him off. "Not this time. This stays on the record. The eco resort goes ahead, but not like this. Knight Enterprises will fund full environmental remediation and pause all construction until a new plan is approved. One that serves the people who live there.

"A local oversight committee will monitor every phase. We'll launch paid training programs, guarantee jobs for Belizean workers, and invest a percentage of profits directly into their communities. What we do, to fix this, will be good, and decent, with long-term infrastructure, not PR fluff.

"Every step will be public. Every report. Every audit. Every promise." I pause to take a breath. "And Raquel Monteiro's name will be cleared, officially and permanently. And while I know you'll never say the words—she will get the apology you owe her, one way or another. That was the deal and if you go back on any of it…" I pause, letting the silence stretch, letting him feel what's coming. "Then I will burn it all down."

The old man walks out.

"Dramatic, bro," Dex whispers alongside me.

"Do you have to be so vicious?" Zach whines.

"Warranted." Jett moves to leave. Then, "Are we celebrating or what?"

"Feels like a win, doesn't it?" I look around. It's just us, the brothers, left. Not only are we in solidarity, but we all seem aligned with the same goal and it feels good. Turning Knight Enterprises into something good, something decent. Not the ruthless machine the old man has built. Something that crushes people in the name of profit, but a company, and a legacy, that is worth fighting for.

RAQUEL

I DON'T BREATHE FOR THE ENTIRE TIME.

At least, it feels like that.

When the live stream ends, I sink back against the couch, my body turning to jelly as I let out a breath I didn't even realize I'd been keeping in.

We all do that. We've all been sitting on the edge of the couch, huddled together, eyes on Cari's laptop sitting on the sleek black coffee table.

When Rio's face flashed across the screen, I stopped breathing. It felt like my insides just vanished. For a moment I didn't know whether to break, or hope. He was amped up, and mad. Ready for a fight. I saw it in the hard set of his jaw and in the way his dark eyes glittered with danger. I felt the weight he bore, even though he appeared calm. The man I loved, still love, looked so tired, but determined. He's always been brave, and what I saw, stern looking men sitting around a table, like Rio was on trial, it made me scared, but he was in it. There, taking them all on.

None of us have touched the wine, or the nibbles.

I've just watched Rio defending me in front of everyone. His father, his brothers, the board.

He did this in public.

My insides are so tangled up, I feel like I might be sick. I was a tightly knotted mess watching it, and I know how big a deal this was for him to go against his father.

He fought for me. He stood up for me. He told me he didn't know his father had manipulated us both, and even I wanted to believe him, but I needed proof. And now, Rio just gave me everything I asked for.

This was about revenge. About keeping the boys in line, punishing them for working together and standing up to him when they helped get Uncle Arminio's company back.

Dani and Cari sit on either side of me, silent. Disbelief hangs in the air. I'm still stunned.

"You okay, hon?" Dani asks.

I sit up slowly, resting my elbows on my knees, and my face on my hands, trying to absorb it all. Cari puts her arm around my waist. Dani slips her arm around my shoulder. We're joined together, in solidarity, in support, in love. I don't realize I'm crying until Dani hands me a tissue and Cari quietly reaches over and closes the laptop.

Watching Rio stand there, I can't imagine how he felt standing up to that monster.

Cari hands me my glass of wine. I mutter a quiet "thank you", before draining it completely. I didn't mean to gulp it all down so fast, but I needed that. I'm so amped up with emotion, my thoughts scattered all over the place.

Rio risked everything for me. Not in secret, not around the table at one of his dinners, not in some whispered apology. He did it out loud, in front of the men who judge. In front of the man who has broken him, and his brothers, and their mothers. The man who wants to play God.

Rio brought him back down to earth, and held him accountable. I see it like a shining, gleaming star. What we had, what I want, what we can be.

The pop of a champagne cork takes me out of my thoughts and look up to find the girls pouring champagne into delicate, long stemmed, glass flutes.

Cari hands me my glass. "Told you the champagne would come later."

"We're definitely celebrating now!" Dani cries.

They look at me, expectantly. "Make a toast hon." Dani nudges me gently. I lift my glass, swallowing the lump in my throat.

"To you both, for having my back." I nod, trying to compose myself. "To justice, for all." I pause and think of Alma, and the people in Belize, who will get their clean water, and the land restored in time. They'll get their cleaner future. It's not hope. I *know*, because Rio will see to it. "And ... to Rio." I take a long, shaky breath, and feel tears running down my cheeks.

I see a flash of us laughing and kissing. Of us holding hands. Or Rio stroking my face. I miss him. I miss him so much. I want him back.

Dani rubs my back softly. "To Rio and Raquel, and to not letting fear stand in the way of going after what we want."

Cari raises her glass next. "To loving the Knight boys, as messy, complicated, and sometimes inconvenient as it is. It's love that's worth fighting for."

"Damn, hon." Dani sounds impressed, as am I.

"That's profound," I say. We all clink our glasses again, before emptying them.

"Let the party begin!" Dani puts on some music, and Cari pours more champagne.

I already know that today is a day I will never forget.

CHAPTER THIRTY-NINE

RAQUEL

I'M WAITING IN RIO'S APARTMENT FOR HIM TO COME HOME.

Dani vouched for me with the concierge and he gave me the keys. I let myself into Rio's apartment and made my way to the pool deck. The sun's beginning to set, streaking the water with gold.

Walking around her I feel like an intruder, my steps echoing in the quiet. Through the glass, the pool glitters in the late light, and I recall the last time I was here. What we did in the pool, and up against the countertop in the kitchen.

A slow, burning heat curls low in my belly, as flashes of us tangled in bed fill my head. The memory of his mouth on mine, his hands all over me, the way he moved inside me, makes me impatient to see him.

I sit and wait nervously.

Dani texts me to say that Dex just walked in, and that Rio's probably on his way. She tell me that they have plans to go for a celebratory dinner, all of them, including her and Cari. She says to wait for Rio to mention it.

Just as I get off the phone to her, I hear the key in the lock, and then ... I see him.

He walks in, and time slows down. I clasp my hands together, my chest tightening as emotion washes over me. My heart fills, with love and longing, because as soon as I set my eyes on him, looking devastating in his suit, head held high, dark eyes widening as he sees me. I'm filled with longing and a hunger that only Rio can satisfy.

I rush to him, and he catches me, wrapping his big, strong arms around me, like he never wants to let go.

I melt into him, clutching his shirt, my tears falling freely now.

He gently pries me away and tilts my face up. Worry fills his eyes. "Did you watch it?"

I nod.

His hands move to my face, gently wiping my tears away.

"Am I forgiven?"

"Completely."

"Do you believe me now? That's all I wanted. That's why I did it," he says, his voice hoarse.

I press my fingers to his lips. "I believe you. I do. I wanted to before, but I needed proof."

He grins. "I know. That's my lawyer lover. My girl. Always needing the facts." A quiet, broken laugh escapes him. "Any lingering doubts?"

"No."

Our lips press together, gently at first. Hesitantly. Then we fall into a kiss, soft and tender, filled with yearning and regret for all the days, hours and minutes we've missed. Our kiss deepens, and I breathe in his scent, taste his mouth, feel like I've come home.

Tears tangle with our fevered breath. His hands skate over my waist, while I cling to his neck. And slowly, between the kissing, we explore. His hands skate over the contours of my hips and bottom and I splay my hands across his chest, looking up at him. "I loved all of it," I whisper. "Everything you did, standing up in front of everyone. Standing up to your father."

"I've missed you," he says. "God, Raquel, have I missed you. You not being around, was like losing a limb."

A multitude of emotions flood through me, and I smile through them.

"I needed time away, to think things through."

He cups my cheek. "I wanted you to take all the time you needed. I was working on things here."

"I've had the best time with Dani and Cari. They've been so good."

His mouth widens to a smile. "They're amazing, aren't they?"

"The best."

"I'm putting things right. I promise." His expression sobers.

I squeeze his hand. "I heard. There's a lot happening behind the scenes."

"I figured Dani would keep you up to date with everything." He takes my hand, leading me out onto the rooftop garden, to the area by the pool. We sit facing one another on the recliners. My legs in between his, holding hands.

"The resort's still going ahead," he says. "But not the way it was planned. I've halted the launch. We're bringing in a third-party environmental team. Full oversight. Maybe you can recommend someone from your NGO network?"

My heart is full. "We can work something out." I need to reach out to Alma, and I will, in time.

"I wanted the old man to apologize to you, but he won't, not in words. I seriously doubt he ever will, but I told him."

I kiss the back of his hand. "I don't expect him to. It doesn't matter. You did what matters. I've always known he wasn't a ... a... good man." I struggled to find the words.

"He's a monster," Rio says easily.

My hand slides up and curls behind his neck. "You're nothing like him, Rio … my love, my everything. Meeting you was the best thing that ever happened to me."

He touches my lips. "Meeting you was fate. It was destined to happen."

I lean into his touch.

"I did it for you, but for the people in Belize, for Tomas, and Vilma, and the villagers. But I also did it for my mom."

His voice cracks.

"Standing up for you—doing this in the open—was standing up for her too. For the woman who didn't get a voice. For everyone he tried to crush. This was me finally saying, no more."

Leaning forward more, I rest my forehead against his, blinking back fresh tears. "You did the right thing. The *only* thing. You exposed him."

He has a faraway look in his eyes. "He'll recover, sure. But something shifted today. Everyone saw it. They saw who he really is. We knew, the brothers, but the board members got to see him for who he is."

"Will it damage the company?"

"He'll smooth it over. He owns the board. But I made it clear where the blame lay. He felt it, and so did everyone else. No doubt about it. The dynamic's starting to change. We're fixing it from the inside, and I think we're all working towards the same goal."

He presses another kiss to my lips.

"I'm not like him," he murmurs, his breath warm and sweet.

"I know."

"Now I finally believe it."

"You were worried that you might be?"

"Sometimes, you become the very thing you try to resist."

I scoff. "You're nothing like him."

He smiles, then says, "Dex says we need to celebrate. He says this was a big step, exposing the old man in front of the board." He pauses.

"You don't feel that way?" I sense his hesitation, and I wonder if he regrets it. Going up against a monster can't be easy, especially if the monster is your father.

"I agree. He's talking about renting out that fancy rooftop place where he proposed to Dani. It'll just be for us. I swear that dude just wants to relive his engagement scene over and over again."

I can't help but giggle. "It's nice of him to suggest that. I think it's a great idea for you all to celebrate this big milestone together." I pause to consider my words carefully. "I don't have any siblings, and neither does Dani. You're lucky to have so many. Even if you didn't all grow up together, it's never too late to forge a bond. You're all brothers and nothing will ever change that."

"Do you want to go?" he asks. "We don't have to. We can hang out here."

I hesitate, not because I don't want to go, because I do. "I'd love to. But more than that you need this time with your brothers. You're healing. You're finding each other again. I don't want to get in the way of that."

He cups my cheek. "You wouldn't. You're part of this now. All of it. You're part of us. Dani and Cari will be there."

My heart swells. I think of Dani. Of Cari. Of the way this strange, powerful, messy family has started to come together. "It would be good to see them again," I whisper. "This feels like a family."

He kisses me again, deeper this time, and as our lips and tongues mesh and entwine, the world begins to make sense again. I begin to find some clarity in the debris of my world.

"I was thinking of getting the ethics board to open an investigation into Pierce and the abuse of power."

I shrink back, but Rio's hold on me tightens. He shakes his head. "I've got you. I don't want you to worry about him."

"It's not worry. It's a dull ache. Something irritating that gnaws at me each time I think of him."

"I know what that feels like. Just tell me what you want me to do."

I consider his proposal, then decide against it. "I would rather let karma come for him in her own sweet time."

The man fired me, and though I didn't want to be let go of in that manner, I was looking to move anyway. Now I have other things to look forward to.

"I was going to get Knight Enterprises to issue a public apology to you on behalf of the company. It's not going to be from the old man directly, but it will clear your name publicly."

I think about that for a moment. "I would like that. More than anything, I want EcoGuardians to know that I wasn't completely careless."

"Completely careless?"

"I shouldn't have used your data. I should have recused when we came back to the US. I shouldn't have gotten involved when I did."

"You make it sound like you did it single handed." He cups my chin. "I was just as complicit, but know this. If you hadn't used the data, the old man would have found another way to bring you down. That's who he is."

Chills zig zag along my skin. "It never ceases to surprise me the lengths bad actors go to. If they only used that energy for good."

We fall silent for a while.

"What are you thinking?" he asks, quietly.

"Of what I should wear to my first interview with Kingston Mansell," I say casually, like it's no big deal, when it's everything to me. Almost everything. "It's a globally renowned law firm in Manhattan."

I wait for the words to land, when they do, Rio's eyes widen like saucers. "In Manhattan?"

"Yes." I try not to burst from the inside out. "They headhunted me. I have an interview next week."

I didn't think his eyes could get any bigger, but they do. "Kingston Mansell? They're *extremely* prestigious."

"Yes. They want me for Senior Counsel, ESG— environmental, social and governance, and International Compliance." When I say it all out loud, it sounds like a big deal. I can't stop myself from smiling, or ignore the way my stomach feels all fluttery, in those moments when I know something good is coming.

Rio jumps to his feet, pulling me up with him, and then he lifts me up in his arms, and spins me around effortlessly. "Babe! Wow. That's .... that's *fucking* incredible."

"I don't have the job yet. It's the first interview," I say, breathless from both the spin and the thrill, and Rio's uncontained joy. "They want me to lead high-profile cases, and advise billon-dollar clients, as well as build international policy strategy. It's ..." I laugh, overwhelmed. "It's like the universe is finally listening."

Not just with the job, and removing me from working for a boss I detested, but by letting Rio strut into my life. I'm filled with joy and disbelief, my heart so full, my skin tingling. I'm experiencing a joy that doesn't come from adrenaline or excitement but from alignment.

He sets me down, his arms still around my waist anchoring

me. "You're going to walk in to that firm like the storm that you are. They'll be lucky to have you. Just like I am."

Then he kisses me, slow and certain, and it's like a new chapter is starting in our lives. We've made it through the worst, and the best is yet to come.

CHAPTER FORTY

RIO

Dex texted to say that tonight we're having a Knight brothers' dinner at the rooftop sky garden in The Bluebell Manhattan, Luke Hunter's hotel. The entire garden has been reserved just for us.

Fitting really, since it was here that Dex proposed to Dani. And it was in the upscale bar inside, The Midnight Lounge, where Dex and Dani had their first date. It was also where I first met Raquel.

Dex organized it all. He claims he's proud of what I did, and we need to celebrate standing up to the old man.

But I didn't just wake up and do this. I saw Jett stand up for what he believed in, and then Dex fought his battle. Sure, we helped, but seeing my brothers rise up, slowly, but surely, pushing back, inspired me to do what needed to be done.

But what I'm celebrating tonight is getting Raquel back.

We're late, and by the time the elevator doors open, and we step out to find everyone seated around a long rectangular table.

Thick white candles in glass jars are dotted around the table. The lighting is low and warm.

All the brothers are there, and Dani and Cari. No sign of the old man. This feels like a family get-together. Not a Knight family dinner night. Jett is sitting at one end, arms folded. Dex is next to him, looking into Dani's eyes like she's the only woman on earth. Dani's laughing about something and the dude is just watching her. Zach stares out at the city skyline probably wishing he wasn't here. I suck in a breath. He's one of the youngest of the Knights, not the youngest, Enzo is, and that dude is far wiser than his twenty-six years. Problem with Zach is that he's deluded when it comes to the old man. He still thinks the old man might change. Another problem is that he loves him and still looks up to him. Matteo is tapping away on his cell phone and Enzo is silently surveying everyone.

"Brother. Raquel. Glad you could both make it." Dex nods. Everyone quiets. Raquel and I are holding hands. I give her hand a gentle squeeze, knowing how daunting it can be to walk in and find seven pairs of eyes on you. Cari and Dani spring out of their seats and rush to Raquel. They don't even acknowledge me.

"You okay, hon?"

"How's it going?"

She's bombarded with questions, and hugs and kisses, even though they were all together earlier, watching the live stream.

"Thank you," I say, when they finally, *finally*, turn to acknowledge me. The girls took care of the livestream, and setting it all up, getting Raquel to come over to Jett's place and getting her to watch it.

"Want to come sit by us?" Dani asks.

"I'm fine, thanks. I'll sit by Rio," she says softly, looking a little shy. She's nothing like the velociraptor in the courtroom—

the fierce, unstoppable woman I know. I hate that because of me, my father was able to get to her.

The girls go back to their seats.

We're still holding hands. "You ready?" I ask.

She nods, Jett gets up first and comes over to shake my hand, before greeting Raquel warmly by giving her a light kiss on her cheek.

The others follow, murmuring, "Hey", and "Hi," and "Good to see you."

Raquel is right. There are so many of us. It takes a while for all the greetings to subside, but by the time the boys all sit back down again, I feel Raquel relax beside me.

I'm touched by these guys. When we meet without the old man, and its only happened once before, it really does feel like we're a family.

We need to make this a regular thing.

At my place setting, a cut-crystal bottle of my favorite aged tequila waits, condensation just starting to form on the glass. Beside it, a matching tumbler, already poured. Dex knows me so well. The champagne has been poured in glasses.

He gets up from his seat. "Welcome, Raquel. Just glad you could make it to dinner."

The girls beam at her, like she's one of them, and I guess she is.

She smiles. "Thank you for inviting me."

"To Rio. For paving the way. Way to go, brother." He raises his glass, and everyone else raises theirs. "And to Raquel, who came tonight, despite knowing our surname." This gets a laugh from everyone. "I'm sorry our old man dragged you, an innocent woman, into his power games."

"She was collateral," I reply, anger rising in my chest. He ruined her life, or tried to, to teach me a lesson. What a psycho.

"She wasn't just collateral," Enzo says. "He probably enjoyed it."

Jett swirls the whiskey around in his glass. "Unfortunate, but strategic, according to father."

"Her career was destroyed," I bite out. "And her name dragged through the mud." My jaw tightens. Raquel squeezes my hand gently.

"Let it go," she whispers. "Don't spoil this evening."

"The old man's an ass," Matteo says. "He shouldn't have taken his grudge against Rio, and the rest of us, on you. You still sure you want to date my brother?"

"More than sure," Raquel answers.

I rise and clear my throat, wanting to make a toast. I lift my glass of tequila, the amber liquid catching the light. "No reporters. No legal teams. No boardroom. Just us. A band of brothers. A family."

The table is quiet, the candlelight catching in every glass.

"Thanks for putting this together, dude," I nod in appreciation at Dex. "It's been tough. Really tough, but it's been hardest on the woman I love."

I look down at Raquel. She does something I've never seen before—she looks coy, her eyes dropping to the table as if she can't meet anyone's gaze. It hits me how much losing her job and her reputation has broken her. Even though I stood up to the old man in the boardroom, I know it's not a quick fix. This will take time to heal.

"You stood up to him, bro. That's a big thing." Dex is trying to make me look good, but I wish he'd tone it down. He means well, but this wasn't all me.

Raquel looks up at me. "It can't have been easy." She reaches for my hand, her fingers curling over mine. Her voice is soft, because she knows. She understands me, knows what it took.

"And on that note," Jett says, standing. "Won't take too much time, Rio, just wanted to say that what you did was a big thing."

"You inspired me," I reply, feeling a lump in my throat that surprises the hell out of me. I'm suddenly overcome with emotion. Suddenly feeling like we're so much more than who we used to be. The corners of Jett's mouth lift just enough for me to know he appreciates the comment.

Looking at Raquel, he says, "I hope you'll be a part of this family. You can ask Cari and Dani—we're not that bad when you get to know us. We're not like our father."

Zach shakes his head and sits back. Jett continues, "I just want to welcome you and hope that whatever wrong's been done to you, we can somehow make it right. Being fired, having your reputation attacked—it's too big a price to pay."

"Thank you," Raquel says quietly. "I appreciate that. But for this man? There's no price I won't pay." Silence falls, and something tightens in my chest. Heat crawls up my spine. She said this in front of everyone, and now she stares at me lovingly.

Glasses are raised, and there's a chorus of cheers.

The servers begin setting out steaming platters of steak and sides, the scent of charred meat filling the air. The conversation picks up again, laughter mixing with the clink of cutlery and glasses.

Raquel's eyes are shining as our gazes lock. The earlier meekness, the timidity—those things that were so unfamiliar in the woman I love—have vanished. Leaning closer, we can't help it, our lips meeting in a quick, heated kiss that sends sparks tingling through me. I know things are going to be okay.

I know we'll be more than okay.

The food is good. The insults fly. Each of the brothers throws in a jab or a laugh. It's loud, it's warm, it's family.

It's everything I never dreamed we could have, and yet, here we are.

Raquel's sitting back in her chair, relaxed and content. Looking happier than I've seen her. My heart warms.

I feel on top of the world.

The servers have cleared the plates, and refilled all our drinks, and they're about to serve dessert.

A phone rings somewhere, then Jett's voice cuts through the air.

"What? When?" The words are sharp, and loud, causing every fork to freeze midair.

"What fresh drama is this?" I mutter under my breath.

Everyone sits forward. The air chills. The sound of laughter and chatter disintegrates with the weight of impending doom.

Jett's face turns white.

"We'll be there." He hangs up, swipes his hand over his face, looks around the table at us all.

"That was the housekeeper. The old—" A muscle ticks in his jaw before he corrects himself. "Father ... was rushed to the hospital. He collapsed. Chest pain and vomiting and confusion. EMT's took him straight to the hospital."

A chair scrapes across the floor. Zach stands, looking deathly pale. "He's alive, isn't he?"

"She didn't say otherwise so I'm assuming, yes." Jett deadpans.

Anger flashes in Zach's eyes. "Can't you have anything good to say about him-"

"Let's calm down, shall we?" I get up. "We should go."

"He just tried to destroy Raquel, and *you*," Matteo counters, sitting back in his chair, like this isn't shocking news.

Enzo stands up. "We should go. He is our ... father. It's the right thing to do."

"Amen, brother." Dex gets up.

Everyone rises, and the warmth and laughter, the easy conversation, the delicious meal, and rare moment of unity, they vanish.

WE WALK THROUGH THE QUIET AND STERILE CORRIDOR OF THE Manhattan private hospital. The rooftop celebration feels like another timeline ago, and the mood has shifted from joy to something heavy and morose.

The girls are in the waiting room, and now we, the Knight boys, file into the private room. The old man's eyes are closed. He's resting. Or maybe he's pretending to be asleep, so he doesn't have to deal with all of us looking at him while he's at his most vulnerable.

We stare at the man who's loomed so large in all our lives.

"Is he ...?" Zach begins to ask.

"Breathing, dude." I gesture at the monitors, the steady beep of the heart rate, the slow rise and fall of his chest; every sign that he's still alive.

"What the hell happened?"

The housekeeper and his private butler are outside, but they couldn't tell us much. A doctor walks in, a few moments later.

"Mr. Knight experienced what we believe was a hypertensive crisis. His blood pressure spiked to dangerous levels, and it caused acute symptoms, like vomiting, confusion, and chest pain."

The words settle over us, like a suffocating blanket. I can't breathe. I can't process what this means, because him? That old man lying in bed looking helpless, is something my brain was never prepared for.

"What happens now?" Jett asks.

"We've stabilized him for now. He's resting."

"Is he resting?" I ask.

Jett peers at him closely. "He's keeping his eyes closed, but whether he's asleep or just not talking… who knows?"

"His labs were concerning," the doctor announces. "His kidney function is significantly impaired. This isn't new—it's likely been progressing for some time."

A silence falls over the room.

"For some time? How long?" Enzo asks quietly.

Matteo frowns. "I would have thought he'd have regular checkups, all the top medical care and maintenance that money can buy."

Dex scratches his chin. We all seem to have trouble grasping this. "Has he been hiding this?"

"Possibly." The doctor looks at us. "But this level of damage doesn't happen overnight. We'll need to run more tests. CT, biopsy, renal panels. It's too early to know the full picture, but…" She pauses.

"But what?" Zach asks, the tension in his voice giving away his worry.

"We're likely looking at chronic kidney disease, at an advanced stage."

We exchange glances, but no one speaks. We're all trying to process what this means. I wonder if I've been too harsh. If what I did somehow set this off.

Then Zach pipes up again. "He'll be okay, though, won't he?"

The doctor pauses, pressing her lips together, before answering. "With treatment, monitoring, and lifestyle changes, possibly. But, he may eventually need dialysis, or a kidney transplant."

"A kidney transplant?" The color drains from Zach's face.

"Another kidney." I can't imagine the old man wanting anyone's kidney.

"He won't like that." Jett swipes a hand over his forehead, staring at the ground.

"No," I agree. "He won't take any of this well."

We all freeze in the silence, the gravity of this announcement settling heavy and hard on each of us as we try to wrap our heads around what this means. How a man forged from stone, all hard edges and unrelenting, a man who's ruled over us with a steel fist all our lives, can suddenly be brought to his knees.

It feels impossible. Unheard of. And until a few hours ago, it was.

"I'll let you spend some time with him, but only five minutes. Your father needs his rest." She closes the file, and leaves.

We stand around the bed, listening to the constant and steady beep of the monitor.

"I can't believe this," Dex says, looking like he's got the weight of the world on his shoulders. "Is this how it starts?"

Matteo shoves his hands in his pockets, looking glum. "His body is turning on him. Fitting."

"Don't," Zach snaps. "Not now. Have some empathy."

"You mean like he does for us, for everyone else?" Matteo growls.

"Maybe he did bring this all on himself," says Enzo quietly. "Years of control, pressure, stress. Power costs, in the end."

I step forward and stare down at the old man. He looks gaunt and haggard. Nothing like the icy unfeeling magnate who's ruled over us with an iron first for so long. The man before me looks fragile, almost breakable. I barely recognize the man who stared me down in the boardroom earlier.

A heavy silence settles in the room, pressing in on us, and daring me to feel something I swore I never would.

I wonder if this empire finally cost him something, and I

wonder if the king is starting to fall. Instead of feeling triumphant, a heavy sadness settles over me. I feel numb.

I don't hate him—not the way I thought I would. I don't want him gone. I don't want him dead. I just want… *peace*. For me. For all of us. Maybe even for him.

That's the part that surprises me. This feels like a momentous event. He's losing his grip, and we're finding our strength. His empire, built on secrets and control, is one we can rebuild, with a conscience. With heart. With transparency.

He never believed these things were important, but I know they are.

Jett and Dex know they are.

Because of Dani.

Because of Cari.

Because of Raquel.

We're finally choosing something different.

I don't know what happens next. I don't know if the old man makes it another five years, or if his health collapses like his moral compass. But I do know this much; we're no longer standing in the shadow of a tyrant. We can build this company differently, with a different set of values. We have the heart and moral courage he never possessed, and just because we share this man's DNA, doesn't mean we walk in his footsteps.

EPILOGUE

Two weeks later ...

RIO

"This is a lovely hotel," Raquel says, gazing around in awe at the landscaped grounds.

We've arrived early at the Casa Adriana, in Verona. I was supposed to meet with Nico Cazale months ago, before the old man sent me to Belize. I have a proposal for him which would benefit both of us, and he'd be smart to take it.

"Not bad." I look around, taking in the manicured gardens dotted with lemon trees, a central fountain sparkling in the sunlight, and wide terraces shaded by striped awnings. It's quiet here, and refined, every stone, every flowerbed, is placed with intent.

Nico Cazale is the king of the luxury hotel empire. He has a portfolio of high-end, upscale, boutique hotels. Nothing gaudy or commercial. Allegedly, a stay at one of his hotels promises relaxation, peace, privacy and indulgence. I've read the write-ups in luxury travel magazines. They're glowing. I hope he agrees to the deal, because it will be good for both of us.

We walk inside, across the black-and-white marble-tiled floor, which gleams under the soft lighting. A receptionist at the front desk looks up and smiles warmly as we head towards her.

"What will you do?" I ask Raquel, stopping beneath an enormous crystal chandelier that sparkles in the sunlight streaming through the tall windows.

It's been two weeks since the old man's health scare. He's now at home, getting rest. I wouldn't say it's brought us, the brothers, closer to him, but we take turns visiting him at his penthouse. There are no Knight family dinners, for now. That's one advantage.

When he was told about his kidney disease, he didn't show fear. He demanded every possible treatment option, grilled the doctors like they were under a corporate audit, and refused to acknowledge weakness. If anything, the diagnosis made him more determined to exert control, as if sheer will could outpace the limits of his own body.

He scared us, but he also made us realize the old man is fallible. He's just a mere human—not the god he likes to think he is.

He's fine now, but the doctors have advised us that he needs ongoing kidney treatment.

He now has a private butler tending to his needs, a private nurse, and the usual housekeeper, chef, and cleaning staff who keep his personal life ticking over.

It's not easy to warm to him, even now, while he sits on his recliner, reading papers and documents, still trying to stay up to speed with everything at the office. Trying to keep his watch over everything.

He hasn't changed one bit, not really. Every day he's getting stronger, and that usual hard, unforgiving streak is back.

"I'll just walk around the grounds. They look spectacular."

"You sure?" Her color and vivacity are back. After four interviews with Kingston Mansell, they offered her the job. She starts in two weeks. She's perfect for it, and I couldn't be more happy or more proud of her.

We're here in Italy for a week—for this meeting in Verona, but also for a long overdue visit to see Mama. I want her to meet Raquel. She's the first, and only, woman I'll take to meet her. I think Mama will love Raquel as much as I do. It's not just so that the two most precious women in the world to me can meet. There's another reason. I wanted to tell her in person about the old man. Matteo, Enzo and I all agreed that it wasn't something we could tell her over the phone.

"I'm sure. Look at these beautiful gardens, Rio. A world away from a law office."

I cup her face. "I won't be long. Mama's expecting us for lunch."

"I can't wait." She presses a kiss and we part ways.

I head towards the reception desk. "Rio Knight, here to see Nico Cazale."

"Good Morning, Mr. Knight. Mr. Cazale is waiting for you. This way, please."

She leads me to his office. The door is open, and sitting at his desk is a smartly dressed man.

He rises as soon as he sees me. "Please, come in."

I walk into the office. The first thing I notice is a picture of a distinguished-looking man right above Mr. Cazale's desk. I'm guessing it's his father, because I can see the resemblance so clearly.

He shakes my hand firmly, and I automatically try to place his age. His salt-and-pepper hair, greying mostly around the ears and speckled in his dark head of hair, makes me think he's in his late forties or early fifties.

"Please, take a seat."

"Good to finally meet. I know we were meant to meet a few months ago, but business called and I had to deal with something."

"I understand. We're all busy, are we not?"

"We certainly are, Mr. Caz—"

"Nico," he says. "Call me Nico."

"It's not about age, it's just a sign of respect."

He nods.

The reason I'm here is because Nico Cazale has a portfolio of some beautiful hotels—mostly boutique, very gorgeous properties scattered around Italy. I've examined the brochures in detail, and the particulars of his business empire. That's how I discovered work has started on his flagship Amalfi hotel, and that there is limited land to expand outward. Knight Enterprises recently acquired adjacent waterfront properties and land that could complement the hotel without competing against it. I already knew about the Cazale empire before this recent acquisition, but it was the perfect opportunity for me to approach him with a plan.

What I proposed would also enable Knight Enterprises to get a foot in the door of a world-famous hotel brand.

After all, why would Knight Enterprises open their own luxury brand of hotels in Amalfi when the Cazale empire is already set up? Knight Enterprises could contribute the land and development expertise. Although I'm pretty sure this guy has a solid development team behind him, he'd bring brand prestige and local connections. We'd back it with serious money. He's rich. But not Knight-level rich.

"You read over my proposal?" I say. I put something together and then refined it with Raquel's help.

He inhales before resting back against his chair, arms casually placed on the armrest. "Tell me why I should work with you. You're based in America. I live in Italy. I was born and bred in Verona. Our prestigious luxury hotel brand has been around for forty years. Italy is ours to conquer. Why would I need you?" He smiles, like he doesn't need this. Like it wouldn't make any difference to his wealth or portfolio.

"Good point. Look, Nico, I'm not here to compete with you. I'm here to make you an offer you probably won't get from anyone else."

He chuckles. "I must say, you're very confident. But I was like you once—confident, maybe bordering on arrogance. I thought I could do it all, have it all. I thought the world was my oyster."

"Was it? Is it?"

"Yes. Now it is, but not in the way I thought when I was younger."

"You're married," I state, seeing the ring on his finger.

"I am."

"Nice."

"Sometimes fate brings you not what you want, but what you need. I was a playboy—"

"I'm not a playboy."

"No, but like I said, it brings you what you need and not always what you want. I think I would have drifted. I was an only child. I had money. Not earned by me—by my father. I inherited all this from him." He waves his hand around the room.

"Is that him?" I nod at the picture of the distinguished-looking gentleman behind him.

"Yes. That is my beloved father, Edmondo Cazale. Not a day goes by when I don't think of him." His voice softens, his eyes turn shiny. "My father built the family business from scratch. He did all the hard work, and I simply inherited it. But there were a lot of personal lessons to learn along the way."

"And you … learned them?" I'm eager to hear what exactly he learned. What price he had to pay.

"I did, but not without pain and loss and suffering. But life rewarded me with riches that weren't monetary. That is why I consider myself to be blessed. Lucky."

It begins to dawn on me that feeling blessed and rich has nothing to do with money. It's about who you share your life with, the people who stand beside you when the bottom drops out, the rare moments that matter more than the numbers in your accounts.

"That's rare," I say. It's extremely rare coming from the world I know, for a business man to say that.

"Knight Enterprises—your father built it from nothing."

"You've done your homework."

"And your father, he still guides you and mentors you?" Nico asks.

Still?

Nothing of the sort. I pause. "He's still around," I say, feeling bittersweet and conflicted.

How do I describe Paul Knight? Nico must sense my unease because I don't smile—not the way he smiled when he spoke of his father so fondly.

I have nothing to say because I'm trying to choose my words carefully. It's impossible to speak warmly of Paul Knight, despite his health scare, and even now that he's come home and is recovering.

"My father is a complicated man," I say carefully.

"So I've heard."

He looks at me, and I wonder what exactly he knows. His eyes narrow, like he's seeing inside me and understands what I can't articulate.

"The people we meet in life always teach us something."

Hell, he's profound.

I rake a hand through my hair. "Maybe. I've learned that people can surprise you—for better or worse. And that sometimes, the right person can make you see everything differently."

"I don't take anything I have for granted. And neither do you, I suspect."

"Not anymore."

We sit silently for a few seconds, mulling things over. I'm intrigued and want to know more about him. I wonder what he's thinking.

"Regarding your offer," he says, finally. "I've been thinking about it. I still am. I can see ways that we could work together, but I want to keep full brand control."

"Absolutely. It would be low risk for you, not to mention highly beneficial."

"It would also be low risk and extremely beneficial for you," Nico states. "I have one of the most respected luxury hotel brands in Italy—a brand that's taken decades to build."

He's proud of what he's achieved, and he's not letting me think I'm doing him a favor.

"True. So it's a win-win. You keep the brand, the standards, the clientele. I just give you the keys to expand without touching a cent of your own capital."

Nico raises his eyebrow. "Without touching a cent of my own capital?"

"Yes."

"What's the catch?"

"There isn't a catch. You said there's always something to learn, and I have learned from my father. For him, money is everything, and he doesn't care about people or who he destroys in his ... sorry, I'm getting too personal."

He tilts his head, looking genuinely interested. "No, continue. If I'm to go into a partnership with you, I need to know everything."

I steady my breathing, try to steady my thoughts so I don't ramble on about the old man.

"We purchased the land near your flagship Amalfi hotel, and I can make sure no one else builds on it. We could expand. You've seen my ideas in the proposal?"

He nods. "There were some good ideas."

"Thank you. I don't see why business needs to be dog eat dog. I don't need to ruin you to get something out of this. And you're right—Knight Enterprises would never venture out here and build a luxury hotel brand. You already have one. That's why I see this as a win-win. I'm overseeing an eco resort in Belize at the moment, and I've learned that business doesn't have to be solely about the money. It has to work for everyone, in different ways."

"Interesting. You must have learned a lesson somewhere."

This guy has wisdom and experience. I wish the old man could be the mentor and guide that Nico's father must have been for him, and a small part of me feels envious. Like I missed out on something I can never have. I glance at the photo again, and clear my throat, forcing myself to look away.

"But I want to make it ethical," I say, meeting his gaze again when I've composed myself. "I want it to work for the people who live there, because they will still be there after all the tourists have gone home."

"I like what you're saying."

"Work has recently started on your hotel, but maybe we could turn the adjacent waterfront properties into exclusive villas and private residences, or add more amenities? That's something we could talk about in more detail at a later time."

"I have hotels which have wine-tasting and cooking classes.

I have world-class spas. I believe we could do something." He sits forward, elbows resting on the table, hands steepled together. "You understand that I don't put my name on just anything, especially not when it carries someone else's fingerprints."

"I understand. That's the point. It wouldn't carry mine, or Knight Enterprises—just yours. The kind of privacy, exclusivity, and luxury location we're talking about... no competition could match it. I'm not here to compete with you, Nico. I'm here to make sure no one else does. But more than that, I want a situation that works for us both."

There's a long pause, and he studies me like a man weighing whether a rival could also be an ally. And I very much want to be that. We are rivals—we want the same thing—but I want to be an ally.

"I'll think it over. Why don't you stay for dinner? We have a lovely restaurant here, and if I've made my mind up by dessert, we can talk details."

"We'd love to—"

"We?" Nico raises an eyebrow.

"My girlfriend Raquel is here. She's exploring the gardens."

"Ah, then she'll probably meet my wife, Ava. Why don't we all meet for dinner?"

I like that idea very much. I like this man more than I thought I could like a stranger, and a business rival at that. I feel like we could be friends.

"That would be nice, but we're meeting my mother for dinner later. She lives here."

"Your mother lives here? But you're in the States."

"Yes, long story. She's in Soave."

"That's not far from here at all. Family always comes first," says Nico. "I tell you what—I'll call you first thing tomorrow morning with my decision."

A knock on the door interrupts us.

"Come in."

In walks a young man, tall, gangly, handsome—a younger version of the man before me. I can't believe I'm seeing three generations of the same family before me.

"Papa, I'm going to take the car. I'm going for football training, then out with Aurora. Mama says to let you know."

"Drive carefully."

"Yes, Papa. Sorry to interrupt." The door closes.

"Aurora?" I say, louder than I intended.

"Alessandro's girlfriend."

"I can see the resemblance, between all of you." I tilt my chin at the photo.

Nico laughs. "People do say we look alike."

I'm intrigued about this man and his life. How he runs a successful empire yet is married and has children. "How many children to you have?"

"Four."

"Four!" I almost bounce out of my chair in shock.

"Elisabetta, my oldest, she's twenty-one. Alessandro is nineteen, Carlotta is thirteen, and Marco is nine. We had him late. My wife, Ava was forty, but it's never too late, is what I say." His smile makes me want to know more. Makes me want to meet them all.

"I'm so happy to hear that," I find myself saying, the possibility of a future like that flashing before my eyes. A wife, children, family, and love. Not just money and business. This man's face lights up when he talks about his family.

"You look content."

"More than content. I'm happy. I have everything I could ever want. The business is a bonus, and I am grateful, but family is everything."

"You have a lovely family, Nico."

He gives a half-smile, almost private. "Thank you. Children… they'll teach you more about yourself than the world ever will. Don't wait too long to learn that."

RAQUEL

I'VE NEVER BEEN TO NORTHERN ITALY BEFORE, AND I FIND Verona beautiful, in a serene, and elegant way. And the Casa Adriana, the hotel where Rio had his meeting with the owner, was simply divine.

While he was busy, I wandered around the gardens, past evergreen shrubs, olive trees, and tall Cypress trees, inhaling the scent of citrus and lemon which floated along the warm breeze.

I saw a gazebo near which sat an elderly lady. Walking towards her she looked frail, her skin lined like delicate maps of a long and memorable life and her hair tied up in a small bun. She was the picture of calm serenity and she looked content, sitting in a chair, painting calmly. Moments later, another, younger woman joined her, and introduced herself as Ava. I learned that she was the wife of the hotelier, and the painter was her mother.

We talked for a while, but they soon let me go about my business. I inhaled deeply, soaking in the air, the ambiance, the peace and quiet as I ambled along winding pathways that led to secluded stone benches and shaded alcoves draped in climbing roses.

It was such a peaceful, perfect piece of paradise. Rio looked so pumped when he finished his meeting. I hope he and the owner find a way to work together because I would love to go back there again one day.

Now we're driving toward Soave, and I feel like I'm stepping into another time. Vineyards spill down the hillsides in perfect green lines. There's a castle in the distance. Every turn of the winding road makes me fall in love with this place even more.

Being here with Rio, accompanying him on a business trip, feels like I've stepped into another life.

We're a couple. We're together. This feels a million miles away from the law firm I've left. I'm filled with a sense of quiet anticipation at starting my new job; an undercurrent of excitement mixed with nerves. It's going to be hectic, even more demanding than Tovey & Roth, which is why I jumped at the chance for a vacation when Rio mentioned this trip.

"That's the Castle of Soave," Rio says, pointing toward the horizon. "Locals say the fortress around it has guarded this valley for a thousand years."

The sunlight catches his dark hair and I almost reach out and stroke his beard but stop, because these roads are winding and a little scary, and I don't want to distract him. "Your mother's lived here her whole life?"

"Most of it. You'll see—Mama belongs here the way roses belong in her garden. She was in Milan when she met the old man."

He tells me the story—how her family lived here, and when she fell pregnant, she settled nearby, in Soave.

"You still have grandparents?"

"They died a few years ago, within months of each other. It's just Mama now. She came back to take care of Nonno and Nonna, my maternal grandparents, once we were in our early twenties. Her heart was always in Italy, but now that they've passed, I think she's feeling a little lonely. She keeps hinting that she's waiting to play with her grandchildren."

I let out a nervous chuckle. I've stood in courtrooms with more confidence than I'm feeling right now. Somehow, meeting Rio's mother feels bigger.

We pull up in front of a buttercream yellow two-story villa, with climbing roses wrapped around the door. His mother is already standing there, as if she's been waiting for us all afternoon.

I let out a little gasp, in awe, because this woman, she looks like she's stepped out of a lifestyle magazine. She's wearing black capri pants with a crisp white linen blouse with sleeves casually rolled up to her elbows. On her feet are simple leather pumps. Petite, yet graceful, with her dark hair pinned back neatly and large, hoop gold earrings catching the light, she has an aura about her that reminds me of Audrey Hepburn. Quiet and understated elegance.

I immediately feel a little underdressed, even though I'm wearing a pale blue linen wrap dress with tan leather sandals and a slim belt.

We get out of the car, and she meets us halfway, pulling Rio into a hug full of love, with a touch of scolding in rapid Italian. Then she turns to me.

"And this must be Raquel," she says warmly, in accented English.

I smile, my heart thudding in my chest. I just want her to like me. "It's so nice to finally meet you, Isabel." My voice wobbles in a way that feels foreign to me.

She takes both my hands in hers—warm and soft—and I feel comforted instantly. Her gaze searches mine in a way that's not intimidating or invasive, but knowing. And understanding.

"You are even lovelier than Rio said."

Heat rises in my cheeks. "He talks about me?"

She glances at her son with a soft, amused smile. "He talks about you a lot. I feel like I already know you."

I tap Rio playfully on the shoulder. "You never said."

"I never said what?" he teases. His smile that is wide and full, as if he's lit up from his core. It's the kind of smile that belongs to man who is grateful to be home again.

"My Rio has never brought a woman home to me before, and that tells me everything I need to know.

I don't know what to say to that, but Rio's gaze lingers on me, and something flutters deep in my belly.

"Come inside. Let's have lunch," Isabel says, and hooks her arm in mine, familiar and friendly. I warm to her instantly.

Her villa is light and airy, with sunlight pouring through open windows. The scent of basil and fresh bread fills the air. I love the smell of fresh bread—I never bake, so I only get it when I walk into a bakery.

Inside, a small wooden table is set with painted ceramic plates, a pitcher of wine glowing deep red in the center.

"Sit, please." She ushers us to our places.

"Let me help you," I say, not sitting down. I don't like to be waited on, as I survey the dishes and platters on the countertop, I can see she's already gone to so much trouble. Then it hits me. "Oh my goodness—we didn't bring you anything."

I forgot.

Rio laughs.

I put a hand to my forehead like I've committed a terrible offense. "I'm so sorry. I meant to pick something up on the way. Some flowers, and some—"

"Mama, she's nervous." Rio finds this amusing. "Raquel is never like this. This woman is like a velociraptor in court—stubborn, feisty—and I love her so much."

Something trips in my stomach, an unexpected flutter that makes my breath hitch. It shocks and delights me how easily these words slip out, in front of his mother. They land right in the center of my chest, and I feel dizzy, as if the world is tilting around me.

With determined focus, I get up to help Isabel while Rio pours the wine, oblivious to the whirlwind of emotions swirling around me.

I carry over bowls of fresh pasta, roasted vegetables, a charcuterie board, salad and baskets of warm bread. I didn't even realize I was hungry, but all of these delicious aromas combine to make my stomach rumble.

"This smells delicious. You've been hard at work," I tell her.

She sets down a bowl of olives. "This is simple, but it's from the heart. I'm so happy you are both here." She clasps her hands to her chest, eyes misting over, as she looks at us both.

Rio gets up. "Sit down, Mama. We're here now."

She gives him a dismissive wave before sitting down. "It's been so long, Rio. Matteo and Enzo were here recently, and it was just ... wonderful." She looks wistful, a little sad even. "I miss my boys."

"Then come back and live with us," Rio offers. "We're family, Mama. Nonno and Nonna are gone now. I don't like the idea of you being alone."

She arranges a white napkin over her lap. "I will. Not yet, but I have been thinking about it."

"About moving back to the US?" The hope in Rio's voice hurts. I know just how much he loves his mother, how much he hates the idea of her being so far away, and all alone.

"Don't rush me. I'm thinking about it."

I touch his thigh. Leave her be.

We eat, and she draws me into conversation, asking about my job—because Rio has told her—and then about the deal he's working on. He explains about the Cazale hotel we just visited. Her questions aren't polite filler; she's genuinely attentive and listens and ask more questions than even my mother does.

Not that my mother worries about me much anymore—not since I've been FaceTiming her with Rio.

She's more relaxed now that I'm not single. Or focused on my work to the exclusion of everything else. I heard her say this to Rio. She loves him, and is even coming to New York soon. I'm moving into a new apartment, and she's going to stay with me for a week. I want her to get to meet him and get to know him, just like he wanted me to meet his mom.

Sometimes Isabel and Rio slip into rapid Italian before remembering I'm here. The resemblance between them is striking. It's not just in their eyes, but in the way they listen and make you feel you have their full attention.

Halfway through the meal, Rio sets down his fork.

"There's something else I should tell you, Mama."

Her attention sharpens, and her hand stills as she breaks the bread. She can tell from his tone that this is serious.

"It's about the old ... Papa," he says, finally. His voice is calm but there's an edge to it.

Her eyes widen.

"He had a health scare a few weeks ago. Kidney problems, and its being dealt with."

He pauses, like he's not sure if he should tell her more.

"Rio?" she says.

"He has stage 4 CKD, chronic kidney disease. It's severe, but not yet total failure."

She sets down the bread, and for a moment she doesn't breathe.

"He has the best medical care, and he's fine, but he'll need ongoing treatment. Maybe even dialysis or a kidney…"

"It's serious, then?"

"He's not dying tomorrow, but this could kill him if it isn't treated."

Something flickers across her face. Pain, a rush of shock. Concern, too, but her composure calms in an instant.

"He will have the best treatment that money can buy."

"He will, Mama. He'll be fine."

She picks up her bread again. "No matter what's happened, he's still your father, and thank you for telling me."

I feel like this woman has known deep pain and now she knows how to school it. I can see why. She's survived heartbreak. I can't imagine how that would be—to be so in love with a man, only to discover he has a secret family and children and a wife. It would break my heart into so many pieces. I don't think I'd ever be able to put it back together.

But this woman has. Rio's gaze drops to his plate. "He's still not an easy man, Mama. He's still not nice or decent."

I slide my hand beneath the table, my fingers brushing against his, and he glances at me briefly, his fingers twining with mine. I squeeze his hand, needing him to know I'm here for him. Whenever. Forever. For all time.

When I look up, Isabel is watching us, her expression soft. "Eat," she says gently, pouring more wine into my glass. "We'll talk more later. For now, I want to enjoy having my son home, and I'm so happy to meet the woman who's made him smile again."

The way Rio looks at me makes me light up from the inside out. Sitting here, in his mother's house, with the man I love, knowing how his early life was ripped apart by the man he loved, I feel like Rio has finally come full circle. It feels as if we're standing at the start of a new chapter where the past no longer haunts him, and the future belongs to us both.

Thank you for reading Rio and Raquel's story! I love the

Knight Empire story world, and all the characters in it. I hope you do, too!

I have written another BONUS EPILOGUE for Rio and Raquel, in which they return to Belize and see Alma again. **You can get it here : www.lilyzante.com/bonusrio**

Please note: If you're already subscribed to my newsletter, there's no need to sign up again. You will automatically get these bonuses.

The next book in this series is ZACH, and it will release in February 2026!

If you're intrigued by Nico Cazale, the hotelier mentioned in the epilogue, you can read his story in HONEYMOON FOR ONE, which is the first book in the HONEYMOON series, based on Nico and Ava. Their story begins when jilted bride Ava is dumped six weeks before her Valentine's Day wedding. She goes on her honeymoon alone, hoping to find peace and get clarity, but life sets her on a new path, one which ultimately leads her to finding the love of her life.

BOOKLIST

Buy direct from Lily and save!

NEW SERIES

Knight Empire: A series of steamy billionaire romances based around a family of six brothers and their tyrannical and controlling father.

The Darkest Knight (prequel)
Jett
Dex
Rio
Zach

The Seven Sins: A series of seven standalone romances based on the seven sins. Emotional, and angsty romances which are loosely connected.

Underdog (prequel)
The Wrath of Eli

The Problem with Lust
The Lies of Pride
The Price of Inertia
The Other Side of Greed
The Seven Sins, Books 1-3

The Billionaire's Love Story: This is a Cinderella story with a touch of Jerry Maguire. What happens when the billionaire with too much money meets the single mom with too much heart?

The Promise (prequel)
The Gift, Boxed Set (Books 1, 2 & 3)
The Offer, Boxed Set (Books 1, 2 & 3)
The Vow, Boxed Set (Books 1, 2 & 3)

Indecent Intentions: This is a spin-off from The Billionaire's Love story. This two-book set consists of two standalone stories about the billionaire's playboy brother. The second story is about a wealthy nightclub owner who shuns relationships.

The Bet
The Hookup

Honeymoon Series: Take a roller-coaster journey of emotional highs and lows in this story of love and loss, family and relationships. When Ava is dumped six weeks before her Valentine's Day wedding, she has no idea of the life that awaits her in Italy.

Honeymoon for One
Honeymoon for Three
Honeymoon Blues

Honeymoon Bliss
Baby Steps

Italian Summer Series: This is a spin-off from the Honeymoon Series. These books tell the stories of the secondary characters who first appeared in the Honeymoon Series. Nico and Ava also appear in these books.

It Takes Two
All That Glitters
Fool's Gold
Roman Encounter
November Sun
New Beginnings

A Perfect Match Series: This is a seven book series in which the first four books feature the same couple. High-flying corporate executive Nadine has no time for romance but her life takes a turn for the better when she meets Ethan, a sexy and struggling metal sculptor five years younger. He works as an escort in order to make the rent. Books 4-6 are standalone romances based on characters from the earlier books. The main couple, Ethan and Nadine, appear in all books:

Lost in Solo (prequel)
The Proposal
Heart Sync
A Leap of Faith
Misplaced Love
Reclaiming Love
Embracing Love

Standalone books:

Tomorrow Belongs to Us
Love Among the Ruins
Love, Inc
An Unexpected Gift

ACKNOWLEDGMENTS

I would like to thank Maria at SteamyDesigns for creating this awesome cover. A huge thanks to Nicole McCurdy at Emerald Edits.

As always, a huge 'Thank You' to my wonderful team of proofreaders:

Charlotte Rebelein
Dena Pugh
Marcia Chamberlain

ABOUT THE AUTHOR

Lily Zante lives with her husband and three children somewhere near London, UK.

Connect with Me

I love hearing from you – so please don't be shy! You can email me, message me on Facebook or connect with me here:

Buy Direct from Lily and SAVE
https://shop.lilyzante.com

TikTok |Instagram | Website | Facebook Email

Newsletter sign-up:
http://www.lilyzante.com/news
Follow me on Bookbub
Follow me on Goodreads

facebook.com/LilyZanteRomanceAuthor

instagram.com/authorlilyzante

bookbub.com/authors/lily-zante

goodreads.com/authorlilyzante

www.ingramcontent.com/pod-product-compliance
Lightning Source LLC
Chambersburg PA
CBHW050612170726
48283CB00001B/212